GENTLEMAN

OF

FORTUNE

The adventures of

Bartholomew Roberts,

Pirate

EVELYN TIDMAN

Gentleman of Fortune,

The Adventures of Bartholomew Roberts, Pirate

No portion of this work may be lent, resold, hired out, circulated or reproduced in any form without the prior permission of the author.

Fiction
Second Edition (December 2013)

Copyright © 2013 Evelyn Tidman
All rights reserved.

ISBN-13: 978-1494493479
ISBN-10: 1494493470

In honest service, there is thin commons, low wages and hard labour. In this, plenty, and satiety, pleasure and ease, liberty and power; and who would not balance creditor on this side, when all the hazard that is run for it at worse, is only a sour look or two at choking. No, a merry life and a short one shall be my motto.

Bartholomew Roberts

For an estimation of today's monetary values in GB pounds, multiply by 100

GENTLEMAN OF FORTUNE

ONE

June 1719, West African Coast

Leaning on the gunwale, Bartholomew Roberts arched his back to ease aching muscles and cursed. He could blame no-one but himself for his relegation to the veritable dog's berth of third mate. The sailors' servant they called it, neither man nor officer, but a creature at the whim of both, expected to have some control over the men, yet at the same time climbing the yards and hauling on ropes.

'Get those blacks below, Mr. Roberts!'

Wearily he straightened up, lifted his old black hat and combed spread fingers through sweat-soaked black curls. The deck was a jumble of crates, casks, ropes, cages, sacks and bundles, and the men worked to get them stacked in the hold. They had worked since sun up without a break to bring them aboard, ivory and gold dust, skins and tobacco, provisions and water, as well as live pigs and chickens. But it was the sorry-looking group of native Africans standing near the helm that made him curse again.

They were males, chained in pairs by the ankles, their naked oiled bodies glistening in the stark glare of the African sun like polished oak. They brought the stench of the holding cells from the castle with them, an acrid ammoniac odour of stale urine, dirt and decay that seemed to ooze from their skin, and upon their faces the blank hopeless stare of the African slave.

From beside him, the captain's voice goaded him quietly. 'Come on, Mr. Roberts, get on with it.'

Captain Plumb turned away, strolling aft to the taffrail and Roberts began the task of checking the slaves, peering at teeth and skin for sores or other signs of illness while they stood quietly submissive. A single case of smallpox would decimate cargo and crew in a few days. He made each one cough while he checked for rupture and then passed them all as fit. Nodding to young John Jessup waiting beside him, he said, 'Get them below.' He was always relieved to get them off the deck and into the hold, for their presence disturbed him.

'Mr. Roberts!' The captain's voice reached him above the squeal of block and tackle and the sing-out calls of the sailors keeping the rhythm of the pull.

With an impatient sigh he crossed the deck to where Captain Plumb stood peering out to sea, the more favoured second mate John Stephenson at his side.

'What do you make of that, Mr. Roberts? There! Just rounding the headland!'

Plumb, of course had the benefit of a telescope. Even so with his naked eye, he could just make out white sail rounding the distant grey headland.

'Captain?'

'Well, what do you make of it, Mr. Roberts?' Plumb demanded impatiently and then to Stephenson added: 'Damn it, give him a glass!'

With a warningly raised eyebrow at Roberts, Stephenson handed him the telescope and even though the *Princess* rocked Roberts focused with practised ease on two three-masted ships forcing their way through the heavy green sea.

And he knew then why his opinion, that of a lowly third mate, had been sought.

'Pirates,' Roberts said with loathing.

'Not navy, Mr. Roberts?'

'The navy hasn't been heard of on the Guinea coast for some considerable time, Captain,' he pointed out.

Plumb had another look. 'They're in a mighty hurry for ordinary merchantmen. Packing too much sail for that'.

'They has to be pirates, Cap'n,' John Stephenson put in urgently.

Captain Plumb did not want to acknowledge it. 'That will be all!' he snapped.

Roberts glanced at John Stephenson who shook his head expressively. Handing back the telescope he turned away.

Pirates! He thought in disgust. Savages! The vermin of the seas! He crossed the deck, his eyes falling on the distant pale beach, just now busy with people loading and unloading boats, the sea between packed with boats and canoes ferrying the goods—and slaves—between ship and shore, the people having no idea of the danger they were in. Beyond the beach was a verdant green paradise, the forested coastland of Anamabo, the native village, and the ugly grey stone Dutch fort on the hill. There, behind those walls, guarded by cannon, were the holding cells for the slaves. Such places as that were strung out like beads on a necklace, all along this coast.

Roberts thumped the gunwale, a ball of dread forming in his belly. *Damned pirates!* They had to be pirates. And the *Princess*, and the other ships moored alongside were trapped. They could not flee—most of the crew were ashore and it would take too long to clear the decks, haul up the anchor and make sail. Besides, the pirate ships were faster than the *Princess* could ever hope to be. They would soon be overtaken, and then the pirates would be less inclined to give quarter. Furthermore, they were seriously outnumbered, so no chance to stand and fight. No, to his mind, Captain Plumb had but one alternative—to yield.

Roberts again crossed the deck to him intent on reasoning with him. In the few minutes since he had last looked, the incoming ships had made much headway and were now close enough to remove all doubt. Wordlessly, grimly, Captain Plumb handed him his own glass. Through it, Roberts could see them clearly.

The lead ship had a rakish appearance, a swift heavily-armed vessel, with perhaps thirty-six guns and twelve deceptively small man-slaughtering grapeshot-spewing swivels mounted on the high gunwales. She was a low ship with a black hull, flush decks, that is without raised forecastle and quarterdeck, and no raised hatches either. This was a fighting ship. The high gunwales afforded protection to her men and the flush decks aided their ability to man the guns and engage in hand-to-hand fighting unimpeded.

The second vessel was a frigate, Dutch by the look of her, boasting thirty guns and over twenty swivels and rode in the wake of the first.

The decks of both ships were packed tightly with men, an army, nearly a hundred on each ship. They meant business.

Captain Plumb swore profanely. For a brief moment Roberts pitied him. They could expect no help from the two ships riding at anchor alongside them, also loading. They too had more than half their men ashore. Plumb stood to lose everything unless he acted swiftly.

He made a decision. 'Mr. Stephenson—send the boats ashore.' He meant the boats ferrying human and other cargo to the ship. It would minimise losses. 'Mr. Roberts, belay loading and clear the decks!'

Immediately John Stephenson strode down the length of the ship, bellowing out the orders, with Roberts following. 'Get these crates below. Clear the decks!'

Pirates! The word buzzed around the ship as men frantically began the task of clearing the decks of any clutter that might cost them dear in a hand-to hand fight.

Captain Plumb paced back and forth, cursing in his agony, not taking his eyes from the incoming ships.

Roberts joined him again. 'Your orders, Captain?'

The other two ships anchored alongside had seen them too, and had sent their boats away back to the shore. The *Morrice* was nearly slaved—her loss would be great. The *Hink* by contrast had hardly begun.

Captain Plumb stopped pacing and leaned his hands on the gunwale staring at the newcomers.

A distant noise, a whisper on the hot air, soft, like a faint heartbeat reached them from across the water. Roberts felt it rather than heard it and the hairs rose on the back of his neck.

The men had heard it too and stopped to lean on the gunwales to stare at the newcomers. 'Clear the decks,' Roberts repeated, then louder: 'Clear the decks!' Reluctantly they obeyed.

'Your orders, Captain?' Roberts demanded again. 'You must yield!'

Plumb had no choice. Yet still he did not answer him. He stood mesmerised by his impending ruin, staring at the intruders, as the sound grew, a rhythmic drumbeat, like the voodoo drums so prevalent on this coast.

The men stopped again, also held by the menace of those drums, the tension in the air thick, like treacle. Roberts' mouth dried. His heart thudded at breakneck speed. They were heavily outnumbered. A show of resistance would cost them dear.

A ball ran up the mast of the lead ship, unfurling at the top to flutter and fill out in the wind, a sinister black silk pendant with the stark white figure of a skeleton holding an hour-glass in one hand and a dart in the other, suspended above a heart dripping blood. Once the jack of Blackbeard himself its chilling message was known to all: *Surrender and we give quarter, if not we spare none.*

The drumming ceased abruptly, the sudden silence as nerve-straining as the noise. On the *Princess* not a man spoke or moved, but each man watched in dread as the pirates came close.

Suddenly every man on the pirate's crowded decks waved their cutlasses in the air, and shrieked like wild animals, a terrifying war cry.

Roberts' stomach jolted and he gripped the gunwale.

The first ship fired one of her murderous bow-chasers. A puff of smoke first and then the gunpowder blast. But they had aimed high and with the ships riding at anchor and without sail, they caused no damage, the small shot splashing in the water.

It was enough for the *Princess*'s men. Without waiting for their captain's command, they leaned over the side crying out in panic: 'Give quarter! Give quarter!'

Captain Plumb swore profanely and beat the gunwale with his fist. 'Damn their cowardly eyes!'

'You must yield, Captain,' Roberts insisted. They were running out of time. Any moment the pirates would be upon them.

Stephenson too said urgently: 'Cap'n—yield!'

Again Plumb swore. He hesitated for precious seconds. But he was a beaten man. Then at last: 'Strike the colours,' he ordered.

Roberts passed on the order and the *Princess*'s flags slid down the mast in defeat.

'What d'ye think they'll do with us, Mr. Roberts?'

Roberts looked down at John Jessup beside him. He was sixteen with the pale bum-fluff of the adolescent not yet old enough to shave. His pale eyes now were wide with a fear he had given up struggling to conceal.

'I think they'll take what they want and leave us,' Roberts said with more in hopefulness than with any degree of certainty.

'We'll all be murdered,' William Hedges hissed from behind him. 'Lord, I wish I'd never come! Me mother, God rest her soul, told me I'd come to no good going to sea!'

'Well she was right then.' Roberts watched as the ships came nearer. The problem with pirates was that you never knew what to expect. Some were intent only on plunder. Others took delight in mistreating the crews of captured ships. And still others were nothing more than murdering scum, intent on the destruction of ship and men. Mercifully the last were in the minority.

The first ship, bearing the legend *The King James* came alongside, her hull meeting the *Princess* with a jarring bump. The second ship, the *Royal Rover*, joining her a few minutes later, came alongside the *Morrice*.

Grappling irons whistled through the air and clanged to grip the gunwales. The *Princess*'s men fell back in a huddle about the foremast as their attackers poured over the side, a fierce rabble of seamen, armed with knives, boarding axes, pikes and pistols, the last of which they levelled threateningly at the *Princess*'s passive crew. Yet they were ordinary seamen, the sort Roberts had to deal with every day, unwashed, mostly unshaven, wearing incongruously fine silk shirts above their sailor's slops and some had gold hoops dangling from elongated earlobes.

Two or three of them were set to guard the prisoners, which they did by waving pistols threateningly, while others of them with gleeful whoops and curses, disappeared below, returning almost immediately with bales of cloth which they gleefully unravelled. They were drunk, high on alcohol and excitement, dangerous.

A pistol shot brought their antics to an abrupt halt. 'Damn yer eyes, that'll do!'

Grumbling, they threw the cloth down, and the sea of men parted to allow their captain to come through the rabble to confront the prisoners.

Howell Davis was in his forties. Not a very large man, he had, nevertheless, developed a comfortable belly and rounded ruddy cheeks. He was well-dressed, no doubt his clothes pilfered from some rich merchant, and he wore a very creditable black wig that curled over his shoulders beneath a large black hat. A blue-dyed ostrich feather floated about the hat, and Flanders lace decorated his wrists and throat. But for all the twinkling grey eyes and broad friendly smile, he was heavily armed with two brace of pistols on red ribbons hung over his shoulders, a sword in the scabbard on the baldric slung across his body, and a knife tucked in his belt. Pirating was profitable.

'I am Captain Howell Davis, gentlemen,' he announced grandly, tucking the spent pistol in his belt at his waist. He grinned at them.

'I am Abraham Plumb, captain of the *Princess*,' Plumb announced from among the men by the mast.

Howell Davis studied this important prisoner, his eyes quickly assessing the man. Then he bowed low, sweeping the deck with his hat, a civility that surprised and impressed the *Princess*'s men. 'Captain Plumb, your most obedient.'

Unimpressed, Plumb drew himself up to his full height of just about five feet six inches. 'Sir! I must protest!'

Captain Davis paid him no attention whatsoever. Instead he smiled on the *Princess*'s men. 'Gentlemen,' his tone was smooth, quiet, reassuring, unexpected. 'We are taking your ship. Your officers shall be my—guests—aboard the *King James*.'

He might have used the word 'hostages' Roberts thought with disgust and he knew that as an officer he would be taken aboard the *King James*. And he realised that Davis was literally taking the *Princess*, that is sailing off with it. It made sense, of course, quick in and quick out, but it meant that the victims would be some days before they were rid of these men.

Davis's smile broadened into a grin as he looked at them. 'Carry on Mr. Dennis.' And another officer, even more gorgeously dressed than the captain nodded and said in an educated voice: 'Aye, aye Captain!'

David Symson walked slowly with a long stride crossed the deck of the *King James* to join his captain near the helm. 'A good haul, Mr. Symson,' Howell Davis said, grinning at him.

'In men too, I'll wager,' Symson said in a thick northern accent. His lids drooped over cold grey eyes, as he surveyed the men coming aboard. 'Who is the big man?'

'One of the mates.'

'Capable?'

'Look into it, if you please Mr. Symson.'

Symson nodded. 'Aye, aye Cap'n,' he said in his lazy way.

Davis nodded and turned his attention to another of his officers.

David Symson approached the prisoners. 'Welcome aboard friends.' The big man, Roberts, raised his chin and met David Symson's hooded eyes squarely with dark intelligent eyes. 'Who says friends,' he demanded quietly, 'when we are prisoners?'

David Symson's long scarred face managed a smile, and revealed two missing teeth. Too bold by half, and definitely too quick. 'Guests, Mr. . . . ?'

Roberts did not answer but continued to study Symson in a disconcertingly frank way. He did not have to give his name of course, but David Symson would find out.

'That be Mr. Roberts,' John Stephenson supplied helpfully. He'd already turned traitor.

'And what might Mr. Roberts do aboard ship?' David Symson

asked.

'He's third mate,' Stephenson said. 'And the best navigator in Guinea, I'll wager.'

The eyes remained hooded but there was a sudden intensity in their depths. 'Navigator, eh?'

Roberts said nothing, but continued to return stare for stare.

David Symson moved, walking a little past the group and then coming back again to stop in front of Roberts. 'You know, Mr. Roberts, we need a sailing master.'

'Oh?'

'The pay's good,' Symson continued.

'So?'

'No tyrannical captain to lord it over you.'

He glanced meaningfully at Captain Plumb who stood silently beside Stephenson.

'Women and wine and rum a-plenty. And gold.'

'Now there's something,' Roberts replied, a hint of sarcasm in his voice.

'A Welshman, eh?'

Roberts considered it unnecessary to answer.

The pirate crew had disengaged themselves from the *Princess* now and men swarmed over the yards, piling sail upon her.

Roberts watched with some surprise at the dexterity and eagerness of the men. A tight run ship, then, but not because of an autocratic captain, but because they had some kind of unity in a common venture. They had pride in their work.

The *King James* began to move as her sails filled with wind, sliding away from the *Princess,* and as men hauled on the yards, she began to come about, the deck canting beneath their feet. A distant pop of guns, and from the fort little puffs of smoke made a show of ineffectual defiance.

And suddenly the *King James* came to life as the officers bellowed out orders and men poured down the hatches to man the guns, while others arranged themselves in groups of six around the guns on the upper deck, navy style.

The decks had been sanded and the guns made ready earlier in case of resistance. All that was needed now was the order to load.

'Run out! Run out!' A man with a voice like gravel bellowed the orders.

David Symson had disappeared but another man ushered the

prisoners back to a position behind the helm near where the captain stood with his sword arm raised.

Men heaved on the side tackles and the guns trundled forward on the carriages, their rusty iron wheels squealing in protest.

As the ship came round further to present her side to the fort, Captain Davis waited for his moment.

Roberts felt the tension in his belly, and his mouth went dry. It had been a long time since he had been in battle. He remembered now the exhilaration of fear coursing through his veins, and realised he had missed it. A man could become addicted to the thrill of fear.

The Dutch Fort William, on the hill overlooking Anamabo had been built to protect the settlement from interloping trade—ships of other nationalities trading without a licence. They fired again on the pirates, but the shot fell short, sending squirts of water into the air some distance away.

And suddenly Captain Davis gave the order, *'Fire!'* and brought his sword down sharply.

The command echoed around the ship as the gun captains relayed it, and applied torches to the fuses. Then every man stood away from the guns waiting, some covering their ears.

One second. Two seconds. The delay was agonising. Then the first gun crashed, recoiling savagely against the ropes that held it fast, followed by the others one after the other down the side of the ship.

The noise blasted their eardrums, and sent tremors through the structure of the ship, shaking her very seams. The air filled with the thick stench of smoke and gunpowder and burning pitch.

'Sponge out! Re-load!' bellowed the gunners. But they were already to it. Roberts remembered it all so well. The war with Spain had come to an end six years ago. Of course he had been a navy man then, laid off when the war finished. But they had been hellish days, glory days, exciting days.

The *King James* had turned away from the fort and was running eastwards along the coast.

'Cease firing! Belay all!' came from the captain.

It was over.

Howell Davis looked at them then, grinning cheerfully. 'Out of range,' he said by way of explanation and abruptly walked away.

TWO

Captain Davis hacked off a lump of fatty roast pork with his dagger, speared it with the point and transferred it to his mouth. 'Now then, where are you from Bart Roberts?' he asked.

The lanterns swinging from the deck head beams made scant impression on the darkness of the great cabin, and a thick fog of tobacco and candle smoke made it almost impossible to see the bulkhead opposite. Even so, the head of every man seated around the great cabin table swivelled in Roberts' direction, and they peered at him with keen interest.

Roberts tore off a piece of meat from the chicken leg, and chewed it. Then he said without looking up: 'Casnewyddbach.'

He had been deliberately cryptic. Who but those familiar with the area would know such a small hamlet? Davis did. 'Haverfordwest, is it? Milford Haven man myself.'

Roberts raised his brows in acknowledgement. Milford Haven and Haverfordwest were no more than eight or ten miles apart.

'Damn my soul, another Welshman,' the man with the gravelly voice growled from across the table.

Wondering if he should take offence, Roberts studied him. He was the archetypal pirate, built like the side of a house, and with a week's worth of black stubble on his face, 'Valentine Ashplant,' the man introduced himself, rising slightly in his chair and holding out one large paw for Roberts to shake. 'Welcome aboard Mr. Roberts.'

It would have been churlish to refuse the friendly gesture, so Roberts rose too, and took the hand. 'Mr. Ashplant.' It might be safer to keep these men sweet.

'You'll be staying with us, Mr. Roberts?' Ashplant growled, resuming his seat, and his pipe.

'I doubt that, Mr. Ashplant. I've no wish to turn pirate.'

'Ain't no need for that now, Mr. Roberts,' Captain Davis reprimanded him gently as he reached for the ladle in the bowl of rum punch and leaned over to pour some into Roberts' mug. 'Gentleman of fortune, if you please.'

Roberts did not acknowledge it, intent instead on stopping him filling his cup. 'I don't drink.'

Once more he was the focus of all the stares. 'Don't drink?' Davis repeated aghast. Then his eyes narrowed. 'Or is it that you don't drink with pirates, then?'

'I don't drink,' Roberts repeated. 'Ain't nothing personal in it.' But he knew how it must look. To sailors in general and pirates in particular, a man who did not drink, smoke or wench like the rest of them was hardly a man at all, a real oddity, definitely not to be trusted.

But he had his reasons. Reasons he was not about to divulge to the interested group around the table.

Captain Plumb sitting on one side of him said: 'And I give thanks to the Lord, gentlemen, for a third mate I can trust not to lose his senses in drink.' He himself was well on the way to 'losing his senses'.

'I prefer to keep my wits about me,' Roberts agreed.

Davis laughed and hacked off another piece of meat. 'Very wise, Mr. Roberts.' He changed the subject abruptly. 'I hear you're a skilled navigator and sailing master.'

'Aye,' Roberts fixed his eye on John Stephenson who carefully avoided his gaze.

''Tis true then?' Davis persisted.

'I were mate of a Barbados sloop last year,' he confirmed. A man who held a mate's certificate had, of necessity to be a skilled navigator and sailing master, ready to take over the running of the ship if anything should happen to the captain.

'He's the finest navigator I ever did come across,' Stephenson said, adding: 'begging yer pardon, Cap'n Plumb. Does it all in his head, I reckon.' And he tapped his own temple expressively.

'And so what happened to your mate's licence?' Davis asked.

'I lost it,' Roberts said, and there was a touch of defiance in his voice.

'Lost it how?'

'That's my business.' An overbearing captain, a drunken brawl, and everything he had worked for gone.

'We need a sailing master,' Davis said. 'And a navigator.'

'Do you now?' Roberts replied with studied disinterest.

'"Artists" are hard to come by.'

'So I understand.'

'Why don't you join us?' a ferrety man Roberts had already noted as quartermaster called Richard Woods spoke up. As quartermaster, responsible for booty and victualling the ship, he also had the job of hiring men.

Roberts helped himself to a banana and began to peel it. 'No, I thank you.'

'You'll find life better with us than on any ship you've ever sailed on,' Davis coaxed.

Woods added: 'An easy life, good food, women, and gold. You'd be a rich man, Bart Roberts.'

'Much good it'd do me if I dangled at Wapping Dock!' Roberts retorted. 'I'm an honest man and I ain't about to change that.'

His words provoked a response from them. Then, above the hubbub a man from the end of the table spoke up: 'What be an honest man, Bart Roberts?'

In the dim light Roberts could just make out the speaker, a small wiry individual, one of those men who had strength in arms, legs and back that defied logic.

'What mean you, friend?'

The man sucked on a clay pipe for several seconds, sending more smoke into the already thick air and shrugged and for a moment Roberts thought he wasn't going to answer. Then he came to life again. 'Rogues, all of 'em.'

'What are you talking about man?' Valentine Ashplant demanded impatiently.

'Captains,' the man said with equal impatience, as though this point should be obvious.

Captain Plumb was moved to protest. 'I say, sir, I must object.'

'You'll have to tell'm why, Jim Phillips,' David Symson drawled, leaning back in a chair which seemed too small for him.

'Well, and I'm coming to that! Now in my opinion, gentlemen, there ain't a captain as commands a slaver that ain't done some double-dealing in his time. A little bartering on the side, shall we say. An' there ain't a captain who don't short-change his men when it comes to their rations, buying bad meat because it's cheap. And there ain't a captain alive who don't beat his men and treat them less than the damned slaves.'

'That be true enough,' Valentine Ashplant agreed, and waved his pipe about in the air expressively.

'Aye,' James Phillips went on doggedly. 'I tell you, gentlemen, that if there be one reason why good men go on the account, it be bad captains.'

Roberts was acutely aware of Captain Plumb sitting very quietly in his chair beside him. Every word of it was true. Autocratic captains were the bane of every sailor's life, and who hadn't longed to be free of the tyranny?

'Are you trying to say that there are not bad captains among pirates?' Roberts asked.

'Gentlemen of fortune, Mr. Roberts, if you please,' Captain Davis corrected him again.

Roberts met his eyes. So they preferred a euphemism. '*A rose by any other name . . .*' he quoted softly.

He saw the flash in Howell Davis's blue eyes, and knew a moment's perverse satisfaction.

'If there were, we wouldn't be here,' Phillips said, sticking doggedly to the issue of bad captains. ''Sides, we can depose a captain at a moment's notice.'

There was a silence as everyone looked at Howell Davis, then someone else seemed to wake from a drunken stupor to say in an unmistakable Irish brogue: 'Knew such a captain once. Sent a man to the topmast in a gale, so he did. Half out of his senses with malaria, so he was, shakin' so bad . . .' he gave a demonstration, holding his hands out in front of him and shaking them violently. 'Couldn't hang on, see. Fell into the drink, and never did we see him again.'

It was common enough, Roberts knew. He'd seen it himself where sick men had been forced to work and had died doing so.

The man who had spoken looked up straight at Roberts. He was a dirty, drunken, scarred, murderous brute with stringy hair which fell past his shoulders. The man's eyes—cold, evil, calculating—struck a chill in Roberts. This man would be better on your side than against you.

There was an awkward silence, for the man had made them all uneasy. Then, as if to fill the gap and break the bad spell, James Phillips spoke. 'Now when I sailed with Captain Teach . . .'

It was the signal for the rest to protest, but John Stephenson cut in excitedly. 'Teach? Blackbeard?'

Pleased, Phillips puffed out his small chest, and took a leisurely drag on his pipe. 'Aye, Blackbeard hisself. I were on the *Revenge* captained by Major Stede Bonnet, but in company with Cap'n Teach.'

'Hell's teeth! Not Blackbeard *again*!'

'I heard they hanged Bonnet at Charlestown a year or so ago,' Roberts put in provokingly.

Sudden silence hung over the company again and Roberts

looked inquiringly at Captain Davis once more, noticing with triumph the anger flash in Davis's blue eyes. One thing he admitted of Davis—he had a firm grip on his emotions.

'After my time,' Phillips went on doggedly apparently insensitive to the sudden change in atmosphere. 'As I were saying. Now Captain Teach were a man! A big man with black hair and long black beard tied in braids with ribbons. A fearsome man, he were. I remember when we were all at dinner when all of a sudden—bang!—and poor Israel Hynde fell to the floor, shot in the knee. Cap'n had shot him. Said it were to keep us all on our toes.'

'I imagine Israel Hynde did little on his toes for a bit,' Roberts said dryly.

'Stories of Teach have spread wide,' Davis said, any hint of rancour gone. 'Probably no truth in any of them.' He helped himself now to half a roast chicken.

'I were there!' James Phillips protested, affronted. 'And I'll blow out the brains of any man who says otherwise!'

'All right, you were there.' Someone else said placatingly.

James Phillips was not to be put off. ''Tis said when they finally caught up with him, they put five balls in him and ten cuts from a sword, but they couldn't kill him. So they took his head clean off! But they say—'

'—his headless corpse swum around the ship seven times!' they all chorused together. They'd heard the story too many times.

Roberts raised a disbelieving black eyebrow. 'Indeed?'

Davis laughed. 'Well, sailors are a superstitious lot. And Teach had evaded capture for sometime, put up a brave fight at the last. No ordinary man could give the navy so much grief, could he now?' And his eyes twinkled.

Valentine Ashplant, slurped at his rum punch, wiped his lips on a dirty sleeve and belched. ''Tis said Edward Teach did marry a young girl . . .' and he went on to relate a graphically ribald story about the pirate's wife.

Before long, under the influence of rum punch the talk had degenerated to the loose women that were the comfort of all sailors, each one trying to outdo his neighbour in ribaldry.

The hour was late when they began to disperse, this one to the head, that one to 'turn in'. By this time they had been well-fed, and well-watered, and well-entertained, and despite drinking only water, Roberts glowed with a sense of well-being. It had been a long time since he had enjoyed such camaraderie.

'They want you, Mr. Roberts,' Captain Plumb said as he made his way topside to relieve himself before turning in. The going was not easy. Plumb had drunk far more than he ought.

'They want us all,' Roberts replied, stepping onto the companionway ladder. 'As much as they want plunder, they want men. For their strength is in their fighting force.'

'You'll have to beware,' Plumb said sourly. 'They mean to have you.'

'I've already said, I have no intention of turning pirate,' Roberts told him. 'And I always keep my word.'

He awoke as the watch changed at eight bells or four o'clock in the morning, but he lay in his hammock listening to the sounds of the ship around him as the *King James* ploughed on steadily through the waves. He wondered how many men on the *Princess* had been persuaded to 'go on the account'. He had heard singing from the *Princess* last night, which suggested the crew were drunk and enjoying themselves mightily at the hands of their captors. It was a common trick, one he had been warned about. Pirates never had to force men, there were always enough volunteers.

The men who had been on watch came below and with as little noise as possible climbed into their hammocks. It was stiflingly hot between decks, despite the hatches being left open to catch the slightest breeze and the proximity of so many unwashed bodies produced the rancid odour of sweat, and dirt, and the stench of sweaty feet. The noise was gruesome too, a crescendo of snores and snorts and mumblings mingling with the creak of the ship's timbers and the boom of wind in the sails, the twang of the stays against the masts.

Roberts stayed in his hammock waiting for it to become light, listening to the sounds and wondering what life on 'the account' might be like. In truth he was sickened even now by the degradation of slavery, the vicious cruelty, both to slaves and sailors alike, and he had often thought wistfully of leaving the sea. But the sea was in his blood. He had been brought up near the ocean, spent all his working life at sea, and it kept him chained to the life as though he too were a slave.

At two bells, five o'clock, just as it was getting light, he rolled out of his hammock, and stowed it away, put on shoes and stockings and went topside.

The sun had not yet risen above the horizon, but the lightening sky filled the sea with a dim grey light.

Valentine Ashplant was the officer of the watch, and he paused in the act of recording on the log board the course steered during the last half an hour, greeting Roberts in his gravely voice: 'Morning, Mr. Roberts.'

'Good morning Mr. Ashplant,' Roberts responded in kind, and climbed onto the leeward gunwale to relieve his over-full bladder into the sea, while Ashplant added the details of wind direction and speed by the log, and then replaced the board on its peg by the helm.

'Going to be damned hot, by my eyes,' Ashplant observed unnecessarily.

'Aye.' Roberts joined him, leaning over the gunwale to watch the first yellow rays appear on the horizon. The provoking mood that had settled on him the night before had given way to a more genial turn of mind. Perhaps it was because of having a good night's sleep for the first time since setting out from London some weeks previously. In any case, he had decided there was no real reason to continue being deliberately obstructive.

'How long have you been with Captain Davis, Mr. Ashplant?' he asked.

Ashplant cast him a sideways glance, as though trying to weigh him up, then rubbed the flat of his hand across his whiskery face thoughtfully. 'Since Cap'n Davis captured me blasted sloop.'

'Your sloop?'

'Aye. I were master of her, and a poor business it were too, I might say. I were already running at a loss, didn't know how I were going to pay the crew's wages. Damned slaves kept dying on me, y'see. Turned most of them over the side.'

'Should have treated them better then,' Roberts observed dryly.

Ashplant turned offended bulbous eyes on him. 'Damn me, there ain't a man in Christendom who treated his blacks better'n me!' He paused and studied Roberts. 'Ain't a damned slave-lover are ye?'

Roberts stiffened. 'Don't matter what the colour of a man's skin might be, or where he hails from. If he does a day's work, he deserves his pay, like everyone else. And he don't need to be taken from his family and treated worse than an animal to do it, neither.'

This was a new thought to Ashplant, for he seemed to consider it carefully. Then he evidently decided not to enter into an argument about it. 'Well, all I can say is, 'twere a blessing for me when Cap'n Davis took the ship and said he were looking fer men. We all signed up! 'Twere the end of my worries, I can tell you.'

Roberts said: 'He wants me to sign.'

'Aye. We need a navigator and a sailing master.'

'I'm an honest man from a God-fearing family.'

'Yeah. Ain't we all!'

Roberts looked at him then and laughed in disbelief. 'How can you say that?'

Ashplant shrugged. 'Well, the way I reckons it, when we take a ship and plunder her, we're only taking what we're owed for all those years of blood sweat and toil for a pig's farthing . . . Ah, here's the Cap'n now.'

Howell Davis dressed in shirtsleeves and breeches, glanced up at the sails with satisfaction. 'Mr. Ashplant, how goes it?'

'All's well, Cap'n. Steady six knots. Wind's freshened from the sou-west.'

'Good. Mr. Roberts—you slept well, I hope?'

'As well as a prisoner may sleep, Captain.'

Davis did not take him up on the remark but removed the quadrant from its carrying case, and lined it up on the Pole Star as it hovered just visible in the lightening sky over the northern horizon, carefully noting down the reading. 'Probably you know our latitude, Mr. Roberts.'

'Probably,' Roberts agreed.

Davis concentrated on getting the angle right. 'Well?'

'Just north of the equator,' Roberts said vaguely, but he raised his eyebrows in mock innocence.

Davis looked at him and laughed suddenly. 'It don't take a genius to work that out!'

Roberts chuckled in spite of himself. 'No indeed.'

'And what do you think to be our longitude, Mr. Roberts?'

'I should think we are near Accra.'

Davis looked at the log board where changes in direction had been noted by the officer of the watch every half an hour, and then tucked it under his arm to take it below. The calculations he had to make would be complicated, using the almanac, every detail noted in the captain's log. Even then the calculation of their position would have to be approximate. For there was no way known to man of calculating longitude. Still he said: 'That's what I think. That also was not a difficult guess to make.'

Roberts grinned just as the sun suddenly peeped over the eastern horizon and flooded the sea and the ship with light and colour. 'Nope.'

He had no intention of confirming Stephenson's glowing report of him as a navigator. Yet he was capable of making the calculations in his head, of guessing the speed by the log, of calculating currents, and without the use of an almanac coming up with a more accurate position than the captain. Dead reckoning or not, sight verification proved him right.

But this was easy. Travelling eastwards, with the wind on a broad reach on the starboard side, the next fort from Anamabo was Accra, about twelve leagues [thirty-six miles] distant, also a Dutch holding, and forty-one leagues beyond that the eerie voodoo coast of Whydah.

'*Sail ho!*'

The sudden cry from the masthead stopped Roberts on his way below. 'Deck there! Sail ho, larboard bow!'

Howell Davis took the telescope from Ashplant, pulled it from its leather case, scanning the horizon with his naked eye while he did so. Then, with impressive athletic ease for a man of his portliness, he swung out over the sea and up the rigging to stop at the crosstrees to peer in the direction pointed out by the lookout.

'Aye, there she is all right,' Davis cried to the men who had congregated on deck. 'A Hollander.' He came down, yelling as he did: 'All hands! Lay aloft! Look alive there! Lay aloft you laggards! Make all sail. Drummers!'

'Does he intend to go after her?' Roberts asked Ashplant.

'Oh aye,' Ashplant growled at him. 'Never a ship is let slip,' he added.

But they already had three ships in their claws, Roberts thought.

The drummers took up a position forward, beating to quarters, but already men poured from the hatch in various states of undress, swarming into the rigging, running out onto the yards.

'Mr. Ashplant, make ready the guns.'

As the men frantically worked to untie the gaskets to release the sails, Davis pulled on shoes and stockings, shrugged himself into the fine blue coat that his black steward, Joseph, had brought for him, put on his baldric and loaded his pistols, all the while watching the horizon.

Roberts retreated to the windward side, as the men expertly piled on more sail and then came down.

The *King James* responded, picking up speed immediately, as the wind caught the sails, lurching forward, bucking and ploughing through the green waves so that the sea cascaded over the bows and washed the deck afresh before emptying out through the scuppers.

The Hollander, now aware of her peril, tried to flee before them, her crew desperately putting on more sail, even using oars to improvise spankers from which to hang more sail. But it was to no avail. The *King James* had the undoubted advantage of packing more sail than the Hollander, and Davis, familiar with the coastal currents and winds, steered her himself, skilfully. The gap between the two ships began to close at a surprising rate.

As the *King James* gained on her, the Hollander began to turn to larboard, towards the coast, running for the shore. Davis saw it, and swore under his breath. 'They'll not get away!' he declared, more in determination than prophecy, and, leaving the helm to another man, marched smartly forward as the men running to prime and load the *King James*'s guns dodged around him.

The Hollander knew she could not outrun them. Her only chance was to run aground, where she knew the pirate would not dare to follow.

Davis came back to the helm and turned the *King James* with a view to coming between the Hollander and the shore.

For tense minutes he held her course, determined to head the Hollander off.

Roberts saw disaster looming, and swiftly crossed the deck to the helm. 'You can't do it!' he cried at Davis. 'Damn you, you'll run us aground!'

'Then what do you suggest, Mr. Roberts?' Davis snapped, his little eyes glittering. But he gave the order to turn the ship away from the shore.

The Hollander now presented her larboard side to the *King James*'s bowsprit.

With every nerve in his body stretched, Roberts left Davis to watch from the other side.

'Prepare a broadside, Mr. Ashplant!' Davis snapped.

Excitement flooded Roberts' veins like the effect of strong drink, as he watched this man skilfully guide the *King James* into the attack.

Davis relinquished the helm. 'Bring us astern of her Mr. Grahams.'

The young man at the helm corrected the course, gave a command to alter the sails, and the *King James* responded immediately.

Men ran to distribute the buckets of water among the guns. Others threw water and sand on the decks to stop men slipping in blood should it come to bloody conflict.

Roberts' heart began to pound in his ears, and he found he was gripping the gunwale so hard his knuckles showed white in the dark tanned skin.

The gun crews charged the guns with powder, wad, the large cannon shot, and more wad, and rammed all home.

'Run out!' Davis bellowed.

'Run out! Run out!' Ashplant echoed, hoarse now with shouting orders.

Two rows of black barrels protruded through the side like a double row of fearsome metal teeth.

The *King James* ploughed onwards gaining quickly on the Hollander, the excitement like a fever sweeping through the ship.

'Steady as she goes,' Davis said, and young Abraham Grahams did his best, correcting as necessary, lining up the *King James* to cross the Hollander's stern.

But it wasn't good enough. Watching, Roberts itched to take the helm from a boy who lacked the feel of the ship. Davis sensed it too, and strode across the deck to again take command of the helm himself. Oh yes, they needed a sailing master, and desperately, for much as men saw Davis as some kind of magician, even he could not be in two places at once.

He positioned the *King James* just right, and Roberts acknowledged that he was a master.

The gap of sea between the two ships closed at a spectacular rate. Davis again handed the helm over to Grahams and marched forward a little and raised his sword, judging the moment.

It was a masterpiece of timing. As the *King James*'s bowsprit crossed the Hollander's stern, Davis brought the sword down sharply. '*Fire!*'

The obligatory two seconds ticked away in nerve-straining tension as the fuses burnt down and the *King James* came up on the crest of a wave putting her nicely in line for aiming the guns. And the first gun fired, recoiling savagely against the ropes, followed rapidly by the others in an almost continuous thunderous roar, spitting fire and smoke and deadly shot. The *King James* shook and shuddered in protest.

'Sponge out! Re-load!' Ashplant bellowed.

With his heart crashing in his ears, Roberts peered through the smoke.

The gallery in the Hollander's stern had smashed, the windows disappeared. He could imagine the damage a cannonball tearing through the gun deck would make, the dead, the dying, the injured, the blood and panic. Not forgetting the damage to the ship, perhaps to the stanchions and knees, the supports holding the ship together. Clearly Davis had no intention of sailing away with this ship.

'Bring her about Mr. Grahams!' he bellowed. For it was over. Crippled, the Hollander sent her colours down the mast, and her men leaned over the taffrail. 'Give quarter! Give quarter!'

THREE

The Hollander proved to be a fine prize, yielding fifteen thousand pounds sterling, and carrying the Dutch Governor of Accra. Davis dropped anchor off the deserted densely-forested coastline, and the pirates celebrated their victories with dancing and singing and drinking throughout the night.

'I'll be sorry to let you go, Bart Roberts,' Davis told him the next morning as the captured ships made ready to leave.

Roberts leaned back in the chair and studied him. There was something in Davis's manner that put him on his guard. He had been just two days in the company of Howell Davis, long enough to be able to see that he had something on his mind.

Roberts had a sneaking admiration for Davis, who was as different to his idea of a pirate as a high-born lady was to a common harlot. He was also different to his notion of any sea captain he had encountered in more than twenty years at sea. Davis was a civilised man, a man who prided himself on honour and good manners, who could afford to be chivalrous, magnanimous even, and took pleasure in doing so. He saw himself as a warrior, a righter of wrongs, a courageous knight. He was genial, not brutal, affable, with a fine sense of humour and expensive taste in clothes.

But, by whatever means, Davis always got what he wanted.

'I do not wish to turn pirate,' Roberts repeated stubbornly. He was also a man used to getting his own way, and part of his success as mate had been because he had the ability to control men with a look, a word, but also to inspire them, to get the best out of them without losing his popularity, nor compromising his authority.

Davis shook his head sadly. ''Tis a pity, now, indeed it is.' He paused, glancing at someone who had slipped quietly into the great cabin and who Roberts suddenly realised had taken up a position behind him. He glanced round himself in sudden alarm, as Davis said: 'Ah, Mr. Symson. Take Mr. Roberts below, if you please.'

Before Roberts had time to react, David Symson moved with uncharacteristic speed, twisting his right arm up behind his back until he thought the bone would snap, the pain shooting through to his fingers, at the same time pushing him forward roughly so that he fell onto the table, his face crushed against the blackened wood.

It took Roberts a second or two to realise that he had been crossed. It was a shock, for he had thought he was free to go if he wished, and had expected Davis to try to win him round by argument. The men who had decided to stay had already been vetted by Woods, the quartermaster, and had signed the pirates' articles or list of laws. So Davis thought himself an honourable chivalrous man, eh?

'What's this?' he demanded angrily as Symson grabbed hold of his hair and pulled him upright again.

The smile had vanished from Davis's eyes. 'I'm sorry Bart,' he said, and he seemed genuinely apologetic. 'But we need a navigator and sailing master, see?'

Anger choked in Roberts' throat. 'Damn you! Damn your double-dealing eyes!'

Davis shook his head. 'Yes, yes, yes. I know it ain't right, now. But I have no option. You'll see when you have been with us a little while that really I had no choice.'

David Symson hoisted him from his seat and propelled him towards the door. It was useless to struggle. Outside the great cabin, Symson finally let him go, propelling him forward so that he fell against the gun deck bulkhead. By the time he had recovered, Symson had pulled a pistol.

It brought Roberts up short. David Symson may exhibit all the outward signs of lethargic good nature, but the glitter in those grey eyes told Roberts he would not hesitate to use the pistol if necessary. These men were amoral, used to murder and torture to get what they wanted.

'Sit down, Mr. Roberts,' Symson advised, and Roberts did so on one of the benches that were suspended on ropes from the deck head beam, as Symson took a seat opposite him, still pointing the pistol.

Roberts felt the anger coiled tightly like a serpent deep in inside him. But he kept it there. Only his eyes had darkened, betraying it, and David Symson smiled knowingly.

Topside Roberts could hear the noises as the various ships were finally let go, the Hollander, the *Hink,* the *Morrice,* and also the *Princess.* He heard Captain Plumb being bidden a good natured farewell by Captain Davis, and all he could do was sit and stare at Symson and the pistol.

'You ought to be flattered, Mr. Roberts,' Symson said with a languid smile. 'Cap'n Davis don't usually force men. It be against his principles, like.'

'But not against yours, I see.'

'Me?' The smile broadened. 'I do as I am told, Mr. Roberts, as I am sure you are aware.'

'Why me? There are other men who can navigate.'

Symson shrugged non-committally. 'See this?' He waved his pistol at the space between decks where they sat. It was a vast empty space, the place where the company ate, and slept and spent their time, but what was strange was that there were no bulkheads at all, save the one that separated the great cabin. The deck was completely open, and, with the tables, benches and hammocks stowed, was now an open gun deck, running the full length and breadth of the ship, save for the great cabin aft, and the galley right in the forecastle or bow. It had been made into a warship, permanently cleared and ready for action.

'What of it?' Roberts countered.

'This is what we are all about. We are a fighting ship, Mr. Roberts. And we are at war. At war with those who have victimised us.'

'I've heard it all before.'

'No doubt. And as in any war, the victor takes the spoils.'

'So?'

'So you'll be getting your share of this day's work.'

Roberts shrugged.

Symson went on slowly, apparently doing some mental arithmetic. 'It should amount to something in the region of, say, seventy pounds.

Surprised, Roberts stared at him. 'Seventy pounds?' It seemed like a fortune and represented more than two years' wages for a third mate whose pay amounted to just two pounds and ten shillings per month—and he could not expect to work every month of the year.

Captain Davis's voice filtered down to them as he gave the orders to make sail, and then he came down the hatch. So, all the captured ships had now departed. Roberts felt his spirits sink, for he realised that a chapter had closed on his life, and a new one was just beginning. For once he had been in company with pirates, there was no way out.

Davis went into the great cabin, followed closely by Richard Woods, the shrew-like quartermaster.

Symson stood up, and now put his pistol away in his belt, and jerked his head in the direction of the cabin.

Roberts did as he was bid and was in time to find Woods extracting a roll of paper from the drawer in the chest.

He knew what it was. He had been present at the reading of the articles the day before when thirty-four men from the three ships signed. Only he had not signed. Now he saw that they intended that he should do so.

Without speaking, Davis brought the heavy silver inkstand onto the large table and unrolled the paper, using the heavy inkstand to weigh down one end and a pistol the other. It was a long roll, a lot of writing at the top, and great list of names at the bottom, some crossed out, others signed with just a mark.

Symson pushed Roberts down into the seat he had vacated earlier.

Davis took the pen, dipped it in the ink, and gave it to Roberts. 'Sign here, Mr. Roberts, if you please.'

Roberts hesitated. Once his signature was on that paper he was committed.

The unmistakable clicks of a pistol hammer being cocked and the kiss of cold steel on the side of his neck helped him come to a decision. The men in the cabin were silent, the tension thick in the air. He knew that if he did not sign, he would be summarily despatched. No-one needed to keep prisoners on a fighting ship.

It was one thing to hold out for what was right. It was another to give one's life for it! And there were worse things than being forced into piracy under the command of Howell Davis. Being dead was one of them.

He took the pen, dipped it again in the ink, and signed his name with a flourish.

Tucked in the elbow of the West African coast, the mangrove-clad bays and channels of High Cameroon afforded the pirates excellent, if pungent cover. To the south the distant peak of a mountain rose mistily from the rainforest, a majestic backdrop to the vivid green of the tangled foliage.

Two hundred men crammed the *Royal Rover's* decks all sweating and stinking in the oppressive heat. It had rained that morning, great heavy droplets of water cold and hard as pebbles, a formidable deluge that sent even hardened sailors scurrying for cover. But the rain stopped as suddenly as it began leaving behind a sulky sky and steaming air.

Roberts perched on the gunwale between John Stephenson and John Jessup who were among the voluntary recruits. His shirt, like theirs was soaked with sweat, and the exposed skin on his arms and face was damp and clammy and even his legs were uncomfortable.

'Why have we been called on deck, Mr. Roberts?' John Jessup asked, looking up at him and screwing up his freckled face against the sun.

Robert shrugged non-committally.

''Tis a meeting,' another man said, turning to address them both. He was a stocky rough-looking fellow of not yet thirty, but aged beyond his years by the harsh seaman's life, his sun-baked face deeply etched with lines and gullies. He had dark hair and the requisite chin stubble. With slow precision he drew on a dirty clay pipe, sending a cloud of white smoke into the heavy air.

'Why do we need a meeting?' Jessup asked. 'Don't the captain make the decisions?'

'Bless yer, no!' the man answered, surprised, and looked at Roberts. 'Little innocent ain't he!'

'Naïve,' Roberts agreed, raising a brow at Jessup.

'Ye're from one of them ships at Anamabo, ain't ye?' he asked.

'From the *Princess*,' John Stephenson confirmed, and he gave the man their names.

He picked up on Roberts. 'So you be the new artist, eh?'

'Evidently,' Roberts replied 'And who are you, then?'

'Robert Birdson. Bin with Cap'n Davis since the day we do leave the *Buck* together.'

'So what's with the meeting?' Roberts asked.

Birdson shrugged and drew several puffs on his pipe before replying. 'Mr. Woods, the quartermaster, share out the gold and goods from the 'Ollander, and if there be a brace o' pistols, he might auction 'em off if no-one have a claim on 'em.'

Roberts wanted pistols—he felt naked in this company without. 'How much would a man expect to pay for pistols?' he asked.

Robert Birdson leaned forward to ladle rum punch into his tankard and took a large swig before answering. 'I dunno. That depend. Ten pound, p'raps, for an ordin'ry pair. For a good pair, fifty.'

Roberts felt his heart sink. Ten pounds was more than he had to his name. Fifty pounds a fortune beyond his reach. However, had not Symson suggested he would receive part of the prize?

'After that,' Birdson went on, 'we have to decide what to do about the *King James.*' The *King James* was leaking badly, and the amount of pumping necessary to keep her afloat was a matter of much aggravation in the company. 'Then there be a matter of appointing artists—that be you, if you be the new sailing master— and then where we do go to next. All got to be discussed, see?'

To the new men used to having decisions made solely by the captain, it was a novel idea. 'So we all make the decisions?'

'Aye, in a manner of speaking. The Cap'n will have talked it over with the 'Lords'—that be the officers—and then they puts it to us. And we all votes on it. Ah—'ere they come, and about time too, I say!'

Captain Davis had dressed for the occasion in billowing white shirtsleeves, royal blue waistcoat and black leather gloves, as he followed out the rougher elements of his 'house of lords' and came to stand on what would have been the quarterdeck, had the decks not been made flush. Roberts was struck by the presence of the man. Everything about him proclaimed him commander, and his men fell silent as they watched his approach.

He didn't address them, but took himself to the side to lean against the gunwale. He was followed by another man, someone Roberts had seen before, gorgeously dressed in a suit of powder blue embroidered silk, a black curled wig falling over his shoulders. 'Who is that man?' Roberts asked Robert Birdson.

'Why, that be Mr. Henry Dennis,' Birdson said. 'He be a gunner on the *Royal Rover.*'

Henry Dennis paused on the deck and his eyes slid over the assembled men, coming to rest on Roberts. If Roberts had not known better he might have thought this well-attired man to be the captain. Whoever this Henry Dennis was, he thought much of himself.

Dennis spoke to James Phillips beside him, and they both looked at Roberts as Phillips answered him. Evidently the news about the new sailing master had spread.

Henry Dennis joined the captain at the gunwale, and Richard Woods came to the foremast, the place for conducting all business, including distributing their ill-gotten gains. Two straining men brought a chest, which, Roberts supposed, contained the Hollander's gold, and they put it down with reverential awe in front of Richard

Woods.

Everyone focused on the box as though it were magical, although it was an ordinary chest, made of oak with a domed lid, and padlocked. Woods drew the hammer back on his pistol, aimed it at the lock and fired.

The report seemed to bounce off the hills behind them, and sent a flock birds into shocked flight, but the attention of every man was fixed on that chest. The lock had broken on the shaft, and swung drunkenly with the shock of the attack. A swift kick and it clattered to the deck.

Woods leaned forward and pulled back the lid. There was a gasp from the company, for the gold was in the form of coins, glittering in a sudden shaft of sunlight like a thousand candles. Roberts felt his stomach tighten in anticipation. It was a fortune, more than he had ever seen in his life before, greater than the fabled riches of El Dorado, he thought.

Richard Woods turned once more to the scroll with the names on it, and began to read.

He already knew how much gold there was from the inventory found on the Hollander and had already worked out how much a share would be, and now he called each man by turn, beginning with the captain, and gave to each one his share.

Roberts, the last man to be called, for his was the last name on the list, received a share of seventy-two pounds, which he put into a cloth purse, for stowing later in his chest. He had never had so much money in his possession all at once, and he liked the feeling of being rich.

The chance came to spend some of it. Woods auctioned three brace of pistols, and Roberts bid for a pair and to his great satisfaction he got them for twenty pounds.

With the most urgent business dealt with, it was time for Captain Davis to address the company. He took a swig of rum punch from his tankard before setting it aside. Looking around him at the eager faces before him, he pushed himself off his perch on the gunwale and took up a place in front of the foremast. The delay heightened the expectation of the waiting men, and a hush descended over the ship. And at that moment the sun broke through the clouds, bathing him in white harsh light, as though to bestow heavenly blessing upon him.

'Gentlemen, we must congratulate ourselves on our success I

think. A toast then, to our victories!'

They raised tankards and cried: 'Victory!'

'And may we have many more. But we have earned shore leave—' this was greeted with approbation by the company, '—and besides, we need to clean ship.'

Valentine Ashplant found the narrow shade of one of the masts and he sat on a barrel resting his elbow on his knee and rubbing his stubbly chin. 'The *King James* ain't salvageable,' he growled.

Every man knew it. The tropical worm had eaten into the hull turning it into a sponge. That's what happened if you did not beach and careen every six weeks or so. Without urgent extensive repairs, they could go no further in her. But it would be easier to replace the ship than repair it.

A cloud passed over Davis's face. He had affection for the brigantine, and had given her the name for his own Jacobean leanings. But he couldn't deny the truthfulness of the charge. 'Aye,' he said regretfully.

'And the *Royal Rover* must be cleaned and fitted,' Birdson said from his place beside Roberts.

'Suggestions, gentlemen?' Davis asked.

Roberts thought about it. They needed deep water close to shore and sturdy trees to allow them to beach the ship and haul her over on her side, so that her bottom could be scraped clean of barnacles, repaired, caulked, and repainted with a mixture of sulphur, tallow and tar.

Young Tom Sutton, good looking and dark haired, reeled off a list of the favoured careening bays on the Guinea coast in his swallowed northern accent. 'Old Calabar, Whydah, Gabon, Cape Lopez, or Prince's. We are already east of Whydah and Old Calabar.' The prevailing winds were south-westerlies. 'So it has to be Gabon, Cape Lopez or Prince's.'

Davis nodded. Gabon and Cape Lopez were well-known stopping points, with easy access and isolated bays where they could trade their goods with the natives. But the local women were considered 'noxious', even downright poisonous, for after a sojourn ashore there half the company was likely to go down with the pox, or malaria, or yellow fever.

Prince's Island, or Principe, as the Portuguese inhabitants called it, was an island paradise belonging to the archipelago which included São Tomé and Annobona to the south. It too was a trading post, exporting thousands of slaves to the New World annually, and willing to trade in other goods, besides having an abundance of fresh fruits and meats and grains and sweet water. Of even greater importance to the pirates, the women there, Portuguese, Creole and Negro knew how to welcome generous sailors. It was a favourite anchorage for the English but had the disadvantage of being well-populated with no hiding places for pirates seeking shelter, for unlike Sierra Leone, it lacked the labyrinth of river channels where they could hide themselves.

All these virtues and drawbacks were discussed at length.

'If we went to Prince's we would have to go in disguise,' Roberts said. 'Perhaps as British navy with a commission to search out and apprehend pirates, and those guilty of trading with pirates.' The subterfuge would account for the flush decks of the *Royal Rover* which were instantly recognisable, and therefore suspicious, to anyone with a glass. And the British navy were known to stop there.

Davis's eyes glittered with appreciation and he smiled thoughtfully. 'Now that I like.'

Henry Dennis nodded, and smiled, and wished he had thought of it. 'It will work,' he said.

'There be gold to be had on Prince's, too,' David Symson said. The wealth of the island from slave-trading was well-known. 'I'd like to see how to get at that!'

'We could go in and slit their throats,' said a man hidden by Ashplant's bulk, but Roberts had no difficulty in recognising the distinctive Irish accent of Walter Kennedy. 'Quiet, like in the dead of night. And when they were all dead, steal their gold from under their noses!'

Davis exchanged uneasy glances with Dennis and Symson, and there was a murmur among the crew. There was something about this Kennedy that made them uneasy. the way he had made Roberts uneasy.

'Well, we ain't in the business of murder,' Davis said sharply. 'We'll see how the land lies when we get there.' He raised his voice addressing the whole company. 'So, then, is it to be Prince's?'

'Aye, aye!'

He grinned.

The men began to talk about it among themselves as they dispersed, but Davis beckoned Roberts to join him.

'I like that idea, Mr. Roberts,' he said, walking towards the hatch so that Roberts had to go with him. 'A smart naval rig is what we will indeed become. And I think if you have no objection, I would like you to accompany me when I go ashore to meet the governor.'

'You will meet with the governor?' Roberts asked, surprised at the audacity of the man.

'But of course, Mr. Roberts. Are you willing?'

Roberts had a brief vision of going straight into the lion's den, but he knew that to turn it down would brand him a coward. Where Davis went, he was more than capable of following.

'Why me?'

Davis waved his hand in the air. 'Because you speak fluent Portuguese. Because you look the part of a gentleman.'

'And because you want me to be involved,' Roberts added.

Davis nodded. 'Yes, that as well. It is well known, Mr. Roberts, that you were a reluctant recruit. The men don't trust you, see?'

'And once I've got my hands muddy it will difficult to extricate myself?'

'Something like that.'

'So I'll hang, whatever happens.'

'Only if we get caught Mr. Roberts. And I don't intend to allow that to happen.'

FOUR

Príncipe, some two hundred miles west of the Gabon coast rose abruptly from the soft turquoise ocean, a breathtakingly beautiful island of smoky mountains and misty hills gowned in primeval rainforest. Towering green-liveried islets emerged from the sea around the coastline like sentinels, and eagles kept a watchful eye, soaring from castellated crags, sounding alarm with eerie cries as they circled the *Royal Rover*.

''Tis to be hoped the governor is less suspicious than the eagles,' David Symson observed languidly watching them from where he leaned on the taffrail.

Roberts glanced up at the red cross of St. George flying at the masthead and then at the men working in silence on the *Royal Rover's* decks. Rule on a British naval rig was unforgiving, as some of them knew. And the Portuguese pilot guiding them into the bay had to be convinced that they were indeed a naval rig.

'Are you observing, Mr. Roberts?' Howell Davis asked quietly as he wandered towards them. 'We might have to find our way out of these shallows on our own.'

Roberts nodded. 'Aye.'

David Symson gave a half-disbelieving laugh. 'You see it once and remember?'

Roberts raised his brows at him. 'Don't you?'

Chuckling, Symson went away.

Davis leaned on the taffrail beside Roberts. 'Don't mind Symson. A good man. Trustworthy. A little temperamental at times, but a good man.'

Roberts said: 'He ain't stupid.'

'No.'

'And he knows the running of the ship.'

'Every timber, every rope. He'd make a good quartermaster.'

'Why ain't he, then?'

'Because Woods got there first! Symson's time will come. Now then, looks like we're just about here.'

The pilot had brought them safely into the elongated natural harbour, and the sailing master gave the orders to furl the sail and drop anchor.

Roberts stood by with his hands clasped behind his back, observing, imitating a lieutenant on a ship he had once served on.

Naval officers did not do any hard work—theirs was all mental—and Roberts was supposed to be a lieutenant.

Henry Dennis too. He joined Roberts, standing beside him. 'So you go ashore, Bart Roberts.'

'Aye.'

'For what purpose?'

'Perhaps you had better ask Captain Davis,' Roberts said. Dennis had a superior way with him that set Roberts' back up.

'Thought you didn't want to be a pirate,' Dennis said.

Roberts was on his guard. 'Aye.'

'So what has changed your mind?'

Roberts looked at him, and raised his brows. 'Why, Mr. Dennis, I thought you knew! I'm a forced man!'

Dennis's eyes narrowed as he tried to decide whether to believe him or not. Finally he said: 'Captain Davis does not believe in forcing men.'

Roberts said: 'As you will, Mr. Dennis.'

Dennis walked away to join David Symson. Roberts saw them talking about him, and guessed they didn't like the way the captain singled him out. He'd already summed up Henry Dennis. An opportunist. He would misuse others to get what he wanted. And what he wanted, Roberts could see, was power. For Henry Dennis thought a little too highly of himself, even among a company of men who all thought themselves better than the next man.

Davis and Roberts and an armed guard of four men went ashore in the pinnace, being rowed by some of the lesser men for there was not enough breeze for sail. They drew up on the beach at the bottom of the harbour, where the town sat mostly hidden on a wooded hill, and hauled the boat up onto the sand.

Davis stood and looked around him, half expecting a welcoming committee from the governor. After all, he could not think their arrival had gone unnoticed. When it did not arrive, he took the path off the beach and up the hill, and the others trudged along behind.

Overlooked by the tall cloud-draped mountain of Pico Papagaio, Santo António the only town on the island consisted of three straight streets of wooden dwellings and brick-built colonial houses. It boasted a cemetery, and a church run by two monks, and the governor's house, a grand affair proclaiming wealth from slave trading.

The governor's house was at the head of the main street, a typical Portuguese colonial house with stuccoed walls and tall arched and shuttered windows, and it boasted a neat garden to the rear overlooking the harbour, and a barren yellow earth square to the front edged by fan-shaped palms where a dozen or so armed musketeers lounged, passing the time of day with the many people who came that way, particularly the young Creole women who flirted openly with them.

A bewigged black footman dressed in white livery met them at the door of Government House, and shutting Davis's armed guard outside, invited them to wait in the spacious hall while he went to enquire of his master.

Glancing up at the ornately-plastered ceiling Roberts raised expressive eyebrows at Captain Davis who nodded dourly. This was no mere peasant residence. The man who lived here had the best of everything, tiled floor, whitewashed walls hung with paintings, upholstered chairs, fancy ornaments. He picked up a gilded ornament of a rearing horse. Expensive. Certainly above the means of a lowly sailor.

Roberts caught a glimpse of his reflection in a gilt framed mirror. Dressed now in 'gentleman's' clothes, with lace at his throat and wrists, and his black curls forced into a black ribbon at the nape of his neck, he certainly looked the part of a naval officer. He liked what he saw. If ever he had the opportunity, he told himself, he would always dress like this.

The servant returned. 'If the *senhores* will be pleased to come this way,' he said on a bow and led them to a room at the rear of the house, where he announced them.

'*Capitão* Howell Davis of his majesty's ship *Royal Rover*, of the English navy, and *lugar-tenente* (lieutenant) Bartolomeo Roberto.'

'Yes, yes, send them in, Fernando.'

This room was larger than Roberts had expected from the size of the house he had seen from the outside, but it was also stark white and sparsely furnished. A window looked out onto a small garden, and a few trees, and beyond that the sea twinkling through the foliage. But it was cool in the study, a great relief from the heat outside.

António Furtado de Mendoça sat behind a large ornately carved mahogany desk leaning back in his chair and reading from a sheet of paper in his hand, but he smiled engagingly at his visitors, put the paper aside and came to his feet as Roberts and Davis bowed, sweeping their hats in front of them.

Roberts summed Mendoça up in an instant. His fine clothes and the general air of opulence in the house proclaimed him to be a successful slave trader. Mendoça smiled and bowed slightly in acknowledgement, but his black eyes darted over them quickly summing them up. This man would not easily be fooled, Roberts thought.

'Welcome to Príncipe *Capitão* Davis. *Senhor* Roberts.' He made no attempt to use English but spoke in Portuguese.

Davis thanked him also in Portuguese and in response to the invitation the visitors sat down on the wooden upright chairs indicated.

'Fernando! Wine for our guests!' He made a big theatrical gesture with his arms as he said it, beamed enthusiastically and then sat down himself behind the desk. 'It is a great honour to have the captain of King George's navy to visit us,' he added with a grin and another expressive wave of his hand. Portuguese custom dictated that the use of the pronoun *you* should not be used except on the most familiar terms, and he kept to the polite, distancing third party expressions, and Davis, of course, followed suit. 'Tell me how we can be of service to the English, *capitão*.'

Davis said: 'I am captain of his majesty's ship the *Royal Rover, senhor*, with a commission to search out and apprehend pirates.'

Mendoça nodded, those black eyes watching Davis intently. *The man already knows who we are*, Roberts thought.

Then, suddenly as if remembering his role, he beamed on them, all good-humour and arm-waving. 'But of course! The visit of *Capitão* Davis is well-timed. I make infrequent visits to Príncipe, being governor also of São Tomé. The *capitão* is indeed fortunate to find me here.' He paused thoughtfully. 'Furthermore, I have as guest in my house the Emissary to his majesty King João and he will be most interested in the *capitão*'s mission.' He smiled serenely, his little dark eyes watching them carefully to see their reaction to this piece of news.

Roberts felt Davis stiffen beside him. The presence of the Portuguese King's Emissary could well complicate matters. Where a governor might be corrupted with a bribe or two, an emissary might not. Davis said smoothly: 'I shall be pleased to meet the King's Emissary, *senhor governador*,' Davis said. 'Perhaps the *senhor* would like to come and view the goods the *Royal Rover* has to offer?'

Mendoça smiled and nodded acknowledgement and would have spoken, but the footman arrived at that point, carrying a silver salver on which stood an expensive cut-glass decanter and goblets which he set down on the sideboard. He poured wine into the goblets, and then passed them to the guests and his master.

Roberts looked at the glistening ruby wine in the cup, and thought of his decision never to drink.

Davis raised his glass and said: 'The health of the *senhor governador*!' which Roberts repeated, and while Davis swigged his wine, Roberts held the glass to his lips but did not drink. Thereafter he sat holding it in his hands, fingering the diamond pattern.

'It is particularly interesting that the English are here just now to seek out pirates,' Mendoça said, 'and we are, of course, always pleased to welcome the navy of King George.' He held up his glass, ostensibly studying the contents, yet at the same time watching them carefully. And Roberts did not miss the slight twitch of a moustachioed mouth. Oh yes, Mendoça knew alright.

Mendoça went on: 'Pirates have been most troublesome in these waters. Only last week one of our ships was taken by a pirate, homeward bound from São Tomé and intercepted off the Guinea coast. Mercifully no-one was killed, but I wonder what might have happened had they not surrendered.' He crossed himself in a show of piety.

Davis shifted in his seat, and Roberts suppressed a grin. They both recognised their own handiwork.

'English does the *senhor* think?' Davis inquired innocently.

'They flew English colours, as well as the pirate flag. I tell the *senhores*, we are at a loss. We do not have the ships, nor the men to go in search of them. Why even the Governor of Accra was attacked just two weeks ago on his way home to Holland. Again no-one was hurt, and it would appear it was the same English band. They took a large amount of gold, though.'

Davis shook his head and clicked his tongue. 'Dear me! Absolutely lamentable. The governor of Accra, eh?' he peered into his wine. 'How much gold?' he asked casually.

Mendoça put his glass down on the desk and spread his hands

expressively. 'I do not know. A goodly sum. What can the English do to rid this coast of these—parasites, *capitão*?'

Not slow to put the first of his plans into action, Davis said: 'Well, to begin with, there is a French ship lying at anchor in the harbour. We have reason to believe that the goods she carries she obtained from pirates.'

'The *capitão* wishes to search her? I give permission.' Mendoça waved his hand dismissively.

'If we find contraband goods on her we will hold her until we are finished here and take her back to Cape Corso Castle.' Corso, or Cape Coast as the English sometimes called it, was the largest English slave trading post on the West African coast, and the British administrative centre for the region.

'Very good! And anything we can do to help the *capitão,* he only needs to ask.'

Davis took up the offer with alacrity. 'Well now, as it happens, *senhor,* we are in need of supplies and water, and we need to clean our ship.'

'The senhor may clean ship in one of the bays,' Mendoça said magnanimously, and with a wave of his hand added: 'As for everything else, the senhor may take whatever he needs.' But he did not mean without payment.

Captain Davis nodded his head graciously. 'And whatever we take, *senhor* our King will pay for,' and he smiled as he disposed of the hated King George's wealth. He put his empty glass back on the silver salver. 'I thank the *senhor governador* for his hospitality to the King's navy.'

Mendoça's smile did not waver. 'I would rather the *senhor capitão* traded for his provisions,' he said gently. 'It may well be some time before King George makes reparation.'

Davis's eyes looked straight into Mendoça's and there was complete understanding between them. 'Of course,' he said after just a moment's pause. 'The *senhor* must come and see what we have to trade.' He was on safe ground here—even naval ships did not leave England without goods to trade.

Mendoça stood up, indicating that the interview was now at an end. 'I shall look forward to it, *senhor capitão*. Rid these waters of pirates, and we shall be ever in the debt of *senhor capitão*. Be sure, King João of Portugal shall hear of this.'

****

'So what do you make of him?' Davis asked as they crossed the searingly hot square outside, with the four armed men falling in behind them.

It had taken Roberts no more than a few seconds to assess the Portuguese governor. 'A slave trader, I reckon. Mendoça is rich, and capable and has a vested interest in the wealth and well-being of the island. And he has brought the King's Emissary here whom he no doubt hopes to impress with his management of the place.'

'You think he is not to be trusted?'

But Roberts thought Davis had already formed his own opinion of the governor.

'I don't think we have anything to fear from Mendoça,' he said carefully. 'But he knows who we are. And he knows that we will trade at good rates. I doubt if Mendoça would let a little thing like morality hinder his making a good profit.'

Davis grinned, well pleased. 'You reckon he'll give us what we want?'

'The provisions? Yes, without a doubt. But as for the gold—the Portuguese are wealthy on slave trading. But their wealth is distributed about the island. We can hardly steal it from a dozen merchants so we must think of another way of getting it.'

They took the shady road between the trees leading down to the harbour where the pinnace waited for them. 'Well, we will have to give that consideration,' Davis said, and stood aside to let two Portuguese women pass, removing his hat and bowing as he did so.

Roberts, who had been too involved in his assessment of Mendoça to pay more than cursory attention to the women, was now forced also to stand aside and remove his hat, and because English gentlemen were supposed to have different manners to common sailors, also executed an extravagant bow.

The women nodded in acknowledgement of the courtesy. The older woman stared at them icily, as though English sailors, whether officers or not, were beneath her matronly consideration.

But the other, a much younger woman, bestowed a smile of gratitude on them. *'Obrigada, os senhores.'*

Never in his life had Roberts set eyes on anyone so beautiful. Her face was perfection, smooth pale honey skin, finely sculpted features—neat little nose, small chin, aristocratic cheekbones. Her lips were the colour of dark red wine, parted now in a slight smile to show fine white even little teeth, and beneath black eyebrows, the eyes that smiled into his were as black as the sea at midnight.

'Our pleasure, my dear,' Davis breathed reverently in English.

Her eyes flicked to him, but immediately flicked back to Roberts.

Then her attention was claimed by her maid and she walked on past them, gliding across the square, and entered the governor's house.

Davis grinned. 'What a beauty!' He glanced at Roberts and laughed out loud. 'Faith! You've been at sea too long, Bart Roberts.'

Roberts grinned. 'Aye. Happen you're right.'

Davis clapped a fatherly hand on his shoulder. 'When was it you left England, then, Bart? April? And now 'tis July.' He clicked his tongue twice. 'Dear me, three whole months without a woman! We'll have to remedy that!'

Roberts let him tease him as they took the road down to the harbour where the boat crew awaited them.

But the woman's face stayed with him.

FIVE

The cool darkness of the governor's house welcomed Lúcia and her maid from the steaming heat of the square outside.

Lúcia waited while Maria took her *mantilha,* or shawl, and her parasol, and the footman appeared followed closely by Mendoça.

He executed a slight incline of the head in greeting. 'Good day to you, *senhora*. I trust you enjoyed your walk.'

Lúcia raised her chin haughtily. '*Senhor.*' He had overstepped the bounds of good manners by using the familiar *tu* in addressing her. She tossed her head. 'I thank the *senhor.*' Deliberately she put the distance between them again.

She asked the footman for a glass of fruit juice, and turned to ascend the stairs but Mendoça stood in the way, leaning lazily on the banister.

'Please let me pass, *senhor.*'

He did not move immediately, but grinned, flashing uneven discoloured teeth.

Lúcia waited with outward coolness but inward seething impatience.

'You will find your father still in his room, although I believe he has asked for his breakfast to be brought to him. I wonder that he declines my hospitality in the dining room.'

'My father is unwell, *senhor*,' she said. 'I hope that the *senhor* will excuse him. Now if the *senhor* will let me pass, I shall go to him.'

Mendoça hesitated just long enough and then stepped aside, bowing gallantly. '*Senhora*,' he murmured.

She swept up the wide staircase in a swish of green silk, her head held high, her long black hair streaming down her back. Maria followed quickly.

'I do not like that man,' Maria said as she closed the door behind her.

Lúcia sat on the bed. '*Senhor* Mendoça is our host while we are here, Maria,' she reminded her, 'and the governor of these islands.'

'Governor! Hah! He is a wicked and cruel man.'

Lúcia had seen evidence to know it to be true. The sooner her father concluded his business here in Principe the better, then they could be gone from this dreadful place. However, she had no intention of encouraging her maid to discuss her betters. So she did not answer her.

Maria pinned a white lace cap on her young mistress's head, ran a brush through her hair, curling the ends around her fingers. 'There! The *senhora* is fit to see the *senhor* now.'

Lúcia stood up abruptly. She saw no reason to doubt Maria's words, so did not even bother to check her reflection in the looking-glass, but left the room.

Her Father's room had the sun coming in the window and was stiflingly hot. He lay draped in a chair by the open window in the sun, swishing a black fan in front of his face, and sweating profusely. He was not a big man, illness making him slender, and he looked frail and old. In the months since they had left Opporto, he seemed to have aged.

He stretched out a hand to her his eyes twinkling. 'My child, you are about early.'

Lúcia crossed the room to plant a kiss on his old brow, and then closed the curtains casting him immediately in the shade.

'Oh don't block out the sun Lúcia,' he complained. 'There is no breeze now.'

'*Pápa*, it is past noon, and you just risen?' she countered briskly, ignoring his pleas.

He chuckled and pulled himself more upright in his chair. 'Ah, you know all about me. Sit with me a while, Lúcia.'

She sat down on a stool at his feet. 'You are better today *Pápa*?'

'Now we are off that dreadful vessel!' They had arrived two days ago from São Tomé, and he had not travelled well.

'It is too bad that you should be sent on this voyage.'

'Now Lúcia, my child, you know that where the king bids, I must go. That is what an emissary does.'

'But you are too—' she was going to say 'old' but ended up saying, '—ill to be travelling the world. It is time you were left in peace.'

'I prefer to be out of the way of the intrigues of court, my child.' He waved his hand. 'But I do regret allowing you to come with me.'

'And who else would look after you?' she demanded hotly.

'Rodrigues,' he countered at once, referring to the retainer who had known him since schooldays. His thick grey brows rose in surprise, as if it went without saying.

'Pshaw! Rodrigues is a man. What does he know about nursing the sick?' But there had been another reason. Her beauty was legendary. Unfortunately, the impoverished state of her father's finances, and his disgrace at court were just as legendary. The recent scandal meant that Pietro Almeira Andrade was a fallen man, a man in disgrace, one it had been expedient for the king to send abroad out of the way. For any man to ally himself with him by marrying his daughter would be political and financial suicide. Which was the reason that at five-and-twenty, Lúcia remained unmarried. It had been expedient then for her to accompany her father.

'You have been out?' Pietro asked.

'I have seen a little of the island,' she told him. 'And yes, Maria went with me,' she added before he could berate her.

'And where did you go?'

'Just for a walk, *Pápa*.'

'Not down to the beach?'

'No. You said I should not. I called on *senhora* Flores.'

'I do not want you to go to the beach, Lúcia, for there are ships in the bay, and I will not have you put in danger from the foreign sailors.'

'There's a British navy ship anchored in the bay,' she said.

'How do you know this? Did you indeed go to the beach?'

Affronted, she was moved to protest. 'No, *Pápa*, I told you I would not do so. *Senhora* Flores told me. And I saw two of their officers leaving here as I came back.'

'They will have come to see the governor as a courtesy, I suppose.'

'But why would the British navy come here?'

He hunched his shoulders and spread his hands expressively. 'Who knows? Am I the font of all knowledge?'

'But of course *Pápa*! But the British are not at war with Portugal, or anyone else, are they?'

'Not that I know of.' He thought for a moment. 'But if they were hunting criminals—pirates—they might be patrolling these waters. Now that's enough of your curiosity, Lúcia. It is time for me to dress myself. Where is Rodrigues?'

Lúcia came to her feet and straightened out her skirt. 'If the English come to trade, may I buy some silk, *Pápa*?'

'Oh Lúcia, you will see me in my grave! We will see. Let me

be, now, for I am a poor old man, and I need to go about my toilette.'

She laughed and kissed his cheek lightly. 'Not such a poor old man, *Pápa.*'

The night was black. A squall of cold unseasonal rain fell in sudden fury upon the men in the boat, and someone uttered a whispered curse. The French ship's stern loomed large above them out of the darkness, dwarfing the boat, the lanterns swinging from her stern illuminating the pinnace's single sail. At any moment they could be discovered.

Roberts' heart pounded in his chest. He realised he had missed the sheer exhilaration of fear when a man's mental and physical abilities were sharpened to the fullest extent. His ears strained for the cry of alarm that would mean they were discovered and bring musket shot raining down upon them. An alert man could not fail to spot them if he looked over the taffrail. He fingered one of the pistols slung on silk ribbons over his shoulders. Of course, they had chosen this hour of the night when men were at their lowest ebb, knowing that the watch would have difficulty in keeping awake.

At the prow, David Symson turned to whisper to Thomas Sutton, and catching sight of Roberts, flashed his remnant teeth in a grin, plainly enjoying this adventure. Between them, the white shirts of the boat crew glowed like ghostly clouds in the sparse light. No-one uttered a sound. Noise carried too easily across a slight sea at night.

From the Frenchman, all was quietness and calm. They hadn't been seen so far, but Roberts felt his nerves stretching as taut as a bowline. In another moment they came under the shadow of the keel, and the little boat bumped with a small elastic thud, which might as well have been a cannon blast in the silence. Swiftly the men forward lowered the single sail.

A head appeared over the gunwale, silhouetted against a pale cloud. 'Who is there?' a boy's voice cried in French.

'What is it, Jean?' someone else called.

'I don't know. I thought I heard something.'

David Symson waved his arm—the order to board—and half a dozen grappling irons and lines sailed through the air and caught on the gunwale with the twang of metal on wood.

Then from the French: 'Mother of God!'

The second man called out a warning, but already the first

pirates swarmed up the ropes with astonishing speed, well aware of the need to take the victims by surprise.

The stocky Robert Birdson came onto the French deck just ahead of Roberts, and acted swiftly grabbing a panicking Frenchman from behind and slipping his arm about his throat, jabbed his pistol barrel in his ear and growled in English: 'One more peep, and I'll blow yer blasted brains out!' If the Frenchman didn't understand the words the import was not lost on him.

The boy stood frozen with shock. But then suddenly realising that he must warn the captain, he started running towards the hatch, yelling as he went.

As he passed, Roberts' hand shot out and grabbed him, pulling him viciously round against him, so that his head snapped backwards, and twisting his arm up between his shoulder blades. The boy cried out with pain, and Roberts let the cold steel of his dagger touch his throat. 'No sound,' he murmured in French. 'Don't move!' And he felt him stiffen in his grasp, gasping in terror.

However, the first warning had woken the others. The men on the watch who had hidden themselves to sleep off a drunken stupor beneath a longboat now came groggily from their hiding place, rubbing their faces and hair to cast away the befuddling fog of drunkenness, and peered about them, shocked. The two Englishmen holding cocked pistols on them precluded any unwise moves.

David Symson jerked his head. Sutton took some men and crept to the hatch, pistols at the ready, but the French captain threw open the hatch at that moment and burst onto the deck in just his under-breeches and shirt.

'What the Devil is going on?'

Symson approached him and said easily in French: 'We are pirates, captain, and we have taken your ship as prize.'

It was quick, and it was easy, but it was wasted effort, for the French ship contained nothing of more value than provisions and a few bales of tobacco.

Davis's disappointment was understandable, especially as his releasing the French now would betray his real purpose to the Portuguese. Until he had concluded his business on Prince's, he could not let them go. So he put a crew of his own on the French ship and had them sail her out to a point near the entrance to the harbour, away from the fort's guns and out of reach of Portuguese help.

*****

With the *Royal Rover* hauled out of the water and tipped over on her side, the pirates began the arduous task of careening. It was hard work, and necessitated their lightening the ship of guns and goods and camping ashore in tents fashioned from the sails for the duration of the clean. The camp attracted the attention of the local people, Portuguese and Creole intent on trading at reasonable rates. And of course, there were the women who came under cover of darkness, eager to vie for the attentions of what they hoped might be generous lovers.

And generous they were too. Davis should have realised that naval men would not have the fortunes to spend that pirates had, and it did not take long for speculation as to their true identity to spread through the island.

Not that it put the local people against them. On the contrary, the native men encouraged their women folk to please the visitors for such bountiful largesse. As for the sailors, they needed no encouragement.

None of which dissuaded Mendoça from paying the English a visit along with his guests, Pietro Andrade and his daughter, as well as some of the dignitaries of the island and their wives.

They came in odd procession across the sand, Portuguese noblemen, wives and slaves, some of the women carried by slaves in strange hammock-type contraptions, a sort of canvas sedan chair, the customary mode of travel for women and frail old men. Others of the women walked, sporting large fringed parasols, and wrapped up from head to foot in the *mantilha*. But they found it difficult walking on the soft sand, and some were worried about their skirts dragging in it. They were accompanied also by a small band of musketeers, which Davis regarded with a sceptically raised eyebrow.

It took some time for the procession to reach them, time enough for Davis to make preparations. Men, freed black slaves for the most part, ran to tidy up the tent area which served as the great cabin, removing empty rum bottles, banana skins, mango stones and empty coconut fragments as well as clearing away certain men's garments it would not have been prudent for gently-reared women to see. Others brought out the goods for sale, textiles, and metal goods, iron and copper and some silver. Davis sent for Roberts who was working on the up-ended ship, and ordered him to tidy himself up for Mendoça was here and would be looking for the 'lieutenant'. By the time Mendoça hailed them from just outside the camp, all was ready.

Davis emerged from his tent the very picture of indolent command, a man in a fine blue coat decorated with gold braid, and a black wig cascading over his shoulders in curls. He bowed, and then came forward to grasp Mendoça's hand and clap him on the shoulder like a lost brother.

Mendoça, resplendent in a coat of gold thread, blossomed under this treatment. 'Ah, *senhor capitão, os senhores!*' he cried and planted huge kisses on Captain Davis's cheeks.

Davis, a little taken aback, nevertheless submitted to the embrace with as much dignity as he could muster, struggling to hide the alarm in his eyes, and Roberts, who had arrived just in time to witness the scene, was pleased to bow with the others to hide the grin that came to his lips.

'*Boa tarde, senhor.*' Davis bowed again to Andrade, and to Lúcia, as Mendoça began the introductions which seemed to go on and on, and necessitated the return introduction of those of the ship's company that might be considered officers, together with much bowing and many civilities.

Then Davis ushered everyone except the slaves and the musketeers into the large tent, and the ladies sat down at the oak table, while the men had to stand for lack of room.

There followed more civilities, the drinking of wine, the toasting different royal families, and death to all pirates. The 'stewards' ran with the wine, but there were not enough elegant goblets. Some of the guests drank wine from delicate china teacups, of which the *Royal Rover* had a surprisingly large number.

While Davis exchanged pleasantries, Roberts found he had an unobstructed view of Lúcia. He had the leisure now to take in every detail of her face; the way her eyes turned up slightly at the outer edges and the long black lashes resting on her cheek he imprinted on his memory. Her eyes were dark depths, lustrous, liquid. She was slightly above average in height for a Portuguese, but with delicate hands and slender fingers. She had a small waist, her breasts confined in one of those bodice things that women wore, so that he would have believed her almost flat were it not for the roundness that spilled over the top of her bodice and bulged beneath the lace shawl.

She sensed him looking at her, and for a fleeting moment she looked up and their eyes met. Immediately she looked away, pulling the *mantilha* closer around her. He smiled. She was captivating, this Portuguese lady.

Davis was generous with the wine, and the Portuguese were not slow to take advantage of English hospitality. Davis knew from experience that a little wine now paid dividends in profits later.

Besides Roberts, one other did not drink the wine, and that was Pietro Andrade. He had allowed the conversation, the pleasantries to flow between Mendoça and Davis uninterrupted for sometime. Now he commanded attention by breaking in on them suddenly:

'Forgive me, Captain Davis, but where did the captain say he came from?' His voice was not loud, but it had a timbre about it that caused a sudden hush. He smiled, but there was a spark in his eyes, a challenge. Everyone looked at him.

There was a strong family resemblance between Andrade and his daughter, Roberts saw. Only the chin was stronger, decorated with a small white pointed beard on the end, the yellow skin sagging and deeply lined.

'We are out of Spithead,' Davis said without hesitation.

Andrade continued to smile, but the eyes were sharp. 'I did not ask where the ship sailed from,' he chided quietly. 'But where the *senhor capitão* is from.'

There was a moment's embarrassed silence, and Lúcia looked down at the glass in her hands.

Davis, though was not put out. He said evenly, his eyes straight on Andrade's: 'Why does the *senhor* wish to know where I come from?'

'It was a civil question. Does the captain not wish to tell us?' There was a challenge in Andrade's eyes.

'I come from Wales,' Davis said.

Andrade's smile did not waver. 'Ah, I see.' Everyone had heard of the Welsh pirate. 'And just why does the *capitão* come to Africa?'

Davis frowned. 'Perhaps the *senhor governador* has explained that we are in search of pirates believed to be operating on this coast.'

Andrade raised his brows expressively. 'A noble cause, Captain. And just how does the *capitão* expect to capture these—ah—pirates?' There was a subtle note of disbelief in his voice.

Davis met Roberts' eyes for a split second, but Andrade

noticed.

Davis said, 'The *senhor* cannot expect me to divulge my orders, surely.'

Andrade examined his fingernails closely. 'And the French ship—I trust the *capitão* was—ah—satisfied?'

The smile froze on Davis's face. 'Of course,' he said because he could think of nothing else to say. He had the feeling he was being interrogated by this smiling, supposedly charming Portuguese man, and he did not like it. He began to wish him at the Devil.

Andrade's smile broadened to show a row of even, surprisingly white, teeth. 'She was a pirate, then?'

'She had traded with pirates.' Davis was seriously rattled now, but controlled himself by sheer willpower.

'And what will happen to her crew, *senhor capitão*? Will the *capitão* hand them to the governor to deal with?'

The tension was palpable, everyone seeming to hold their breath.

The smile was gone from Davis now, replaced by a look of sheer murder. Andrade continued to smile, safe in the knowledge that Davis could not touch him.

'We'll take her to Corso, *senhor* where her crew will stand trial.'

'Oh. I see. English justice then.' He smiled at everyone around the table, turning to do so. 'English justice,' he repeated. 'I shall make a note of it, *senhor capitão,* and write to England—to thank them for their efforts at controlling the scourge of the seas.'

Davis slammed his goblet down on the table with such force that everyone jumped.

Mendoça, seeing his prospects of buying goods at very reasonable rates vanishing, rushed into speech in an effort to divert attention away from Andrade. 'But perhaps, the *senhor capitão* would care to show us his goods?'

Davis smiled icily at him, but it was enough to ease the tension. Straight away Roberts jerked his head at the others, and they moved towards the tent doorway, in a tacit signal to encourage everyone to leave. 'Yes, of course,' Davis said.

The goods were spread out on sails over the sand. Bolts of silk and cotton in crimson, emerald, topaz and various shades of blue. As they pored over the goods, Roberts stood back, watching Andrade as he walked with difficulty towards the hammock in which he had arrived. He may appear a frail old man, but there was nothing frail in the wits of Pietro Andrade, King's Emissary. He knew who they were, and he had just put Davis on warning. But Roberts did not think Andrade posed much of a threat. Mendoça was governor, not Andrade, and he evidently did not quibble about trading with them, as long as it was profitable to him.

'If the *senhor* pleases . . ?' He turned and found himself looking into dark liquid eyes that made the breath catch in his throat.

'*Senhora?*'

'If the *senhor* pleases, I should like to see the blue silk,' Lúcia said at her most demure.

'Of course *senhora*.' He had to elbow his way through the dignitaries to retrieve it and bring it out to her, a bolt of peacock blue material. He held it out to her, and she put out a delicate hand to touch it.

'It would make a beautiful dress,' he suggested gently.

She ignored him, and spoke to the maid beside her. 'I thought a ball-gown. My father said I might buy some.' She glanced up at him, and a flush crept over her pale honey skin, from her breasts to her cheeks, and his stomach slid. 'Or, perhaps the dark blue?'

He put the first down at her feet, and went to retrieve the other, and held that out to her. It was of a slightly inferior quality.

'Oh, I do not know. The lighter blue is prettier,' she said to the maid.

He said gently: 'The lighter colour contrasts better with your eyes, *senhor*.'

The words and the pattern of speech were deliberately less formal, *your*, instead of *the senhora's*. Her eyes now flew to his face and she hesitated.

The maid tugged at her arm. 'Come away, *senhora*,'

Roberts wasn't to be put off. He unravelled some of the cloth and held it up to her. 'There! Bewitching!'

She put her chin up and tossed her head haughtily. Her eyes flashed dangerously. 'I think not,' she said coldly.

He was too close, and she took a step backwards. Immediately he put the material down, and stepped back himself removing the threat. She glared at him. Oh, but she was beautiful!

'Forgive me, *senhora*, perhaps the peacock silk . . ?' He picked it up again.

'Daughter! Come away this instant!'

She jumped, and turned. '*Pápa*? You said I might buy some—'
'No.'

Immediately she fired up. '*Pápa*, you promised. You cannot go back on your word. You said I could buy some cloth—'

'Not from these people!' Andrade said firmly. 'I tell you now, Lúcia, come away. We are leaving.'

'*Pápa*!' but she turned away from Roberts with her maid. Immediately Andrade took her arm and compelled her to go with him taking her to where his hammock awaited him. As they walked away Roberts heard a heated exchange between father and daughter that made him laugh inwardly. Oh, but she was a spitfire! Beautiful and dangerous.

Henry Dennis joined him. 'What's with the emissary?'

Roberts shrugged. 'Damned if I know.'

'Offended at your flirting with his daughter, no doubt,' Dennis pursued. 'Not on, Bart. Nobility, you know.'

Roberts frowned. 'He knows who we are,' he said.

'Even worse,' Dennis said.

At the Governor's house Pietro Andrade retired to his room for a *sesta*. It had been a long hot day, trying too, and now Lúcia was not speaking to him. She had flounced off in high dudgeon to her room, but he knew her bad humour would not last. It rarely did.

He sighed dramatically. He had offered her no explanation. She was a woman after all, and unable to keep her mouth shut. Stood to reason. Best not to disclose his hand until he had to. He had to think about this, and the best place to do the thinking was lying on his bed in the cool in his own room.

But no sooner had Rodrigues, his manservant closed the door on his chamber than he heard a loud knocking at the front door, and the dark brown voice of Fernando the footman arguing with an agitated caller.

Andrade growled his bad humour. He was hot, tired, and wished to rest. When the argument below showed no signs of abating, he called Rodrigues. 'See what all the fuss is about!'

Rodrigues bowed and went. He was an old and faithful retainer, to whom deserting his master during exile would be like cutting off his own leg. He nursed and looked after Andrade, never deserting him, always seeing to his comfort. And he never seemed to take it amiss when his master took his bad humour out on him.

He came back after a few minutes and said: 'There is a man, a trader, in great distress who demands to see the governor.'

Andrade sighed again. 'Where is the governor?'

'Still on the beach with the English.'

The man's voice again penetrated the room from downstairs. 'Well it seems there will be no peace until someone deals with him!' Andrade said irritably. 'Can no-one give me peace? Send him up to me!'

Again Rodrigues bowed and left him, and Andrade went to the chair by the open window to await the caller.

The man came in, bowing low, well aware that he had interrupted the governor's important visitor, yet too agitated to keep his peace. 'Forgive the intrusion, Excellency,' he began, but Andrade cut him short.

'The *senhor* has intruded now, so perhaps he will be kind enough to tell me what it is that ails him!'

The man bowed again. '*Senhor*, I am but a poor trader.'

'Huh! In my experience, *senhor*, poor traders are a figment of their own imaginations!'

'I beg the *senhor* to hear me. It concerns the governor.'

'*Senhor* Mendoça?'

The man's eyes darkened at the mention of the name, the reason for his agitation, and he changed from polite courtesy to smouldering anger. 'Mendoça is a criminal,' he fumed, beginning to pace back and forth in front of Andrade's bemused gaze. 'He's a villain! I would see him hang for what he has done!'

Andrade frowned. 'Tell me, *senhor*, please. And for the sake of all that is holy, *sit down*! All this pacing about makes my head ache!'

The man sat, and leaned forward earnestly towards Andrade. 'I tell the *senhor*, that if the *senhor* knew what kind of man it is that is his host then the *senhor* would quit this place forthwith!'

'I am surprised to hear the *senhor* speak of the governor in such terms,' Andrade said, not in the least surprised. 'What has he done?'

'The man is the very Devil—'

'Yes, yes,' Andrade waved his hand impatiently. 'But what has he *done*?'

The visitor stood up, unable to sit still any longer. 'I trade in slaves, *senhor*. But on this island, as on São Tomé, since Mendoça became governor, no-one may buy or sell slaves except through him, at a fixed rate that is a worse price than if we traded properly. Indeed, it is impossible to buy or sell anything to anyone but the governor, for he has made it law here, and strictly enforces it. Then he, of course, sells the slaves to the ships which take them across the Atlantic at a fat profit.'

Andrade frowned and folded his finger over his lips thoughtfully. 'You are sure of this?'

'Sure? I tell the *senhor* emissary that no man may buy or sell here except through the governor. He has the monopoly on everything that comes through here.'

The man went on to give him several instances, and while Andrade listened, his mind was racing. The information shed a whole new light on Mendoça, for such a monopoly was not only unfair, it was illegal. No wonder the governor had musketeers stationed all around him at all times. Half the population of the island would like to see him dead! He said when the man came to a halt: 'The King shall hear of this! I would beg a favour of the *senhor*.'

'If it will bring the downfall of this man, name it!'

'I ask you to say nothing of your visit here to anyone else. I need time to think about this and what I should do. But believe me, Mendoça shall not escape this.'

'*Senhor*, I am pleased to hear it. I thank the *senhor*.'

'Yes, yes, yes.' He waved the man away.

After the man had gone, Andrade considered what he should do with this information. Of course there would be a report to the King. However, he wanted more. He wanted to remove Mendoça, but he could not immediately see how. In any case it would not be wise to disclose his knowledge to Mendoça. Indeed, to do so could put himself and Lúcia in danger.

SIX

'So—what's the plan?' Valentine Ashplant sucked on his pipe and then blew a white cloud into air already thick with the aroma of tar, sweat, rum, damp and the suffocating stench from the bilge. 'How do we get our 'ands on the gold, then?'

Captain Howell Davis spread his hands and smiled benignly on them all. 'Have I ever failed you, my children?' he asked mildly.

Henry Dennis looked up from contemplation of the bottom of his mug, his face glowing eerily in the direct overhead light from the swinging lantern, and met Davis's eyes. 'If you ask me, 'tis time we were somewhere else, Captain,' he said. 'Every day we linger here increases our chances of discovery. The Portuguese are going to be asking about the Frenchman ere long. Ash—will ye put some of that punch in here?' he added, holding out the mug.

As Ashplant ladled from the bowl, Davis said dismissively: 'The Portuguese are happy with the explanation we gave them. I think we have a few days yet.'

Roberts, standing behind the seated Symson, shifted uneasily. 'The Portuguese know who we are,' he repeated. 'I say we should be gone from here. We have tarried long enough.'

'Nay, we're safe,' Ashplant said.

Birdson agreed and the rest of the Lords began noisily debating it.

Davis banged on the table with the hilt of his dagger. When they gave him their attention he said: 'Mendoça does know. But he ain't worried. He wants to trade.'

Roberts leaned forward to put his hands on the table between Symson and Woods. 'It ain't Mendoça who worries me, it's Andrade. He's no fool. He knows what we are, and probably even why we are here. If he gets Mendoça to send men out to the Frenchie he'll be forced to act, and we're sunk. Every day we spend here increases the danger.'

The Irishman, Walter Kennedy was so drunk he couldn't sit up straight, but sprawled over the table, his head resting on his arm, to all observers fast asleep. But he heard enough to bring his head up to look blearily at the others and make some contribution to the meeting. 'I do think it be time we be gone. Dangerous to stay. Send some men in. Kill the fellows and let's be on our way!' His voice was slurred and his accent didn't enhance his diction, so that only those very closely acquainted with him made any sense of what he had said.

Davis smiled at him indulgently.

Valentine Ashplant rubbed his whiskery beard. 'Don't rightly think we should kill them,' he growled. 'Ain't got no reason to.'

James Phillips said: 'Now when I were with Blackbeard—' and was shouted down for his efforts.

Davis was obliged to call for order, banging the hilt of his dagger on the table once more until he attracted their attention again. 'Look you! We ain't here just to get a few poxy goods from the Frenchman!'

'Aye. But if we want the gold, we'll have to look to ourselves and be sharp about it!' Henry Dennis said.

Once more Davis was interrupted by the sudden outbreak of everyone else's views. Once more he banged on the table, with more gusto than before, showing that he was losing his customary good temper. 'Listen to me, damn ye! Stop yer chattering!' The voices subsided again, and he took a breath to calm himself. 'Now Mendoça—he's been mighty friendly to us, ain't he? Giving us provisions and such. I reckon it'd be mighty fitting if we invited him and his cronies to an entertainment on board. Aye,' he added on sudden inspiration, 'And we'll give him a dozen of the blacks into the bargain—as a token of good faith.'

Roberts thought of the poor wretches Davis had 'liberated' from the *Princess* and who had thought themselves relatively free with the pirates. Nothing he could do about it, though. And there was another reason why he was not happy. 'Too much delay,' he said. 'I think it's risky.'

Some agreed with him, others noisily protested. Davis banged on the table again.

'If we go now, we miss out on the gold, and I reckon there's plenty to be had on this island. We can't get to it, don't know where it's kept, even. But we can get it this way. I think it's worth the risk.'

Roberts compressed his lips. He didn't like it.

'What entertainment?' Ashplant growled belatedly.

'Keep yer mummer shut!' Christopher Moody put in. He was the boatswain, a coarse Londoner. 'Damn, I'll put yer daylights out if yer don't.'

'An' if you do I'll put yer damn teeth down yer throat!' Ashplant responded, jumping to his feet and reaching across the table before several pairs of hands restrained him and sat him down again.

'Stow it!' Dennis said. 'Sit down, Ash.'

Davis looked up at the deckhead beams as though praying for patience. 'It don't matter what entertainment. Dancing, music, it don't matter. There ain't going to be any entertainment.'

Ashplant couldn't keep up. 'But you said—'

'Yes, I know what I said! When we get Mendoça and his cronies on board, we'll clap 'em in irons, and we'll hold 'em till the island pays. What d'ye say? Forty thousand pounds?'

'Why not make it a hundred thousand?' Dennis asked dryly.

Davis glowered at him. 'Now let's not get greedy!'

Roberts stifled a laugh. Forty thousand pounds was a fortune in anybody's language. It would give them about two hundred each when all was done—if they were not hanged in the process that is.

'An' if they don't pay I'll slit their blasted throats, so I will!' Kennedy slurred with relish.

'No!' Davis snapped, his patience at an end. 'We don't hold with murder! No. They'll pay up. And if they don't we'll sail off with them and put 'em ashore somewhere.'

'They'll pay,' Roberts said with certainty, and they looked round at him. His eyes flicked over their drink-sodden faces, and saw naked greed there. Part of him was disgusted, yet he recognised the gold-lust in his own belly too. After all, greed was the reason they went on the account in the first place.

'Aye,' Davis agreed on a grin. 'They can't afford not to.'

'Get them damned lights out!' Ashplant's stentorian growl filtered up to the deck through the open hatch, and Roberts smiled to himself as he thought of the hardened criminals below hastening to obey orders. Failure to do so could earn a man a drubbing or a lashing for the risk of fire was ever present, and Ashplant would not be reticent about recommending any man for punishment. The articles said lights out at eight, and so lights out at eight it was.

On deck the men assigned to the first watch came up to relieve those who had served the second half of the dog watch, and now took up their places aft and forward, and brought a pack of cards with them to while away the long hours until the watch changed again at midnight. There was a brief exchange in hushed voices and then they too fell silent.

Roberts leaned on the quarterdeck rail, watching the little lights flashing in the moving water below like a million fireflies. The only sounds now were the whistling of the wind in the stays and lines, the gentle lapping of the waves and the continual creaks and groans of the ship, sounds so familiar as to go unnoticed. Occasionally someone snored grotesquely and someone else complained about it.

Roberts sighed contentedly. He liked this time of the evening, when the ship was quiet and he could find the opportunity for solitude that hitherto had rarely come his way. He was not on watch tonight, and he could make the most of the time to himself. For a ship was a crowded place and the only chance to be alone was inside one's own head.

Beyond the glitter of the phosphorous, the black water moved and caught the rising moonlight. It was a full moon, glorious and over-large, and tinged with vermilion. A blood moon, he thought, and shivered. He was not usually superstitious, but it seemed like an omen.

Directly above him, the first stars of the night flashed at him. They were familiar friends, his aid to travelling the world. The pole star would hardly be visible on the northern horizon here, not that he could see it, because they were in the lee of the bay and the trees on the point hid the northern horizon from view.

The town he could see off the other side of the ship, high up in the hills, a hundred candles flickering in a hundred windows, and he thought of the Portuguese girl in Mendoça's house. She was a beauty, and he considered himself to be a connoisseur. But the women he knew inhabited the brothels and inns in the various ports he had visited. Some of them were favourites, visited often. But this woman was different. She intrigued him. She was a lady, not a common trollop, haughty, fiery, and yet there was an innocence about her he had never come across before. No other woman he had ever met was like this girl. Her very innocence intrigued him. He shifted his position, suddenly restless. They had to leave soon. It was dangerous even to stay long enough to pursue Davis's goal of getting the gold. But how he would have liked to stay, to become better acquainted with that young woman!

A gentle splash from the leeward side of the ship caught his attention. A fish rising, perhaps? He didn't think so. Quickly jumping over blocks and lines, he crossed to the other side of the ship and peered over the guard-rail into the inky blackness of the sea.

The lantern light didn't go far enough, so he took it off its hook and held it aloft over the side.

The night seemed to swallow up the light. Straining his eyes to see, Roberts thought there was a movement, a ripple of the waves in the twinkling phosphorous, but he couldn't be sure.

Richard Woods the quartermaster joined him at the rail. 'What is it?'

'I thought I heard something,' Roberts said, still peering into the night.

'Probably a rat.'

Roberts shook his head. 'Too big for that. Almost as though it were a man.'

Woods frowned at him. 'One of the darkies, perhaps?'

'Why should one of them want to jump ship when we give them freedom?'

Woods was unconcerned. 'Who's to know what goes on in their 'eads. Perhaps they think this ain't freedom. Anyway, sharks'll probably get 'im. Often have blacks jumping ship. Some English too, come to that.'

'Well, there ain't no finding him now,' Roberts said, putting the lantern back on the hook. 'I think I'll turn in.'

Below, he felt his way in the darkness to where he had earlier slung his hammock.

David Symson was still awake. 'What's amiss, Bart?'

Roberts chuckled in the darkness. 'Don't miss a thing, do ye?'

'I heard voices,' Symson explained.

Roberts pulled off a shoe. 'Someone went over the side. Probably one of the blacks.'

'Does Woods know?'

Hopping on one leg, Roberts pulled off the other shoe. 'Oh aye.'

'That's all right then.' Symson settled down and Roberts, clutching the overhead beam, hauled himself into the hammock. 'What would they want to jump ship for?' Symson was aggrieved. 'Don't we treat 'em right or something?'

'Perhaps they don't appreciate our kindness,' Roberts said, and closed his eyes. Ten seconds later he was snoring.

*****

Captain Davis had taken a long time over his toilette, eventually deciding to wear a pale green coat with gold embroidery and a dark wig. Surveying himself in the great cabin mirror, he was pleased with the effect. Mendoça should be impressed that Davis himself was to conduct him and his dignitaries to the *Royal Rover* for the promised entertainment. But what a surprise Mendoça would get when he found himself the prisoner of English pirates! He chuckled to himself. That should make the oily ever-present smile on his foreign face falter!

The boat was ready for him. In it six other officers of the *Royal Rover* waited patiently for him, and he cast his eyes over them. William Stephens, the chief surgeon; William Woods, the quartermaster; Peter Aston the other boatswain; Abraham Grahams the acting sailing master; William Kirk; and David Symson. Good men, all of them. Dependable. He would have liked to take Roberts and Dennis, but Dennis had been drinking heavily and was, to all accounts, still unconscious, while Roberts was thought to have upset the Portuguese by flirting with the emissary's daughter. Reluctantly, Davis decided to leave them both behind.

At the order, the oarsmen began to row towards the town, and Davis sat in silent contemplation of the plan, smiling at a mental vision of Mendoça's very shocked face. They wouldn't hurt them, of course, even if they didn't pay up. But he didn't want to think of that eventuality.

As the boat approached the beach it occurred to him that the shoreline was unusually empty. He had expected the beach to be full of people eager to sell what they could to the ships that anchored in the port.

'Where are they all?' he asked.

Doctor Stephens raised his brows. ''Tis Sunday, Captain. They will all be doing duty in church.'

'All of them?'

'But of course! Don't you think the Venetian monks will rule them with a rod of iron? Inquisition and all that! Conversion, captain, that is their object. And woe betide anyone who doesn't go to church.'

Davis could think of no other explanation, so he accepted it even though the unaccustomed silence fuelled a feeling of unease as the boat grated onto the eerily empty beach. Even Mendoça and his dignitaries who should have been here waiting to be conducted back to the *Royal Rover* had not put in an appearance.

Stepping out of the pinnace into the clear water, he wondered what could have happened. He pulled out the watch from his waistcoat pocket and checked that the time was just a little after midday. They were not late. Once more his eyes swept the deserted beach. The pale sand had been washed smooth by the tide and there were no footprints to suggest that Mendoça or his men had come, given up waiting and gone again.

He listened, putting up his hand to quiet his men. As they stopped murmuring among themselves, only the sound of the surf rushing up the steep beach broke the silence. Even the nearby forest was silent.

He looked back at David Symson, frowning. Where were they?

Symson nodded in the direction of the road that led up to the town, where a black servant in white livery had appeared and now waited nervously, evidently unwilling to advance towards them.

There was nothing else for it but to walk to the servant, and they trudged up the beach, sinking into the soft sand at every step. The servant took two or three hesitant steps to meet them, and then he bowed low, and the little tail of his tie wig flipped over his shoulder.

'The governor sends Captain Davis and his men his respects and bids them to take some refreshment with him before going back to the ship,' he said.

His eyes flicked anxiously from one to the other of them, perhaps because he was unsure of their reactions, and he licked his thick purple-black lips.

Davis nodded. 'Very well, lead on.'

The servant bowed again, turned and skipped up the beach and away to the road that led up the hill towards the town.

Davis followed. This display of hospitality on the part of the Portuguese dispelled his earlier misgivings. He allowed himself once more to relish the shock the revelation would ultimately give Mendoça. He already sensed the success of this venture. The gold was almost his. Poor fools! Poor simple fools! He grinned at Symson who lurched awkwardly up the beach with legs that moved slower than everyone else's, but which took longer strides. He looked like a stick man, Davis thought, the kind that children draw.

Symson didn't grin back. Instead his narrowed grey eyes searched the forest edge keenly and Davis sensed his disquiet.

The forest seemed to close in on them, and a bird suddenly screeched and took off in the forest nearby, making Davis jump.

'Nimble, these blacks, ain't they,' he said conversationally to Symson in an attempt to ease the growing tension.

'Aye.' Symson's voice was low, and it certainly did not reassure Davis. 'Nimble and treacherous.'

Davis looked at him sharply. 'Treacherous?'

Symson met his eyes. 'Didn't Woods tell you? One of 'em escaped from the *Rover*. Slipped over the side in the night. Thought you knew.'

'Woods?' Davis enquired of the quartermaster.

Woods glared at Symson. ''Twere only a slave,' he growled. ''Tweren't nothing.'

Davis's mouth went dry. This he didn't like. His instinct warned him to go no further, and he hesitated. Nevertheless, it seemed churlish to abandon a good plan just because a slave jumping ship had spooked him. And there was the small matter of forty thousand pounds to take into consideration.

He took a deep breath. 'Keep your wits about you,' he whispered, and despite himself he put his hand on the pistol tucked into his belt.

They went further up the path, deeper into the forest, but there was no sign of Mendoça's slave. The man seemed to have disappeared.

The forest was dense, like fog. It not only blocked out most of the sunlight, but also prevented them seeing further than a few feet in any direction, and it was gloomy and silent.

'I don't like it,' Stephens the chief surgeon whispered from behind.

No, neither did Davis. Fear slithered up his back to his neck, making him shiver despite the humid heat, and coiled its tentacles around his insides. Damn, it was so quiet! Too damned quiet!

The forest suddenly gave way to the town, the square outside Government House. The musketeers loitered in the street as usual, trying to look casual, talking in groups of two or three, smoking. Yet there was tension in their bearing.

Davis sensed the trap.

'Go back!' he cried suddenly. 'Back to the ship!'

As the words left his lips, he felt a hot wisp of air brush his face, and Stephens, the surgeon, fell dead, a neat black little hole in the centre of his forehead beneath his wig, his eyes staring in surprise.

At first Davis couldn't comprehend what had happened. Then he realised that they had been caught in an ambush. Musket fire rained down upon them in a terrifying hail of hot lead, whistling like a strange stirring wind, whipping up the sand beneath their feet, rattling and shredding the forest leaves.

Betrayed! Mendoça! The escaped slave . . !

Abraham Grahams, the acting sailing master, died next, clawing briefly at a dark hole in his throat. William Kirk stopped two balls, the first in his thigh, felling him, the second opening up a gaping bloody wound in his chest.

Davis, Symson, Woods, and Peter Aston fled the demons that chased them, running for all they were worth to the cover of the forest. But the musketeers were there too, concealed in the undergrowth, and they had to run the gauntlet of their fire. Woods fell as they ran, dropping as though he had run into an invisible wall. Davis hurtled over his body, not daring to pause to look back at his men in their finery littering the sandy floor.

A blinding agony of pain told him that he had stopped a ball in his shoulder, crunching the bone and splashing his cheek with his own blood, and the force of it knocked him to the ground. He was up again in a moment, fear giving speed to his feet as the musket fire continued all around him.

Ahead of him Symson, running faster than any of them could on his long legs, gained the beach and then turned back. Davis saw him yelling frantically, begging his captain to follow, but his voice was lost in the constant fire. Davis wanted to call after him: *Wait for me!* He felt the panic, the blind terror of imminent death. Yet his legs felt like lead.

Searing pain in his stomach told him he had stopped another ball. He fell to the ground again, clutching at his belly, and warm sticky fluid spread over his fingers.

With his heart pounding in his ears, he struggled to his feet. Yet every movement brought a fresh flood from his belly, turning his buff breeches a deep grotesque crimson, dripping onto the pale sandy earth. But he wasn't done for yet. He staggered down the beach behind Peter Aston the only other man left, but he fell suddenly with a cry, and Davis stumbled over his body. Once more he struggled in pain and anger to his feet, staggering drunkenly from loss of blood.

As he stumbled out of the forest he saw that Symson had reached the safety of the waiting boat, but when he saw his captain he started back, leaving the boat, to help him, pistols drawn. But the Portuguese crashed through the undergrowth behind Davis, shrieking in murderous glee.

Howell Davis shook his head at Symson, and waved him on with his pistol. Damn Symson! Didn't he know that he must save himself?

His legs trembled beneath him as he weakened, and his head felt heavy, dizzy. He gasped for breath and each gasp was an agony. His own heart beat in his ears as it struggled to keep up with the exertion, and blood spurted from his belly as though someone had forgotten to put the bung in the ale keg.

Just a few feet away, David Symson had reluctantly gone back to the boat. The men had already cast off, but waited only for their captain. Just a few feet more. No more than twenty at most.

It might as well have been a hundred leagues.

As the blood drained away his strength went with it, and he staggered like a drunken man. Another ball crashed into his chest, splintering the bone, making him cry out, and he fell against the trunk of a tree. With strength borne of desperation, he pushed himself up again, staggering forward blindly, reaching out for the boat with outstretched hands. Now he could taste blood in his mouth and the breath rattled in his throat.

He was done for. He could go no further.

The Portuguese were upon him. A fourth ball hit him on his right side, and spun him around, but he stayed upright. Through the agony, he staggered back two more paces. He could see only through a mist, his vision closing as though he looked down a deep tunnel. At the end of that tunnel were the Portuguese musketeers.

A fifth musket ball tore into his chest and his legs buckled. He fell to his knees. 'Sweet Jesus!' he whispered.

In a last desperate effort, determined to make them pay for their treachery, he levelled both cocked pistols and fired, and two of the pursuers fell.

And in that moment, Captain Howell Davis died.

SEVEN

Bartholomew Roberts wiped the beading sweat from his forehead with the back of his hand, and for the umpteenth time brushed his soft black hair out of his eyes. Despite the open stern windows, the heat in the great cabin seemed to grow with every man who squeezed in to join the discussion. The rank odour of a dozen sweating unwashed bodies mingling with the smoke of several clay pipes and the fumes from the rum punch sliding about in the bowl on the table, obliterated any remaining stench from the bilges.

They all knew why Henry Dennis had summoned them, and men spoke in low voices out of respect for the memory of their late captain and his officers. Howell Davis had achieved miracles of daring that had brought the company riches and fame, chivalry and adventure, and imbued them with a sense of their own immortality. His passing not only struck at the very essence of that immortality but, more pressingly, left a void that had to be filled.

Roberts leaned back against the bulkhead squeezed between the damp wide body of Michael Maer on one side and that of Dennis Topping on the other who glowed with the heat like hot coals. He tried to move so there was a little space between them, but they were jammed in like packing cases in the hold, and he resigned himself to suffering in silence, while the sweat spurted from every pore in his body, drenching his shirt and breeches and soaking his hair.

He had a detached interest in the proceedings. With only six weeks in the company, he could have no expectations himself, but he had been especially invited by Mr. Dennis, which honour he duly recognised, and he had as much a vote as any man. He supposed Dennis also had in mind the appointment of officers besides that of a captain, for they had lost so many men in the ambush, and Roberts fully expected to be promoted to sailing master, the reason for his being forced in the first place.

Around the table sitting on the upholstered chairs were the candidates for the captaincy, the officers with experience of piracy, the old-timers, those with reasonable expectations. They stood out from the rabble, by their braided coats and waistcoats, silk shirts and plumed hats. Even in this heat, and in this confined space, there was no deviation from superiority afforded by expensive clothes, and Roberts smiled to himself. What vanity man?

Thomas Anstis was one of them, a man Roberts had little to do with until now. He had a blond cannon-ball head, his pale hair cropped short beneath a green kerchief topped by a tricorn hat. He had a reputation as a capable seaman, with a bluff and rowdy character which fitted nicely into the pirate way of life. He had experience of navigation, although he remained to be tried in that quarter, and was known as a brave man. Altogether a fitting candidate.

Valentine Ashplant, sitting next to him, and puffing lazily on his pipe was also an experienced man, and once the captain of a brig, although still only twenty-nine. However, he lacked refinement, being a loud coarse Londoner, given to heavy drinking, and, worse, had only the vaguest grasp of what was going on at any one time. Perhaps that was the drink. Whatever the cause, Valentine Ashplant was happier following orders than giving them.

Henry Dennis himself also had the makings of a captain and was well-respected by the crew. Dennis had a way with words, was able to talk anyone into practically anything, but he did not always take counsel and he was a risk-taker to boot. That combination could be dangerous. Besides, Dennis's navigation skills were limited.

Walter Kennedy, permanently sozzled, dirty, unkempt and illiterate, and consequently without a clue as to navigation, stood no chance, and Roberts was inclined to dismiss him contemptuously. However, there was a side to Kennedy that appealed to certain ones in the company. The man was a rebel, a trouble-maker, true, but those very qualities made him completely fearless, which the men admired. But the man was a blood-thirsty villain. If Kennedy were captain, captured ships would find no mercy at his hands. There would be bloodshed and cruelty, and where he led, the men would follow.

To Roberts' mind, the best man for the job of captain was David Symson. Behind his lethargic exterior, he had courage, drive, ambition, and surprisingly quick wits, and he was well-respected by the company. An excellent seamen, he knew better than Davis had done how to run the ship. And what he didn't know about navigation, he would soon learn. Yes, out of them all, Roberts thought that probably David Symson would get the job.

So did Symson. He sat back in his chair, one long arm stretched over the table to the drinking mug, a look of quiet expectation on his angular face.

Henry Dennis took a swig of rum punch, wiped his mouth on a

delicate handkerchief pulled from a capacious pocket and came to his feet. The cabin fell silent, and he stood for a moment watching them all, enjoying this moment.

'Well now, gentlemen,' he began. 'First it is needful to drink to Captain Davis.'

They all raised their mugs solemnly, repeating the words: 'Captain Davis,' and took large swallows. Then they looked at Dennis expectantly.

'Gentlemen, you know why we meet today. We need to choose a captain.'

They murmured in agreement.

He nodded, then went on not quite truthfully: 'And it don't matter who gets the title of captain. For as we all know, power is with the community, and the community may depute and revoke as it suits them best.'

Again the sounds of agreement.

He held up his hands to quieten them, clearing his throat. 'Just so,' he said, trying to pick up his thread. 'Well, we are the ones who decide, and should any captain be so saucy as to exceed his authority at any time, then down with him, I say! It will be a caution to his successors, after he is dead, of what the results of any sort of assuming may be!'

'Aye, aye!' they all agreed.

'Well, I reckon that while we are still sober, we decide upon a man of courage, skilled in navigation, one who by his counsel and bravery seems best able to defend this commonwealth, and ward us from the dangers and tempests of an instable element and the fatal consequences of anarchy.'

He paused, pleased with his own rhetoric, peering at each of them in turn. Then his eyes came to rest on Roberts who read a message in them that he couldn't fathom, but as Dennis's eyes flicked away again, the suspicion entered his head that Dennis intended to suggest him for captain.

Roberts felt his stomach slide sickeningly as the thought occurred to him. He hadn't even considered the possibility. What reason could Dennis have for appointing him? Only six weeks among them, a reluctant recruit at that, they weren't even sure of him.

His heart began to thud in his chest, and he stood up straighter, staring at Dennis in astonishment, waiting for him.

Dennis cleared his throat, and after a suitable pause said into the silence. 'Such a one I take Bartholomew Roberts to be!' He extended his hand toward Roberts. 'A fellow, I think, in all respects, worth your esteem and favour.'

Roberts could only stare at him in shock, as his heart pounded in his ears and he struggled to understand how it had happened. All around him the cabin was in uproar as men cheered and clapped and banged on the table with fists and tankards, evidently pleased, and in agreement with the choice.

Taken completely off guard, Roberts needed time to think. Did he want the honour? But he couldn't think. His brain seemed to have turned to treacle, and he could only watch the men around him clapping him on the shoulder, pushing him forward to the head of the table. They had chosen him. A glow of pleasure spread through him. He realised he had wanted this all his life; his own command, his own ship, his own crew. He had worked towards this goal since he signed up on his first voyage at fourteen. True, it would have been preferable if ship and crew were engaged in legitimate business, but somehow the very nature of the *Royal Rover*'s business made it all the more attractive.

The tumult quietened as they waited for the new captain to speak, but in the sudden hush, David Symson came noisily to his feet, kicking his chair backwards, disappointment making him surly. Roberts had guessed how much he wanted the command, and it was adding insult to injury to appoint a man only six weeks among them.

'Damned if I care who you choose to be captain!' he cried. 'Just as long as it ain't a damned papist! I hate papists! Ever since me father suffered at Monmouth's rebellion!' And he flounced from the cabin slamming the door behind him.

Roberts felt the first clouds of dismay. He liked Symson, knew he could be trusted, and he wanted him on his side. The disappointment must be bitter medicine.

Dennis, keen to ease the sudden embarrassed silence that followed reached up to clap Roberts on the shoulder. 'What say you, Bart?'

Roberts looked around them all, and then grinned. 'You've done me a great honour,' he said. 'I accept!'

They roared their approval again, and they surged towards him like an unstoppable wave, washing him along with them, out of the dark and pungent atmosphere of the cabin and into the bright glare of open deck.

On the main deck, the rest of the company—the 'commoners' had assembled to await the decision of their 'lords'. As Henry Dennis had indicated, without the vote of the entire company, the whole process would have to begin again.

Roberts looked at them, men he had climbed the yards with, men he had scrubbed decks with, men he had exchanged yarns with. There was John Stephenson, his superior on the *Princess*, and John Jessup, and others. They all regarded him with interest, as though it hadn't occurred to them either that he might be a candidate for the captaincy.

In the middle of them, a head above the rest, stood David Symson, not looking at Roberts, but evidently the bearer of the news to the men.

As Henry Dennis repeated the import of his speech, telling them the decision of their 'lords', Roberts felt suddenly alone. He was no longer one of them, but their captain. Unless they were suited for a place as officers, he would never exchange yarns with them again.

Henry Dennis finished speaking and they burst into shouting their *Ayes* breaking into wild cheering, waving arms and hats in the air. Their enthusiasm gave him a surge of pride and certainty. He would control them, enthuse them, protect them. This villainous rabble were *his* crew, and the *Royal Rover* was *his* ship.

He gripped the quarterdeck rail as they cheered, his heart so full of pride that for a moment he could only look at them. Then he held up his hands for silence and they obeyed immediately.

'It's no secret,' he told them. 'All of you know I had no desire to go on the account. But since I have dipped my hands into muddy waters and must be a pirate—well—' he grinned at them all '—I'd far rather be a commander than a common man! I accept the honour!'

He raised his voice at the last to be heard above the loud cheering which broke out again, and he stood still with his head held high, his body braced against the ship's movements, accepting their accolade. They cheered endlessly, and he thought that no man had taken command of a ship under such glorious approval.

The rest of the day was taken up with the necessary task of electing to the 'House of Lords', officers to replace the ones they had lost with Davis. After much drinking, raising of toasts to praise the courage of captain Davis and bestow their blessings on their new captain, they elevated twenty-two year old Richard Hardy, another Welshman, the big Devonshire man Robert Birdson, Michael Maer from Ghent, and twenty-one year old Thomas Sutton. George Hunter who had served under Stephens as assistant surgeon became chief surgeon.

Apportioning out duties was not easy, but the new captain had the authority to choose as his first officer, mate or lieutenant, Walter Kennedy. He chose him for two reasons—one, because he needed a man who would not fear to carry out any order Roberts might give him. Kennedy had the necessary courage to lead an attack, whether on land or at sea. But also, it made sense to keep Kennedy sweet, to keep him on his side.

The other appointments were soon filled. Valentine Ashplant and Henry Dennis became secondary lieutenants in command of gun crews, Tom Sutton master gunner; John Stephenson became sailing master, Richard Hardy his mate; Christopher Moody was appointed Boatswain, responsible for the labour on the ship as well as the ground tackle, and Michael Maer his mate, while James Phillips and Thomas Anstis became the officers of the starboard and larboard watches respectively.

However, the highest honour of all went to David Symson as quartermaster, the man with more power even than the captain.

The quartermaster worked closely with the captain, advising him when necessary and usually he selected the new recruits. He had the authority to punish by beating or whipping any minor offences not covered by the ship's articles, such as disobeying commands, quarrelling, misuse of prisoners and not keeping weapons in proper order. He led the boarding party on any prize, and was able to take the best items for his own use, he alone deciding what they should take from a captured ship and what to leave behind—and woe betide any who went beyond his order!

When he saw the glow of pleasure in Symson's pale eyes, and the quiet smile twitching at the corners of his thin mouth, Roberts knew he had made the right decision to put his name forward. The honour more than made up for his loss of the captaincy, and he hoped it would make Symson one of his closest allies.

But still they had not finished. As the afternoon wore on, and the sun began to slide towards the west, Roberts wondered how much longer it would take.

The rum punch disappeared at a great rate making them more belligerent. The hunger to avenge the death of their last captain erupted in swearing and cursing and they drank death to the Portuguese. Roberts felt the mood change, as if the wind had changed direction to blow a chill breeze from the mountains, and he became uneasy.

'I say death to them that killed Cap'n Davis!'

Recognising the Irish accent, Roberts felt his heart sink. Making Kennedy his lieutenant might have been a mistake.

As usual, Kennedy had drunk too much. His eyes had the glazed wild expression of a man excited by drink but he still had possession of some of his senses and when he spoke his voice was not slurred.

He pushed his way forward through to where Roberts stood, and turned to address the company. Holding tightly to the gunwale, he glared at them all, then belched loudly.

'They damned well killed the Cap'n, so they did. An' Stephens and Aston, and the rest of 'em. An' damn me, gentlemen, I say life oughta go for life.'

Roberts groaned inwardly. He had known Kennedy would be trouble, but he had hoped to have a little while before having to deal with such a situation.

Kennedy grinned, the blood-lust sparking in his eyes. It made him look truly evil.

The men, carried along by drink and a thirst for bloody revenge, yelled their agreement.

Roberts' mind raced. He thought of the woman. If they took their revenge on Mendoça, and there was every reason to expect it, it would be doubtful if she would escape. There were others, too, black and Portuguese and Creole, women and children, innocents. The thought of so much bloodshed revolted him. And he was under no illusions. Kennedy would have no mercy.

'What do you suggest, Mr. Kennedy?' he asked, and the calmness in his voice, at complete variance to Kennedy's shrill excitement, had a soothing effect on them all.

Kennedy pursed his lips, and his eyes narrowed as he understood Roberts' intention, and his voice rose deliberately. 'I reckon we should kill them that killed Cap'n Davis. No man should kill our captain and yet live!'

He waited. Any plan of action needed the new captain's sanction, and Roberts recognised the first challenge to his command. Kennedy was testing his mettle. Would the new captain turn weakly away from shedding blood when necessary? Would he prove unfit to govern this company? He could hear Dennis's warning ringing in his ears: *Power is with the community, and the community may depute and revoke as it suits them best.* And: *Should any captain be so saucy as to exceed his authority at any time, then down with him, I say! It will be a caution to his successors, after he is dead, of what the results of any sort of assuming may be!*

'How do you propose to carry that out, Mr. Kennedy?' Roberts' voice was still calm, but the men shifted irritably. There was warning in their actions.

Ashplant rubbed his bristly chin. 'Aye, Cap'n Davis was a fair man, an' easy on us. 'E gave us many vict'ries. An' 'e'll be sorely missed.'

Christopher Moody nodded. 'Aye—them Portuguee didn't oughta get away wi't!'

Others joined in the chorus of agreement, as Kennedy stirred them up to action. 'We'll fight 'em!' he cried. 'We'll rip their tongues from their treacherous mouths, and tear out their innards—we'll teach them cowardly sons of whores not to murder our men!'

'Aye, aye, aye!'

'Let's burn the town!'

The company burst into a roar of approval.

Roberts had a fleeting mental picture of the three streets that comprised Santo António, with Pico Papagaio in the distance, and the governor's house. And within those walls, the woman. It would be rape and pillage and slaughter. He would not allow it.

Henry Dennis, by now seriously alarmed, gripped the rail and interrupted them. 'Listen to me! You ain't going to get at the men responsible . . .'

But they were in no mood to listen. If Roberts were going to prevent a massacre he had to act quickly, and in a different direction.

As captain, he had the final vote. He could sanction or veto. However, emotions ran hot and he would rather not have a lead ball in his brain. He had no intention of being the shortest reigning captain in history.

David Symson quietened the men by waving his hands for order, then he addressed the new captain. 'What say you, Cap'n

Roberts?'

Roberts came forward to stand in the midst of them on the main deck. 'I'll agree to your plan,' he said, '*if* you can accomplish it without your own destruction.'

There was silence. Then Kennedy: 'What do you mean? We're as good an army as any might be!'

'Aye. But look you!' Roberts crouched down and drew his dagger from his belt, and they edged away from him to give him room. With it he scratched a diagram on the deck polished white with the holystone. 'Here is the town of Santo António. Here, here and here, forest surrounding the town completely. All of it on a hill. If they place gunners here and here—' he pointed with his dagger, '—and if I were defending the town, that's what I would do—then you won't get within half a mile of it. You know the cover the forest will give to the defenders. Already we lost Davis and the others there. And you can't kill men you can't see. They will be on their home territory, and if you think they will run away from you with such an advantage, you are sorely mistaken. You will all be dead men before you reach the town, and for what? A few miserable houses! For you can be sure that by then the inhabitants will have fled into the forest where you cannot follow. Now if you have some plan that will avoid you all being killed, I'll gladly agree. But I will not agree to suicide.'

He stood up, and there was a profound silence as they considered it, some jostling for a position to peer at the diagram.

Briefly Roberts met Henry Dennis's eyes and saw him give a slight nod of approval.

When no-one else spoke, he offered them an alternative. 'We can, however, fire on the town from the safety of the bay.'

Experience had taught him that cannon fire was largely overrated, and only marginally effective—perhaps enough to batter some houses, but with few casualties. But a good salvo from the *Rover* may well satisfy their lust for revenge.

'The water's too shoal,' John Jessup grumbled.

'And the *Rover*'s draught too great,' Roberts finished for him. 'But what about the smaller Frenchie? We could mount her with, say, a dozen guns, lighten her, wait for high tide, and then she'll sail in sweet as can be!'

It hadn't occurred to them before, but now they had the idea put to them, they liked it, and they agreed to it in a vote. Roberts glanced at Kennedy, and saw the smouldering anger. He had made an enemy of Kennedy, and it had not been his intention. Well, he would have to live with it—and watch out for himself.

It was a triumph for his leadership. The town's lookouts would spot the Frenchman coming in, and would have time to warn the inhabitants of the town. He thought of the woman again, and whilst he would have been happier knowing she had left the island, he felt he had done the best he could to ensure that she came to no harm.

The day after tomorrow was decided upon, but before the day ended the Frenchman's crew found themselves in the *Royal Rover*'s hold, and the pirates got on with the task of lightening the ship of everything not required.

EIGHT

The sun's heat had not diminished at all. If anything, as the island woke from its *sesta*, the heat increased, for an earlier breeze had dropped away, and now the houses shuddered in the heat haze.

Under the shade of the roof overhang Lúcia stood on the saloon balcony looking out at the two ships lying at anchor right out at the harbour entrance, the Frenchman and the English pirate.

She compressed her lips in anger. *He* was on that ship, and he was a pirate, not the English gentleman-officer she had thought him, but a murdering, thieving, greedy, unprincipled pirate.

The revelation had come as a shock. She had been lied to. Yet her father had known all along, and so had Mendoça. They too had been complicit in the lie. In fact it seemed that everyone had known who the English really were except herself. But typically, men viewed women as inferior unimportant beings who must at all times be kept in the dark about important matters. That infuriated her just as much as the original lie.

Of course she had known nothing about the ambush before the event, but when she did learn of it, she was horrified by that too. Mendoça's doing no doubt, but she could not help wondering if her father had agreed to it in any way. Not that the English didn't deserve to die, she thought fiercely. Those pirates had intended to take the island's dignitaries captive. She would not have worried about Mendoça, but her own dear father could well have been among the captives, and there was no telling how English pirates would have dealt with him. She shuddered. Still, she had made enquiries and discovered the English 'lieutenant' had not been among the dead. A pity, she thought fiercely. It was what he deserved!

From nowhere the wind picked up again. At the entrance to the harbour the French ship made sail, and seemed to be sailing into the harbour. The pirates had let them go, then.

'*Filha*, daughter!'

She turned. '*Pápa!*' and went to him, kissing his sallow cheek in greeting, and he accepted it as his due.

'What are you doing here?' he demanded, by no means pleased. 'I told you to go to the village. Lúcia, if you do not listen to me, how can I hope to protect you? You are the most unruly, disobedient child!'

She gave a characteristic toss of her head. 'I am not a child,

Pápa. Clearly, you have not been to the village or you would not expect me to spend another hour there!'

'Do you not know that the English pirates could attack Santo Antonio at any moment?'

'No, I do *not* know!' she cried angrily. 'For you do not tell me anything! I am not a child, and neither am I an idiot. Why you cannot tell me . . .'

His own temper began to rise. 'Could you not, just this once, obey me without question?' he demanded through his teeth.

Lúcia stamped her foot, and let fly a torrent of words at a speed that Pietro Andrade found hard to follow. He looked imploringly up to heaven, yet let her say her piece until she suddenly remembered to whom she spoke and stopped as suddenly as she started.

'*Pápa* . . .'

'Lúcia, Lúcia, you make my head ache!' he told her wearily.

She adopted a much softer wheedling tone. '*Pápa*, it was the most dismal place! A single hut for both myself and Maria and a family of six as well as two dogs and a goat! And they were Creoles, father, and so *dirty*. The food was inedible. The bugs bit at night, and the mosquitoes whined all the time. I had to sleep on a blanket on the floor with Maria! I *cannot* think you want me to go back to that place.'

'Lúcia,' he snapped, 'a little discomfort for your own safety. Could you not, just this once, put up with it?'

'Safety! What safety? Your precious Mendoça has killed the English captain and his men! Do you think they will leave any part of the island safe?'

Andrade walked out onto the balcony. 'You see that my dear?' He pointed out over the leafy canopy with his cane at the second of the ships. 'That is the English ship. The pirate ship. They have not left, you see. They are still here.'

She had seen that for herself. 'And so, *Pápa*?'

'And so, Lúcia, while they are here, they are a threat to our safety. It is the town they will take their vengeance on. Mendoça has done us no favours in ambushing and killing those men in that way.'

'You do not agree with it, *Pápa*?'

'No,' he said flatly. 'There is an honourable way of doing things, and a dishonourable way. Mendoça chose the latter.'

'But they were going to kidnap Mendoça, and others, and perhaps you.'

'Yes, that is true. But Mendoça had been forewarned.' He paused and said carefully, 'There is much that goes on in these islands that the King does not know about.'

'No, he doesn't!' Mendoça's voice from the open doorway made them both jump, and they spun to face him. 'And he isn't going to find out either, is he *Senhor* Andrade?'

Mendoça's face smiled, but his dark eyes glittered. Lúcia's stomach contracted, and she gripped the balcony rail behind her.

Pietro Andrade came forward. 'I would think he already knows,' he said airily. 'I sent a full report to him four days ago when you murdered the English.'

Mendoça thought about it. A ship had left for Brazil just then. There would be no chance of stopping a letter that had already sailed, although it gave him a few weeks before he could expect some redress from Portugal.

'And what do you think the King will say to it? Trading with pirates—everyone does it. And you have to prove that I knew they were not English navy.' Andrade smiled. 'Oh, *senhor*,' he said smoothly, 'there was more to my letter than that. A certain man—I forget his name, but it is all in the letter—a short fellow, whiskers, thus!' He indicated a full beard, and Mendoça said: 'Ferdinand.'

'Just so.' Andrade laughed mirthlessly, pleased to have this point clarified. He waved his hand in the air theatrically. 'I found bills of lading in your drawer. Several of them, as it happens. Very careless of you, to leave them lying around like that!' He wagged his finger at Mendoça as though he were talking to an errant child.

Mendoça paled. 'So?'

'So it is illegal, my dear Mendoça, to work such a monopoly. You have intimidated the traders, so that no-one can buy or sell slaves except to you. The King will remove you from office himself, *senhor* and you will no doubt be recalled to Lisbon to answer these charges.'

Lúcia moved away from the balcony, uneasily watching Mendoça's growing anger. He did not answer, but Pietro Andrade said: 'You killed the English to distract me. Instead of arresting them and giving them a fair trial, you shot them down in cold blood. You could have arrested them, quite easily. They were more than outnumbered. What is a pirate's life worth anyway, eh, *senhor*?'

'May you be damned . . !' Mendoça cried furiously and drew his sword. But he got no further for a sudden crash sent stone, mortar and splinters of wood flying through the air like deadly grapeshot from a gun.

A deep silence followed, broken by a trickle of dust and the shifting of more masonry. Lúcia had been thrown to the ground, and lay there stunned among the debris. Brick and plaster dust continued to fall like gently trickling water. Then, somewhere in the depths of the house a woman began screaming hysterically.

Lúcia tried to regain her scattered wits. She coughed, choking on the dust, and struggled to her knees. Behind her, the balcony where she had stood a few minutes previously had vanished, leaving a gaping hole in the wall and a sheer drop to the ground below.

'*Pápa?*'

'I am all right, *filha*,' he said although his voice was muffled, and he too coughed.

'Cursed English!' Mendoça swore as he pulled himself out of the debris. 'You see what your lover has done?' he added to Lúcia.

Outraged, a string of invectives came to her tongue, but before she could speak, the cannon bellowed again from the direction of the sea, shaking the earth. She covered her head with her hands, but the guns had turned. From the commotion in the street, she concluded that it must have hit another house.

She struggled to her feet, hampered by her skirts, and tried to wipe the dust from her face with the back of her hand, with little success before picking her way through the debris to her father. 'You think so?' she retorted above the noise. 'You think it was the English? I wonder why? Perhaps, *senhor*, it has something to do with your murdering their captain and officers!'

'See! She defends the pirates!' Mendoça cried.

'I do not condone murder, *senhor*, she told him with a haughty toss of her head, but tears of shock and anger had come into her eyes.

Outside the English kept up their bombardment, a continual barrage of noise.

She helped her father to his feet and he stood amid the debris, brushing the white dust from his own coat and breeches. 'Ruined!' he said to himself. 'My best coat.' Then to Mendoça: 'You see what you have done?'

'I am governor here,' Mendoça said straightly, 'and I must protect the island.'

'And your own interest, too.'

Andrade, and Lúcia picked their way through the lumps of masonry towards the door.

At that moment, alarmed servants arrived to offer what assistance they could. It precluded further discussion, and Mendoça turned away, too angry to speak, as Andrade followed Lúcia from the room, leaving him alone amid the debris of his riches.

'We have to leave,' Andrade said urgently to Lúcia as soon as they were out of earshot. 'We are not safe here.'

She frowned. 'Where do we go, *Pápa*?'

'Brazil,' he said. 'There is another merchantman in the bay sailing in a few days. Tell Maria to pack your things.'

The manservant who came to enquire solicitously if Mendoça were hurt received a curt denial, and an order to clean up the mess.

He strode from the room, furious with Andrade, and the English pirates and even Lúcia herself. It crossed his mind that he could rid himself of Andrade in much the same way as he rid himself of Howell Davis, but he dismissed the thought. It was one thing to murder pirates, but another to do the same to the King's emissary and his daughter.

For a while he entertained himself with the idea of exacting revenge on the English. However, he was not fool enough to risk pitting his small if willing army against a large highly-trained fighting force, no matter how much it might assuage his hurt pride. So he dismissed it reluctantly. Rather, he had to think of saving himself.

While he watched, the English in the French ship turned away. He would have to leave São Tomé and Príncipe now while he could keep some of the fortune he had made. He would take with him his slaves and his gold, and he would set himself up as a trader on the African coast, long before Andrade's report arrived back in Opporto. He would simply disappear.

He allowed himself a small satisfied smile. António Furtado de Mendoça would survive.

Captain Bartholomew Roberts rested his hands on the guard rail and watched the little orange glow grow in the darkness of the night. Like a flower unfolding its petals, the flames flickered in the coiled rope on the Portuguese deck and spread out. In an instant, it found the oiled stays and sped up them to the yards. Furled sails exploded into flame. Orange smoke swelled into the night. It burned his nostrils, and caught in the back of his throat, and the men returning in the boat coughed and choked in the thick air. Burning wood crackled and spit, steam hissed in the roar of the flames, and sparks showered into the darkness.

On the other side of the narrow entrance to the bay, the other captured ship also began to burn, and he could see his men clearly in the artificial light as they scrambled down the side to the waiting boat.

He grinned with satisfaction at this last defiant act towards Mendoça.

'All hands! Lay aloft!'

Before the order was out, eager men sprang into the rigging and ran up the shrouds, their white shirts reflecting the orange glow of the burning ships, and they were quite visible as they ran out onto the yards to cast off the gaskets. Fifteen men took the handspikes and slotted them into the capstan pigeon holes. This time, as the men strained their backs and the capstan began to turn with a heave and a jerk as the pawls clanked into place, they sang for the rhythm, strong English voices carrying across the water to the town at the head of the bay. First a single voice, beginning with a yelp:

'*Old Stormy he is dead and gorn.*'

And the rest responded:

'*To me way you Stormalong.*'
'*Old Stormy he is dead and gorn.*'
'*Aye! Aye! Aye! Mister Stormalong.*'

The wind found the newly-released sails causing them to thunder and flap as men fought to make the bunts fast. Roberts marched swiftly forward to the helm. By the light of the two ships he could see the way through the strait, and recalled the route the pilot had brought them in by, grateful that he had paid attention.

'*He slipped his cable off Cape Horn.*'
'*To me way you Stormalong.*'
'*Close by the place where he was born.*'
'*Aye! Aye! Aye! Mister Stormalong!*'

The *Royal Rover* jerked forward and Roberts gave the order to bring her about.

Like a queen in full regalia, the *Royal Rover* was under weigh, leaving the island of Príncipe for the last time, accompanied by her lady in waiting, the little Frenchman.

NINE

December 1719, Brazilian Coast

Captain Bartholomew Roberts spread the chart on the great cabin table, weighing it down with a lantern on one corner, the silver teapot on another and the bottom two corners with his hands to stop it rolling up on its own accord, and peered at it for the umpteenth time, as though it might tell him something new.

For nine long, hot, frustratingly fruitless weeks they had patrolled the shipping routes off the coast of Brazil looking for a likely target without even the suspicion of a sail. Yet they had been certain of success here, for the Portuguese were lively in trading between Africa, Brazil and Opporto, and their preferred commodity was gold. Now, however, their supplies of food and water had run low and he knew they could waste no more time. They had to leave and find a vessel which would supply not riches, but needs.

The ship creaked and groaned in the oppressive silence, and the sea's gentle wash against the rudder intruded upon his thoughts. He straightened up and looked at the silent gloomy faces of his officers.

He had seen the mood change in the weeks since they left the island of Ferdinando where they had cleaned the ship. The optimism which had accompanied their first successes after leaving Prince's Island, such as when they had taken a Dutch Guineaman and an English ketch soon waned, for they yielded little in the way of anything satisfactory. The Dutchman they had released, along with the captured Frenchman, but the ketch's crew all signed the pirates' articles and joined the company, and since it had only two masts and was not to Roberts' liking, they set fire to it.

'Perhaps it is worth trying the West Indies,' Roberts said now, struggling to hide his intense disappointment, well aware that the trade in the West Indies was mostly of common goods and slaves, not gold, like the Portuguese preferred. The decision was not popular. He could see it in their faces, their disappointment as intense as his own.

The decision to try the Brazilian coast had been made by the company, but the navigation was his responsibility, and it was his responsibility also to deliver the goods. If he didn't do so soon, they would find themselves a new captain, dispatching the old one to the bottom of the Atlantic. He knew that not one of them would risk his own life to save that of a failed captain. Roberts needed success and he needed it urgently.

'Seems to me that we ought to do something other than sit here waiting for the Portuguese!' Henry Dennis said, breaking the melancholy silence.

Roberts glared at him. 'What would you suggest, Mr. Dennis?'

'Try an incantation,' Thomas Anstis suggested sarcastically. 'Perhaps you can magic up a Portuguese ship!'

Irish Kennedy laughed, but the others regarded him coldly. It hadn't taken Roberts long to realise that while it may be politic to keep the trouble-makers on his side by appointing them as officers, the choice did not always sit well with the others.

'Well, I don't wish to worry you, Cap'n,' David Symson put in slowly, 'but we ain't got provisions for more'n a week, and certainly not enough water. We could get as far as Cayenne, or maybe Devil's Island if we leave now, but if we wait, we'll not make it.'

Roberts ran his fingers through his loose black hair, and made a decision. 'That's it, then. Very well, gentlemen, I think we should quit this coast and vote on Devil's Island.'

Devil's Island had been a favourite haunt of pirates for some years, offering soft women and hard liquor. Some time spent carousing would go a long way to appease the men. It was a prospect he anticipated with as much pleasure as any of them.

Ashplant finished off his rum, wiping his whiskery mouth on his sleeve, and stood up. 'So it be the Caribbean, then.'

'Ah ye daft Londoner!' Irish Kennedy put in. 'We've settled on Devil's Island.'

'Ah. Devil's Island. Ain't Sally Grey on Devil's Island?'

Roberts raised his brows. 'I knew a Sally Grey, once, ran a bawdy house on the Deptford Road. Red hair, as I recall, eyes as blue as the sky. Enormous—' he held his hands out expressively in front of him.

They all laughed.

'That's her! She be on Devil's Island now, and I tell ye she runs a bawdy house!'

'Calls it a tavern, though,' David Symson put in, and grinned. 'Married a Frenchman, a trader, and he took her to the Guiana coast as settlers. Oh, must be five year ago. He trades with the Indians, both at Devil's Island, and on the river at Kourou.'

'*Sail Ho!* Deck there, sail ho!'

It was so unexpected after the long weeks of waiting, that Roberts thought at first he had misheard. Then, as it dawned on him that there might indeed be a ship awaiting their attention, he grabbed the telescope and ran from the cabin and up the companionway steps followed by his officers.

'Whither away?' he called to the man at the masthead.

'Larboard bow!'

Squinting at first against the painful glare of the sun, Roberts crossed to the larboard side, jumped up onto the gunwale and swung out over the water and up the shrouds to the crosstrees.

William Hedges, the lookout, lowered the telescope and pointed to the north west. 'Portuguese, Cap'n, off the larboard bow. 'Undreds of 'em!'

Roberts stretched the telescope and peered in the direction Hedges indicated. Then he saw them, a large number of stick-like masts on the horizon.

Hope sprouted into relief, and bloomed into excitement. Not quite hundreds, but he counted forty-two ships hove-to off Bahia, or more correctly, All Saints Bay, Salvador. And where there were Portuguese ships, there would be gold. All that remained was to work out how to get at that gold.

He frowned. They couldn't go in, death's head flying, drums beating, guns pounding. No, this required a more subtle approach.

He came down from the crosstrees, gave command to the man at the helm to hold the course and shorten sail. He needed time to think about this.

'By my reckoning, forty-two Portuguese ships hove-to off *Bahia de Todos os Santos,*' he announced. 'Sitting there, just waiting for us.'

'Aye, and waiting for their escort, too, I've no doubt. If there is gold, there will be men of war to take care of it.' Henry Dennis said. 'Can't be done, Bart.'

Roberts nodded thoughtfully. With the increase in piracy in the last few years, many nations had taken the proverb 'safety in numbers' literally, and a great many ships sailed in convoy. It was enough to deter even the most desperate pirate.

He watched the horizon with his naked eye, although they had not yet come into view from the deck, and worked out a way to extract the gold. They could not take it all. He would have to single out the ship carrying the most gold.

The familiar fizzing of excitement in his veins and the small slide of fear in his belly made his eyes shine. He knew just how to do it. It would be daring, dangerous, even, yet he could not turn away from what promised to be a rich prize. 'Mr. Stephenson!'

The sandy-haired sailing master was at his elbow. 'Aye, Cap'n?'

'Join us to the fleet, Mr. Stephenson. Keep us out of sight, and bring us about to the rear of the fleet. We want them to think we're another Portuguese vessel joining them.'

John Stephenson grinned. 'Aye, aye, Cap'n.'

'Mr. Moody!'

The boatswain came forward. 'Cap'n?'

'Get all the men below, save those necessary for sailing the ship. Choose men for the sailing who can speak a little Portuguese. Make sure those hidden are armed and ready.'

'Aye, aye, Cap'n.'

'Mr. Hardy—raise the Portuguese flag!'

The excitement was contagious, and men, eager to do his bidding, ran in all directions as their officers shouted the orders.

Stephenson had already got men heaving on the great yards to bring them round, and with the help of the big Belgian, Michael Maer, who shouted the orders, got as much sail on the ship as she could bear.

As they secured all, and the cries came back 'Well all!' the white sails filled with wind and the ship came about. The deck canted sharply, the wind came on the broad reach which the *Royal Rover* liked best, and John Stephenson ordered the yards round again and the trimming of the sails.

She picked up speed with a will, jerking slightly as the wind caught her, the clear green sea streaming by her bows.

Roberts stood beside the helm, his feet braced against the deck's plunge and tilt, giving his orders to Stephenson who had taken the helm himself, adjusting the course as necessary. To outward appearance he was calm, only the light in his eyes betraying his excitement. But his heart pounded and every muscle tensed, and his mouth had gone dry as though he had tried to eat sand.

As the *Royal Rover* turned again, her wake described a huge arc. It took considerable skill to bring the ship into position without being sighted by the target, and Roberts was short with Stephenson when he did not execute his orders immediately, but eventually they slipped unseen behind the Portuguese.

Yet again it was 'Man the braces!' and the yards again swung round protestingly, and the *Royal Rover* turned to bring them to the edge of the squadron.

Forty-two ships, mostly of the old-fashioned square-rigged galleon type so beloved of the Portuguese waited quietly at anchor for their armed escort. They were not very tightly packed, but such a vast number that they stretched into the distance off the starboard bow. Of the men-of-war, there was no sign, and Roberts smiled to himself. They may have been forty-two heavily armed ships, but they were unprepared. Just ripe for harvesting in fact.

'Tell the men to lie low,' Roberts said to Moody, 'and all speech to be in Portuguese from now on. No chants.' The Portuguese did not sing like the English did, and sounds carried a surprising distance. An English word would certainly betray them.

The pounding in his heart quickened as they sailed daringly within hailing distance of a fat galleon. Discovery would find them trapped, with Portuguese on every side, and he studied the ships around him for signs of activity that might warn him of impending disaster. But the Portuguese went quietly about their business, which was not very much, for they were already loaded and waiting only for their escorts.

Roberts gave the order to heave to, and Richard Hardy who had a little knowledge of Portuguese repeated the order, while Christopher Moody graphically demonstrated with his hands.

John Stephenson at the helm, brought the bows into the wind, and immediately the sails collapsed and fluttered helplessly in the hot breeze. Once more men jumped into the rigging and strung out on the yards to haul in sail.

The *Royal Rover* slowed immediately and dropped her anchor.

So far, so good, Roberts thought. No outraged cries, no messages of alarm. But all the same his stomach turned while the excitement flooded his veins.

'Mr. Hardy!'

'Cap'n?' Richard Hardy was at his side, his dark eyes shining with youthful enthusiasm.

'How good is your Portuguese?'

'I get by.'

'Then go to the forecastle and hail that ship!'

'What'll I say to them?'

'I'll tell you.'

Richard Hardy nodded and coloured a little, for although he had been promoted to the House of Lords and had taken his new position very much to heart, he was still young enough to feel proud to have been singled out for this honour. He marched swiftly forward. Roberts followed at a more leisurely pace, in company with Walter Kennedy, Henry Dennis and David Symson.

The Portuguese ship was larger than the *Royal Rover*, with a high quarterdeck and forecastle, and a fat hull, like an old lady with a fat bottom. She had three square-rigged masts, but no trysail, which was the *Royal Rover*'s ace card, and therefore was slower and not as manoeuvrable.

Richard Hardy leaned over the forecastle guard-rail. 'Ahoy there!'

'Allo!'

'What ship is that pray?'

'The *Santa Catriana*, Captain Cordoso commanding. Who are you?'

'The *Aventuro Real*,' Hardy called back at Roberts' prompting. 'Captain Bartolomeo Roberto commanding. We request that you send your master to us to dine with us.'

There was a long wait.

'What's happening?' Henry Dennis demanded in an impatient whisper.

'They are surprised, I reckon, and they are thinking about it,' Roberts replied, outwardly unruffled, but he watched the *Santa Catriana's* decks closely.

David Symson fingered his pistol. 'We're naked here.'

'Aye,' Roberts agreed. A good musketeer could pick them off from this distance with no trouble.

The Portuguese hailed them again. 'Why should we send our captain to you?'

'Open the gun ports, Mr. Dennis,' Roberts commanded calmly, but he felt his insides squeeze tight. To the Portuguese he said himself: 'Because if you don't, we will blow the Saint Catherine out of the water.'

He waved his hand as he spoke and immediately all the *Royal Rover*'s one hundred and twenty crew appeared from behind the raised gunwales waving cutlasses in the air in silent menace, and at the same time the gun ports in the ship's side opened. Then at another signal from Roberts, the cutlass-waving men vanished from sight again, and the gun ports closed. 'Now, if the *senhores* please. Captain Cordoso will come to no harm. But if you raise the alarm, we will give you no quarter!'

He waited and watched. He had gambled and now he relied on Portuguese cowardice to see him through. But if they did not do as he asked, he would be forced to take their ship. He had in mind how he could do it and escape. It would be tight, and it would cost them the gold and possibly the lives of some of the crew, but it could be done.

Minutes ticked by. Roberts watched for any attempt at retaliation, but the galleon remained quiet.

'They ain't gonna do it,' Symson breathed.

'They will,' Roberts said with more confidence than he felt. 'If they have passengers, and I guess that they must have, they will not risk it.'

The Portuguese captain appeared at the entry port. 'Be prepared to welcome *capitão* Cordoso aboard.'

Roberts grinned at the others. 'You see?' To the Portuguese he said: '*Capitão* Cordoso will come to no harm. But we would not like to see any alarm signals or other resistance. Understood?'

Captain Cordoso himself answered him. 'We understand.'

The Portuguese hauled out their boat, and Roberts said jubilantly: 'Prepare to welcome the captain aboard, Mr. Hardy, if you please.'

Henry Dennis shook his head, but it was Walter Kennedy who exclaimed admiringly: 'Holy mother of God! I ain't never seen the like of it, that I ain't.'

'How did you know they'd do it, Bart?' Dennis asked.

Roberts grinned at him and said nothing. The fact was, he had taken a gamble and won.

The Portuguese captain came onto the deck through the entry-port. Meeting him, Roberts bowed low, removed his hat, and then shook the man's hand. After all, Captain Cordoso was a brave man to put himself into the hands of people he now knew to be English pirates.

'Welcome aboard, *capitão*.'

The Portuguese captain met the smile with cold disdain. He was a small man, and he had delicate hands as though he had never done a day's real work in his life. His features, too were small, save for a large hooked nose in his tanned face. 'What is it you want with me? Do you intend to hold me for ransom? Or is it murder?'

'Not if you tell me what I want to know,' Roberts replied imperturbably.

'Who are you?'

'We are English—gentlemen of fortune.'

'Cursed pirates!'

'If you wish.' And Roberts bowed his head in gracious acknowledgement. 'All we require from you, Captain Cordoso, is information.'

'You won't get it!'

Roberts sighed, and shook his head in mock disbelief. 'I see you intend to make this difficult for yourself. Very well.' He switched to English and changed from the calculatingly calm tone to an abrupt order. 'Mr. Kennedy—take him below.'

Kennedy pushed the prisoner roughly ahead of them through the doors leading to the great cabin and by the time Roberts followed them he had him seated in Roberts' own chair in front of the great cabin window.

Roberts leaned over towards the man, putting his weight on the arms of the chair, his face an inch from his. 'Now, captain, down here your crew have no idea whether you are alive or dead. And truth to tell, it matters little.' He smiled, but the coldness in his eyes made his prisoner shudder involuntarily. 'See my lieutenant?'

Cordoso slid his eyes to Kennedy just beside them.

'Well, my dear *capitão, senhor* Kennedy will not hesitate to slit your throat the moment I give the word. Understand?'

Kennedy grinned hopefully, and slid his thumb along the curved blade of a twelve-inch dagger. But Roberts had no intention of killing his prisoner. Instead, still leaning on the arms of the chair, his face still intimidatingly close to that of Cordoso, his voice deceptively low, he said:

'Tell me, *capitão*—which ship carries the most gold?'

Captain Cordoso sweated profusely, and his fingers, locked together across his stomach in a futile attempt at calmness, shook with fear. 'I cannot give the *senhor* that information.'

Roberts stood up straight, and walked away from him. 'Ah— you are a brave man, *senhor*. And loyal. I like that.' He turned and once more his voice changed to hard menace. 'But you are a foolish man. If you do not give me the information, my lieutenant will slit your throat, and I will find someone who will. Now tell me, which is the richest ship in the fleet?'

Droplets of dew-like sweat stood out on Cordoso's upper lip and brow. 'I cannot tell you.'

'Very well. *Senhor* Kennedy, you know what to do. Let us rid ourselves of this fool!'

Since Kennedy's command of Portuguese was limited, he did not immediately respond, but the speaking look cast at him by his captain was enough to remind him to play his part. He grabbed Cordoso's black hair and yanked his head backwards exposing a pale throat and a large Adam's apple. He prodded the pale skin under the man's left ear with his dagger.

Captain Cordoso screamed in terror. *'Não! Não!* I beg you, *senhor capitão!'* Roberts had turned away and was intent on adjusting the lace at his cuffs, apparently unconcerned.

Cordoso cried out again. 'I beg the s*enhor capitão* have mercy! I will tell the *senhor* what he wants to know.'

Roberts looked at him then with renewed interest, and jerked his head towards Kennedy who reluctantly released the victim. 'Yes?'

Involuntarily, Cordoso's thin hand went to his throat, and he swallowed with relief. 'At the head of the squadron, the ship with topgallants on three masts and a royal on the mainmast. The *Sagrada Familia.'*

'Thank you, captain. And what does she carry?'

'Forty-thousand *moidores* as well as jewels and trinkets.'

Roberts exchanged glances with David Symson. 'How much is that in sterling?' he asked in English.

David Symson paused for some difficult mental arithmetic, but before he'd sorted out the conversion rate, Roberts answered his own question. 'About seventy-thousand pounds.' He whistled in surprise. 'That is a good deal of gold.' He grinned his delight at Captain Cordoso. *'Obrigado, senhor capitão.* Mr. Kennedy—see that he is comfortable, if you please.' Then again to the captive: 'The *senhor* will be our guest for a little longer, but then he will be returned to his ship.'

He turned and left the cabin, well satisfied. Regrettable, of course, that one had to resort to threats, but he had no intention of allowing one little man to come between him and a fortune.

TEN

Lúcia sighed yet again, holding her hand to her forehead. 'What is the delay?' she demanded. It was hot in the cabin, claustrophobic, and the continual rocking made her stomach heave and her head ache.

Maria, also struggling with growing seasickness, roused herself sufficiently from her misery to look at her charge. 'Captain Castro has already explained that we are waiting for the armed escort,' she said huffily.

'So—where are they?' Perhaps when they started to move, she might be able to go on deck and so relieve the pain behind her eyes.

She stood up abruptly and went to the open window to get some relief from the heat and the aroma of bilges, rotting wood and cordage, tar and tallow, as well as other less savoury odours. She could see other ships littering the sea, all of them alike waiting for their armed escort, the crews of which were probably lying drunk in some tavern.

She thought of her father left behind in Bahia, unable himself to go home to Portugal, but more than happy to send her to her fate. She was still furious with him, but behind the fury, she had a deep searing unhappiness. She longed to stay with him, for his illness had not improved in the weeks since they had arrived from Príncipe. She had no confidence in Rodrigues that he would care for her father as she would.

'Infuriating man!' she said under her breath. She had known all along that to argue with Pietro Andrade would get her nowhere. He had the annoying habit of always having the upper hand, even when he was sick.

'I am worried for you my daughter,' he had begun. 'I am a dying man.'

'*Pápa*, you are not dying,' she insisted. And indeed, he did not look at death's door.

Still, he said: 'What is to become of you when I am gone?' He silenced her protest. 'Now then, my child. We all have to die. It is just my turn!'

'No, *Pápa*!' She refused to believe it.

'Your mother has written to me with some wonderful news. She has found you a husband at last. One Césario Guerreiro.' He smiled with satisfaction.

It was not wonderful news. She had met Césario Guerreiro in Lisbon. 'I do not need a husband,' she announced her eyes flashing dangerously. 'And as for Césario Guerreiro why, that small pasty-faced young idiot! He's a hunchback, and half my size! And,' she added with feeling, 'he has smelly breath and clammy hands! How I do wish Mother would not interfere!'

'I am sure you can live with all those things,' her father said dismissively. 'Césario Guerreiro comes from a good family, is heir to a fortune and many estates near Lisbon and reportedly is desperate to marry. And you know, Lúcia, that you are hardly in a position to be choosy. Besides, I have already agreed to accept his offer.'

'I will not marry him!' Lúcia insisted, and proceeded to inform him at great speed and at the top of her voice, that she would rather die than be married to Guerreiro, that she thought her father had sold her to the highest bidder, that he had not taken her feelings into consideration, accused him of wishing to be rid of her, and finished up by bursting into angry tears.

All of which left Pietro Andrade singularly unmoved.

'I am sick, Lúcia,' he had said again with studied patience. 'And you *will* go.' He shook his head sadly. 'I should never have brought you out here in the first place.'

'I will not go,' she announced with finality.

Much good that did her. For here she was on the *Sagrada Familia* waiting to set sail, unable to do anything about it.

However, marriage was somewhere still in the future. Of more immediate concern was that she had only said goodbye to her father yesterday as he had put her on the boat. She had pleaded and cajoled, and cried, and screamed, all to no avail. Maria had reprimanded her for not behaving with the dignity that befitted a lady, but she had never felt less like a lady. She could not bear to be parted from that old rogue.

'Perhaps he will be handsome and charming,' Maria suggested helpfully, as Lúcia blinked away tears again. She did not bother to inform her maid of the true character of her fiancé.

'Oh *Pápa*!' she whispered. 'How could you send me away just when you need me?'

'He has Rodrigues.' Maria reminded her. She went on: 'Even ugly men have their good points you know. Perhaps you will find something to love in him.'

'And if I don't?'

'Many ladies of your station take lovers,' Maria suggested.

Lúcia closed her eyes. Was that it, then? To marry for position and wealth, to take a lover for what a husband should provide?

Her thoughts went back to Príncipe, to recent events. Mendoça had fled the island even before the Andrades had boarded the ship bound for Brazil, leaving the island in the hands of a council of men. And then there was the pirate, that rogue!

She closed her eyes against the headache which had grown, and wished she were with her father in Bahia. Obstinate old devil! But she loved him dearly, and she missed him already. The thought of never seeing him again was more than she could bear. And as she thought it, two large tears squeezed out from beneath her closed lids and slid down her face.

Roberts gripped the gunwale and studied the awkward bulk of the *Sagrada Familia*. She was a huge ugly old-fashioned three-masted vessel, broad across the beam, another old woman with a fat backside. She had a castellated stern where her great cabin was housed in a high quarterdeck, accessed by a door from the waist. Not only was she old and ugly, but Roberts knew she would be unwieldy and sluggish to sail, which made his task all the more difficult, since to unload her would take far too much time, and he had decided to sail off with her and her treasure.

She was heavily armed, too, with forty cannon and a hundred and fifty men, giving credence to Captain Cordoso's assertion that she did indeed carry gold. She should have been more than a match for the *Royal Rover* which had fewer guns and less men, but the Portuguese were ordinary sailors, not fighting men, which gave the pirates a distinct advantage. Besides, they were foreigners, not Englishmen, and everyone knew no Portuguese was a match for an Englishman!

His mind flicked back to their last encounter with the Portuguese on Prince's and the memory of Howell Davis's death still stung. This was where the Portuguese would pay, he told himself. Here they would lose what was dearest to their hearts—gold. Better still, it was King João's gold, which did much to salve any lasting conscience Roberts might have had, making the robbery more acceptable. Like Robin Hood, robbing the rich to give to the poor—a kind of equalising. The King, on the other hand, would hardly miss it.

'Bring her in close, Mr. Stephenson,' he said quietly, and John Stephenson turned the wheel. With so much at stake he would not entrust the helm to a lesser mortal.

As the *Sagrada Familia* loomed closer, Roberts said: 'Bring her athwart the stern, Mr. Stephenson.'

Gradually Stephenson guided the *Royal Rover* behind the Portuguese ship, so that she was amidships to the Portuguese stern which towered over her, and the men on the yards hauled in the sails.

Captain Cordoso joined Roberts near the helm. A very good dinner and a liberal quantity of wine had restored the Portuguese captain's courage so that he no longer shook visibly yet when Roberts addressed him, he jumped.

'The *capitão* is acquainted with the master of the *Sagrada Familia*?'

'No.'

'Well, no matter. He can still speak to him. Mr. Dennis!'

Dennis, who had been keeping watch from the forecastle, strode aft to the helm. 'Cap'n?'

'Make ready the starboard guns,' Roberts ordered. 'But don't open the ports until I give the order. And keep the men out of sight.'

'Aye, aye, Cap'n.'

'Mr. Symson? Are the men armed and ready?'

'Aye, Cap'n and in position.'

Roberts nodded. The tension on the ship was palpable. They were close enough to suffer terrible losses if the Portuguese fired their stern swivels. His own stomach had tightened and the excitement chased through his blood. Everything seemed to be in sharper focus. He saw clearly how to position his ship, and if necessary, how to get himself out of trouble. He felt no fear, only calm certainty.

The crew had scattered themselves over the decks, behind the bulwarks, behind the boats, all of them armed with at least one pair of loaded pistols, dagger, cutlass and a musket. Only a small crew actually sailed the ship.

'Smile, *senhor capitão*,' Roberts commanded Captain Cordoso, and when he looked at him he saw a fixed mirthless grin on the man's dark face—and Kennedy's pistol barrel dug into his back. 'If they suspect anything, *senhor*, then you are dead,' Roberts warned him. 'Mr. Hardy!'

Richard Hardy was already waiting on the forecastle for his

orders. 'Captain?'

'Hail the *Sagrada Familia*, if you please.'

Richard Hardy immediately cupped his hands to his mouth and leaned over the rail. 'Ahoy there! Ahoy!'

'*Olá!*'

'Are you the *Sagrada Familia, capitão* Alvaro Castro commanding?'

'We are. Who are you?'

'The *Aventuro Real.* We have *capitão* Cordoso aboard of the *Santa Catriana* who wishes to speak with *capitão* Castro.'

'A small moment, if you please.'

Roberts smiled at Cordoso. 'Now, *capitão*, you know what you are to say.'

Cordoso was not a happy man, but he took a decisive breath, and then nodded reluctantly.

They waited a few tense minutes, but presently another man came on deck, and Roberts concluded this must be the *Sagrada Familia*'s captain.

'We have *capitão* Cordoso with us,' Hardy called.

Roberts pushed Cordoso forward towards Hardy. 'Go on,' he prompted.

'I am the *capitã*o's servant,' Cordoso said. 'I have a matter of consequence to discuss with him, and I desire, therefore, that he comes aboard.'

The *Sagrada Familia*'s captain spoke with a man beside him.

Roberts said to Cordoso: 'See, that wasn't so difficult, was it?'

Cordoso met his eyes. 'Now that I have done what the captain asked, what will he do with me?'

'In a little while, we shall send you back to your ship.'

'And *capitão* Castro?'

'We shall let him go too. You see, *senhor,* not all gentlemen of fortune are murderers.'

The *Sagrada Familia* hailed them again. 'Ahoy there, *Aventuro Real!*'

'*Ola!*'

'*Capitão* Castro sends his compliments and will wait upon you directly.'

'Excellent!' Roberts said, well pleased. 'You can take our guest below now, Mr. Kennedy.'

He continued to watch the *Sagrada Familia*, as Henry Dennis joined him.

'Looks like it's worked.'

'Aye,' Roberts spoke thoughtfully, his eyes on the Portuguese ship. Something, he felt, wasn't quite right. He wasn't sure what it was, but an inner instinct warned him.

All at once, with a slide in his stomach, he saw that the *Sagrada Familia*'s decks were crowded with men as their officers bellowed out orders in Portuguese. Men summoned from sleep, some of them only half-dressed, ran about excitedly, tucking shirts into slops as they went. They were armed.

Roberts' stomach turned over. They were clearing for action, making ready their guns.

'We've been discovered!' he cried. 'Damn his blood! The man's somehow betrayed us!'

'Hell's teeth!'

Anger shot through him. If Cordoso had been to hand then he would have killed him himself. 'That son of the devil!'

With an effort he forced the anger down. He couldn't worry about Cordoso now. He must keep a cool head.

He barked out his orders: 'Mr. Symson—prepare a boarding party. Mr. Stephenson, bring her about for a broadside then alongside to board. Mr. Dennis, Mr. Ashplant, prepare a broadside. Raise the ports! Run out the guns!'

The orders were taken up by the officers. 'Look alive there! Let go the sails!'

'*Run out! Run out!*' The men on the guns heaved on the side tackles and the guns rolled forward until their muzzles protruded from the *Royal Rover's* side, like deadly black fingers. Already the men on the yards had released the sails and as others sheeted home, the *Royal Rover* which had been drifting lightly in current and wind, moved with a will. John Stephenson brought her round quickly until she was parallel to her victim not twenty yards apart.

Roberts gave the order not to cripple her. He wanted to sail her out. His guns were to aim high, over her gunwales, not hole her so that she needed time-consuming repairs, or sank. From this distance, even a blind man couldn't miss!

On the *Sagrada Familia* the activity had become a panic as the luckless crew saw the pirates bearing down on them, her guns ready. It would take them two or three minutes to prepare their guns while the *Royal Rover* was already prepared. Roberts grinned gleefully. He would teach them to resist Bart Roberts!

As the *Royal Rover* came level with the *Sagrada Familia*'s stern, Roberts raised his sword high above his head, awaiting his moment. He realised he was looking forward to the action now.

'Fire!' His sword arm dropped.

That terrible two-second delay, and he saw the *Sagrada Familia*'s distress signal hoisted. It was of no consequence now. As the *Royal Rover*'s guns bellowed, every ship in the fleet would be aware of trouble and the men-of-war would rush to the aid of their distressed sister.

Abruptly, the first of the *Royal Rover*'s guns fired and the others followed one by one down her side, followed by the second tier. The air filled with the acrid taint of burning powder, and smoke obliterated the Portuguese ship from view. The noise went on and on, and the ship trembled as though she would be shaken apart.

'Cease firing!' Then after a pause: 'Bring her alongside Mr. Stephenson!'

John Stephenson turned the wheel to bring the *Royal Rover* in tight to the *Sagrada Familia*.

'Boarders ready!'

With daggers held in their teeth and pistols slung on ribbons over their shoulders, the pirates filled the *Royal Rover's* decks, grappling hooks and lines ready, while the *Sagrada Familia*'s men fired muskets haphazardly through the smoke. Musket balls hit masts and deck timbers, raising splinters of wood, but missed the large body of men waiting for the order.

As a puff of wind blew away the smoke, Roberts had a clear view of the Portuguese ship, no more than a few feet away. Her mizzen mast had snapped near the top and it bobbed about drunkenly like a man dangling on the gallows. He uttered an oath. He had hoped the shot would have missed, for he intended to sail off with her. Oh well, it could have been worse.

As the two ships eased together, the Portuguese abandoned their attempts to load and fire their guns. From his vantage point, now half way up the shrouds, Roberts could see right onto their decks. A hundred and fifty men waited for them, swords drawn, and some fired pistols at the invaders, while the Portuguese captain stood near the helm, raging at his men. The pirates were outnumbered.

Roberts took a breath. The moment had come. 'Boarders away!'

David Symson took up the cry, bellowing: 'Over the side!'

Grappling hooks whistled through the air and clung to the *Sagrada Familia*'s bulwarks with a metallic thud, and although the defenders struck at the attached ropes with axes, it was too little to stop them pulling the two ships together. With the scrape of wood on wood, the ships met and were locked together in a murderous embrace.

Roberts waved his sword in the air. 'Board! Board! Over the side!' he cried again, his voice rising frantically.

He doubted whether they could hear him for they roared and screamed their war cry, but the waving sword was their signal, while the other officers took up the cry: 'Over the side!'

The pirates poured over the gunwales and onto the Portuguese ship, an unstoppable tide of screaming fierce and savage humanity and the defenders came gamely forward to meet them, well armed and determined, but with eyes wide with fear.

From his place in the shrouds, Roberts picked his target, a large man with a beard, a curved cutlass in one hand, a dagger in the other, a look of grim determination on his face. For a brief moment, their eyes met across the small space between them, and Roberts recognised the terror in the other man's eyes. Good! That's how it should be!

Grabbing a line slung from the main yard, he clenched his dagger between his teeth and swung across the bulwarks. For a few seconds he was suspended in the air, but then he slid deckwards. He had a brief view of the *Sagrada Familia*'s decks, a confusion of men and swords locked in a fight for survival. He had a momentary vision of his target and the vicious crooked blade of an upward pointing cutlass, ready for an undefended belly. With all his strength he kicked out. The toe of his shoe connected with the side of the man's jaw, and he heard it crack. The Portuguese fell to the side, his eyes rolling in his head and his jaw misshapen, with blood trickling from his mouth. He was out of it.

Roberts landed lightly on his feet beyond him, but ready for the next man that came at him from his right. With his face contorted in a grimace, his opponent ran at him, cutlass raised above his head with both hands on the hilt, intent on cleaving his head in two. Stepping neatly aside, Roberts saw his chance and thrust the point of his sword into the man's unprotected over-large belly. It sank into the flesh with little resistance and the man fell to his knees, held upright only by the sword, surprise on his fat face.

Roberts withdrew his sword with difficulty, for the flesh clung to the blade sucking at it grotesquely. The man fell forward onto his face.

The Portuguese seemed to be everywhere at once. Two more came at him and he engaged them both, forcing them backwards with hacking cuts and swift brute strength. One man fell backwards over some coiled rope and hit his head on a metal ring protruding from the mast housing, knocking him out. The second man jumped back and leapt up onto the gunwale, where he perched with calm assurance. It was a bad manoeuvre, for Roberts could see his vulnerability. Keeping low himself, he moved in swiftly, saw his chance and sliced at the man's legs. Leaping to avoid the blow, the man landed badly, wobbled, teetering on the edge, and then fell backwards with a cry. A moment later he splashed into the clear blue sea twenty-five feet below.

Roberts turned, gasping for breath. Sweat squirted from his skin, running into his eyes, and dripping off his chin, soaking his hair and shirt as though he had been dipped in water. Around him the deck planking was crimson, as though it had been painted red. It was a brutal mêlée of blood and bodies and severed limbs. His men were well-trained, experts with sword, dagger and pistol. The untrained Portuguese sailors were no match for them. They fell before them like skittles.

Henry Dennis called to him, and jerked his head in the direction of a man at the taffrail, and Roberts had no trouble recognising the *Sagrada Familia*'s captain, a man whose acquaintance he desired to make. Captain Castro had his back to the sea, watching with undisguised horror the war on the decks before him while his sword lay idle in his hands. A damned coward, Roberts thought contemptuously, keeping out of the way while his men died.

Roberts couldn't get through the crowded decks, so he took himself up on the gunwale, quickly and nimbly making his way aft, and surprised the Portuguese commander by dropping lightly in front of him.

Instantly Captain Castro put up his sword defensively, his teeth gritted his eyes wide with terror, but determined. But he was an inexpert swordsman, and two-handedly swung the blade, putting his whole weight behind the stroke. Roberts ducked, avoiding the intended decapitation, and, missing his target, Castro over-balanced and lost his footing. With a cry of alarm he fell and landed heavily on his back.

The fall knocked the wind from his body, and gave Roberts his opportunity. As the man lay sprawled on the deck he pressed the point of his blade to his throat. 'Yield!' he cried. 'Yield, or you will all die!'

Castro froze in terror.

Roberts, panting for breath, stared at him, his eyes wild, his teeth gritted. He had already killed one man, possibly two, and the scent of blood was in his nostrils. 'Yield!' he growled again, 'or I'll kill you right now!' To enforce the words, he dug the point of his blade harder into the man's throat, just below his prominent Adam's apple. A tiny speck of crimson showed on the tanned skin. 'Yield, damn you!' Another second and he would kill him.

The Portuguese captain's dark eyes widened. 'All right! We yield. Give quarter!'

'Louder!'

'Give quarter! Give quarter!' the poor man howled. His voice carried to those nearest, and they took up the cry: 'Give quarter!'

The remaining Portuguese threw down their weapons in surrender.

ELEVEN

It had taken no more than five minutes from the time they boarded, but Roberts' sword arm ached and trembled with the demands he had placed on it and the men were exhausted on both sides. Henry Dennis leaned on a barrel heaving air into his lungs, and Ashplant had to sit down. 'Getting too old for this,' he grumbled from the full complement of his twenty-nine years, but he grinned as he said it.

'More like too much rum and easy living,' David Symson retorted, training his pistols on the captives. He left the Portuguese captives to Robert Birdson, took Tom Sutton and went below. Roberts ordered Captain Castro to his feet.

The deck was littered with bodies. The Portuguese lost twenty-five dead and others injured, and blood and human tissue congealed on the deck-planking, drying quickly in the Brazilian sun. The air tasted of blood and death, and as the killing instinct died in Roberts it was replaced by the euphoria of victory. But they were not safe yet.

Captain Castro came slowly to his feet and pulled himself erect, putting his head up and regaining some of his lost dignity. His face was oily with sweat, but he had lost the wild terror-stricken expression now that he knew he would live.

Roberts grinned at him. Oh, victory was sweet! 'You should not have thought to resist, Captain. We always give good quarter to those who yield.'

Castro glared at him. 'Who are you, *senhor*?'

Roberts carefully wiped the blade of his sword on the sleeve of a dead man's shirt and returned it to the scabbard on his hip. He bowed elaborately. 'Captain Bartholomew Roberts of the *Royal Rover*.'

Castro, who had never heard of him, was unimpressed. 'What do you intend to do with us?' he demanded. 'Do you intend to kill us?'

Roberts' eyes narrowed. 'Not if you tell us where you keep the gold.'

David Symson, emerged from the great cabin, turned and ran up the steps to the quarterdeck. 'There are three padlocked chests in the ante-room to the captain's cabin, Cap'n,' he said. 'Easily heavy enough to contain a large amount of gold.'

'Do you keep the gold in your ante-room, *capitão*?' Roberts asked.

'You seem to know all about it,' Castro growled.

Roberts grinned, the swaggering courageous victor. 'Very well! Mr. Symson—get these curs off the ship and into the boats, if you please, and don't forget Captain Cordoso on the *Royal Rover*.' He cast Castro a derisive glance. 'Forgive me, *senhor*, but I intend to take your ship.'

Before Castro could protest, he turned away from him. 'Take over Mr. Symson. Let's get out of here!'

As quartermaster, it was Symson's job to command the prize ship. It was time for Roberts to make his own departure.

In the distance he could hear the rumble of guns as the other ships in the squadron passed the warning messages down the line, reminding him that the men-of-war, the defenders of the squadron, would be coming for them. He couldn't waste time. He snapped out his orders: 'Get these people into the boats. Clear the decks!' They had work to do.

He made his way to the side as he spoke. He was still riding high, the blood still fizzing in his veins, mixed with the euphoria of victory. But he had to get them away safely.

He heard the shrieks of protest rising from below, and turned just as the huge Belgian, Michael Maer arrived on deck with a protesting, struggling woman under each arm. He dropped them unceremoniously down on the deck.

'Women!' someone breathed close to Roberts.

'I can see that!' Roberts snapped.

Michael Maer grinned at him. 'I did find the women in the cabin, Captain,' he said in his thick accent.

One of the women struggled to her feet, and left them in no doubt as to what she thought of them. 'You son of a rabid dog! You filthy hog!'

Roberts came forward, for he thought he recognised her, but he couldn't quite place her. She recognised him too, and stood mesmerised for a second, her little black eyes in the fat face glaring at him, then she spat in his face.

He could have killed her with one well-placed blow. Instead he wiped the spit off his cheek with his shirtsleeve, and then said coldly to Michael Maer: 'Put them in the boat!'

The fat woman let out a string of invectives as Maer did as he was ordered. Leaving the other woman sitting on the deck he tucked the first under his arm and lifted her bodily so that she was horizontal, as though she weighed just two or three stones rather than the twelve or thirteen she must have done. Her protesting shrieks went unheeded.

Richard Hardy took hold of the other woman's arm and raised her to her feet. Her hair which was not pinned up, had fallen over her face, but she brushed it back now, and stood erect, her chin up glaring at Roberts.

The deck seemed to rock beneath his feet. He had thought never to set eyes on her again, had thought her left behind in Príncipe with her father and Mendoça, but here she was standing on the deck.

Her eyes widened in recognition. '*You!*'

Richard Hardy pushed her in the direction of the side where the boats waited, but she resisted, standing still on the deck.

In the distance, the guns had fallen silent which meant the men-of-war were on their way. Roberts, though, could only focus on the woman. How often he had regretted not seeking her out on the island, not pursuing her. They had left the island, and he had left her behind. Now here she was, blessed Fate delivering her into his hand again. He wouldn't make the same mistake twice.

'Damn my soul if it ain't the Portuguese woman!' Ashplant finally realised who she was.

'Take her aboard the *Royal Rover*, Mr. Hardy,' Roberts snapped.

David Symson was moved to protest, and took his arm. 'You can't bring a woman aboard,' he said. 'It's in the articles.'

Roberts looked at him. 'The articles say 'not for the purpose of seduction', Mr. Symson, and the lady is not for the purpose of seduction.'

Symson raised two very sceptical eyebrows at him. 'Oh no?'

Roberts ignored him. 'Mr. Hardy, take the *senhora* and post a guard on her and take her to Mr. Symson's cabin.' Symson as quartermaster now commanded the prize ship.

'Then, since she is to have my cabin, just what are you going to do with her?' Symson insisted.

Roberts looked at him and said evenly: 'Do you forget Mr. Symson what the Portuguese did to Captain Davis?'

'No.'

Well then.'

'But . . .'

'Do you intend to stand arguing all day, Mr. Symson?' Roberts snapped. He turned and walked across the deck, and clambered onto the *Royal Rover*. Behind him as Hardy propelled Lúcia towards the gunwale, he heard her protests: 'Take your hands off me, you great lump! How dare you touch me!' Then: 'Where are you taking me?' Of course, she did not speak English, so she had not understood Roberts' orders.

'The *senhora* is coming with us,' Hardy said to her in her own language.

'*I will not!* How dare you! Let me go this instant! I am not going with you! I will not allow this . . .'

Roberts glanced back to see Hardy manhandle the lady over the gunwales, while willing hands helped her to her feet. She stood there on the *Royal Rover*'s decks glaring at the grinning men who encircled her. 'Don't you dare lay hands on me!'

Roberts thought it prudent to intervene. 'Mr. Hardy!' he called across the deck.

'Cap'n?'

'Get the *senhora* below if you please. Mr. Moody—make ready to sail!'

Taking the *senhora*'s arm, Hardy propelled her to the hatch, and, still protesting he took her below. Christopher Moody gave the orders to disengage and men ran up to the yards while others retrieved the grappling irons.

A few moments later Hardy reappeared, and called over to the *Sagrada Familia* for the *senhora*'s trunk.

Michael Maer had followed Roberts onto the *Royal Rover*. 'How many dead?' Roberts asked him.

'Twenty-five Portuguese, captain. Two of our own. James Hedges and Dennis Topping.'

He swallowed the sadness. James Hedges had been with Roberts on the *Princess* and Dennis Topping was one of the original members of the company having turned pirate with Howell Davis from the *Buck*.

'Are the wounded aboard?'

Michael Maer opened his mouth, but before he could speak the expected cry came from the masthead. 'Sail ho!'

Roberts jumped onto the gunwale. 'Whither away?' he demanded.

Johnson at the top of the mast, pointed west. 'One sail,' he bellowed.

Running quickly half way up the mizzen shrouds Roberts took the telescope from its leather case. There on the western horizon was the first of the men-of-war.

He had been expecting it, but he had hoped for more time. He glanced down at the *Sagrada Familia's* deck. She was just about ready to sail. He cursed under his breath. He would have to hold them off while the *Sagrada Familia* got away.

The excitement in the pit of his stomach which had begun to subside a little boiled up again. For this possibility, too, he had prepared. 'Make sail!' he ordered John Stephenson. At the same time, David Symson on the Portuguese prize ordered any men not of the prize crew off the ship and onto the *Royal Rover*, and gave his own orders to make sail.

Roberts ordered: 'Bring her about!'

Once more the men played out the ritual of releasing the sails, while he watched the newcomer through the glass.

The Portuguese ship was making good headway, coming in fast.

On the *Sagrada Familia* eager English sailors strung out onto the yards to cast off the gaskets and make the bunts fast by the jigger. Then as Davis Symson gave the order, the ship was instantly covered in canvas and the sails sheeted home. Good!

'Weigh anchor!' Men willingly took on the back-breaking job of heaving up the *Sagrada Familia's* anchor to the encouraging cry of 'Heave and *pawl!*'

As the wind found her sails the crippled Portuguese ship began to move ponderously through the water.

The *Royal Rover* too began to move.

Roberts turned his attention again to the man-of-war, as it came swiftly towards them, and he compressed his lips in a determined line. They had already had one short sharp battle. This time it would be to the death.

'Run out English colours,' he ordered curtly, and added: 'And the red flag.'

The boatswain, Christopher Moody caught his eye. 'The red flag?'

'We give no quarter,' Roberts said grimly, and he saw him exchange glances with Ashplant. The tension in Roberts flared as anger. 'Damn you! Do as I say!'

Both Moody and Ashplant turned away from him, reluctant to incur his further wrath. Without any further explanation to them, he joined Stephenson at the helm.

The beauty of the pirate ship was in her manoeuvrability, made possible by the fore-and-aft sail on the mizzen mast, and she came quickly into position across the road of the oncoming battle ship, shielding the prize ship, and hove to.

'Make ready the larboard guns, Mr. Ashplant,' Roberts commanded.

Henry Dennis was on the *Sagrada Familia* which left Ashplant in sole control of the guns. 'Look lively there!' he growled, and the gun crews took up their positions.

'*Load!*'

As disciplined as any naval ship, the pirate gun crews primed the guns and heaved the heavy balls into the muzzles.

'*Open the ports!*'

'Run out!' Roberts ordered.

'*Run out! Run out!*' Ashplant bellowed excitedly, and two banks of menacing black muzzles protruded from the *Royal Rover's* side.

On the decks the crew were armed and ready for this, the second fight of the day.

'Deck there!' cried the man on lookout. 'Sail ho!' and he pointed in the same direction as the man-of-war.

Roberts raised the glass to peer once more at the horizon, and his heart sank. Sure enough, just on the horizon, the second ship had appeared. One ship they could cope with, but two?

His heart pounded in his chest. He had no choice. But he felt no real fear, just cold determination. At all costs, his men must get away with the *Sagrada Familia*. If he could pull this off, he knew he would be confirmed as their commander. If he couldn't, it would be certain death for all of them

On the deck no-one spoke, but every eye was fixed on the foremost of the men-of-war. She was out of range—just. In a few more minutes she would be in range. He waited, calculating the distance, gauging the rhythm of the rise and fall of the ship, waiting for the time to fire. If he timed it right he might be able to put her out of action with the first salvo.

Walter Kennedy, stinking of rum, tobacco and unwashed

humanity, joined Roberts at the helm. 'What the devil's happening?' he demanded gruffly. 'Surely they ain't holding off?'

Roberts' stomach turned over. He had seen it too. The first man-of-war had turned her bows into the wind, and her men were busily hauling in the sails.

'They're hove to,' he cried, 'Damn me! They *are* holding off!'

Kennedy almost snatched the glass from his hand, and Roberts allowed him to, continuing to watch with his naked eye.

'Hell's teeth,' Kennedy swore. I don't believe me own eyes, that I don't!'

Again Roberts studied them through the telescope. The first man-of-war was waiting for the second to catch up—and the second didn't appear to be in a hurry to do so.

He considered his options. Almost on the north-eastern horizon the *Sagrada Familia* had made better speed than he dared hope. In a few more minutes she would be out of sight. In another hour it would be dark when, if the Portuguese gave chase, they would be able to lose them.

With sudden relief he realised he could make good his exit.

'Time to take our leave, gentlemen!' he cried exultantly. 'Mr. Stephenson—make all sail!'

TWELVE

Lúcia paced the tiny cabin in impotent fury. How *dared* he take her, the daughter of the Emissary of the King of Portugal, prisoner! Just who did this man think he was? It was an outrage! And in the name of all that was sacred, just where were those dolts, the two men-of-war assigned to protect the fleet?

If she'd had a window, as on the *Sagrada Familia*, she would have peered out. As it was, she was blind, locked in a tiny coffin of a cabin, with a bunk, a washbasin and a bucket. There was just enough room to pace to and fro alongside the bunk, and she had to duck to avoid the deck-head beam with the ring-bolt sticking out of it.

She smarted too, under the hand of the boy who had brought her to the cabin. He had paid no attention to her protests, had used his superior strength to catch and hold the hands that lashed out at him, and had lifted her up and thrown her on the bunk! Her dignity had suffered for that, especially when he closed the door and she found she was locked in total darkness. Her screams brought him back with a lantern which swung now precariously above the wash bowl, but, despite her treatment of him, when she mentioned her trunk, he had brought it to her, and it now stood in the only available space, beside the washstand at the foot of the bunk.

She stopped pacing, and sat down abruptly on the bunk, the anger turning to fear. She was alone, so completely alone, on a ship somewhere in the Atlantic, with a hundred or so filthy English pirates for company. Why had he done it? What devil had made him suddenly decide to take her with him? Her lower lip trembled, but she forced back the tears. No amount of hysterics was going to get her out of this ship. She needed to think, and she forced her mind to stop panicking and do so. It occurred to her that fear and anger were an excellent antidote to seasickness.

Above her she could hear him giving orders, the responses and echoed orders, guessed they were getting away, and was sure of it when the wind took the sails and the ship lurched forward. There was absolutely no escape. Her survival depended now on her wits. If she antagonized them, she would find herself cruelly treated. If she were friendly—well that would be unthinkable! Not after what they had done! No, she would have to be distantly polite. She was a prisoner, and she was fighting not just for her life, but for her honour too. And as for that man . . !

The door unbolted, and she jumped to her feet. 'Captain Roberts wishes to speak with the *senhora*,' Hardy said stiffly, and held the door for her.

She looked at him trying to see not a villainous pirate, but a lad younger than she was. It didn't work, for Hardy, sporting a week's worth of dark stubble, and a red scarf holding his long lank hair in place, looked every inch what he was. As it was, the dark eyes that looked her over were insolent, and the curve to his lips left her in no doubt as to his views about her. And this one, she thought, was to be her guard. With a toss of her head, she picked up her skirts and swept imperiously from the cabin.

The great cabin was on the same deck, just a few feet away, and Richard Hardy held the door open for her to go in.

Roberts stood with his back to her, looking out of the great stern window, so Richard Hardy said: 'The *senhora* Cap'n,' before withdrawing and closing the door behind him.

Roberts turned and looked at her. Even through fear and anger, the sight of him made her stomach slide. His presence filled the cabin, those dark eyes penetrating right into her soul. He seemed somehow superhuman and all the more fearful for it.

'Ah, *senhora*, we meet again!'

Summoning every ounce of courage, she squared her shoulders and put her chin up. 'I demand that the *capitão* sets me ashore immediately.'

He came forward, and he truly was magnificent, in snowy white silk shirt and scarlet damask waistcoat. He raised a black eyebrow. 'You demand? You are hardly in a position to demand anything!'

He used the familiar *tu*, deliberately provoking her. She took an uncertain step backwards. 'You took me by force!' Her heart thudded hard in her throat and she trembled.

'I did,' he agreed.

'Why?'

He raised both brows now as though the answer were obvious. 'Why? Why do you think, *senhora?* Because I wanted to.' He paused, his eyes hardening. 'Perhaps you have forgotten what your countrymen did to our people? Captain Davis and several others are dead, murdered in ambush.'

'I do not need reminding,' she told him. 'So how is capturing me going to redress that? Do you intend to kill me in retribution?'

He chuckled. 'No, *senhora*, you are quite safe with me. Far too pretty to be dropped over the side. No, but your capture should give others pause.'

'If you mean my father, he had nothing to do with what happened to your Captain Davis. In fact, he deplored it, and told *Senhor* Mendoça so. It was all Mendoça's doing. My Father wrote to King João to a full report, informing him of all that *Senhor* Mendoça had done.'

'Did he indeed?' Roberts replied mildly surprised.

'And besides, did you not take enough revenge on the island when you bombarded us and set alight two ships?'

He laughed gently. 'My dear girl . . .'

'I am not your girl,' she retorted, her temper temporarily getting the better of her, 'dear or otherwise!'

He nodded appreciatively. 'My dear girl,' he said again, 'I well know that we caused some damage to the buildings, but I doubt many were hurt.'

'I myself was thrown to the floor and covered in dust,' she informed him.

'You were hurt?'

'A few bruises.' She took a breath. 'What are you going to do with me?'

His dark eyes smouldered as they ran over her body, and a slow smile spread across his lips. 'That depends.'

She didn't dare ask on what it might depend. His meaning was obvious. Her mouth had gone dry, and her legs seemed to have turned to jelly. How could a man be so attractive and at the same time so terrifying?

'I ask, *capitão*, that you return me to Bahia.'

'No,' he said flatly. 'I am taking you to Devil's Island. And there you shall be released to make your way back to your father.'

He took another step towards her, and suddenly his hand shot out with a longer reach than she had thought possible, and grabbed one of her wrists. Her heart crashed to her feet.

'Please, *senhor*, let me go,' she whispered, and felt the colour drain from her lips.

He jerked her towards him and caught her and held her close against him. She could feel the beat of his heart in his chest, smell the sweet man-scent of him. She was paralysed with terror. Sweet Mary, did he intend to rape her?

His eyes were dark, laughing, mocking. 'Well, *querida*, (sweetheart), what do you think I should do with you?'

She panicked. 'Let me go, *senhor*!' she hissed.

His grip tightened on her, and he laughed. 'Afraid, *querida?*'

'Let me go! *Let me go!*'

The look in his eyes changed, becoming suddenly intense. It was all the warning she had before he pressed his mouth roughly over hers.

She tried to scream and succeeded in making a choking noise. She hit him with her fists again and struggled, and tried to kick out with her foot, but he was far too strong for her. *Sweet Mary, help me!*

He released her abruptly, and stood there laughing at her.

Her fear vanished in a sudden boiling fury, and quite without warning, before she had even thought, her hand came up and slapped his cheek with as much strength behind the blow as she could muster. His face slapped round to his right, and a handprint appeared on his cheek in red. 'How *dare* you!' She was shaking with shock. Never in all her life had anyone done such a thing to her!

He laughed again. 'Oh, I see. Five-and-twenty and never been kissed!'

'You know nothing about me!'

Those raised black brows again. 'Don't I *querida?*'

'You have the manners of an English pig!'

He laughed all the more.

'You filthy son of a whore!' She gave him the benefit of her views on his character and birth at high speed and in language he had not thought a lady of her breeding should be able to use. It amused him, but when she lashed out a second time he caught both her wrists, but not before she had dragged her nails down his cheek.

'Let me go, you son of a dog!' She kicked him on the shin. He seemed unmoved.

'You want me to kiss you again?' he asked, and promptly did so.

When he drew back this time, he kept hold of her wrists, and his eyes glittered like steel. She knew then what he was telling her. She was no match for him, no matter how she fought and swore, and parried with him, he was ruler here, and all did his bidding. Like her father really, although his tactics were different, the end result was the same. Perhaps all men were like that.

He saw her capitulation, and released her.

'I hate you!' she told him.

He put the back of his hand to his cheek and it came away with blood on it.

'Very likely, *querida*, but you won't always.' He went to the door. 'Mr. Hardy!'

Richard Hardy had been waiting outside, and had probably heard the exchange. 'Is everything alright, Cap'n?' he asked looking from one to the other of them.

Roberts grinned. 'The *senhora* and I have had a difference of opinion.'

'I *hate* you!' she said again with feeling.

Roberts said: 'Take the *senhora* back to her cabin, if you please.'

'Aye, aye, Cap'n.'

'And Mr. Hardy!'

'Cap'n?'

'Fit a bolt on the *inside* of the cabin door, if you please. If *anyone* touches the woman, I will hold you responsible. Do I make myself clear?'

'Aye, aye, Cap'n.' Richard Hardy held the door open for Lúcia who swept past him and preceded him to her own cabin, where she threw herself on the bunk and gave way to a good deal of weeping.

'Lord, I ain't never seen the like!' Ashplant said admiringly, as he took another swig of tea from the delicate white and blue china cup in his huge hand. 'Sailed in among them Portuguee, and took the gold right from under their noses! Damned my soul, I never did!'

'What happened to you?' the surgeon George Hunter asked Roberts, casting his professional eyes over three parallel lines running down his cheek.

Roberts picked up the teapot. 'A hellcat!' he said evasively

Valentine Ashplant peered into his empty cup and frowned. 'So who is she, anyway?' He held out the cup for Roberts to pour tea into it. Ashplant wasn't a great tea-drinker himself, but occasionally imbibed as the mood took him, and after a night's drinking, tea refreshed a mouth that resembled the ship's barnacled bottom.

'Daughter of the emissary of the King of Portugal,' Roberts said, replacing the silver teapot on the salver. He picked up his own cup, and leaned back in the captain's chair, resting one heel on the corner of the table and crossing the other leg over it at the ankles.

'Now where have I heard that before?' Ashplant wondered, rubbing his whiskery chin.

Christopher Moody shook his sandy head. 'On Prince's.' He spat the word, remembering the betrayal there. He tried to lighten his mood. 'Got too close, eh, Cap'n?'

Roberts met his eyes but did not answer.

A fresh thought percolated through Ashplant's rum befuddled brain. 'Didn't think women were allowed aboard.'

Moody, bit into a piece of pineapple. He saw it as his job to keep the peace. 'Stow it, Ash! Cap'n knows what he's doing!'

It was true, Roberts acknowledged inwardly. He may have acted on the spur of the moment under the intoxication of victory, but he knew exactly what he was about. He had seen the woman, and wanted her, and it was as simple as that. She was not going to escape from him a second time.

''Tain't right,' the Irishman spoke. He was drunk, as usual, and drink always made him belligerent.

'What's not right, Mr. Kennedy?' Roberts asked quietly.

'Well, you got a woman!' Kennedy said with feeling. 'The rest of us ain't! Ought to be fair shares for all, so it did.'

Roberts' eyes narrowed. He said quietly: 'You mistake the matter, Mr. Kennedy. The woman is our prisoner, retribution for Prince's.'

Kennedy's little piggy eyes glared at him for a moment. 'How d'ye mean?'

Roberts traced the pattern on his teacup. 'What do you think the King's Emissary would pay for her safe return, Mr. Kennedy? She must be worth ten thousand *moidores* at least.'

Kennedy was silenced.

Ashplant caught up with the conversation. ''Tis the same woman as on Prince's, ain't it.'

James Phillips raised his head. 'Mendoça's woman?'

'No,' Roberts said. 'Not Mendoça's woman.'

'She's Portuguese,' Phillips persisted. 'And the Portuguese killed Cap'n Davis. Mendoça killed Cap'n Davis.'

'We've avenged Captain Davis,' Roberts said. 'The woman had nothing to do with it.'

'How d'ye know that?' Ashplant asked.

'Would you take a woman into your confidence if you intended to commit murder?' Roberts demanded reasonably.

'Not likely!' Ashplant growled. 'After all, they ain't known fer keeping their mummers shut!'

'If she ain't Mendoça's woman, p'raps she's someone else's,' Irish Kennedy persisted slyly.

Roberts felt his hackles rise. 'If you have something to say, Mr. Kennedy, then do not let good manners hold you back!'

Irish Kennedy leaned back in his chair, his drink clouded eyes on the captain. 'A man could have a fancy for a woman like that,' he said.

Indignation became anger at the accusation, and Roberts came to his feet. 'Damn your eyes!' he snarled. 'You think I'd bring a woman on board to . . .' The ship's articles were clear. To bring a woman aboard for the purpose of seduction was punishable by death—and even the captain wasn't exempt. If they thought to rid themselves of him by such an accusation, they were far out. And he had just given them a grand victory, gold and treasures beyond the imagination. His position right now was strong. He said with emphasis: 'The woman is for ransom.'

'Well, then,' Walter Kennedy asked, 'What about them marks on yer cheek there?'

Roberts said nothing. The marks told their own tale.

Ashplant, still trying to catch up filled the silence. 'Damn it all, Cap'n,' he growled, 'we left her in Africa. What's she doing in Brazil?'

Roberts transferred his steady gaze to him but before he could answer James Phillips said reminiscently: 'I remember when Blackbeard . . .'

'Spare us!' Roberts snapped, his temper dangerously stretched.

''Tweren't a pretty sight,' James Phillips went on relentlessly. 'Not by the time they'd finished with him. Oh dear me no!'

'Are you threatening me?' Roberts demanded awfully, and his hand went automatically to the pistol in his coat pocket.

As if at a given signal they all jumped up from the table, and backed warily away from it. They knew by now to respect any captain's uncertain temper.

'Stow it, Jim,' Ashplant recommended, fear sharpening his wits. 'Pay him no heed, Cap'n. He's had too much to drink! Damn ye, Jim, apologise!'

Irish Kennedy said: 'Do ye deny it, Cap'n?'

'I don't have to explain anything to any of you!' Roberts thundered. 'I'll be damned if I'm afraid of any of you, and I'll go ashore with pistols or sword with any man!'

Alarmed, Ashplant said placatingly: 'Damn me! There ain't no need for that, now. Seems to me the Cap'n couldn't know the lady was on the Portuguee. Nor even that she was in Brazil. Lord, it's bin six months since we left Prince's. So I think that ought t'be the end of the matter.'

Roberts allowed himself to be placated and sat down again. 'Aye. But I tell you all that if any man so much as thinks of laying a finger on the woman while she is on this ship, I'll blow his blasted brains out!'

Phillips cast him a look of arrogant rebellion, and strode from the cabin. It signalled the end of the meeting and others followed.

Still angry, Roberts turned to Ashplant. 'What's that all about?'

Ashplant rubbed his bristles with the flat of his hand. 'The men've been a long time at sea without a woman. They be jealous that the cap'n might have something they don't. It'll be all right when we get to Devil's Island. Damn me, you just pulled off the neatest trick I ever did see. For cunning and daring, damn, not even Cap'n Davis can match you. They reckon the Devil hisself looks after you!'

Roberts grinned at the tribute, his anger evaporating. He was proud of his achievement.

Above them, on open deck, the musicians had started playing. A great victory demanded a great celebration, and the rum punch was already in place. 'I suggest we join the others,' Roberts said, and stood up.

Ashplant went out before him, but George Hunter stayed behind. 'You took a risk, bringing her aboard,' he said.

Roberts nodded. 'Aye.'

'Asking for trouble. They won't believe she's here for a ransom.'

'By the time they realise that, we will be at Devil's Island and they will have their own women to worry about.'

'And you?'

Roberts picked up a mango from the dish. 'I know what I'm doing.'

'You always do.' He followed Ashplant out.

Roberts followed at his leisure, but paused outside the

woman's cabin. She was quiet inside, and he imagined her lying on the bunk, having cried herself to sleep. He had invited her to sup with them of course, but she had refused, and had not eaten the dinner he had sent to her either. So she was going to sulk.

Well let her. She would not be able to sulk forever. He went up the companionway ladder to join the celebrations.

Despite the late night revels, Roberts was awake just as dawn broke, and he went on deck to take a reading from the Southern Cross with the quadrant.

The sky was just turning a lighter grey on the eastern horizon, heralding the dawn, but the stars still twinkled brightly in the remaining indigo sky.

At this latitude, there was no such thing as cool air, but early dawn came as near as possible to the definition, some of the heaviness of the previous day not yet returned. Yet he sweated, as he had all night, and he combed his black hair from his eyes with his fingers.

'How goes it?' he asked John Jessup at the helm, at the same time checking the compass in the binnacle.

'Steady, Cap'n. Wind be fair and the Portuguee's keeping up.'

Roberts glanced at the prize ship, her sails glowing ghostly pale in the growing greyness of dawn, and felt a rush of pride. It had to be the most daring attack in the history of piracy!

The watch struck three bells—half past five. It would be some time before the cook boiled the water for tea, before breakfast.

He went aft to the taffrail. The phosphorous disappeared with the growing light, but he was not thinking about the little twinkling lights in the water, but about the woman.

Since yesterday she had been in the tiny cabin. Well, she had more resolution than most men, for it was hot and claustrophobic in there, and he had expected her to emerge before this. Well, if she wanted to sulk, let her sulk. She would come out eventually.

George Hunter joined him at the taffrail. 'Damned hot,' he said.

Roberts continued looking out to sea. 'Aye.'

George Hunter leaned on the taffrail, and said offhandedly: 'Saw the woman this morning.'

'Is she ill?' Roberts asked quickly.

'No. She is awake, and lively and still cursing you for a pirate!

She is demanding to see you.'

At last!

'Shall I send her up to you?' Hunter asked.

'If you please,' Roberts answered. It would be private enough here at the taffrail, but not too private.

Hunter left him. Belatedly it occurred to him that he had not shaved, and he was wearing only shirt and breeches, a state of undress to receive any woman in! Still, she wanted to see him. That was progress.

When Lúcia came on deck she did not present a picture of a woman pining to death. She wore the green dress which emphasised the tan of her skin, and her black hair was loose, newly brushed, and fell about her shoulders like a mantle. She had a quiet dignity about her, a dignity that he knew would dissolve the moment someone crossed her.

He inclined his head curtly. '*Senhora.*'

She hesitated, her dark eyes glowering at him, then she came to join him at the taffrail. '*Senhor capitão,* I must protest!'

Not again. 'Oh?'

She retained her dignity. 'As the captain's prisoner, I would ask a favour.'

'The *senhora* is mistaken. She is not a prisoner, but a guest.'

Her eyes flashed. 'How can I be a guest when a man guards my door and I am not allowed to leave my cabin?' she demanded, her voice gaining pace and rising in pitch.

He grinned. It was so easy to rouse her! 'You are allowed to leave your cabin! I invited you to join us for dinner in the great cabin if you remember.'

'But that is all. Besides, I was feeling a little seasick.'

He said: '*Senhor* Hardy is your sentinel, for your own protection. He will conduct you where you wish to go. But I do ask that you make sure he stays with you at all times. I hope I do not have to explain further that my men have been some months at sea without pause.'

Her skin darkened in a flush. 'As you have yourself, Captain.'

'Indeed.' He changed tack. 'I trust you have now found your sea legs?'

'As you see.' She struggled with herself. 'What are you going to do with me, *capitão*?'

'If you wish to go back to Bahia, I will put you on the first ship we encounter which is bound there.' The chances of that were remote.

She widened her eyes, like a pleading child. 'Can you not take me back now?' So, she was prepared to use anything in her armoury to get her own way!

He said: 'You wish to go back now?'

'Certainly I do! How could it be otherwise?'

'I hope that is not an observation about our hospitality,' he said dryly.

'Of course not!' she retorted with obvious sarcasm. 'I have been so well treated in all respects!'

'Good. Well, I hope you understand that we cannot take you back to Brazil.'

'You do not understand, *capitão*,' she wheedled. My father is ill, and will be worried about me. And I am to be married.'

His heart missed a beat. 'Married?'

'I was on my way to Lisbon for my wedding.'

'Do you think I will take you back to Bahia, so that you may marry another man?' he demanded.

She was taken aback. 'Well, what is that to you?'

'You are here for a reason, Lúcia.'

'And what is that, pray?'

'To be my woman,' he said.

She gasped, anger jumping into her eyes. Oh it was so easy! 'Why you arrogant dog!'

'Very possibly,' he agreed.

She struggled again, and won, swallowing her anger. 'Take me back to Bahia, *capitão*,' she pleaded.

He shook his head. 'I cannot do that, *querida*.'

'Yes you can. You can turn this ship around and . . .'

He was serious. 'No. I cannot take you back. Do you think your countrymen will look kindly on us who stole their king's treasure? It is too dangerous for us to return to Bahia, I cannot risk my men or my ship.'

'Then set me ashore here!'

'Here?'

'Yes, here. I understand we are sailing up the coast. We cannot be too far from land.'

He shook his head and began to laugh. '*Senhora*, this coast is largely uninhabited. It is jungle. You would not be alive five minutes after we sent you ashore. The local inhabitants are Indians. Cannibals,' he added for good measure, for it was generally considered that the indigenous people of all these newly-discovered lands were man-eaters. 'Nothing, not even your sweet good-nature, would prevail upon me to abandon you on this coast.'

'I doubt it would be greater danger than I will encounter on this ship,' she retorted.

'You mistake the matter. You are in no danger on this ship.'

'Except from you.'

'Except from me,' he acknowledged.

She stamped her foot. 'You are the most insufferable man!'

He bowed his head in acknowledgement. '*Querida*!'

She clamped her lips shut, and turned abruptly away from him, marching towards the hatch where Richard Hardy had just emerged to look for her.

Roberts turned back to his contemplation of the sea, chuckling to himself. But the laughter died as he thought how much he wanted her, and it was more than a physical need. He could take her body any time he wished. That was not his need. His need was something deep inside him, a strange longing that ate away at his peace of mind.

THIRTEEN

January 1720, Guiana

The decks of the *Sagrada Familia,* having been scrubbed clean of crimson stains and freshly holystoned, glowed white in the setting sun. Since leaving Brazil, the carpenters had sawn and chiselled and hammered to make repairs, and with the mizzen mast jury-rigged, she looked fairly creditable. Even so, Roberts thought dourly as he stepped through the entry-port, she was still old-fashioned, ugly and sluggish, a typical Spanish-type galleon that he would get rid of as soon as he could.

David Symson, acting as master, and Henry Dennis were waiting to greet him, and he had brought the other officers across from the *Royal Rover.* 'Welcome aboard, Cap'n.'

Roberts looked about him and nodded in satisfaction, but he had just one concern. He turned back to David Symson. 'How much?' he asked.

'Forty-thousand *moidores,*' Symson answered promptly, and he could not conceal his glee. 'And two chests of trinkets. Diamonds, pearls, gold. In the hold, skins, sugar, tobacco.'

Roberts nodded. Gold, and treasure. They were rich men.

Valentine Ashplant let his breath go in a whistle through his discoloured teeth. 'And all for the rich king o'Portugal,' he growled.

Roberts wanted to see for himself. 'Where is it? Show me.'

David Symson nodded, and led the way across the deck to the companionway. 'How does she sail?' Roberts asked conversationally, looking up at the patched-up mizzen.

'Sluggish,' Symson said and went on to give a more detailed account of the ship, its handling, and the repairs they had made.

The *Sagrada Familia*'s great cabin was larger than the *Royal Rover*'s and more luxurious, reflecting the wealth of the Portuguese owners, grown rich by trading in gold and slaves. Ornately carved panels decorated the bulkheads, and gold candelabra were fixed to the stanchions. Rich damask drapes hung by the large stern window and the bench seat beneath the window was upholstered in black velvet, as were the ten matching armed chairs around the table. A large gold cross with a figure of Christ on it was bolted to the bulkhead. The blatant idolatry disgusted Roberts. He was not a religious man—few sailors were—but it stirred a childhood memory of fervent anti-popery.

Symson, following the direction of his gaze curled his lip disdainfully. 'Damned Papists!' he spat with loathing.

'I take it your hatred does not extend to Papist gold?' Roberts chided quietly.

Symson grinned. 'I'll overcome my prejudice!'

He opened a door on their left leading to the inner cabin, the captain's personal quarters. No expense had been spared here either. The small swinging cot, draped in embroidered cotton, like a large baby's crib, rocked gently beneath the window, and for a fleeting moment Roberts found himself wondering if David Symson had tried to fit into it, glanced at Symson, presently ducking to avoid the overhead beams, and decided he couldn't have. But Captain Castro had been small, he remembered.

Beyond the captain's cabin was the ante room, accessed only through the captain's cabin. The original padlock on the door had been forced but a new bar and lock had been fitted and Symson had the key with a bunch of others, on a chain suspended from his belt. He unlocked the door.

'You posted a guard, I hope,' Roberts said.

'Aye,' Symson assured him.

The ante-room was no more than six feet by four, with no window and very low angled deckhead. Holding the lantern aloft, Symson went in, and hooked it to a ring-bolt on one side out of the way, and he could not stand up straight. Neither could Roberts.

Three large chests with domed lids stood against the three bulkheads. 'There weren't no key,' David Symson informed him, 'so we forced the locks and put new ones on.' And a pretty good job they had done of it too, Roberts thought, with thick iron bands girding the trunks and huge padlocks. Well, you couldn't trust a bunch of pirates!

Symson knelt down in the small space left in the middle of the room, turning towards the chest on the left, swinging the domed lid back.

Roberts' heart jumped in his chest. Gold. More gold than a man had a right to see at one time, more gold than the miserable third mate of a slaver could earn in a dozen lifetimes, was heaped up in the chest. In a glittering yellow mountain lay the full summit of their hopes, their dreams, the sole reason for their existence.

No-one spoke. In silence they stared at the glittering golden heap with something akin to religious awe. Never in his life had Roberts seen a sight like it. He thought how glorious, how wonderful, how humbling it was to be in the presence of so much wealth.

Ashplant broke the intense silence. 'So that's what forty-thousand *moidores* looks like.'

David Symson thrust both hands into the heap, pulling out two hands full of coins, allowing them to trickle slowly through his fingers in a shining yellow shower. 'Seventy-thousand pounds, gentlemen.'

Someone giggled nervously. The presence of so much gold made them all jumpy.

Roberts picked up a coin and examined it. It was an irregular shape, with a head embossed on one side, writing on the other, and it felt heavier than he had expected. He held it up to the light, momentarily mesmerised by it, then flicked the coin back into the chest, and it was immediately lost among the others.

Roberts did some mental calculations. 'Just the gold will give each man a share of about four hundred and twenty-five pounds,' he said. Which made Roberts' own share something in the region of eight hundred and fifty pounds. Riches indeed. And that was just the gold.

'We'll give each man twenty *moidores* each to be going on with until we can distribute it properly,' Symson suggested.

The others thought it a good idea. It would take time to distribute forty-thousand *moidores*. But twenty apiece should keep them all well entertained until then. And all gold coins were legal tender on these coasts.

In the other chests there was other treasure. As though reading the captain's mind, Symson unlocked the second chest, and Roberts' heart missed a beat. Gems and trinkets of all kind lay in a tangled gaudy, glittering, heap. It was treasure beyond the thinking, its worth incalculable, but worth more even than the gold. Diamonds, rubies, topazes, amethysts, sapphires and pearls vied for attention in an assortment of vivid colours, worked in gold settings. Roberts reached in and pulled out a large gold diamond-studded cross, fully six inches long, from which dangled a heavy gold chain.

'There's another one of them,' Symson said. 'Keep it, Cap'n. For luck!'

Roberts didn't answer him, but stared at it as it glittered in his hand, the gold chain hanging from his fingers.

'I reckon ye've earned it, Cap'n,' Ashplant growled. 'I swear I ain't never seen the like o' what happened!' It had been his favourite saying since Bahia: *I ain't never seen the like!*

Pride swelled in Roberts' chest until he thought it might strangle him. It had been daring, a gamble, but he had won.

'There's more,' David Symson said, and opened the third chest to reveal more trinkets.

Seeing that his audience was speechless, Symson added: 'And in the hold, sugar, skins, tobacco. Worth a fortune in themselves.'

Roberts nodded and found his voice again. 'We'll sell what we can in Cayenne, and Devil's Island, and on to the Caribbean.' The trinkets were going to be more difficult to turn into cash, but sometimes you could barter with jewels. Worry about that later.

The first thing was to make the acquaintance of Cayenne's governor.

Guiana was a land as yet untamed. Sandwiched between Brazil to the east and south and Venezuela on the west, the English, Dutch and French had struggled for almost two centuries to get some kind of foothold in an inhospitable plague-infested jungle and had succeeded only in creating a few colonies dotted along the coast on the rivers. Here men fought to make a living, clawing land from the ever-encroaching forest for sugar, tobacco, cotton and anatto plantations, assisted by strong black African slaves.

The Dutch had spread the farthest west, as far as the salt pans of Venezuela; the English had a wealthy and sprawling colony at Suriname; and the French had wrested Cayenne from the Dutch in 1664, and established another settlement between the Sinnamary River and Kourou some sixty miles west of Cayenne, which included the three small islands known by the name of the most northerly, Devil's Island.

The settlements depended on trading with ships for vital supplies, and the traders in turn conducted a brisk business with the peaceable Indians to mutual advantage. Here then, was a market for the goods in the *Sagrada* Familia's hold. Unrestricted by morals and virtually ignored by the mother country, the French in particular, were eager to trade where they could, and no questions asked. Whether the French governor, Monsieur D'Orvillers guessed what the English were, mattered little. Like Mendoça before him, he could pretend he did not know.

Roberts invited D'Orvillers and his important men to dine on the *Sagrada Familia*, before showing them what he had to offer. A decent meal and good wine from the Portuguese's hold would pay dividends in sales later.

He invited Lúcia as well, or rather, he ordered her to attend.

'Why should I?' she demanded.

Roberts stood in the doorway to her cabin, and leaned on the doorpost. 'Because, if you don't, I may decide to drop you over the side!'

'You wouldn't dare!'

'I wouldn't test me, if I were you,' he warned.

Her eyes flashed dangerously, but she was learning to keep her temper more in check. After a moment she said: 'Why do you want me to meet the French? Are you not afraid that I should tell them who you are?'

'I expect *Monsieur* D'Orvillers already knows who I am,' he said. 'So you can tell him what you like. Not that he will understand you anyway. You speak only Portuguese, he speaks only French! I doubt you would be able to understand one another. No, *querida*, you are to be merely decoration.'

'Don't call me *querida*!'

He went out from her, laughing.

The dinner went better than Roberts dared hope. The Cook had surpassed himself, with pies and tarts, and a dish of salmagundi which was the captain's favourite, roast fowls, of which the Sagrada Familia had plenty, and fresh fruit.

Lúcia behaved with distant decorum throughout, only once causing Roberts a moment's anxiety when he introduced her. '*Messieurs,* allow me to present you to *senhora* Lúcia Margarida Carvalho Andrade. The *senhora* is travelling with us as a passenger.'

She picked up on her name and the French word for *passenger* which was close to the Portuguese, and straight away said: 'Not *passageira*, but *prisoneira*!' which was also close to the French *prisonniere*, and at which D'Orvillers raised his brows.

Roberts laughed. 'The lady jests,' he said, and because D'Orvillers wanted to believe him, he did.

To Lúcia Roberts said quietly: 'One more word from you, and you will go back to the *Rover*.'

She glared at him rebelliously for a moment, and then turned her attention to the Frenchman.

D'Orvillers though, all punctilious courtesy took Lúcia's hand in his and kissed her fingers. '*Enchanté, madame.*'

Lúcia acknowledged the compliment with a slight incline of her head and sat down.

'Such a beautiful woman, *capitaine*,' The Frenchman said. 'Where did you find her?'

'At Prince's Island,' Roberts said truthfully. 'The lady is Portuguese and alas, does not speak French.'

'And I do not speak Portuguese,' D'Orvillers replied.

She smiled disarmingly at the French governor, and said to Roberts: 'Then I am relieved of the necessity of making conversation with a Frenchman who paints his face and powders his hair!'

Henry Dennis choked on his rum punch. Roberts felt a smile tugging at the corners of his mouth. He said to the Frenchman: 'The *senhora* is desolated, *monsieur,* that she will not be able to converse with you.'

D'Orvillers raised his glass to her. 'And so am I, *senhora.*'

Roberts skilfully turned the conversation by asking: 'I hear you are a frigate captain, *monsieur* D'Orvillers?' Which effectively launched the kind of conversation sailors liked best of all, tales of voyages and peoples and the war which ended seven years previously. D'Orvillers relaxed and began to enjoy himself. The rum punch loosened his tongue, and caused him to flirt freely with Lúcia. Roberts' dark eyes glittered dangerously, but he watched the Frenchman closely.

Unable to understand, and in any case effectively silenced by the captain's threat, Lúcia concentrated first of all on her plate, and then on the men seated around the huge table. The French she disregarded; they were of no consequence. She thought their speech odd, their mannerisms affected. With their painted faces, and strange powdered wigs, and lace, she thought them effeminate. Not like the English. They, on the other hand were coarse and brutish, unrefined, and for the most part unwashed. Ashplant alarmed her, and Irish Kennedy terrified her every time his eyes moved in her direction, which was often. And although she did not understand what they said, their actions and attitudes were often threatening—towards each other!

Which was why their captain was so remarkable, she thought. He was a man of education, a man well-respected by the company, clever, Richard Hardy had told her. She took the opportunity to study him.

He was sideways on to her, lounging in his chair, one long leg crossed nonchalantly over the other, his ankle on his knee. He laughed suddenly at something David Symson had said, and then, as D'Orvillers started to speak, he listened intently, giving him his full attention, leaning his elbow on the arm of the chair, and resting his finger across his lips in a gesture of concentration. He was a fascinating man, and not just because he was handsome. There was power in this man, the strength and determination of a man born to rule. He had a magnetism that drew people of all sorts to him. Even the French had fallen under his spell.

And so had she.

He must have felt her eyes on him, for he suddenly looked at her, and she felt her heart thump in her chest. 'More wine, *senhora*?' he asked.

She picked up her goblet and held it out for him to pour for her, but her hand shook. He noticed it, took the glass from her, and poured the wine himself, before putting it down on the table in front of her.

D'Orvillers stood up and announced that he would like to see what the English had to sell.

It was well after dark when the French, well fed, and well entertained, and having driven a hard bargain, took to the boats to take them back to Cayenne.

Lúcia's mouth set in a mutinous line. 'I *will not* go!'

Roberts raised his eyes to the black night sky, and one of the rowers sniggered. If ever there was such a provoking woman, he had yet to encounter her. He said with forced patience: 'It is a ball, *senhora*, not a hanging! *Monsieur* D'Orvillers particularly invited you.'

'Huh!'

Richard Hardy said : 'Seems to me, it would be better to go to the ball than be cooped up on the ship.'

'I have nothing to wear,' she declared using the excuse women have used from time immemorial.

'And that is a patent lie,' Roberts said. 'You have a whole chest full of gowns. You will go to the ball, *senhora,* if I have to drag you there by your hair!'

She glared at him. 'I *hate* you!' she said with feeling, which was what she always said when he won an argument.

'Very likely.' He met Ashplant's eye. 'And what are *you* grinning at!'

'Nuthin'!' But Ashplant continued to grin.

Since she had no choice in the matter, Lúcia decided to make the best of it. Deep in the chest was a silk dress of midnight blue, which opened down the front to reveal a paler blue petticoat, decorated in ribbon and lace. It was low cut, perhaps a little immodest, but she had a white lace kerchief which she could use to fill in the décolletage. And because the gown laced up at the front, she could manage to dress herself.

She had little experience of dressing her own hair, preferring to plait it while on the ship, but for the ball she wound the plait around her head, and fixed it with pins which gave her a serene and somewhat aristocratic air. It might not have been the most fashionable of styles, but then she wasn't concerned with that.

So just who was she trying to impress? *Monsieur* D'Orvillers? The French? Or the pirate captain?

She glared at her own reflection in the broken mirror Hardy had found for her. It should not matter what he thought of her. He was an arrogant man, a swaggering pirate, a lawbreaker who had taken her hostage. In short, he was the enemy. So what had he to say to anything? A slow smile spread across her face. There would be a certain perverse satisfaction in bringing such a lofty man to her feet.

There was a knock at the door. 'Come!' she said and used the English word. Learning English from Richard Hardy had whiled away the long hours at sea.

Roberts opened the door, and halted on the threshold. She turned and looked at him, and her insides swooped unexpectedly. He certainly cut an impressive figure. He looked every inch the gentleman he pretended to be, the equal of the governor and his cronies, those he wished to impress if he were to continue trading with them. Lace foamed at his throat, a pale blue silk coat and white embroidered silk waistcoat, white knee-breeches and hose, as befitting a legitimate captain. His curls had been brushed from his face and forced into a small black ribbon at the nape of his neck. It changed him from the wild wind-swept sea-captain into a gentleman.

'Well, *capitão,* will I do for your precious governor?'

For a long moment he did not speak, but there was naked admiration in his eyes. 'I brought you something.'

'Oh?'

He held out his hand, offering her a black velvet pouch. She hesitated fractionally. Then she reached out and took it, opening it and tipping the contents into the palm of her hand, a pair of pearl earrings shaped like teardrops, and a pearl necklace. She knew where they had come from. 'Part of the *Sagrada Familia's* treasure, I suppose.'

The pearls represented more wealth than he had ever had in all his life, and he all but snarled at her: 'They are a gift from me to you. But of course, if you do not want them . . .' He reached out his hand, but she snatched them away from him.

'I did not say I did not want them, *senhor capitão*! I merely asked where they came from.'

He grinned, satisfied. She was as mercenary as he was!

She peered at herself in the mirror fragment and fitted the earrings in place then held up the necklace to her throat. 'Perhaps you will help me with the necklace, *senhor*?' she invited.

He came into the cabin and took up a position behind her and took the two ends of the necklace. She watched him in the mirror, and felt his touch on her skin, his breath in her ear and he sent the blood fizzing round her body, raising the colour in her cheeks, making her legs suddenly weak. Oh, but this man had a power she found difficult to resist!

The clasp was delicate, but at last it was done, and he let it fall onto her neck. He let his hand also drop onto her neck, and gently caressed the smoothness of her throat.

She held her breath, and caught his eyes in the mirror, her own wide, almost disbelieving, his serious, intense.

He turned away abruptly. 'Come. The boat is waiting.'

D'Orvillers had gone to much trouble. The huge ballroom at the back of the house on the first upstairs floor, was lit by a thousand candles. Pale blue silk draped the walls, and a small but very creditable orchestra played on the dais. Black slaves, some only boys, dressed in white livery with white turbans on their heads and bearing salvers with drinks on them, moved among the guests with the practised ease of those used to making themselves invisible. Where all the guests came from, Roberts had no idea. There must have been every white settler in Cayenne present in their best finery. Roberts himself had brought only Dennis, and Symson with him, men who could adopt good enough manners for such exalted company, and the only ones he could persuade to leave the black beauties in the brothels. And of course Lúcia.

She was perfection itself. No other woman in the room matched her for beauty, no other attracted as much attention. Everyone wanted to dance with her, and Roberts, who of course had never learnt the dances of the upper classes, watched from the sidelines as she performed minuets and gavottes with consummate skill, flirting with first one Frenchman, then another. This was her world as far away from his as it was possible to get. The gap between them yawned as wide as the Atlantic Ocean itself. Not that he was going to be put off by a culture difference.

D'Orvillers joined him. 'You do not dance, *Capitaine?*'

Roberts shook his head. 'Two left feet,' he said.

The Frenchman pursed his lips and nodded. 'That is what all Englishmen say. You will be leaving soon, I think.'

Roberts said: 'Tomorrow.'

'A pity. We have so few visitors here. It would have been amusing to have fellow sailors to converse with.'

Roberts laughed, and the Frenchman wandered off, then as he watched Lúcia, the laughter died.

When the dance ended, the young man who had been her partner, brought her across to Roberts thanking her.

Roberts said to her: 'Not so bad after all, *senhora?*'

She used a black lace fan to cool her face. 'Not so bad,' she agreed. But I cannot quite come to terms with a man who paints his face!'

He was surprised into a laugh.

'Well!' she went on. 'Are they men or are they women? I must say I do not understand the French!'

'Few people do,' he agreed, still chuckling.

'It is so hot in here!'

'You wish to go outside?' Deliberately he used the familiar *tu* for *you*.

She glanced up at him, and she seemed to consider. 'Yes, please.'

The ballroom had many French windows or glazed double doors which opened out onto small balconies overlooking the garden, and he directed her to the nearest.

Outside the air was a little less hot, although not cool, and it seemed relatively quiet after the noise of the ballroom. The musicians had taken a break, and the guests sought out the food the governor had provided, so that they were quite alone.

She rested her hands on the stone balustrade, and took a breath. 'Ah, that is better.'

He stood beside her. Below them, just visible in the lights from the house, the neat formal garden seemed to stretch until it met the wild forest. Cicadas and crickets and frogs contributed to the noise from the forest, and at the same time contributed to the feeling of isolation.

He said: 'You are not afraid to be here with me, *senhora*?'

She looked up at him, her eyes black inviting pools, and he felt his heart jump. 'I don't think I am afraid of you any more, *senhor capitão*. Should I be?'

He searched her face, looking for clues. She continued to look up at him, irresistibly beautiful in the light. The blood pounded in his ears.

He reached out and slipped his hand around her waist. He could feel the warmth of her body through the tight silk. She did not resist and he pulled her against him. 'Perhaps you should,' he said, his voice low.

She put her hands on his shoulders, her eyes searching his face. One little hand reached up, and touched his cheek, very gently. 'Why, what are you going to do with me, Bartolomeo?' she whispered, but it was not the same question she had asked when he had first taken her.

He hesitated, even though he recognised the invitation. He had held back for so long, and he wanted her so badly, that he hardly dared to go further. Would she turn away from him? But he could not resist. Gently, hardly daring to breathe, he brushed her lips with his own. Immediately, he felt her response. It wasn't what he had expected, and he pulled back to look at her.

'Oh Bartolomeo,' she whispered.

The gulf that existed between them, of age, of culture, of wealth, vanished in that moment. He pulled her into his arms and kissed her, losing himself in the intoxication of his love for her.

FOURTEEN

January 1720, Devil's Island

With a following wind and favourable currents, they made good speed. At just seven hours out of Cayenne, the lookout bellowed the cry: *'Land ho!'* and sure enough on the horizon, in the shivering heat haze, grey and indistinct shapes grew out of the blue water—the Îles du Salut, better known to the English by the name of most northerly of the three islands, Devil's Island.

The second of the three islands, Royale, a tree-swaddled tropical paradise rising out of the turquoise sea beckoned invitingly. The *Royal Rover's* crew knew they would get a warm welcome there, that there would be women and drink, and food, and comfortable beds.

Roberts sent the first watches ashore, and looked forward to respite for himself from the responsibility of command.

''Tis busier than I remember,' Ashplant observed as the boat came towards the island. The quay was cluttered with warehouses, taverns, shacks, all nestling beneath the hill, and a market at one end of the black shingle beach where the islanders haggled over the goods from the ships. People had seen them coming and crowded together on the wharf to greet them, a mixture of whites, negroes and a few nearly-naked Indians. The vivid colours of their clothing contrasted with the dull grey stone that was the fabric of the island. Noise—shrieks and gabbled French and English, mingling with the protests of chickens, pigs and geese—drifted across the water.

With a bump the boat finally ran against the jetty and the oarsmen stowed the blades away as a black man ran forward to catch the rope and tie it off, hoping for a penny for his trouble. Henry Dennis carelessly tossed him a coin as he stepped out onto the jetty—and it was considerably more than a penny.

Willing hands helped Lúcia ashore, and Roberts followed. By now some of the goods from the *Sagrada Familia* had come ashore and found their way to the marketplace, so that is where Roberts ushered Lúcia.

For such a small group of islands, the marketplace was surprisingly busy. French, English and Indian mingled together, haggling over the pirate goods. Cloth, tobacco, oil, wine, skins, already bought and paid for by the merchants who had been quick aboard the *Sagrada Familia,* now vied for the attention of the inhabitants. The lithe dark-skinned Indians, their black hair hanging lankly to their shoulders and both sexes wearing just a small loin-cloth to preserve their modesty, haggled as hard as anyone over the cloth, grinning with mouths full of overlarge sparkling white teeth when they got their bargain, then loading the bales into their canoes to take to the mainland. As a people who had little use for clothes, Roberts wondered fleetingly what they wanted them for.

Lúcia, could not resist the urge to shop, and Roberts stood by ready to pay for whatever she wished to buy. But he was impatient to find lodgings for himself and for Lúcia, and he had it in mind to find a maid for her. He looked around him with a view to finding someone when a woman in a bright red dress caught his attention as she haggled with a small dark-skinned man over a young pig.

He stared at her intently. Time had made a plump figure grossly fat, and the once-pretty face had deep wrinkles etched by sun and drink, tobacco smoke and debauchery, but there was no mistaking Sally Grey. He had last seen her twenty years previously in a bawdy house on the Deptford Road in London. She had been his initiation into the lures of the fair sex.

A grin spread across his face.

'Damn you, José!' she swore in English, adding in French: 'I tell you I paid for him and he's mine.' And to lend weight to the argument she pulled on the front legs of the unfortunate pig.

José had a grasp of the hind quarters like a new recruit clinging to the top yard in a gale. 'Not so, *madame,* you bought the little one!'

'Go fly to the Devil, José. The little one wouldn't feed a cockroach!'

Roberts' grin grew wider. 'Then you'd better have the larger one, Sal,' he said in English, 'afore you pull the poor creature in half between you!'

Sally Grey spun around, her little pale eyes staring at him in astonishment. Then abruptly letting go of the pig, she threw her arms wide. '*Bart!*' she shrieked. 'Bart Roberts! You old Welshie! As I live and breathe! Where the Devil did you come from?'

He found himself locked in an embrace that would not have disgraced a giant squid, holding him so tightly he couldn't breathe. But he was genuinely pleased to see her and when he disengaged himself, he planted a kiss on her too-red lips. 'Sally, my old darling!'

She held him off. 'Lord, let me look at you. You've grown into a fine figure of a man. I knew you would. You was nobbut a kidwy when I last seed you. How long ago was it?'

'Twenty years.'

'I allus said you'd be a prime cove! What are you doing here?'

'I am a gentleman of fortune,' he told her, and executed a bow, sweeping his hat before him.

'A pirate? You? Nay—I don't believe it! You was allus quoting the Good Book, and telling me I be a sinner! And you turned pirate. Why?'

'Because the pay's better.'

She laughed, but she halted her mirth abruptly as her eyes alighted on Lúcia standing back a little, watching the interchange with interest. 'Who's the beauty?'

Lúcia answered her herself. 'I am Lúcia Margarida Carvalho Andrade,' she said in English, surprising Roberts. 'I am pleased to meet you.'

'Sally Grey,' said Sally, and recognising quality, she bobbed a curtsey.

Roberts told Lúcia: 'Mrs. Grey is an old friend.'

'Your woman?' Sally asked Roberts.

'A passenger,' he said blithely.

'Passenger eh? Since when have pirates taken passengers?' Sally pursed her lips. 'I don't know what to make of you, Bart Roberts. You ain't the kidwy you was. You was the Puritan that couldn't be turned.'

'I seem to remember you managed it,' he remarked.

Her eyes strayed beyond him. Then: 'Ash! Davy boy!' she shrieked.

Ashplant ran up to her, wrapped his arms about her and squeezed her tight. 'Sally Grey! Me old darlin'.'

David Symson also planted a kiss on her lips. 'Ah, darling Sal!'

'What're you rogues doing with the Welsh puritan?' she demanded. 'No wonder he's bin led astray. I'll wager it were all your doin' Valentine Ashplant!'

''Twern't nothing to do with me,' Ashplant retorted. ''Twere Cap'n Davis as took a shine to'm.' He looked straight at Roberts. 'Cap'n, the men want to know if they can stay ashore.'

Roberts nodded. He couldn't prevent them anyway, not if he

didn't want his brains scattered all over the landscape. 'Aye.'

As Ashplant wandered off, Sally said: 'You're their captain? I don't believe it! Bart Roberts captain of pirates!' She broke off, catching sight of Henry Dennis. 'Henry! You old sea dog!'

She subjected Henry Dennis to the same treatment they had all received. When she finally put him down, she beamed around at them all. 'But what're ye all doing here in the marketplace. I got rooms. You stay at my place. And the food's good. Ask anyone.'

'And women?' Ashplant, having relayed the captain's permission to the crew returned just in time to hear the last bit.

Sally grinned. 'Naturally.'

Sally's house clung precariously to the hillside as though to lose the slightest hold would send it plummeting to the depths below. It boasted a verandah and overhanging balcony, and one side looked out to sea, the other over the forest.

She found a room for Roberts, and another for Lúcia, and also sent one of her black waitresses called Éva to act as maid to Lúcia. The others found rooms with her girls, for Sally's place doubled as a bawdy house, and the taproom with wooden refectory tables, flagstones darkened by wear and spilled drink and food and the walls blackened by the combined effects of candle smoke and tobacco was the noisiest and jolliest on the island.

But to Lúcia it was a haven, and she was grateful for a bed that didn't spend the entire night rocking, and room enough to dress in, to say nothing of the luxury of a maid, be she ever so inexperienced, and quite idle to boot.

She sat down on the bed, which, much to her surprise, had freshly laundered linen. She had forgotten the feel and smell of clean sheets.

But her thoughts were not of the house, or of the bed, but of the man in the bedroom next door.

She ought to be ashamed of herself, she told herself roundly. To allow herself to be kissed like she was a common trollop, and by a sailor, a pirate, what was she thinking of? What could come of it? He was a sailor—he would be leaving again soon, and she could not go with him. That is what sailors did. They hardly ever went home. She absolutely must not lose her heart to him. But she knew she already had.

Sally served dinner in the taproom, a kind of stew that Lúcia did not recognise, but which she ate without hesitation, for she was hungry. She was squeezed in between Henry Dennis and Roberts on one of the grimy benches on one side of the table while Ashplant, Sutton, Hardy and Symson occupied the bench opposite. The taproom was filled with people, sailors and merchants, and serving women who Lúcia assumed were of ill-repute, for their clothing was not what she would call decent. Not that the customers seemed to mind. She watched one young woman deliver a tray full of tankards to a table, where the men grabbed her gleefully and she shrieked in delighted laughter. Lúcia was appalled, and even more so when she found the eyes of the men on her table watching her reaction with amusement.

'What sort of place is this?' she asked Roberts.

Tom Sutton guffawed with laughter, and Ashplant also seemed to find her funny.

Roberts said with aplomb: 'The only decent hotel on the island.'

'Well I think I might take my dinner in my room in future,' she said.

'As you wish.'

The men fell into unaccustomed silence, aware of a lady's presence, when what they wanted to say and do might offend her. She was touched by their tact, but they need not have bothered. While her command of English was not enough to understand what anyone around her said, she gathered the import. As soon as she had finished eating and had swallowed some ale, which she found particularly refreshing, she stood up.

Roberts also stood to let her pass. 'If you will excuse me, gentlemen, I am tired and I wish to retire,' she said.

They all watched her go to the stairs just in case she was molested, and then as she disappeared around the bend, Dennis said: 'No place for a lady, this.'

Roberts agreed. 'Unfortunately, the only other place for her to stay is aboard the *Royal Rover*. And she needs time ashore as we all do.'

Symson grabbed a passing wench, and kissed her. 'Later, my beauty,' she told him, laughing, and he patted her on the backside and let her go.

Someone began to play the fiddle, and, recognising the tune, someone else began to sing the song. Before long they all joined in a drunken chorus.

Roberts watched, but he did not join the revelries. His men were here to enjoy themselves, to spend their cash on women, drink and gambling. And he would have done the same, had it not been for the woman upstairs.

He couldn't keep his mind off her. He had been careful while on the ship but he was not tied to the pirates' articles while on land, and seduction was very much the purpose he had in mind. In fact his need for her had become an obsession. But how to proceed he had no idea. That she liked him he knew. But she had been strictly reared, and he had no idea how to proceed with a shy young virgin.

He stayed a short while longer in the taproom, keeping company with his men, but he was preoccupied, and when he saw they no longer noticed whether he were there or not, he slipped away too.

The raucous noise permeated through the ceiling beams up to the rooms above. Roberts paused on the landing, looking at the array of closed doors. Lúcia's room was the one at the end, the one furthest from the stairs, next to his own. He had seen to it that she had a bolt on the door. Now he wished he hadn't. His instinct was to go straight into her room, but he was not dealing with a common whore here. So he hesitated, wondering how best to deal with her.

At that moment, her door opened, and the maid came out. Seeing Roberts, she passed him, a knowing smile on her face, and hurried down the stairs. Then Lúcia appeared in the doorway, and called out to her. 'Éva, you have forgotten—' But whatever it was that the maid had forgotten remained forgotten, for she spotted Roberts.

It was dark, only a single candle in the sconce on the landing and the candle in the room behind her casting any light. But he was acutely aware of her being clad in a white shift, her black hair tumbling about her shoulders. The breath caught in his throat.

He expected her to scurry inside and bolt the door, but she hesitated, as surprised to see him as he was to see her. 'Bartolomeo!'

Her use of his forename encouraged him.

Roberts came towards her and said: 'What are you doing out here? It is dangerous for you to be out here on your own. That's why I provided a bolt on the door, and a maid.'

She turned to go back into the room. 'The maid was anxious to be gone. I thank you for your concern.'

Backlit as she was he could see the outline of her body through the shift, and his heart began pounding in his chest. He followed, and took hold of her arm, turning her again towards him. 'There is danger for you here, *querida*.'

'I am in no danger,' she said softly and smiled, 'as long as you are with me.'

He wondered if she had any idea of the effect she had on him. 'If only you knew!' he said in English and slipped his hand around her waist. He could feel her skin warm and firm beneath the shift. Of her own will she moved closer, and he felt her hands tremble as they rested on his chest. 'Oh, Lúcia . . .'

Footsteps on the stairs alerted him, and he pushed her quickly into the room, kicking the door closed behind him.

She was in his arms then her body soft and yielding against his. He kissed her hungrily. Her response was passionate, all hint of shyness gone. He kissed her lips, her neck, her throat, his senses filled with the heady scent of her, the feel of her.

'Lúcia.'

'Bartolomeo,' she whispered, 'bolt the door!'

Lúcia was a woman transformed. Gone was the aristocratic lady. In her stead was a girl freed from the stifling restraints of what was proper for a woman of her station. Gone too was her innocence, and that had been his doing.

But he could not regret it. She was happiness and gaiety, laughter and joy, beauty and love. It shone in her eyes, danced on her smiling lips, twinkled in her laugh. And he was intoxicated by her.

The days passed quickly. They spent every day together, often sitting in the shade of the palm trees on the south beach while he taught her English, getting her to repeat phrases and laughing at her mispronunciations. Unable to sit still for long, she would run off through the forest, expecting him to follow, squealing in delight when he caught her unawares to steal a soft warm kiss. She paddled in the transparent sea, bunching up her skirts to show him tantalising glimpses of neat ankles and creamy calves, and then kicked water at him.

For the first time in his life he considered the possibility of settling down, of marriage. It would mean leaving the sea, of course; he could hardly remain a pirate with the responsibility of a wife and family. Yet to leave the sea was unimaginable. It was a problem he could not deal with, so he put it to the back of his mind, and just enjoyed the here and now.

But he could not put it off forever. Every passing day brought him nearer to the time he must make a decision. The crew were growing restless with drinking and wenching, and idleness was fast becoming boredom.

He didn't know what woke him, but when he opened his eyes, he realised that it was not quite dawn. The room was filled with a grey light which preceded sunrise for just a few minutes each day, before the sun came up over the sea.

The windows were open, and a slight breeze ruffled the thin curtains. Something was wrong. He could sense it, but he wasn't sure what it was.

Beside him the bed was empty. He pulled himself up onto one elbow and saw her on the balcony, leaning on the safety rail, looking out at the sea, at the promised sunrise. She was so beautiful, with her black hair cascading in untidy curls down to her waist. She wore the white thin shift, but with the growing light behind it, he could see the outline shape of her body, of her hips, of her thighs.

She had been restless in the night, troubled. Perhaps he should have expected it. They had been here six weeks, and everyone was beginning to feel agitated.

It had been idyllic, a paradise. Quickly they had sold the remaining goods in the *Sagrada Familia* to the French traders who worked from the islands who in turn would trade with the Indians and other settlers at Kourou on the mainland. And then the company had set about carousing in earnest, searching out the prostitutes who were eager to please their rich lovers, gambling with their fortunes—which they were not allowed to do on ship—and drinking themselves senseless. It had been six weeks of indulging in every desire of the flesh and now they were satiated with women, good food and drink, and gambling. They were adventurers. Prolonged carousing led to restless boredom, and degenerated into fights and duels which stretched Christopher Moody as Boatswain and David Symson as quartermaster to their limits as they tried to keep the peace. The time had come to take their leave.

Furthermore the supplies they had brought with them in the ships were all but exhausted, and the island just could not support another one hundred and fifty insatiable bellies. The men were itching to go.

On one level Roberts was eager to go, too. It had been wonderful, a paradise of love. Lúcia was passionate, and loving, and amusing. She brought sunshine and laughter into his life. Yet they both knew it would have to end. They didn't speak of it, but then they didn't speak of the future at all. He made her no promises, and she did not ask for any. They knew that their lives were separate, that they could not be together forever. Each had a destiny somewhere apart from the other, in a different world. It was enough to love and be loved, to enjoy what time they had.

But now the day of reckoning had come.

He slipped out from beneath the sheet, and went out onto the balcony just as he was, mother naked. She turned her head slightly, acknowledging that he was there, but otherwise did not move.

The sun glowed orange on the edge of the sea. On the hillside, the mist hung in ribbons draped in the trees. The air was unusually still, and even the birds and insects and animals of the forest were silent. Already the temperature soared.

He slipped his arms around her, and she leaned back against him resting her head on his shoulder. He kissed her temple, where the hair met the skin.

For a long time neither of them spoke. The sun came up sending a blinding shaft of light onto the balcony, but they were shaded by the corner of the house. He thought how precious this moment was, a single moment in a lifetime, a magical moment. His heart was so full of love for her that he thought it would burst. He didn't want to let her go. Not now, not ever.

'You know what I was thinking?' she asked suddenly.

'What were you thinking, *querida*?'

She sighed. 'I was thinking how I would like to stay here, with you, forever.'

He said nothing, but his arms tightened around her. They were silent again. Then she said: 'There is a ship in the anchorage.'

His insides swooped in alarm, and yet he knew it must happen. 'I know of it. A Quaker is her master. From Rhode Island.' It was a foolish captain who put into Devil's Island when Roberts and his company were there. However, Captain Brown's *Pilgrim* had already been robbed at sea, and had only victuals and a few slaves left in her hold, so they left her alone. One robbery per voyage was enough for any man, and they had nothing against Quakers.

'She is destined for Brazil,' Lúcia said quietly.

He already knew it, but he felt a sharp pain shoot through him. He said nothing.

'I have booked a passage for myself,' she added, and her voice was dry. 'I feel I may trust Captain Brown to treat me with respect.'

Dear God, no! 'When?'

'Tomorrow. At noon.'

He felt sick inside. Yet he had known all along that it would come to this. He let go of her suddenly, and turned and went inside. She followed him. 'You are angry?' she asked.

He pulled on his under-breeches, and reached for his breeches. 'No.' But he was.

She stood by the window, watching him, but he could not look at her. She said: 'You and I are lovers, Bartolomeo. Yet we have always known it must end. You have not told me that you wish anything different.'

He reached for his shirt, draped over a chair. 'I do wish differently,' he snapped, crossing the room to confront her. 'I wish we could be together for always. I wish we could marry, that you would be the mother of my children. I wish I were not what I am, or that you were not a lady. I wish that I were good enough for you. But wishing don't make it happen, Lúcia.' He touched her cheek, his mood softening. 'You just don't know how much I love you. But, I must let you go even though it rips the insides out of me to know you will belong to another man.'

'I will never belong to another man the way I belong to you, Bartolomeo,' she said. Her lower lip trembled and her dark eyes filled with tears. 'I will never ever forget you.'

He reached out for her, and pulled her into his arms. 'Or I you, *querida.*'

The *Pilgrim* sailed just after noon the following day. Roberts stood on the shingle at the southern end of the island of Royale and watched as she paid off into the wind. Aboard, she had a cargo more precious than gold or slaves.

Lúcia stood at the taffrail, dressed in customary black, her hair confined in a net. There, on the *Pilgrim*'s deck he had kissed her for the last time, there he had almost begged her not to leave him.

She had seen it in him, and resolutely not given him the chance. Now, as the ship gained speed, he watched her disappearing forever from his life. And the pain was like torn flesh inside him.

FIFTEEN

Roberts looked at the eager faces of his men as they sought places to sit in the shade of the spread sail on the *Sagrada Familia*'s main deck. They grumbled because of the heat, and grumbled because they had become bored with constant carousing. They were eager for action.

He wouldn't be sorry to go now either. Without Lúcia, the islands held no attraction for him, and the constant drunkenness, fights and jollity of his men grated. He needed the diversion of action, and he itched to get to it.

Removing his hat, he wiped the sweat from his brow with his forearm. It was midday, and the sun roasted them from out of a deep blue cloudless sky. The searing heat reflected off the white holystoned deck and evaporated the splashes of sea-water cast up onto the *Sagrada Familia*'s structure as waves splashed against the hull, leaving white gritty salt stains. They said that at midday on this coast, the sun was so hot it could boil a man's brains in his head. Roberts believed it.

David Symson as quartermaster, had called the meeting on the *Sagrada Familia*, so, standing at the quarterdeck rail of the Portuguese ship, he addressed the ship's company. He was a good man, David Symson. Reliable. Capable. Big enough to enforce discipline by brute strength if need be. They called him Little David, with typical inverted British humour.

'Gentlemen!' Symson began in his diluted north-country accent. 'Six weeks we been here and as fine a place to rest up I never did see! But provisions are short, and 'tis time we found a vessel that'll provide belly-timber.'

'What, and leave Antoinette behind?' someone bellowed from the back.

Roberts compressed his lips, in no mood to join the laughter for it reminded him of his own loss which was still an acute, raw pain. Half of the crew had enjoyed Antoinette's favours, Symson included, and he had displayed a certain amount of jealousy over her. They would pull his leg about it for days to come, Roberts guessed.

It was true enough, though. They did need provisions. They had exhausted what the Portuguese ship had in her hold, and the islanders could not feed such a large force indefinitely. Almost all the food on the islands was imported, save for a few chickens and a pig or two, although red mullet and lobster abounded in the seas. And who, indeed, was not tired of fish and lobster, even though the cook did his best to vary the menu? There were a hundred and fifty men in the company, and they had to be fed.

'Where'll we get provisions then?' Robert Birdson asked, his voice rising from the crowd on the foredeck.

David Symson wiped a drip of sweat from the end of his long beak and turned his head to look at Roberts. 'Well, Cap'n?'

Roberts had already considered it. Drawing on his past experience as the mate of a Barbados sloop, knowing that there would be more chance of finding 'belly- timber' in the busy shipping lanes of the West Indies than on the South American coast, the decision was really of no debate. He came forward from the gunwale. 'There's only one place, the Caribbean. There will be more chance of encountering a laden ship there than anywhere else, and there are places there where we can trade the rest of the Portuguese goods.'

There were nods of agreement. They knew the logic of seeking ships in the busier waters of the Caribbean. So they voted for it.

Then they came to the major reason for their meeting, that of sharing out the remainder of the booty. Already David Symson, as quartermaster, had shared out the gold, each share, once the common fund had been extracted, amounting to 250 *moidores* or just about five hundred pounds. Roberts received a double share, as did Symson. But there was the little matter of two chests of jewels, and the monies realised from the sale of the *Sagrada Familia*'s goods. The jewels they would have to keep until they could sell them on the market. The monies from the sale of goods, however, needed to be distributed.

Symson was good with figures, but he had taken sometime over the mathematics of the case, but now he wanted to get on with it.

It promised to be a lengthy procedure, and meanwhile the men were cooking in the equatorial sun. The company shifted with expectation as two men heaved a chest onto the deck. David Symson lifted the lid so that it swung upright on its hinges, making a cavernous backdrop to the gold coins inside, the profits from the sales. The harsh equatorial sun struck the gold with the movement of the ship, reflecting stabs of light into the eyes of the waiting men.

They had managed to sell some of the jewels also. One of the six-inch crosses had been given to the governor of Cayenne, and Roberts had the other one on a chain around his neck, which hung to his waist. He was not particularly religious, although brought up Nonconformist, but he thought it might bring him luck in a job where luck was needed more than skill.

They might have thought themselves inured to the sight of gold, but it still brought a communal gasp from them. Their greed was tangible. Roberts felt it too. It coiled inside him like a terrible voracious serpent, and sent a shiver of delightful expectation down his spine. For brief blessed moments, it distracted him from the black mood that had settled on him since Lúcia's departure.

David Symson unrolled his list of men and laid it on the top of a barrel, weighing it down with a pistol, which served the double purpose of warning any who thought to take without permission. The scroll, however, did not fit, and a curl of paper hung down the front of the barrel, flapping in the breeze. Symson had brought from the great cabin a pen and inkstand, and now he trimmed the nib to his liking with his knife.

Then he began the task of calling each man in turn and giving him his share, starting with the captain.

Roberts took the coins counted out to him, signed for them, and put them in the large purse he kept for the purpose. There was no reason for him to stay on board really, and he was irritated by not being able to leave. His chest, his belongings, the rest of his share of the prize was in his cabin on the *Royal Rover*. However, for now he must kick his heels while David Symson carried out the job of paying the crew.

Roberts tucked the purse inside his waistcoat. He had five hundred gold coins, and they weighed heavy. He moved to go below to the great cabin when a sudden cry from the masthead stopped him. 'Sail Ho!'

Shinning nimbly up the shrouds, he reached the crosstrees and pulled out the telescope from its leather carrying case, to get a better look. A small sloop was clearly visible to the north-east, her bows turned towards the islands.

David Symson made a note of where he had got up to, and they all waited.

Roberts slid down to the deck again, his delight that this small ship should sail unsuspectingly into his clutches shining in his eyes.

But he played it down. 'A sloop. She won't be worth much.'

A slow smile dawned on Symson's face. 'We need bellytimber.'

Roberts nodded, and couldn't keep back the grin. 'Aye.' This might mean that they need not pursue provisions in the Caribbean after all, but turn their attentions to more lucrative trade elsewhere. The thought appealed.

There was no rush. They had time enough to finish their business.

During the afternoon the sloop slipped into the anchorage off Royale alongside the *Royal Rover*. She was a small ship, single masted, fore-and-aft rigged with a gaff mainsail and jib. A neat little vessel, built for speed rather than carrying capacity, very nifty.

'She won't be worth much,' Henry Dennis confirmed his thoughts as he peered through the *Sagrada Familia*'s large open stern window at the newcomer.

She had not been looked after, Roberts silently agreed. Her decks had not been holystoned, her sails were untidily furled with reefs and ropes dangling where they ought to be tied, and the vessel had a general air of dirt and decay about it. It indicated a slack crew, with no pride in their work, their overseers as bad as the rest.

'There'll be provisions,' Roberts said bracingly. And he needed the diversion of work. 'We'll wait until tonight, and then we'll send in the longboat.'

They asked for twenty men. Forty volunteered, each one of them eager to show off his courage to prove himself a man. Who would not volunteer indeed, with the additional reward of a new suit of clothes from the prize if any could be found on such a small vessel? David Symson had to limit them by list.

David Symson led the boarding party, and, caught unawares, there was little the sloop captain could do, but surrender. Roberts followed his men onto the captured ship, and stood for a moment looking at the crew standing by the mast. 'Which of you is the captain?' he demanded.

'I am!' A man stepped forward. He was in his mid to late thirties, but the relative inactivity of command had cost him the hardness of his muscles and his stomach sagged comfortably over his breeches. He seemed to size Roberts up, then he grinned affably and came forward, holding out his hand. 'Captain Cane, sir, at your service. From Rhode Island. Welcome aboard, sir.' He looked meaningfully at the pistol Walter Kennedy had levelled at him. 'And there ain't no need for that, now.'

Roberts jerked his head at Kennedy, who lowered the pistol, and released the hammer. 'You yield to us?' he asked suspiciously.

'Oh aye,' Captain Cane replied easily. 'As long as you give good quarter.'

Roberts studied him for a long minute. Captain Cane might smile as friendly as you please, but a muscle twitched in his cheek beneath his right eye, and his hands shook. The man was scared witless. 'You are hardly in a position to bargain, Captain,' Roberts reminded him. 'But we give good quarter, and you, Captain Cane, will be our guest.'

'And who are you, sir?'

Roberts bowed grandly, mockingly. 'Bartholomew Roberts, at your service. Commander of the *Royal Rover.*'

'My ship is yours, Captain Roberts,' Captain Cane said expansively and grinned again. 'Anything I have, you may have, sir. I don't carry much beyond provisions, but you may take what you need and welcome. Indeed, I only wish my poor vessel were larger so that you may find more.'

As his tongue rattled on quickly, beads of sweat glistened on his upper lip and the little grey eyes in his fat round face implored mercy. The sloop carried little of value to risk lives for and the rest was insured. No point is risking lives in resisting.

'You may be easy, Captain Cane. We want no violence. You and your officers will be our guests aboard the *Royal Rover*. Mr. Hardy! Conduct Captain Cane and his crew aboard the *Royal Rover* if you please.'

However, the sloop brought more than supplies. Captain Cane's affability increased as they plied him with copious amounts of wine and rum during that night and the following day, which investment yielded information that made Roberts' eyes shine. The sloop had not left Rhode Island alone, but had sailed in company with a richly-laden brigantine, bound for the English colony at Suriname.

Peering through the telescope, Roberts felt his heart quicken. There, at last, was the brigantine.

She rode the waves in stately splendour, like a virginal bride, ready for the taking. A week they had waited for her, while they stripped the sloop of all but the most basic foodstuffs and all her goods, and Roberts had begun to think that Cane was either a lying rogue or the brigantine's commander had changed his mind about Suriname.

Patience, though, had brought its reward, and he snapped the telescope shut and slid down to the deck, brisk and ready for business.

''Tis the brigantine all right,' he confirmed to the company summoned by the lookout's cry,

Irish Kennedy said: 'She's heading away from us.'

Indeed, as they watched, the brigantine veered off for the north-west, as though she knew they lay in wait for her.

Roberts swore under his breath. It would take more effort now. 'She's hugging the coast for Suriname. We can overtake her easily.'

'Not with the Portuguese in tow,' Thomas Anstis growled. 'Nor even with the *Rover.*' He scratched his cannonball head. 'But if we was to use the sloop now . . .' Captain Cane's sloop was small with a shallower draft, therefore lighter and swifter. She already had ten guns which would be enough for their purpose.

Henry Dennis's face was turned towards the sun hovering just above the horizon. It seemed to be twice its normal size, a bright golden orb staining the sky in pinks and reds and orange. He said: 'Night is coming on. By the time we set sail, it will be dark.'

'And by morning she will be gone,' Roberts snapped impatiently. 'But we know where she is heading, and we'll follow and overtake her.'

'I don't like it,' Dennis said.

The assembled company murmured and shifted uneasily, and Roberts felt his anger rise. 'What the Devil is wrong with you all? We have kicked our heels here far longer than necessary on the promise of this brig. She is within our grasp.' He glared at them. 'Should we let them get away now? What say you all? Who will go?'

Forty men volunteered, and Roberts shot a triumphant look at Dennis, who hunched his shoulders and continued to search the sky line.

Roberts barked out his orders, and men ran to do his bidding. If they were to catch the brigantine they had to get moving straight away before night fell.

As he gathered together his charts, telescope, quadrant and other navigational necessities, he gave his orders to Kennedy, his lieutenant, left in charge of the prize, and to Symson, the quartermaster, to keep an eye on Kennedy whom he trusted about as much as he trusted the great sharks that patrolled the waters.

There was no time for more. Not even to check the provisions. The forty men transferred to the sloop.

'We'll have her by morning,' Roberts prophesied. Christopher Moody bellowed the order and men hauled on the lines to raise sail and before the sun reached the western horizon, Captain Cane's sloop had raised its anchor and was well under weigh.

SIXTEEN

Walter Kennedy cast an experienced and very happy eye over the *Royal Rover*. She was a fine ship, one a man could be proud to sail on. Or proud to command.

Already the sloop had cleared the islands, sailing far to the west, her sails billowing in the decent breeze, sheets of white against a pale yellow and crimson sky as the sun sank. But the sloop held his attention for only a moment. The real focus of his interest was the Portuguese ship lying just a few yards away across a stretch of darkening water. For on the *Sagrada Familia* he knew, there were still two thousand gold *moidores* in the communal chest, as well as a chest of valuable jewels and trinkets, diamonds and pearls, besides the goods they had not yet sold. The ship was still half-laden. And Kennedy's little eyes glowed. To share it between a hundred and fifty men would be a very good living. To share it between half that number would be even better.

He licked his lips, an unconscious gesture of greed. He wanted it. He wanted it all. Not just the gold and trinkets, but the ships as well. He wanted the command. He had always wanted it, and he felt his heart swelling once more with the sheer injustice of Fate that had sent Bart Roberts to them just before the position of captain fell vacant.

Envy had turned to hatred in a very short time. Roberts had everything Kennedy desired, even the Portuguese woman. Lord, how he had desired the Portuguese woman! If he could have got away with it, he would have found some way of putting an end to the captain's life. Then the woman, the company, the gold, would all be his. But desperate though he might be, he was certainly no fool. The captain was twice his size, and seemed possessed of a sixth sense that alerted him to danger. Kennedy was not stupid enough to think he was a match for Bart Roberts with sword or pistol, or even fists. Furthermore, he had a superstitious dread of that sixth sense.

This was altogether a much better idea. Roberts had played right into his hands. His mouth twisted into a thin line, a parody of a smile, his eyes forming two slits in his face.

He went below to the Great Cabin and from habit paused on the threshold. Then he reminded himself that he didn't need to now. He was captain. Roberts had gone.

He crossed to the stern window and peered out into the sudden darkness, just in case Roberts had changed his mind and turned back. But the sloop was nowhere to be seen. Nothing, he decided, and no-one could stop him now. Certainly not Bartholomew Roberts.

David Symson grinned affably at the men assembled in the *Royal Rover*'s great cabin. He was, as the saying went, *in the gun*, having seen off a large quantity of wine already. Raising the glass of dark plum-coloured liquid to the flame of the lantern he examined it thinking that although it wasn't rum, it was surprising what you could get used to when necessary. He smacked his lips. 'Mighty fine wine, this, Irish,' he told Walter Kennedy.

Kennedy folded his arms across his chest and his mouth twisted. 'Portuguese wine,' he said.

Through the fog of drink, Symson thought about it for a moment. 'From the *Sagrada Familia*?' Kennedy had no right to raid the Portuguese ship without his, the quartermaster's, say so, and he was annoyed as well as puzzled. There was wine in plenty on the *Rover*, wasn't there? Why take the stores from the *Sagrada Familia*?

Walter Kennedy sat in the captain's chair at the head of the table, his back to the great stern window, his legs crossed at the ankles on the corner of the table in an attitude reminiscent of the captain. Belatedly, through the fog of inebriation, it occurred to Symson that something wasn't right, but trying to work it out in his sluggish brain was like wading through molasses. He struggled to make his brain work. If only he hadn't drunk so much!

Gradually, he realised that all those sitting around the table had been carefully chosen. Jack Pinder, known for his dislike of Roberts since the *Princess*, and anxious to free himself from the company and make his way home to his wife and child. Himself, because it was well-known that he had once coveted the captain's chair. Tom Sutton because wherever Symson went, so did Sutton. In fact, all of them had been the prize crew on the *Sagrada Familia*, men who had built up an allegiance to Kennedy.

Symson looked at him, noting now the wicked self-satisfied smile, the cruel little eyes screwed up into thin slits. As they rested on him, Symson felt the prickles run up his neck, the stirrings of unease. He had never liked the Irishman, had never liked the cold detached way he took another man's life, as though it were of no value.

Something in Symson's face must have given away his

thoughts, for immediately Kennedy's smile vanished and he took his feet from off the table and sat upright, business-like.

'Something bothering you, Davy boy?' he asked softly.

'No.'

'No—*Captain,*' Kennedy corrected.

All conversation halted abruptly, for the Irishman had their full attention.

Symson's heart began to thud with alarm, and he fought to make his brain work, to understand. But when he spoke, he slurred his words slightly. 'Captain is it? But the captain ain't here.'

'I'm captain now, Davy.'

Symson took a deep breath, once more studying the glass twisting in his long fingers in front of him, but his alarm seemed magically to clear his head. He cursed the quantity of drink inside him, for he knew his life might depend on keeping a clear head now.

Beside him Tom Sutton shifted uneasily in his seat.

'It needs a vote to appoint you captain,' Sutton said.

Now Symson could see why those sitting around the table had been carefully chosen. Those known to favour Roberts had been excluded. No doubt Kennedy expected Symson to cast his lot in with the mutineers. If that were so, Kennedy had misjudged his man, Symson thought fiercely.

'We'll put it to the vote, then,' Kennedy said. 'What say you men? Stay with me and you'll have all the gold and trinkets in the Portuguee and we'll be free to do what we want. We don't need Bart Roberts! We've never needed Bart Roberts and his dainty conscience. Follow me and I'll lead you to England.'

The noise around him told Symson what he didn't want to hear. The vote was in favour of mutiny.

He thought of Captain Roberts, of his brilliance as a leader, as a navigator, tactician. Would there ever be another Captain to be his equal? Certainly not Kennedy! Surely Captain Roberts was owed the loyalty of his men? Symson himself would defend him to his last breath.

With the thought came anger that Kennedy had not the same loyalty towards a man who had fought side by side with them both. It brought him swiftly to his feet, his chair scraping on the bare boards, and then tilting over against the bulkhead with a crash

Kennedy smiled maddeningly. 'Sit down, Davy boy, sit down. I ain't talking to a great mast like you!'

Symson swayed unsteadily, towering over them all. 'You're a traitor, Walter Kennedy!' he cried. 'Damn me, I'll hang you myself if I ever catch up with you!'

Kennedy's hand went into the capacious pocket in his long frock-coat. The threat was implicit. Kennedy would not think twice about using the pistol Symson knew was cocked and primed there. 'Oh aye?'

'Aye!' Symson cried with more bravado than wisdom. 'You bucket of pigs' puke! You couldn't navigate as far as Kourou, let alone England.'

Since Kourou was just ten miles south of their present position on the coast of Guiana and visible from there with the naked eye, it was an insult that brought Kennedy to his feet too.

'I'll show you! I'll show you all. We're going home, back to Ireland, back to England. And I'm taking the *Royal Rover* and the Portuguee. And no-one is going to stop me. Certainly not you, Symson.'

'You won't make it,' Symson retorted angrily.

'Shut your mummer!'

Symson glared at the men crammed into the *Royal Rover*'s hold. It wasn't just the gold, although that was bad enough, and surely Roberts had a right to expect him to defend it with his life, but the ships, the company, everything he had built up into a fighting unit. Roberts had made the *Royal Rover* his flagship, and the *Sagrada Familia* would be disposed of in due course, being too big and sluggish to be of use. Roberts had been on his way to making the company the most formidable pirate fleet in the world. And now Kennedy was breaking it all up.

'So you rob your own shipmates,' he cried, addressing them all, 'men who've fought with you. Cap'n Roberts is the best man you'll ever sail under, don't you know? But you throw your lot in with this—this ape with half a brain! When Roberts comes back he'll hunt you down and kill you himself.'

'But we wants to go home, Mr. Symson,' John Adams whined. 'We got wives, and kidwys, and we wants to go home.'

'And be hanged, damn you!'

Kennedy smiled that evil parody of a smile. 'When Roberts comes back we'll be long gone,' he prophesied.

'You stinking pool of hyena's . . !' Symson reached across the table to grab Kennedy by the throat, intent on strangling the life out of this venomous snake. In his anger his drink-clouded brain forgot the pistol in Kennedy's pocket.

The cabin seemed to explode and Symson felt a thud in the side of his chest. The force of it spun him round away from Kennedy, but he couldn't quite work out what had happened.

Sutton sprang out of his seat in alarm in time to catch Symson's arm to stop him falling. 'Davy? Davy? Are you hit?'

Symson tried to stand, but his legs felt like soggy ropes, and he sagged in Sutton's arms.

Then the pain bit into him, searing agony which made him reel with the force of it. Sweat broke out on his forehead and upper lip, but he shivered with shock.

Unable to hold him Sutton gently set him down on the deck, propping him up against the drinks cupboard in the corner.

Symson put a hand on the wound and brought it away again wet with his own blood. He stared at it transfixed with shock and cursed himself for a fool. He should have remembered the hand on the pistol in Kennedy's pocket. If he hadn't been so drunk, he would have.

Glancing back at Kennedy he saw the neat little hole in his coat pocket, burnt black around its edges where the powder had singed the brown material. His eyes rose to Kennedy's grinning face.

'You can tell Bartholomew Roberts that I'm taking his ships, his crew, and his gold,' he taunted.

Symson tried to answer, but his mouth wouldn't work. Instead, Kennedy seemed to have gone far away. Dimly he heard Sutton cursing and swearing at Kennedy in his panic, as he pressed a kerchief over the wound in Symson's side in an attempt to stop the bleeding.

David Symson lost consciousness.

Kennedy looked at his prone form dispassionately. 'Get rid o'm!'

'Kill 'em? John Adams asked horrified.

Kennedy smiled. He didn't have a grudge against Symson particularly, save for his allegiance to Roberts. For once he could afford to be merciful. 'No. Just send 'em and any who want to go with 'em ashore.'

SEVENTEEN

On the sloop, Roberts made himself at home as best he could in the captain's minute cabin. He could hardly dignify it by the title of Great Cabin, but there was room enough to spread his charts out on the small table. The bunk, too, was small, wedged into a corner of the cabin, so that it was impossible for a man of Roberts' size to stretch himself out comfortably. He would have to find space to hang his hammock. For the short time he intended to be using the sloop, it would do.

He went on deck again, and searched the dark sea around him for any sign of the brigantine which had disappeared in the time it had taken them to get under weigh. He looked in vain for her stern lights which confirmed his suspicions that they had recognised the sloop as a pirate vessel and had killed the lights in order to give them the slip. It was standard practice when pursued. Perhaps she had turned her bowsprit northwards for the Caribbean, safe in the knowledge that the pursuers must continue west-north-west to follow the coastline to Suriname in the hope of overtaking her. There was a feeling in the pit of his belly that told him that might be the case. Still, it was too early to be certain of that. There was always the hope that the brigantine had kept to her original heading, making good speed which had taken her out of sight. If so, they might overtake her yet.

He cursed softly under his breath. On Cane's word he had kept the company tied up at Devil's Island in the hope of following up his Portuguese trick with another decent prize. And more than anything else, he hated failure. He needed this prize, and the next, and the one after that if he were to keep his credibility as captain.

He needed this victory also for his own self-esteem. Letting Lúcia go had hit him hard. There was a great void in his life where she should have been, and he missed her with a physical ache. He should never have let her go, but there had been no alternative. They had both known it was not a permanent arrangement. How could it be, when his only means of making a living was at sea, when he might die in action, or be hanged for a criminal? It was an unwritten rule that new recruits to the company must be unmarried men. But knowing it did not ease the depression that dogged him and made him short-tempered and irritable.

He needed to be busy, to feel the excitement of the chase in his veins, the flush of success at victory. Then he might forget.

It was well past midnight before he turned in, and he slept only a little. Before the grey light of dawn seeped into his cabin from the stern window he was on deck again, feeling as though he hadn't slept at all, with the fear that they had lost the quarry nagging at him.

Glancing first up at the triangular sails, comfortably full with a decent following wind, and then at the wake fanning out astern, he joined Robert Birdson at the helm.

'Speed Mr. Birdson?'

'We just drew in the log, Cap'n. Twelve knots.'

Roberts clicked his tongue thoughtfully as he glanced at the compass in the binnacle. It was fast. More than he had anticipated with such a small area of sail, even allowing for the sloop's small size. 'Current?'

'A strong undertow, Cap'n, taking us west-nor-west.' Birdson had a good many years of sailing experience and had been chosen as the first helmsman of the watch by Thomas Anstis the officer in charge of the starboard watch for his reputation of being able to see in the dark.

'Any sighting of the brigantine.'

'Nope.'

Where the hell is she? Roberts went forward to the forecastle, and stretched out the telescope to a depressingly empty murky grey sea and the still-black western horizon.

Ashplant arrived at his elbow in a puff of tobacco smoke and a whiff of stale rum. 'Anything?'

'No.' But still he trained the telescope on the horizon. If he spotted sail before the man at the masthead, he would have him flogged!

Ashplant grunted and unbuttoned his breeches to relieve himself over the side. 'Know what I think?' he growled helpfully, rebuttoning.

'What?' Roberts snapped.

'Reckon she's clean away. She must have spotted us.'

Certainly there should have been a sign of the ship by now. Oh, she was long gone.

He handed the glass to Ashplant. 'See if you can see anything,' he recommended. The sky was lightening all the time, and visibility improved quickly.

While Ashplant stared through the glass, Roberts leaned on the rail himself. The heat of the previous day had lessened only a little; these latitudes did not produce any real coolness at night. He seemed to live his life soaked with sweat, his shirts clinging to him with the damp. Impatiently he combed his damp hair from his eyes with his fingers and replaced his hat.

Ashplant folded the glass and shot him a sideways glance, judging his mood. 'Nothing.' He gave him back the telescope.

Roberts swore profanely beneath his breath in sheer frustration. Where the Devil was she? Abruptly he turned and went below.

Henry Dennis followed him into the captain's cabin, having just risen from his own hammock. 'Any sign, Bart?' It was a purely rhetorical question, for if there had been a sign, he'd have known about it.

'We've lost her,' Roberts snapped, unable to hide his frustration.

Ashplant ambled in and filled up the remaining space in the captain's cabin, having followed Roberts at a more leisurely pace from the quarterdeck. He was reluctant to leave the chase. 'She can't be far off. She were heading in this direction, and I reckon we should look a bit longer.'

'She's put her lights out and turned the bowsprit northwards,' Roberts said with forced patience. That's what he would have done in the master's position.

'Reckon she knew who we were, then?'

'The way she took off when she saw us, I reckon so,' Dennis agreed.

'What say you?' Roberts asked. 'Do we go back, or do we stay?'

Dennis shrugged. 'She must have given us the slip. We ain't got much in the way of provisions, and Kennedy and Symson will be expecting us.'

Roberts made the decision. 'We'll wait until it is properly light and if there is still no sign, then we'll turn back.'

As they left him, he retrieved the charts for this coast from the chart locker. Before he spread them on the table, he spun the large globe until the great land mass of South America faced him. Devil's Island wasn't even marked. Not that he was surprised. The islands were tiny, hardly worth the cartographer's pen mark.

He spread the charts, weighed them down with his pistols, and frowned at them, looking for likely places where the brigantine might have hidden herself. The charts showed the trading posts established by the English, Dutch and French, from the river Oiapoque in the east, the small Dutch settlement at Aprouage on the Aprouage River, the island of Cayenne, Kourou and Devil's Island. And the English colony of Suriname on the Suriname River. Yes, that was where the brigantine was heading. And if she hadn't turned her bow northwards, she was probably already there and out of reach.

He studied the charts, looking now for shoals, channels and currents as well as landmarks that would identify their position.

Joseph brought him a bowl of porridge and Roberts pushed the charts aside to make room for the wooden dish, and then, on sudden suspicion sniffed the contents. They had left Cook on the *Royal Rover*, but the man they had taken with them in his place had learned at Cook's elbow. Not well enough, though. He must have had the galley fire too hot overnight, for the porridge had the bitter sickly taste and smell of burning, was a strange brown colour, and by the time it reached him, it was already cold.

Roberts eyed it with disfavour and glanced at Joseph, who shook his head. 'He did his best, Cap'n. He says it ain't easy on such a small ship.'

Roberts shook his head too. Taking a deep breath, he forced it down, determined not to let it come up again. He knew better than to waste food. He had suffered worse in the past anyway. He followed it down with water, and then spread the charts on the table again as Joseph took away the wooden bowl and mug.

Dennis and Ashplant joined him a short time later. 'What's our position, then?' Dennis asked, nodding at the charts on the table.

'I've had sight of the coastline,' Roberts said. 'And we are here.'

He pointed with one long finger to a spot on the drawn coastline that had no name, some ten leagues—thirty miles—west of the Moroni River. It was a shock. They had travelled further in the night than any of them would have thought possible. 'We are some thirty-six leagues from Kourou, and Devil's Island. The current is strong here. And the wind.' Both wind and current travelled in the same direction, causing them to move so fast that in one night they had covered a hundred and eight miles. Roberts had an uncomfortable feeling about it, a suspicion that all was not as it should be. He sat down, his back to the window, and puzzled over it.

Dennis said: 'We have definitely lost her then.' He took an agitated turn about the cabin. 'Damn it all, Bart, it ain't like you to make this sort of mistake!'

Roberts felt the sudden swoop of anger inside him. 'Oh?' he prompted.

Ashplant said placatingly: 'We lost sight of her, that's all. 'Twere damned bad luck.'

'Aye. She bolted,' Dennis retorted angrily. 'Anyone could tell you it ain't time to give chase just as night comes on! They put the lights out and sail under cover of darkness, don't you know? And if your head weren't so full of the Portuguese wench, you would have known it!'

Anger turned to cold fury within Roberts at the mention of Lúcia. Whether he knew it or not, Dennis had touched a raw wound. 'Watch your mouth, Mr. Dennis,' Roberts recommended, his voice dangerously quiet.

Ashplant shifted nervously. 'Come on, Henry . . .' he began, but Dennis wasn't listening.

He went on recklessly: 'I'd remind you—*Captain*—that if it weren't for me, you'd still be climbing the blasted yards!'

Roberts glared at him, his anger growing murderous and vindictive. With superhuman effort he kept it under control. 'That will be all, Mr. Dennis,' he said quietly, and rested his hand on one of the pistols in front of him.

Dennis seemed not to notice the implicit warning. 'You ain't fool-proof, Bart Roberts! And I'd remind you that just as the company voted you into office, they can vote you out again!' He didn't add *With a pistol if need be*, but the threat hung in the air.

The metallic clicks of a pistol-hammer being cocked echoed around the small cabin. Henry Dennis froze. The pistol in Roberts' hand pointed at his belly.

'Care to repeat that, Mr. Dennis?' Roberts asked, his voice as cold and menacing as the steel of the pistol.

Valentine Ashplant hovered nervously on the edge of Roberts' vision, uncertain as to what to do.

Dennis wavered nervously, his eyes flicking from the captain to Ashplant and back again as he realised that anger had pushed him too far. Self-preservation came to his aid. He smiled tremulously, and waved both hands at once. 'Hey, Bart, there ain't no need for that now. I didn't mean anything by it!'

'Then you will apologise,' Roberts said evenly.

The smile on Dennis's face flickered. He had no reason to think Roberts would not use the pistol. 'Yes, of course,' Dennis said hastily. 'I apologise. Spoke out of turn.'

He spoke too easily, Roberts thought. It meant nothing. He kept his eyes on Dennis. Dennis struggled. 'Dammit, Bart, you're the best commander I ever sailed under, and that's a fact.'

Roberts continued to study him a little longer. Then he let the hammer down gently, laying the pistol on the table, within reach if necessary.

Ashplant let his breath go in a sigh of relief. Dennis sagged. He had engaged in a battle of wills with the captain, and he had lost. Faith! All he ever wanted was an easy life!

Roberts came to his feet, and tucked the pistols in his belt. 'Call all hands, Mr. Ashplant. We are going back.'

The wind increased, booming in the sails in spurts, like cannon fire, howling through the stays and blocks, bending the mast into an arc and whipping the sea into mountainous peaks that creamed over the little ship's bows in a green wash and drained out through the scuppers.

Roberts glared at the bellying sails as though they were a mortal enemy. But then, at that point, they were, for the wind drove them west when they needed to go east.

'We can't make headway in this, Cap'n,' John Stephenson complained. They had been tacking into the wind all morning, and tacking was akin to slave labour on any vessel. It meant heaving round the sails to alter the set of them in order for them to catch the wind and drive them forward in a zigzagging fashion when the wind came from dead ahead. At best it was slow progress. At worst ineffective. More than once the sails collapsed into uselessness and the ship continued to drift westwards, the wrong direction, in the strong undertow.

Roberts felt the strain. After an hour his voice was hoarse from shouting orders to be heard above the wind. At the end of the morning he was close to losing his voice altogether.

The strong easterly winds buffeted the little sloop sending her crew slithering dangerously across her narrow deck. A brief rainstorm deluged them with all the fury of a Noachian flood and the green sea poured over the bows and washed away in the scuppers with each plunge of the vessel. The men were exhausted from the backbreaking work of hauling round the sails every half an hour or so.

Henry Dennis pushed his luck again by protesting. 'We can't do it, Captain. The wind's in the wrong direction, and the current too strong.'

Roberts said nothing, but he raised the telescope and searched the shoreline.

There was little here to distinguish one part of the mangrove swamp from another, but he could just make out the irregularity of the coastline, the same coastline he had seen first thing that morning. His heart plummeted. They hadn't progressed at all, but rather, had stood still somewhere between the Suriname and the Moroni Rivers.

He gave the order to heave-to, turning the bows directly into the wind, and furl the sails. But even without sail, the current drew them westward and closer towards the land. And it was a treacherous coast.

'Away anchor!' he commanded.

He couldn't risk running aground. The shores, submerged at high tide, were thick oozing mud at low tide, the silt washed up by the currents from the Amazon—and, he'd heard, deep enough to swallow a beached ship. He certainly had no intention of finding out if it were true.

At noon the wind dropped suddenly and the sea flattened miraculously, giving the illusion of solidity, as though a man could walk on it. The heat reflected off the white holystoned decks, turning the sloop into a furnace.

Tired and dispirited, Roberts went below.

When the wind picked up, they tried again. And again. Until the men could hardly stand and the officers could hardly speak. Yet after several days, they still looked out on the same piece of mangrove swamp. They were fighting wind direction and current, and when they were not, they were completely becalmed, a bright white sun scorching them from out of a hot sapphire-blue sky without a breath of wind to ease the furnace-like heat. The sails hung pathetically limp like damp washing, not even stirring. The sea, too, was calm, the little westward-travelling ripples making the water look like thick treacle.

Time and again Roberts panned the shoreline with the

telescope.

Eight days dragged by, and the hardtack ran out.

Despite all their efforts, when Roberts examined the shoreline, the wide flat delta told him they were only at the mouth of the Moroni River. In all, their efforts had advanced them no more than two leagues.

With the food exhausted, Roberts knew he could wait no longer. They must send the boat out now if they were to survive.

He called all hands and put it to them.

'We are here,' he told them, pointing to a place on the chart, which he had brought on deck to show them. They all craned their necks to see, shading their eyes from the white glare of the sun.

'How far?' Robert Birdson asked.

Roberts took a long breath. 'Thirty leagues. At least.' He looked around at their expectant faces. They saw him as some kind of god, he thought despairingly, able to magic them out of any situation. He said, 'We cannot sail back. We are weak now, with no provisions. The ship is being taken by the current against all our efforts and the wind is contrary when it does come up. We have two choices. Either we forget the *Royal Rover* and the Portuguese ship and sail north to the West Indies where we will be bound to find a ship with provisions—' he was interrupted by a groan of protest, and he waited until it subsided, '—or we can send out the boat back to Devil's Island and bring the *Royal Rover* and the prize back here, then sail on to the Caribbean.'

'Thirty leagues is a long way for men to row against wind and current,' Christopher Moody pointed out.

Roberts took a breath. 'Aye.'

They all fell silent as they considered the option. It was a desperate solution.

Seeing their hesitation, Roberts said quietly: 'If we don't do it now, we'll all perish.'

James Phillips moved and Roberts saw the challenge in his eyes. 'You've killed us all! Damn you, Bart Roberts! Damn you to hell!'

Roberts stiffened, angry at the accusation, and his lips drew into a thin line. 'Indeed?' His eyes blazed dangerously.

'You've brung us all on a fool's errand,' Phillips went on recklessly, 'chasing after a brigantine that ain't. And now we're all as good as dead.'

There were murmurs of assent, and Roberts glared at them all, reducing them to instant silence. 'I would remind you, Mr. Phillips, that every man here volunteered,' he said awfully. 'No-one was forced. Any one of you could have stayed behind with Kennedy and Symson. We all knew the risks, the same risks as on any venture. Not one of you recommended caution.'

'Mr. Dennis did!'

Roberts looked around him for the speaker and his smouldering gaze fell on young John Jessup. 'Aye. Mr. Dennis did. And perhaps we should've listened to him. But we chose not to. We chose instead to chase the brigantine while we could. And we all decided together.'

Certainly, he told himself, with the decision a majority vote, they could not lay the blame on him. But he knew he had a persuasive tongue, and that he must therefore bear the largest portion of guilt.

'You're the navigator,' Phillips persisted, growling in his throat. 'You shoulda known about the currents and winds.'

'Have you sailed these waters before, Mr. Phillips?'

'Aye.'

'Did you know about the currents and winds?'

'No, but—'

'Neither did I! I can only know what is written on the charts,' Roberts snapped. What did they expect of him? 'I ain't no seer. Unlike the god-like Captain Teach, I don't have the dubious gift of knowing the unknowable.'

Stung by the reference to his habit of often quoting his former captain, Phillips lapsed into silence. Instead, the big Belgian, Michael Maer spoke up. 'Ninety miles back to the *Royal Rover*,' he repeated, in his thick low-countries accent. He folded his great hard-muscled arms across his bare sun-blackened chest. 'So you intend to send the boat, Cap'n?'

'If I have volunteers enough,' Roberts confirmed.

'I'll go,' Maer said.

His example encouraged others. Another voice cried: 'And I.'

'Me too!'

'And me!'

In the end, eight men crewed the small rowing boat, working in relays.

*****

'There ain't no water left, Cap'n.'

Roberts paused in the act of buttoning his shirt and stared at the man who had taken the place of Cook. Peter Isaacs was a small man, with a peg-leg, which left him unfit for active service, but his willingness to join them from the *Experiment* just out of Prince's and his assurances that he would make a good cook, had persuaded David Symson to sign him on. Unfortunately, his boasts had proved to be little more than wishful thinking. The man was incompetent, not keeping a watchful eye on the stores in his care, nor over the cooking of them on the ship's galley fire.

'None? None at all?'

Isaacs shifted uneasily beneath the captain's glare. 'Well, Cap'n, we gave the last to the boat crew,' he said apologetically.

'Damn you!' Roberts exploded in anger at the enormity of the man's confession. It rubbed salt into wounds left raw and bleeding from the difficult meeting yesterday.

They were two miles off shore, and he had already noted that one of the smaller river tributaries emptied into the sea here. Fresh water was there before them, but their only boat was half way to Devil's Island. They had no means of retrieving it. It would be a week before the boat returned, by which time they would all be dead of thirst.

In his fury he hit the table with his fist with such a crack that Isaacs jumped. 'Damn you, you stupid stinking dung-eating hyena! Do I have to see to everything myself? Didn't it occur to you to keep an eye on it, or to suggest rationing? How do you think we are going to get water now with the boat gone back to Devil's Island?'

Isaacs quailed visibly at the tirade, the colour draining from his face. Bartholomew Roberts in a fury was enough to melt the innards of any man. ''Tain't my fault, Cap'n!' he growled sulkily.

'Then whose fault is it?' Roberts bellowed. His, he supposed, in the long run, like everything else was. Thinking to be away no more than a day or two, they had left Devil's Island without making provision for a long trip. They had water, plenty of it to start with, but there had been no rationing. *Do I have to think of everything?* he demanded of himself. Wasn't that why they had a cook and a quartermaster, as well as a boatswain, and others, so that he could concentrate on the more important tasks?

Isaacs clamped his lips tightly shut.

Roberts combed his hair off his face with his fingers in a

despairing gesture. 'Damn you!' he swore again. 'Don't you realise we will all die because of you? We won't last until the others get back in this heat! Don't you know the lives of every man on board depend on your doing your job properly?'

'I thought we still had a full hogshead—'

'You lazy skulking son of a bitch! If we get out of this I'll have you flogged, damn me if I don't! Get out!'

Isaacs did not need to be told twice. The threat of a flogging was enough to give wings to his one good leg. He turned, grateful to hop out of the danger area on his peg-leg and crutches.

Roberts paced the room in frustration. In his mind's eye he could see the river as it had appeared in the telescope, a different, muddy colour to the clear sea around it, washing silt from the interior to add to the swampy mud flats of the coast. Fresh water. And suddenly an idea occurred to him, so obvious that he wondered that he hadn't seen it before.

'Isaacs!'

The man reluctantly turned back. 'Cap'n?'

'Scald all the barrels, ready to take on water!'

Isaacs stared at him then grinned with relief. 'Aye, aye, Cap'n.'

'And send Mr. Dennis and Mr. Ashplant to see me. And the carpenter. We are going to build a raft, Mr. Isaacs.'

Isaacs grin widened. 'Aye, aye, Cap'n.'

By noon the following day they had fresh water.

The first speck on the eastern horizon brought a cheer from the company, and a rush of relief to Roberts. It had been six days since they sent out the boat, a long agonising wait, and he had hoped for a sighting of the *Royal Rover* before this.

He ran nimbly up the ratlines to the crosstrees—and felt the sudden lurch of dread in his belly. Even with the naked eye he could see it wasn't the *Royal Rover*. It was too small, and the spread of sail almost inconspicuous. And only one vessel. Raising the telescope confirmed it. Only a single triangular sail met his searching eye, the single sail of the pinnace.

Tight-lipped, he searched the skyline in vain for signs of the ships—any ship—sick dread forming like a solid ball in his belly. Something had happened, and his first wild guess was not far short of the truth.

His crew, at first cheering with delight at the approaching vessel, fell silent as it came nearer their disappointment tangible in the searing air.

Roberts came down to wait on the quarterdeck, his lips stretched into a grim line, his face set as though carved out of rock, and his eyes mere slits as he screwed them up against the sun.

'Where's the *Royal Rover*?' someone whispered. 'Where's the Portuguee?'

It took an hour and a half for the boat to pull alongside the sloop, and Roberts and the entire company waited in silence.

The boat crew suffered from heat and toil. They were exhausted, and it showed in their sun-darkened faces and bloodshot eyes. Besides the eight men that had gone out, they brought back three others—David Symson, Tom Sutton and the surgeon George Hunter. That was all.

Roberts waited impatiently for them to come aboard, the big Belgian Michael Maer first, followed by Symson and Sutton and Hunter. For David Symson it was a struggle to climb the ladder, and he needed help to clamber onto the sloop's deck. As he stood in front of the captain he looked tired and pale and haggard, older than his thirty-five years.

Roberts broke the oppressive silence. 'Where's the *Royal Rover* and the *Sagrada Familia*, Mr. Symson?' he asked, and his voice was dangerously calm, his eyes narrowed ominously.

Drawing a painful breath, Symson met Roberts' eyes apologetically. 'Kennedy's taken the *Rover* and the Portuguee and the gold and gone,' he said.

Kennedy! *That murdering double-dealing son of an Irish whore*! The company erupted into outraged protest. Every man had left his chest on board the *Rover* with their share of the gold in it.

Roberts turned away from them, bracing himself with clenched fists on the gunwale. He felt this new blow twist his insides. In a few weeks he had lost Lúcia, caught an almost worthless sloop, chased a non-existent brigantine, been caught in contrary winds and current, almost lost his crew to thirst and near starvation and now this. He seemed dogged by the worst possible luck.

Unnerved by the captain's silence, young Tom Sutton spoke up above the outraged crew. 'Davy did try to stop 'em, Cap'n. Kennedy shot him.'

'Damn near killed him, too,' George Hunter added. 'A little

more to the right . . .'

'How many went with him?' Henry Dennis asked as Roberts still did not speak.

'All the rest. Forty or more.'

'John Adams?'

'Aye. They all voted on it. Said they wanted to get home to England, and their women.'

'What they wanted was the rest of the booty,' Dennis said, and the others joined in noisy agreement.

Ashplant rubbed his whiskery chin. 'Kennedy can't navigate. How're they going to get to England?'

'P'raps they'll wreck somewhere, and good riddance!' Richard Hardy put in with vicious anticipation.

Roberts found his voice. 'Damn their eyes! Damn their double-dealing murdering eyes! Blood and thunder! In the name of all that is sacred . . .!' He struggled for some semblance of self-control. But it was a severe blow, not just in material terms, but also to his authority, his command. There were no words to express the fury inside him. He turned and thumped the solid mast with his fist, bruising his hand and wrist, but not noticing the pain. 'Damn his treacherous blood! Damn him to hell! Damn all of them!'

EIGHTEEN

April 1720, Caribbean

Roberts cast his eyes over the sloop's decks and felt a good deal of satisfaction. The watch had sweated up to tighten the lines to the accompaniment of a chorus or two of a good sing-out, and now the wake panned out in a lugubrious white froth astern. The little ship, which they had christened the *Fortune* had a decent cruising speed, her bowsprit slicing through the green waves as they roared over the forecastle deck and washed away in the scuppers.

Already in the last three days they had taken two sloops and a brigantine which had supplied their immediate needs. It felt good to have a belly-full of decent food and in the hold a welcome supply of provisions. Still, it wasn't enough. It was never enough. Provisioning the ship was always a constant worry for the quartermaster and captain of any vessel and it never ceased to amaze Roberts at the rate a well-stocked hold emptied. But then his crew was not rationed the way some, particularly English sailors, were.

A day after these successes they had taken a Bristol galley called the *York*, coincidentally commanded by a man called James Phillips, bound for Barbados. The *York* proved to be a fine ship, broad-built and flush from bow to stern, and certainly larger than the *Fortune* sloop, and perhaps better fitted for their purposes. Roberts considered the possibility and kept her for three days while his crew gleefully relieved her of a large quantity of clothes, money, goods, gunpowder, cables and a hawser, and provisions, as well as five men who eagerly signed the new articles Roberts had had drawn up to give cohesion to his fragmented company.

The galley, however, was too sluggish for Roberts' needs, the sloop having the advantage of speed and manoeuvrability, and he allowed Captain Phillips to take her away. It was a mistake that would cost him.

However, the galley had been a good prize. He had regained the confidence of his men, and the disaster of the *Sagrada Familia* and Walter Kennedy slipped away into the past.

Ashplant's head suddenly appeared above the level of the quarterdeck and he stumbled up the steps, clutching his greasy black hat to his head in case it blew off in the stiff breeze. He looked about him, blinking owlishly in the harsh sunlight, and lurched towards the side to catch hold of the gunwale. Each roll of the ship exaggerated his unsteadiness.

Too much rum, Roberts thought with an inward shake of his head. That was the trouble with finding supplies. Most of the crew were *in the gun* most of the time, and he thought ruefully of the articles he had just drawn up which had allowed them unlimited access to the rum, wine and ale, while it lasted. But then, they wouldn't work on less.

As he staggered towards the captain, Ashplant fixed him with clouded grey eyes. Not a man who was fair of face, drink and debauchery had taken their toll on Ashplant's russet-coloured skin, and with bulging red-rimmed eyes and a week's worth of black stubble on his chin, Roberts thought he had to be one of the ugliest brutes he had ever encountered.

Ashplant rasped his whiskery chin with his open hand, continued rubbing his bulbous nose, and then his forehead, knocking his hat further back on his head in the process, as though to rub away the thudding Roberts knew must be going on behind those bloodshot eyes.

'Feeling rough, Ash?' Roberts asked with an unsympathetic grin.

Ashplant eyed him suspiciously. ''Twere a damned good night,' he growled with satisfaction. Smoking and drinking had roughened his voice still further so that it sounded like gravel crunching underfoot.

Roberts laughed. 'Not such a good day, though. You should try sobriety, my friend.'

Ashplant stared at him as though his brain couldn't comprehend such a thought. 'Sobriety? Ah—ye daft Welshman. I sure as hell didn't go adventuring to get sober!' And he turned away disgusted.

Roberts chuckled. He had learned to put up with them, and their excesses didn't detract from his enjoyment of the adventurer's life, the constant excitement, the riches, the freedom. And that most precious commodity, his own command. While he could keep the crew in check, all would go well. Only the memory of Lúcia clouded his sense of well-being, slipping in at odd moments, despite his best efforts, to worry and nag him anew.

'*Sail ho*! Deck there, *Sail ho!*'

Immediately Roberts jumped up onto the gunwale and

scrambled up the ratlines where he clung with practised ease, while he levelled the telescope to scan the horizon. Sure enough, two triangles of white sat on the horizon.

He felt the familiar blood-rush in his veins. True, a good many ships surrendered willingly to the pirates, hoping thereby to be treated leniently, but the thrill of the chase and the unexpected never dulled.

As he came down he began bellowing his commands, and also called the musicians. 'Beat to quarters!' and immediately the roll of the drum brought from below those laggards who had not been roused by the lookout's cry.

Roberts went to the helm. 'Mr. Stephenson—bring her about if you please.'

John Stephenson gave the order to the boatswain, and Christopher Moody filled his great lungs and bellowed: 'Look alive there!'

Men, still groggy from too much rum, heaved on the halyards, their bodies at an angle to the deck, the muscles of their sun-scorched torsos bulging and glistening with oily sweat. Swiftly the boom swung round, and as they sheeted home, the wind filled the sail.

'Helm down!' John Jessup at the helm bellowed, and Roberts braced himself as the ship began to turn, and the deck beneath his feet canted sharply.

Slowly, slowly, the little sloop came about, paying off to leeward.

But it took too long. Only a man asleep could have failed to spot the pirate sloop's turn, and Roberts struggled to swallow his impatience.

'Make ready the guns!' he ordered, and Ashplant, suddenly cold sober in all the excitement, strode with almost steady steps forward, growling his orders to the gun crews.

Watching them scurrying back and forth with buckets of sand and water, clearing the decks of clutter, and loading for the first round of fire, Roberts felt a good deal of pride in them. Ashplant, Dennis and Symson had trained them in slack times, and their reward lay in the quick efficiency with which they cleared for action. It took just ten minutes from the time they first spotted the quarry.

The intended victims, a galley showing her stern to the pirates and beside her, yardarm to yardarm, a sloop, matching her for speed, flying English and Barbadian colours, held their course, evidently unaware of the danger the oncoming sloop presented. Roberts smiled to himself. Perhaps the lookouts were asleep after all. Or perhaps they were fooled by the sloop's smallness. But the little ship's swiftness lay in her size. She gained on the unsuspecting victims quickly.

'Raise the black jack,' Roberts ordered, and the black flag with the white death's head and hour-glass and the crossed swords, the one the crew had facetiously dubbed *the Jolly Roger* fluttered from the mast as the expanse of water between the ships shrank. Roberts grinned. It had become so routine now.

He glanced down the ship to the forecastle where men crouched beside the small forward-pointing swivel, the bow-chaser, ready and waiting for the order. He couldn't fault them.

They came closer to the intended victims, just a little over a quarter of a mile from them. They must have been seen by now, with the death's head promising quarter if they yielded.

But the two ships did not strike their colours.

'Do they think to outrun us?' Dennis asked, his brows meeting above his nose.

'They can try.' But since leaving Guiana no ship had challenged the black flag. All had surrendered. And he was surprised that in this case the English ships had not already struck their colours.

'Bow chaser ready?'

'Ready, Cap'n.' It was loaded with man-slaughtering grapeshot, as were all the swivels.

'Steady as she goes,' Roberts told the man at the helm.

He judged the distance, the rise and fall of the vessel, not wishing for a hit, but a warning.

'Fire!'

The moments ticked by, then the small gun mounted on the forecastle gunwale belched smoke and flame.

As he had expected the shot splashed harmlessly into the sea, neatly between the two victim ships.

He watched them closely through the telescope, expecting the colours to slide down the masts, but the flags fluttered still at the mastheads.

Something was wrong. He trained the telescope on the decks of the galley, and his stomach turned over, for the galley's deck was alive with men, far more than he would expect on a merchant vessel, and a group of them were leaning back, heaving on the braces, heaving round the yards to turn the ship.

'Hell's teeth!' With the danger suddenly apparent, he had to act quickly. He could stand and fight, but with only ten guns to the galley's twenty, and the sloop's ten, he was seriously out-gunned.

'Bring her about!' he bellowed. 'Hell's teeth! Mr. Stephenson, bring her about!'

Immediately, others took up the cry and the *Fortune*'s decks came alive as men ran in all directions to bring the sails round to turn her.

Now Roberts could see the quarter-circle described in the sea by the galley's wake as she turned. Her gun ports opened and two rows of gleaming black muzzles stuck out from her side.

Now very much alarmed, Roberts felt his heart thud in his chest. They were caught naked, exposed, with the *Fortune*'s side to the galley's guns, a sitting target.

'Get those damned yards round, for God's sake!' Roberts bellowed like a man possessed.

Now at last the sloop began to respond, turning agonisingly slowly to starboard in the opposite direction to the galley, putting the wind behind them to run with the wind on the beam reach which the *Fortune* liked best of all, and which he hoped the galley wouldn't, although her fore-and-aft rigging didn't allow this hope to rise too high.

The galley's guns roared into life as each gun along her larboard side exploded in fire and smoke in succession. The dreadful noise seemed to go on forever, as did the scream of cannonballs tearing through the air like demons of death. Time seemed to stop and Roberts held his breath, waiting in horror for the first of them to find a home in the little sloop's side. They were close enough to receive the full force of the shot. All he could hope for was that the waves unsettled the aim.

A ball crashed through the sloop's side in a screech of splintering wood. Dennis stared at it in horror, and Roberts felt as though the deck beneath his feet had turned to mud. Fortunately the hole was above the water line, but each plunge of the *Fortune* would send water into her.

The deck erupted in chaos. Men were injured by the splintering wood, and other flying fragments. They screamed and cried, and blood poured from them over the decks. Two men were dead.

Roberts had to close his mind to their agony. He had a job to do, and he snapped out his orders in quick succession. 'Get those men below! Man the pump! Sand the decks! For God's sake, Mr. Stephenson, get us out of here!'

As the *Fortune* came about, the gunners had come to the five guns on the starboard side. It was pathetic enough. The galley had shown him ten guns on the larboard side. He could show only five.

'Make ready the gun! Load!' He raised his sword and waited for the rise of the wave, and then brought his arm down. '*Fire!*'

The sloop shuddered as though her very seams would be shaken apart and the galley was obscured by a smoke pall until it blew away on the wind.

They had missed.

As the sloop came fully round, Roberts began to breathe again. Now she presented a smaller target and she was running away from them, gaining speed. They couldn't fire a broadside at this angle, but with relief came anger. Damn them! They had attacked him! How dared they even consider it?

'Give us more sail, Mr. Stephenson!'

Stephenson bellowed his orders, and men rigged up extra spars from the boat oars and lashed them in place, lashing the spare sails to them.

Roberts left them to it, turning his attention again to his pursuers. And the relief died. The galley had come in behind him, and was gaining, her master using the sweeps or oars now protruding from her side to give him more speed.

Roberts' heart became a solid ball in his chest with dread. Worse, the almost-forgotten Barbadian sloop appeared off the larboard side, and was now broadside to broadside. And its guns began bellowing at him.

But it was the swivels that caused the most damage, cutting down his men with their murderous grape and chain shot. His only chance was to get ahead of them. Yet he knew the two sloops were evenly matched for speed. He hoped the bigger and heavier galley would be more sluggish, although she carried a good deal more sail than either sloop.

As the Barbadian sloop ran out her guns Roberts swore profanely. His orders were lost in the terrifying explosion of the Barbadian's guns, and Roberts waited for the crash and splintering of wood which would signal that they had been hit. If they took down one of the masts, the game would be up.

But once more they were spared as the sloop had fired at the wrong rise of the wave and the balls fell beside the pirate sending a plume of water into the air which soaked everyone on board.

Word came: 'Larboard guns ready.'

'Fire as your guns bear.'

Once more the *Fortune* gave back fire. Acrid smoke filled the air as gun after gun fired. The very air shuddered with the noise.

But now the *Fortune* had found her wind, and the extra sails rigged up filled, pushing her forward.

Astern the galley had made the mistake of sailing into the wind as she came about and her sails collapsed so that she lost precious time, allowing Roberts to put some distance between him and his pursuers. Through the glass he could see the men struggling with rebellious sail as she foundered. In a few minutes they had her on course again, but it gave Roberts a breathing space.

The Barbadian sloop still fired at them, but now only from her forward guns. Clearly her men were not competent, despite her captain's best efforts, and the shots fell wide. But she stayed on his tail, doggedly giving chase, the way he had once seen a cheetah stay on the heels of an antelope as it ducked and weaved until it eventually brought it down in death.

For all the pirates' efforts, and the little sloop responded well, they could not pull any further ahead. Now the galley gained on them, also firing from her bow.

The sloop's guns were useless like this, and Ashplant abandoned his post as gunner. 'We can't outrun them, Cap'n,' he said.

Roberts' mouth was set in a grim line. He remembered the *York,* bound for Barbados, and Captain Phillips, and his anger seethed. No doubt he had given a full report to Governor Lowther. *This is what you get for showing mercy and letting them go free,* he told himself. *You'll get yourself hanged, Bart Roberts.*

He made a decision. 'Lighten the ship. Throw the guns overboard. And the shot. And the goods in the hold.'

Dennis, Ashplant, Phillips, Symson and Anstis, the five most senior officers, turned to him. They knew what it meant. Nothing to defend themselves with. Nothing to trade with. All they had worked and fought for and risked life and limb for, gone overboard.

But Roberts was the captain. Any man who disobeyed his orders during action would be liable to be shot.

A cannonball whistled past and Roberts found he was praying to a God he had long since forgotten.

'Lighten the ship!' he repeated the order, and then bellowed to the crew above the din: 'Lighten the ship!'

Frantically the hands got to it. As Symson went below with some others to supervise the emptying of the hold, the gun crew slashed the ropes that held the first black cannon fast, waited for the roll of the ship and then heaved on the side tackles, cutting it free at the last moment. The ship heeled over and the first cannon burst through the gunwale in a screech of splintering wood. The gun seemed to hover on the edge and then slowly tipped over and into the sea.

Tight-lipped, Roberts watched them go one after the other. A pirate's advantage lay in his guns and the trained men to fire them. He tried to console himself with the two swivels mounted on the gunwale at the bow, but it wasn't the same as cannon.

He turned his attention aft. The Barbadian sloop sat doggedly on his stern. His disappointment was intense, and for a moment it surfaced in anger. One day he would make the Barbadians pay for this. And as for any Bristol merchantman, well they could expect no mercy from Bartholomew Roberts in future!

With an effort, he concentrated on the job in hand. Later he could plan his revenge, but for now he must put his anger aside. Everything depended on his keeping a cool clear head.

They needed more speed. With the guns gone, it was the turn of the cargo. Symson chose wisely, keeping easily-sold goods as future insurance. But the gunpowder went, and twenty-five bales of other goods.

Now when Roberts looked back, to his unspeakable relief, he could see the distance between them and the Barbadians had lengthened. At last he dared hope they might get away.

Still the sloop fired her bow chasers intermittently, but they had only a short range, and the *Fortune* had pulled beyond it. But those murderous swivels had done their job, as the blood painted on the decks bore eloquent testimony.

Gradually the Barbadian sloop fell further behind and at last gave up the chase, finally disappearing below the horizon.

Roberts left the taffrail, and closed the telescope. His legs seemed to be soft, like sponge, and he gripped the telescope tightly lest it should be noticed that his hands trembled. Still, he strode purposefully to where John Stephenson peered at the compass in the binnacle.

The crew had assembled on the deck, and at the sight of him they began to cheer as though they had won a great victory rather than escaped from certain death, and he felt a great rush of affection for them all. They had worked well, obeying his orders without question. He cast his eyes over the shattered guard-rails, and the decks spread with blood and skin tissue and a wave of nausea washed over him. It could have been a good deal worse, of course. The Barbadians could have sunk them. Or brought down a mast. It would have been hand to hand fighting then, and with the number of dead and wounded, they would not have been able to fight them off.

'What's the toll?' he asked.

'Five dead,' Tom Sutton told him. And he listed them.

Roberts listened gravely. Good men all. Four of them had been with Davis.

'And two the doc says won't make it.'

Roberts nodded.

'And eight more wounded. Damned grapeshot!'

Roberts shook his head. Fifteen men down, that left him thirty-five. It was a heavy toll, and he needed to replace those men as soon as possible.

'Course, Cap'n?'

He turned to John Stephenson waiting by the helm.

Roberts thought about it. He needed to replace the guns, and to make repairs, besides giving his men some time off. In their escape from the Barbadians they had run with the wind abaft the beam on the starboard side, driving them north by north-west. In his mind's eye he visualised the islands northwards. Saint Lucia and Martinique he rejected as too populous, each with a governor.

'Dominica,' he said at last. 'I'll give you the heading directly.'

With the need to acquire provisions and water and men of equal importance as finding a place to careen and repair the sloop, Roberts sailed into Dominica's Prince Rupert's Bay and anchored in Portsmouth harbour. Half a dozen ships were anchored there, for it was a favourite watering and provisioning stop. French and English ships stood side by side in the clear blue waters of the bay, their reefed masts like a winter forest of nude trees.

But this time he wasn't interested in accosting other shipping. His need was to re-arm his ship and allow his men some well-earned shore-leave. Besides, he was unhappy with Dominica. The encounter with the Barbadians had put him on edge and he was anxious to be gone. Accordingly, as soon as he had made the necessary repairs, and re-armed and re-provisioned the sloop, he cancelled shore leave and sailed away for Carriacou in the Grenadines where he could careen in safety.

On the day that Roberts sailed out of Dominica, the governor of Martinique received a visit from the captain of a French ship just arrived from Dominica. Accordingly the governor equipped two sloops and gave them a commission to look for the English pirate Bartholomew Roberts in Carriacou which, the French captain was reliably informed, was the pirates' next destination.

However, Carriacou did not suit the pirates' needs, for there were no women and no wine. As a result they careened with dispatch and sailed within a week.

When the Martinican sloops hauled into Carriacou, they found the pirates gone. They had missed them by no more than a few hours.

NINETEEN

Autumn, 1720, London

The First Lord of the Admiralty pointed his fat buttocks towards the blazing logs in the grate, raising the skirts of his coat so that he could feel the benefits of the invigorating warmth. The weather had turned surprisingly cold, with a brisk north wind blowing sheets of rain across the country, and the cold damp had penetrated every corner of the Admiralty offices.

His lordship suffered with the cold more than most. Certainly the other men seated around the large highly-polished walnut-veneered table seemed less prone to the cold than his lordship. If anything they seemed to consider it warm in the Admiralty office. Sir William even mopped his brow with a lace handkerchief beneath the flowing white curls of his powdered wig.

'One thing is certain,' Sir William said to the First Lord and the Rear Admiral, 'if we do not put a stop to this abomination no ship is safe in any waters.'

'You think Ogle is the man for the job?' the First Lord asked. There had been much debate as to whom should command this enterprise.

'Ogle has proved himself in times past. I think he has as much chance as any.'

The First Lord's secretary coughed deprecatingly from the door. 'Captain Chaloner Ogle and Captain Mungo Heardman, my lord.'

His lordship eyed the large oval table in the centre of the room. It would be cold over there, away from the fire. He sighed resignedly and nodded to his secretary, taking a step away from the fire and straightening up. 'Very well. Send them in.'

The secretary bowed and disappeared.

'What do we know of Captain Ogle?' the Rear Admiral asked.

The First Lord came and sat down. 'Thirty years old, he distinguished himself in the war with successful sorties. A man more than capable of dealing with a few pirates.'

'Captain Chaloner Ogle and Captain Mungo Heardman, my lord,' the secretary announced gravely.

Even if the First Lord had not already been acquainted with Captain Chaloner Ogle he would not have had any difficulty recognising him as the more senior and experienced of the two captains standing before him. He had a calm authority about him and was alternately feared, hated, and respected by his men. His lordship could well believe it.

Not above average height, he had put on a little weight since his lordship had last seen him. But he was not fat, only a little full in the face. Beneath a neat small white powdered wig, his brown eyes surveyed all around him with analytical thoroughness, a habit which his lordship found particularly unnerving, especially as he was the object of that disconcerting gaze for several moments before Ogle bowed solemnly. 'Your servant, my lord.'

Captain Mungo Heardman was different altogether. Five years younger than Ogle, he still had the fresh enthusiasm of youth. He wore no wig, but his red-gold curls were forced off his freckled face into a ribbon at the nape of his neck. He was not personally known to his lordship, and only recently promoted to his own command, he had not had the opportunity to distinguish himself. He too bowed and muttered politely.

His lordship introduced them to their lordships of the admiralty, and indicated chairs for them around the table.

'Well, gentlemen, we have called you here on a matter of the utmost urgency.' he began. 'This is a trading nation. We depend on the trade from overseas, and we depend on outgoing trade reaching its destination. But as you have no doubt heard, Captain Ogle, a great deal of that trade is going astray.'

'There have been questions asked in Parliament,' Sir William put in. 'Even the King has asked us to intervene.'

Captain Ogle studied the First Lord with that disconcerting gaze. 'I collect you are referring to the recent increase in pirate attacks, my lord.'

It was the talk of the taverns, how the pirates ruled the Atlantic, how no man was safe at sea, how ship owners could be ruined because of their depredations, and how insurers had put up their premiums to cover claims. And now that Edward Teach, alias Blackbeard, was dead, and Kidd now long in the past, one name came up more times than any other—Bartholomew Roberts.

The First Lord nodded sagely. 'I am indeed. We have received complaints from the Caribbean, Guinea, and even the Indian Ocean.' He sifted through the pile of papers in front of him. 'From the Caribbean we have complaints from Governor Lowther of Barbados about a certain Bartholomew Roberts and his crew, and also from a Captain Carey of the *Samuel*, whose ship was taken by the same company. This Roberts attacked the fisheries at Newfoundland which terrified everyone and ruined the fisheries this year. Even the damned French have complained about him.'

'Do we know anything about him?' Captain Mungo Heardman asked, and dabbed unobtrusively at his upper lip with his handkerchief; the heat in the room was intense, and the sweat poured out of him.

The Rear Admiral said: 'Most of what we know comes from a Captain Carey whose ship the *Samuel* was taken by Roberts in the summer. He says that he is a tall good-looking man, dark, speaks with a Welsh accent, and that he sailed in company with the pirate Howell Davis whose company decimated the African coast until he was killed and Roberts assumed command. Roberts is a far bigger threat to British trade than Davis, or in fact any other man. He has been known to take three ships in one day! The Portuguese governor of Salvador in Brazil complains that he attacked a squadron of forty-two ships and sailed off with the richest which contained a fortune in gold and jewels bound for the King of Portugal.'

'Did he indeed?' Sir William put in, impressed.

The First Lord went on: 'The governor of Barbados—'

'General Lowther, my lord,' whispered his secretary.

'—General Lowther, sent out two ships after this Roberts, but he escaped. The governor of Martinique sent out two sloops also, but they did not find him. He has raided the New England coast and Governor Spottswood of Virginia has put up batteries with forty-five pieces of cannon at strategic points as a protection against this man. He raided the French off the Newfoundland Banks destroying all their ships.' He sifted through his papers. 'Lieutenant-General Matthew here writes that Roberts attacked him at Basseterre in St. Kitts, destroying shipping and causing havoc.' He looked up at them all. 'This man must be stopped.'

'Is he still on the American eastern seaboard?' Ogle asked.

Once more his lordship rifled through the papers in front of him. 'Captain Carey of the *Samuel* writes that they had the intention of sailing for the Guinea Coast.'

Sir William said: 'That is where we want you to search for him, Captain Ogle.'

Ogle frowned. 'Certainly, with all the governors in the

Caribbean ranged against him it will be difficult for him to sell his plunder there.'

Mungo Heardman said to Ogle: 'Sierra Leone?'

Ogle nodded. 'There is a colony of English and French and Portuguese at Sierra Leone, gentlemen, living among the Negroes, who trade with any ship that anchors and no questions asked. Indeed, it is said that some of them are retired pirates themselves. It would be a good place to begin looking. I doubt there is a pirate on that coast that has not put into Sierra Leone.'

'You seem to know the area, Captain,' the Rear Admiral said.

Ogle nodded. 'It is a labyrinth of swampy rivers and channels, mangrove swamp mostly, a disease-ridden hole. Ideal, if you want to lose a ship, or you have goods to trade. And the women are amenable, too.'

The First Lord coughed. 'Well, quite so.'

'What I mean is, it is just the sort of place a man like Roberts would take his company. You are sure he intends to go to Africa?'

The First Lord frowned at the report in front of him. 'Yes indeed. Captain Carey says that they told one of the men they pressed into service—his mate, a man called Harold Glasby who is a sailing master and who had no wish to join them—that they intended to go to Guinea. He reported this to Captain Carey.'

'So we are bound for Guinea?' Ogle asked confirmation.

'Just so. Here are your orders.' He handed him a folded and sealed sheet, and another to Mungo Heardman, 'And you, Captain Ogle are to command the *Swallow* and Captain Heardman the *Weymouth*. You will sail in company with six other merchant vessels for the Guinea Coast in search of Roberts, or indeed any other pirates, and you will put yourself at the disposal of Governor General James Phipps of Cape Coast.'

Sir William added: 'You, Captain Ogle, will command the squadron as commodore.'

Captain Chaloner Ogle was singularly unimpressed with his promotion, and to search for outlaws was hardly on a par with battling it out with an enemy squadron. On the other hand, who had not heard of Bartholomew Roberts? News of his deeds, greatly exaggerated, no doubt, had spread the length of the British Isles.

He thought about it as his lordship droned on about the ships which would sail in company with him. Bartholomew Roberts was a clever rogue. He had the wit and the experience to get clear of the

Barbadian ships sent to apprehend him. He knew the waters around the Caribbean like the back of his hand, and probably around the Guinea Coast, too. He had attacked a Portuguese squadron of forty-two ships off the Brazilian coast and come away with their prize ship. This was no mere amateur. This man knew his job. Not eight years previously when the Spanish war of Succession came to an end with the signing of the Treaty of Utrecht, thousands of sailors who had fought in the British navy in war had suddenly found themselves out of work. These were men trained in the art of warfare at sea—as well-trained as any naval company. It would not do for Captain Ogle to underestimate his quarry. Captain Roberts was just as likely to have served in one of His Majesty's ships during the war, and if he had any kind of brain, he would know the strategies of warfare as Ogle did himself, as would many in his company.

The Rear Admiral spoke up. 'This Roberts has taken over a hundred ships at the last count—possibly nearer two hundred.'

Mungo Heardman let his breath go in a long whistle.

The First Lord said: 'Catch this pirate, Captain Ogle, and England shall be forever in your debt.'

Ogle and Heardman came to their feet and bowed politely. Mungo Heardman said: 'By God's grace, my lord, we shall see Bartholomew Roberts hang.'

'May God go with you, gentlemen,' the First Lord said.

Outside the fog had descended on London in a thick choking blanket, hanging cold and dark around them.

'The *Weymouth*, eh?' Mungo Heardman said, by no means displeased.

'And the *Swallow*.' Ogle too was pleased. The *Swallow*, like the *Weymouth* was a third-rater, with sixty guns on two decks. But the *Swallow* was just two years out of the Chatham dockyard, and was swifter than the *Weymouth*. Good ships, both of them.

Heardman opened the seal on his orders. 'We sail from Spithead in January.'

Ogle nodded. 'Good.' It gave Ogle time to see his family, before the task of bringing together his officers and raising a crew and provisioning his ship.

However, neither their lordships of the Admiralty, nor the captains would have been so confident had they known that Bartholomew Roberts was not where they thought he was.

TWENTY

1720, off the West African Coast

David Symson came into the Great Cabin after noon, and stood with his hand on the overhead beam, staring at the charts on the table as if he could make sense of them from that distance, before raising his eyes questioningly to the captain's face.

'We're off course,' Roberts said depressively. 'We cannot hope now to make landfall. How is it topside?'

Symson shook his head. 'Harry Glasby's run the legs off 'em, but we can't make headway.'

Roberts compressed his lips. He felt sick to the pit of his stomach. He had ordered Christopher Moody the boatswain to make out a tacking and wearing bill, in an effort to make it to the coast. He had known what their protests must be before even they voiced them. 'We can't do it, Captain,' he'd protested, 'we're in the teeth of a dead nuzzler.'

'Do it,' he had snapped, at the end of his patience with them.

He said now: 'And the *Fortune's* no better, I suppose?' They had attempted once before to tack the sloop into a contrary wind with no success. Why should it be different this time? And the new ship, the *Royal Fortune*, was more difficult to manoeuvre when it came to tacking, being square rigged and carrying more sails. She was also slower to respond.

'Nope.' Symson approached the table. 'Where are we, do you think?'

Robert shrugged his shoulders and drew a circle on the chart with his forefinger which encompassed a thousand square miles of the eastern Atlantic. 'Anywhere here. But one thing I do know. We are not *here!*' and he stabbed the Cape Verde Islands off the west coast of Africa viciously with his forefinger.

How could they have missed those islands? Because the drunken sots who had deserted their posts during the night and tied up the *Royal Fortune's* wheel had allowed it to happen. Now they had come too far south, and hit the north-east trade winds which sailors relied on to take them from Africa to the Americas. But they had just come from the Caribbean.

'What food and water do we have?' he demanded curtly.'

Anticipating the question, Symson had already checked.

'Food—three barrels of salt beef, oatmeal, hardtack.' He paused and met Roberts' eyes squarely. 'A single hogshead of water.'

Roberts' stomach slid sickeningly as the import of this information hit him. He swore. There were a hundred and twenty-four men on the *Royal Fortune*, and a hogshead of water would not last long between them. It wouldn't help in the decision he knew he must make. 'What about the sloop?'

The *Fortune* sloop had a crew of ninety-six.

'About the same.'

'Hell's teeth!' He knew then that they could not make it. He paused as the door opened and all the other officers of the company filed in solemnly, including those who had rowed over from the sloop.

'Sit down, gentlemen,' Roberts invited. This was not going to be easy. There were no words that could soften the blow.

'Gentlemen,' Roberts began at last, 'I have to tell you that we are somewhere here.' He stabbed at the chart with his finger. 'As you know we have been some hours tacking into the wind in order to make landfall on the African coast, without making headway.' He paused and looked at them all. They relied on him. He felt sick at the thought. 'Gentlemen, our situation is dire. We have just one hogshead of water between all one hundred and twenty-four men on this ship, and about the same for the ninety-six men on the *Fortune*.' Thomas Anstis nodded his cannonball head in confirmation of this fact. 'If we keep striving for the shore, we will all perish. As I see it, we have just one option—to turn back for the Caribbean.'

'That's six weeks away,' Henry Dennis pointed out quietly.

Roberts nodded, and tried to sound positive. 'A month with favourable winds. If we carefully ration the water to, say, one mouthful a man in twenty-four hours . . .'

The suggestion appalled them all, and they immediately roared their disapproval. Roberts didn't answer them, but waited for them to stop protesting and start thinking. As they fell silent, they looked at each other, working it out, just as he had done, seeking another option.

George Hunter, the surgeon, was the first to speak. 'We won't make it. A man cannot survive a month on one mouthful of water a day. Certainly not in this heat. You are condemning us all to death!'

'Then what would you suggest?' Roberts asked quietly. 'Because if any of you knows of some other way, let us all hear it.'

George Hunter glared at him from across the table. 'I ain't a sailor. I don't know.'

'The fact is, gentlemen, we have no choice but to try to make it back to the Caribbean.'

The surgeon's patience snapped, and he stood up, leaning on the table towards the captain. 'Well if you are determined on this course, I cannot stop you. But I tell you, Captain Roberts, it cannot be done! We will all perish!'

Roberts said steadily: 'While we value your opinion, Mr. Hunter, nevertheless you have not signed the articles.' He paused to let the reprimand find a home. As a surgeon, Hunter was not strictly speaking part of the company. He had not signed the ship's articles, and therefore, did not have a say in the running of the company. He looked earnestly at the rest of them. 'If we continue trying to make the African coast, we *will* all die. The winds won't let us make landfall. We have to make the decision now.'

Hunter marched to the door. 'Well, I'm glad I haven't got it on my conscience. But as long as you are bent on this course, you can tell them from me that if any man drinks seawater, or urine, he will go insane and die. Tell them that!' He opened the door, but turned back to say awfully: 'May God forgive you, Captain Roberts!'

The door snapped shut on the latch behind him, and Roberts looked down at his hands resting flat on the table. A large ruby ring glittered on the third finger of his left hand, a jewel from the *Sagrada Familia*'s hold. He would gladly have sacrificed it for more water—or for favourable winds.

The surgeon was right, of course. A man couldn't live a month on just a mouthful of water a day. He knew there was little chance of any of them making it to the Americas alive. He knew too that death by thirst had to be one of the most agonising. He was sentencing them all to die.

Harry Glasby came unexpectedly to his rescue: 'I know these waters, and I know this wind. We cannot make it to land here. We have to turn back.'

Roberts looked at him gratefully.

Valentine Ashplant rubbed the flat of his hand across his bristly chin. 'Well, if Harry Glasby says so, then damn me, there ain't nothing else to do!'

William Main, five feet eleven and fifteen stone, had a shrewd and calculating way about him. He had been picked up off

Newfoundland and was an appointed officer on the *Fortune* sloop. He thoughtfully traced an invisible pattern on the table with his forefinger, and he asked without looking up: 'What put us off course, Commander?'

Symson replied in Roberts' stead. 'The watch was drunk. They tied up the wheel and it worked loose. We drifted in the night.'

The cabin erupted into a volley of oaths that Roberts quietened by waving his hands. 'The men responsible shall be dealt with.'

'I don't like it,' Anstis said.

'None of us likes it, Mr. Anstis,' Roberts said tartly. 'But we've got no choice. While we sit here arguing, we are wasting precious time. The wind blows fair for America. If we make haste to come about, we might just make it.'

Dennis said quietly: 'We will lose some of the men.'

A solid ball formed in Roberts' belly. 'Aye.'

Anstis came to his feet angrily. 'Damn you, Bart Roberts, Damn you to hell!'

'Very likely,' Roberts agreed grimly. 'Perhaps we shall all be in hell before this is over.'

Spiders! Huge spiders! At least a foot across with long hairy legs and huge mandibles sawing threateningly in the air, their black bodies stuck to the deckhead directly above him.

Roberts awoke with a start, staring fearfully at a now-empty deckhead. It took a long minute for him to realise that he had been dreaming, and even then he wasn't so sure.

He turned on his side in an effort to allay the pain that shot down the side of his head, making his teeth ache, his neck ache, and his head throb sickeningly. He forgot himself, and tried to swallow, and his throat closed and stuck fast so that he thought he had breathed his last. But then it opened again with an audible click, and he gasped at the air like a drowning man.

It was a little after ten o'clock in the morning. Twenty-eight days ago they had been forced to turn back towards the Americas.

He cursed again at the waste of life. How many men had they thrown over the side since then? Despite George Hunter's orders, some, crazed with thirst, had been tempted to drink sea-water or their own urine. They had died in wretched writhing agony. And all because the men on watch had left their posts, tying up the wheel at the helm, so that they could indulge their drunkenness.

The water had run out two days ago. Dead reckoning had suggested they should have made landfall in Guiana by now, but then calculating longitude had always been an inexact science. There had been no water this morning, nor yesterday, not even a mouthful, nor even a drop to moisten his tongue. His throat and tongue were sore and swollen, his skin dry and wrinkled, like it didn't fit him any more, and he had grown so thin he could count his ribs, for they found that if they did not eat, they could bear the thirst easier. He hadn't passed water nor visited the head for days, as though his body had forgotten how to, and his eyes felt gritty and sore because the tears had all dried up. He had a fever, and muscle cramps and a sharp pain like toothache across his loins accompanied his every movement.

Damn them! Damn them to hell, who had not kept to their watch! If they had not been among the dead he would have had them flogged. But their bodies had been among the first to go over the side. He couldn't even remember their names now. Drunken sots.

He raised a thin shaking hand to his face. He was so weak. He knew none of them had more than a day left, perhaps less in this heat. He thought about it without fear. Strange. He had thought his day of reckoning would come at the end of a rope below the water line at Wapping dock. That's where pirates finished up, didn't they? Then what? Hell fire? It was no more than he deserved. He had the deaths of all those thrown overboard during this dreadful voyage on his conscience. And those on the Portuguese ship, and those killed in battle with the Barbadians. He had killed them all, really. They were his responsibility.

He tipped himself out of the bunk and shuffled to the washstand. A small mirror was screwed to the bulkhead and he looked at himself. He was thirty-seven years old, but looked nearer sixty, the lines in his face etched deeply, as his skin clung to his skull. With his eyes sunken into dark hollows, and his lips and tongue turned black, he looked like a dead body, except that he still breathed. He poured some seawater into the washbasin and splashed his face with it, and his shirt, in an attempt to keep cool, and then wiped it off his lips. He knew how deadly the salt would be. But oh, the temptation! How cool the water was!

He struggled up the companionway to the deck and his head pounded sickeningly. He screwed his eyes up against the offending brilliance of the equatorial sun. The mainsail bellied nicely, flapping occasionally in the wind where the stay was in need of sweating up to make it taught, the wind, usually music to a man's ears, now mimicking a full complement of marching men on the deck.

By the entry-port, a heap of old rags was piled up against the safety rails and he peered at it surprised. And then he saw that it wasn't rags, but bodies and at the realisation, his heart thudded suddenly, sending tortuous pain through his brain.

Two men had the job of sliding the bodies over the side. There was no prayer, no ceremony, nothing to note their passing. Roberts watched in ghoulish fascination until young Tom Sutton joined him.

'Ten,' he whispered and held up his spread fingers. He meant ten men dead that morning. Died in the night.

Roberts dared to nod slightly, which set his head spinning again and he had to hold on to one of the stays until it stopped. Sutton didn't notice. He had his own misery to deal with.

'Three of the flux,' Sutton whispered painfully through black lips. 'Two of thirst. One drank his own piss.'

'Where's Davy?' Roberts couldn't make his tongue move, and no sound, not even a whisper came out, but Sutton understood him.

'Bad.'

Sutton's youth was in his favour. The young fared better in this.

The two men shoving the bodies over the side finished, the effort leaving them weak and breathless and clinging to the gunwale for support, before closing the entry-port.

John Walden, sat on a stool by the helm struggling with the effort to keep the ship on some kind of course. Since leaving Guiana, the company had doubled in size, and John Walden was one man who had signed the company's articles from the *Blessing* at Newfoundland, and had instantly been promoted to officer. He was twenty-one, but with an evil temper that had brought Symson's wrath on his head on more than one occasion. An amoral man, Roberts thought, one he would have preferred not to have had in the company. But then perhaps he was better fitted to piracy than any of them because of it, and he was willing. With youth on his side, he too bore up better.

Roberts peered ahead. If only they could sight land! It could not be far, surely. They should have hit Guiana long since. But it was only guesswork.

With an effort Roberts crossed the deck to peer at the binnacle compass. He wanted to say: 'We'll make it if we keep on at this speed,' but he couldn't. Instead he slapped Walden on the shoulder.

Walden looked up at him with red-rimmed eyes and almost smiled at the encouragement. His cracked and blackened lips wouldn't let him.

Roberts had taken a reading from the quadrant earlier, and knew they were on the right latitude for Guiana. Cayenne, perhaps. Where the hell was it?

Roberts could bear the heat no longer. He knew that he was a dying man. He staggered below again, knowing that he had to go back to his bunk. They were all dying. The mess deck was littered with dying men, in hammocks, on the deck. Roberts paused a moment and then went on.

The door to Symson's tiny cabin swung idly with the motion of the ship, and Roberts looked in.

David Symson lay quite still on the bunk, his long legs drawn up so that his knees flopped to one side against the bulkhead, his eyes closed. He was quite still.

A sudden dread made Roberts' heart check and then lurch on. *Not Davy! Surely to God, not Davy!*

But hearing his foot on the deck board, Symson opened his eyes, and heaved himself into a sitting position, his shoulders and head resting on the bulkhead.

With agonisingly slow movements, Roberts dipped a cloth in the sea-water in the bowl and wrung it out before laying it across Symson's forehead. Taking the cloth with his own hands and wiping it over his face, Symson beckoned his captain closer, and Roberts bent his head. He could not catch the words hardly whispered.

He went back to his own bunk and slept again. It was the only thing to do. He awoke some time later by someone shaking him. Blankly he stared at the unshaven face of John Walden.

'Cap'n! Land!'

Topside, the tell-tale splashes told him more bodies were being thrown over the side. He counted five. That made forty-eight.

It was dark outside, but the moon reflected off the moving sea and sent a flickering glow into the cabin.

Roberts sat up. The pain in his waist, his kidneys, made him pause, but then slowly, very slowly, like an old man, he came to his feet.

With painfully slow steps he came on deck. The lanterns had

been lit. There was nothing to see in the darkness, save for the lights of the similarly stricken *Fortune* sloop a few yards away, struggling to keep up with them, and the moon's reflection on the sea. There could have been land a few hundred feet away, but they could not have seen it.

They took a depth sounding. Seven fathoms—forty-two feet. Too shallow to risk going in closer until they could see what they were doing. They might run aground in the night, and if Roberts' calculations were correct and they were on the Guiana or Suriname coast, they could find themselves caught in the thick oozing mud that surrounded the shore.

He gave the order to heave to, and accordingly the *Royal Fortune* turned into the wind and dropped the anchors.

It took effort. Weak dying men struggled up the yards to haul in the sails and tie them off, but the knowledge that they must be near land was encouragement enough. The euphoria was contagious. They had reached land!

But they could not send out a boat until the morning. It would still be twelve or fourteen hours before they could get water back to the ship.

The night passed with agonising slowness. Roberts drifted in and out of a delirious sleep, and dreamed of a waterfall of glorious clear water which he couldn't reach. At times he thought the morning would never come. It seemed to him that every time he looked at the clock the hands had hardly moved.

Three more men died in the night.

But the morning brought hope of salvation—and a bitter disappointment. The coast of Suriname lay ahead, but as the mists of dawn receded they discovered it to be a mere grey shadow on the horizon.

The task of bringing the anchors up to the cathead, of turning the capstans would kill men already half dead, as would sending them up to the yards to make sail. Equally, to send out the boat some twelve or fourteen miles was asking a lot. Still, the boat was equipped with a sail and the wind and current would be with them, although they would have to row back. But by then, hopefully, they would have found sweet water and recovered some of their strength.

They put it to the vote and there was no shortage of volunteers to go. The men who went were no more than pathetic skeletons, skin and bones, their eyes sunken into deep hollows, lips black and swollen and cracked with thirst, and tongues swollen into a choking mass. Roberts knew he was asking an almost impossible task. He had no choice.

Another man died while they were gone. He had been unconscious for a day already. He sank suddenly and seemed to fade away.

The *Fortune's* crew which had dwindled to a mere fifty men joined them coming aboard shortly after the boat left. The officers went below to the great cabin to get out of the sun, and Roberts was shocked at the state of them. The previously overweight Ashplant was so thin and gaunt that Roberts hardly recognised him, and his skin had taken on a greyish tinge. He couldn't walk unaided. Dennis had lost his belly, and it seemed, some more of his hair. His once-rounded cheeks sagged into deep lined jowls and his small grey eyes were swollen almost shut. He leaned forward on the table, resting his aching forehead on his arm. Thomas Anstis, collapsed in the corner and fell to the deck, asleep, his swollen lips quivering. They left him there.

The day moved on slowly. Hour after agonising hour they waited. The broiling sun came overhead and then began its descent in the west. They sat in silence, sometimes watching the clock hand as it moved so slowly.

Roberts' faith in the water party began to fail. Something had happened to them. They hadn't made it. They had succumbed to thirst, maybe, out there unprotected from the fierce sun, or perhaps the sharks got them, or the caimans which inhabited the South American waters. They did not have another boat to send. The despair of it overwhelmed him, and he had to push it aside resolutely.

However, late in the afternoon the word spread through the ship: *The boat is here.* The men at the oars had undergone a remarkable transformation. From the sad, lethargic and sick young men who had left at dawn that morning, they had become strong with bright eyes, and they talked. 'We found water. Sweet water. At the mouth of the river.'

Roberts swallowed involuntarily in anticipation of the water, and his throat stuck. But he felt that he hadn't heard human voices before that sounded as sweet.

With superhuman effort, and requiring half a dozen weak men, they hauled the first barrel onto the deck, and it had hardly settled when every man tried to get to it first. David Symson ordered them into a queue, and allowed them to fill their mugs. Hunter, the surgeon, confined to bed, sent a message to say that it should be sipped slowly. Some didn't heed the warning and vomited it up again.

Roberts forced himself to drink slowly, sipping at the precious life-giving fluid, and felt the cold trickle of it in his mouth easing his tongue, his gums and the sore scratchy membranes at the back of his throat. He let it run around his mouth and trickle down his throat, delighting in the coolness of it, the wetness.

It wasn't until night came that he passed water for the first time in many days, and he noticed too that he sweated once more in the heat. The headache subsided with such relief that he felt as though he had just come out of the teeth of a gale into fresh clean air.

Recovery was rapid after that. Men began to eat again, filling out sagging skin. But it couldn't bring the dead back. In all over fifty men had died. Their deaths weighed heavily on his conscience.

Still, he had the living to think about. They needed provisions and he turned the *Royal Fortune*'s bows once more for the Caribbean.

TWENTY-ONE

September 1720, Caribbean

'Cap'n, Harry Glasby's gone!'

Roberts looked up from the log he had been writing in, pausing with the pen in the air. 'Gone? How gone? Is he dead?'

'No.' Christopher Moody frowned at him. 'Gone. Taken off, like, with two other men.'

'Damnation!' Roberts put the pen in the ink stand and came to his feet. What was Glasby thinking of? True, he was a pressed man, taken under duress from the *Samuel* back in July for his skill as a sailing master, and true, the excesses of the company depressed him. Glasby was a God-fearing sober man, a quiet man, one Roberts had thought he could depend on. But he had had a hankering for home, and his wife and child. It was always a mistake to sign up a married man, be he ever so capable.

'There ain't anywhere for them to go,' Roberts said, thinking about it. Since leaving Suriname, they had found 'belly timber' in a series of successful sorties in the Caribbean and now they were anchored off Hispaniola where they had cleaned ship and had spent a little time enjoying the pleasures the island had to offer, particularly the women. However, there was little enough here to aid escapees. Much of it was thick forest.

'We've sent some fellows after them,' Moody said. 'Thought you ought to know.'

Roberts sat down again, and picked up his pen, sucking the end of it thoughtfully, his thoughts on Harry Glasby. It was a capital offence to desert, for when a man knew their plans, it could put everyone in peril. The men would not take it lightly.

They had been in Hispaniola two weeks. They had cleaned the *Fortune* sloop, but the *Royal Fortune* was still hauled over on her side while her men cleaned and caulked her seams and covered her bottom with pitch and tallow and sulphur. Roberts had taken up temporary quarters in the *Fortune* sloop, but they had not been idle. They had taken a sloop called *Relief* in the harbour, which presumably brought her captain little relief for they compelled Captain Robert Dunn to supply them with turtles, the harvesting of which was the reason for the *Relief*'s visit.

Roberts' thoughts were still with Harry Glasby. He needed

Glasby. John Stephenson was a good navigator and sailing master, but he was just one man, and when he went off watch, there was no-one to replace him. Besides, Roberts intended to expand the size of his command to at least one other ship. Without Glasby, that would be impossible. Still, he didn't see what he could do to stop them passing the death sentence on a deserter. That was out of his hands. And he was sorry for it. He thought they probably would not catch up with the fugitives.

He reckoned without the determination of John Walden, who added to his cruel streak a degree of intelligence that had been lacking in Walter Kennedy. They caught the three deserters the next day, when it had been forcibly borne upon them that the way of escape did not lie in the thick tangle of forest, and brought them back to the *Royal Fortune* where they confined them in the cordage.

A day after that they left Hispaniola and straight away took a French ship laden with brandy and wine—never a good haul as far as Roberts was concerned, for it meant his men would be in a constant state of inebriation for the foreseeable future. And before nightfall they took another ship, which surrendered without a fight.

Roberts, meeting her captain as he came aboard, was astonished. 'Upon my soul! Captain Cane!'

Captain Cane grinned. 'We meet again, Captain Roberts. Still got my little sloop, I see.' He glanced at the *Fortune* sloop riding alongside. 'Made some improvements, but I'd recognise her anywhere.'

Roberts said: 'She has served us well.' He looked at the ship he had just taken, and raised a brow at Captain Cane. 'You have risen in the world, I see.'

'Aye, indeed that is so, Captain Roberts. In fact, I might say, you did me a good turn.'

'Oh?'

'Well, after you left Devil's Island in my sloop, that fellow Kennedy took your own ship, and after taking everything of value off the Portuguese ship, gave her to me which, as you know, under Admiralty law, I could sell. And so I bought me this fine vessel for which I don't have to apologise, no sir.'

Roberts slapped him on the shoulder. 'Captain Cane, you will be our guest tonight. And tomorrow we let you go. Yes?'

'Aye!' the company agreed, for Cane had been so generous to them when they had captured his sloop at Devil's Island. They viewed him as a good-un, and the following day, after a night's drinking, dancing and singing, they let him go unmolested.

Swinging gently with the rocking of the ship, the lantern cast its beam varyingly on the men's solemn faces, on wooden beams and upright solid wooden pillars, but leaving in darkness the recesses where the light could not reach. White smoke from a dozen clay pipes curled into air thick with the stench of the bilge and human sweat, burning candles and rum punch.

On the table, the favourite tipple slipped about in the bowl in time with the lantern's swinging and the creaking of the *Royal Fortune*'s timbers as she rocked in the swell, yet no-one had partaken for the company had assembled for serious business, and the mess-deck was crowded with sailors tucked into every available space and sitting on anything that proved to be handy.

Close around the table the officers sat solemnly staring at the three manacled prisoners who stood at one end of the table.

Harry Glasby was sick to the pit of his stomach. He had spent a week in the cable-tier, chained to an overhead beam through a ring-bolt until the company could turn to this business. He had not been ill-treated. Indeed, they had fed the prisoners well and allowed them on deck for exercise and fresh air, and to relieve themselves, but it had been uncomfortable, and irksome, and had given Harry Glasby and his companions ample time to consider their crime. A brief meeting with the captain had made him hang his head in shame. Roberts had been pained that Glasby hadn't applied to him, for he had granted many men their freedom, giving them the vital letters that had told (lyingly) of their being forced men. In fact, Roberts did not believe in forcing men, sailing masters apart, for their loyalty could not be guaranteed, and they were a divisive influence on the company. The other two men had signed willingly, and then thought better of it. That would go against them.

Glasby's chains rattled now as he nervously brushed a lock of fair hair from his forehead, and he licked his lips which had suddenly gone dry. He looked around him at comrades and friends, people he had worked with for the last few months, all of them staring at him accusingly. They had never understood him, he thought bitterly. He didn't smoke or drink the way they did, and he avoided the women because he was in love with his wife, but they looked on him with suspicion. Valentine Ashplant understood him, he knew, and perhaps the captain. But the captain had distanced himself, leaving the judging to others.

His judges were the 'Lords': Henry Dennis, as always, the chairman, Valentine Ashplant, David Symson, Thomas Anstis, Christopher Moody, George Smith who had signed up from the *Martha and Mary* and quickly promoted to the House of Lords, Thomas Sutton and Richard Hardy, and behind them, in the shadows, an observer only, was the captain.

Beside Glasby Peter Gilmot shuffled. His head hung low, and he didn't dare look about him at his accusers. On his other side, Sam Watts stood quietly.

Henry Dennis sucked on his pipe, blowing smoke into the air to mingle with the fog others created, and stood up to open the proceedings. With an air of importance, he unrolled a scroll of paper and read out:

'Samuel Watts, Peter Gilmot and Henry Glasby—you are charged with a violation of the articles of the company under the command of captain Bartholomew Roberts of the *Royal Fortune*, namely the breaking of article number seven: *Any man deserting the ship or his station during battle will be punished by death or marooning.* And number nine: *No man shall talk of leaving until each has had a share of one thousand pounds.* You, the defendants, were caught in the act and we can find no defence nor reason for showing mercy. And so, with the agreement of all, we have decided to pass sentence as follows . . .'

'Hold on there, Mr. Dennis,' David Symson interrupted him. 'I reckon we should hear what these fellows have to say for themselves.'

Valentine Ashplant added his growl. 'Aye, I reckon so too.' He packed tobacco into the bowl of his clay pipe.

There was a general murmur of approval while each of the judges in turn seemed inclined to lengthen the pause by lighting their own pipes, and Harry Glasby took his chance.

Taking a step forward, he looked at each of them in turn, his eyes resting slightly longer on Ashplant than on any of them. The beating in his heart was as strong as ever, for he knew what the sentence must be, and his very life hung on whether he could talk his way out of it.

He coughed to clear his dry throat, and said clearly:

'Captain, my lords, gentlemen, all of you—I ain't made no

secret of the fact that I want to get home to my wife. Indeed, all of you know that I be no rogue, nor be I a cruel man, nor do I *not* care for the good of the company. On the contrary, I have performed my duties with care. But, gentlemen, I have a wife. A beautiful wife who I loves dearer than my own life, and who is on hard times until I can get home to her, and my dear little daughter. I ain't seen them in over two years. I know I be foolish, and I know now I could never have made it back to England in that way, but I be a desperate man. As any of you know, if you've the love of a good woman . . .' He paused and searched their faces. Dennis had found a crack in the grain of the table that he traced with concentration with one thumbnail; the captain stared down at a spot between his feet, a strange look on his face; Ashplant's face grimaced, and he brought out a red handkerchief, and blew his nose, wiping it with a flourish. Harry Glasby knew he had hit the right note. 'I love my wife, and I miss her, and I want to go back to her. She ain't got nothing but what I can give to her, and I fear she be suffering privation now. But I can't get home with you gentlemen, I know that. It be too dangerous. I didn't know how seriously you would take my leaving. I didn't pay too much attention to the articles, because I were forced. I thought I were free to come and go as I please.'

The captain raised his head and spoke from the darkness. 'Mr. Glasby—the articles were read out to you. As you know, when you sign on with a merchantman you sign on for the whole voyage until the work is done and the goods delivered. Whatever the master asks of you, you do. Thus is the way of the sea. It is the same with us. Until the end of the cruise and you have made a thousand pounds prize, you cannot leave. If you did and you were caught, you would be forced to inform on us. Yet if you had asked I would have given you letters. You did not have to run off and desert. And besides, we had prisoners with us at the time, which means we were, technically, in action.'

Harry Glasby's eyes filled. 'I just wanted to get home to my wife, Cap'n. I didn't mean nuthin' by't. And please, remember, gentlemen, I stopped Gilmot from shooting John Walden.' This was true. Peter Gilmot had reacted at his capture by drawing his pistol on Walden.

'Alright Glasby,' Henry Dennis said. 'We've heard enough from you. Gilmot, what say you?'

Gilmot took his cue from Glasby, but he had no wife or

children to argue in his favour, and besides, Glasby had reminded the company of his intention to kill John Walden. And unlike Glasby, he failed to win the sympathy of the company who were determined to have vengeance for the wrong they thought had been done them.

Sam Watts was not well-liked by the company, and his plea fell on unsympathetic ears.

When the last prisoner fell silent, so did the judges and for some minutes all the sounds were from outside the mess deck, from the sea, the creaking of the ship, the slap of the stays against the masts while each man considered what he had heard. Then Henry Dennis leaned forwards and the judges went into a huddle.

For a brief moment, Harry Glasby's eyes met those of the captain above their heads and he thought he saw understanding there.

Dennis stood up. 'Well, you have all put your cases, and the court does understand,' he said. 'However, you have deserted your posts and your crime is so abhorrent that we cannot show you mercy. Therefore . . .'

Harry Glasby closed his eyes, and waited for the pronouncement of death.

Suddenly a scrape of chair legs on the floor caused him to open them again, for Ashplant had also come to his feet. 'I have something to offer the court in behalf of one of the prisoners,' he stated in his gravelly voice staring about him with his protuberant eyes.

Henry Dennis sat down with a resigned sigh, and Ashplant steeled himself, taking a large breath which doubled the size of his belly, rubbed his whiskery chin, and uttered meaningfully: 'Harry Glasby shall not die; damn me if he shall!' And he sat down again.

No-one spoke, but they sat in stunned silence, while Ashplant sucked on his pipe. Then quite suddenly he hit the table with his fist and stood up again.

'Damn ye, gentlemen!' he cried. 'I'm as good a man as the best of you. Damn my soul if ever I turned my back to any man in my life or ever will! Glasby is an honest fellow, notwithstanding this misfortune, and I love him, Devil damn me if I don't! I hope he'll live and repent of what he's done, but damn me, if he must die, I will die along with him!'

He eyed them all again fiercely, then pulled a pair of pistols with ivory carved stocks from the capacious pockets of his coat, and presented them to the rest of the judges. 'Take 'em and do your worst!'

The captain put his head in his hands despairingly.

Henry Dennis stared horrified at the pistols for a moment. There wasn't anyone who would have the temerity to pull the trigger against Ashplant—there would be a full mutiny if they did.

Harry Glasby dared to look around him, at the men who were nodding their heads in agreement with the arguments Ashplant had put forward. Once more Henry Dennis went into a whispered huddle with his co-judges. Then he stood up.

'You may sit down again, Mr. Ashplant,' he said and Ashplant did so, resuming his pipe once more.

Dennis addressed the company. 'It is the decision of this court that Harry Glasby be acquitted of his crime. As for Samuel Watts and Peter Gilmot, the sentence is that they be tied to the mast and shot dead. You, the prisoners, may choose any four of the company as executioners.

'Court dismissed.'

Relief flooded over Harry Glasby. Someone led him to the anvil where his chains were cut off, but he couldn't remove his eyes from the face of Valentine Ashplant. He owed the man his life, and he would never forget it.

For a moment Ashplant met his eyes, and grinned, and then he left the mess deck before they had finished removing Glasby's chains.

Sentence on the two condemned men was carried out at first light. Every man in the company, including the captain who was known to avoid being present for punishments if he could, was assembled on the deck, the company silent as the prisoners were brought up from the cable-tier.

Glasby's eyes met those of Sam Watts briefly and he saw the haunted look of a man about to die. He couldn't bear it, and he looked away as Watts was taken and tied to the mast.

He heard the low mumbled intoning of prayer. 'Our father, which art in heaven . . .'

At a signal from Henry Dennis, four men raised their muskets, and at the order, fired, not quite in unison.

A crimson hole appeared in Watts' chest over his heart, and a spurt of blood gushed out. For a shocked moment he stared at Glasby, his eyes wide with horror and then slowly the glaze of death came over them and his head fell forward.

Harry Glasby felt his legs buckling under him, and the sudden firm grip of Ashplant's hand under his arm. 'Steady, lad.'

They tied the other man, Peter Gilmot, to the mast. He uttered no prayer, but began to beg in the manner that pirates scorned, struggling against the ropes, crying out for mercy. 'Please—please, let me go. I promise . . . I only wanted to go home.'

The shots rang out again, silencing his cries immediately. His body shuddered.

Harry Glasby leaned over the *Royal Fortune*'s side and vomited.

The same day, they sailed for St. Christopher's.

TWENTY-TWO

Lúcia Margarida Carvalho Andrade rested her hands on the guard-rail of the *Santo António,* and looked out at the empty turquoise sea. They had left the convoy and sailed alone, a situation Pietro Andrade roundly condemned. But his censures fell on deaf ears. Captain Henrique Sequeira was king of his own ship, and no land-loving passenger, however high and mighty he might think himself, was going to tell him how to sail it!

Lúcia smiled to herself. Even a convoy was no guarantee of security. Look at the *Sagrada Familia*! Then she sighed. If only Bartolomeo would choose to attack this ship! She wondered where he was now. The Atlantic was such a huge ocean, the world such a large place. Yet he must surely have sweltered under the same sun as she did, and studied the same stars. He had told her how, at dawn, he would take a reading from the Pole Star in the north, or in the south the Southern Cross, and she made a point every evening and every morning of looking for one or the other of them.

How long ago it all seemed now, those idyllic days on Devil's Island, the nights of love and passion. They had known it could not last. She had known from the first that it was an impossible dream. She was betrothed to someone else, and she was honour-bound to carry out her part of the bargain. To fail in that would be to betray her heritage, her father, everything she had believed in. For, much as she loved him—and she did love him to the depths of her soul—Bartolomeo could hardly be considered a suitable husband for any woman. An English—Welsh—pirate, low born, and apart from the prize money he received, relatively poor. It was a far cry from the nobleman who had offered her his name and title and landed estates and a life of luxury even if he were an ugly hunchback. Roberts could not even think of a life ashore, for not only had he no means of earning a living, but he would be vulnerable ashore, and should he be caught, he would certainly hang. What life could he offer her?

Well, it was all very well knowing these things in one's head, but it was another matter to make the heart do the head's bidding. Thankfully he had never spoken to her of it, never mentioned the future. If he had, the heart would certainly have won. His silence had been her fortitude, and when she had thought, on that final night, that he was close to breaking their unspoken resolve, she had not given him the opportunity.

She had done the right thing. She knew it. Why then did she regret it so very much? Why did she so long to go back to those idyllic days and stay there? Why did she look for him on the depressingly empty sea, day after day, in the hope he might just stumble across her a second time?

Fate was not so obliging.

'The captain says we are within a day of Madeira,' Pietro Andrade said, joining her at the gunwale.

She looked round at him. He seemed to have aged ten years since Bartolomeo abducted her. He had lost weight, and his skin no longer seemed to fit him. His face was yellow in colour, as were the whites of his eyes, and there was a sadness about him that she could not dispel.

The sadness was two-fold. First, the time she had spent with the pirates. The agony of worry at what had happened to her had ruined his already failing health. Strangely, the joy of her return to him had been short-lived, smothered by anxiety about what he suspected had happened to her. She knew he tortured himself, imagining she had been raped and ill-treated, blaming himself for not stopping it. That's what fathers did, she supposed. Their protective instinct towards their womenfolk gave them a guilt they could not bear.

He had never asked her about that time. When she had tried to tell him, he had stopped her, changed the subject, and on one occasion walked out of the room. One day she would have to tell him the truth, which would be worse for him than his own imaginings.

The other sadness was that at Madeira they would part, he to sail on to Africa, she to go back to Portugal. She knew then that she would never set eyes on him again, and yet it had been such a short time since they had found each other.

She said: 'I wish I did not have to leave you, *Pápa.*'

He looked at her. 'Now Lúcia, we have had this conversation before, and my mind is quite made up.'

She put her hands on her hips. 'You know, you are not legally my father. I do not have to do anything you say.'

His dark eyes glittered. 'Oh no? You are an Andrade, my girl, and you will do as your father tells you!' He shook his head. 'Else you would put your poor father in his grave.'

'*Pápa*! That is outright blackmail!'

He wagged his head. 'So it is!'

She took a breath. No-one, had the ability to make her as angry as her father did. It was always a struggle to keep her temper. In fact, she suspected he enjoyed provoking her.

She said with an attempt at winning him over: 'It does not have to be this way.'

The laughter died in his eyes, and he was serious. 'Look at me, Lúcia. I am grown old, and I am sick. I know I am not long for this world. You must know that. You must see death in my face.'

'*Pápa!*'

'No. Just for once in your life, Lúcia, let me have *my* say!' He paused to recover his thought. 'You always contradict!' he complained.

'Because you always say what I do not wish to hear. I will have no talk of death.'

'It is a reality of life, Lúcia. And we must make provision for it.' He frowned, trying once more to get his thoughts on track. 'Do you remember that night at the King's ball? I knew nothing of you then, nothing of your existence. Your mother had not told me, but had lived the lie, saying that that dolt Joaquim de Santana was your father. Then we met, and when I looked at you, we both knew, did we not?'

She nodded, remembering the shock of learning that he was her father, not the man who had brought her up. The revelation had thrown her life into chaos. Allessandro had broken off their engagement while her mother's husband had threatened to put his wife in a convent, despite the other six children she had borne him. Joaquim had thrown Lúcia out of the house and so she had turned to Pietro Andrade for help, which caused a bigger scandal than the rest had done, for he took her in under his roof. The King, who no doubt had several nubile mistresses himself, had stripped him of his inheritance and dispatched him with a vague commission to act as his Emissary, in reality a banishment from Portugal for ever.

She said now: 'Did you love my mother?'

He leaned over the side and stared down into the creamy depths below the ship. 'More than you could ever know,' he said. 'She was beautiful, clever—and you are so like her, you know. Oh I'd have given up everything for her if she had asked me. I would have taken her away, I would have taken care of her.'

'But you could never have married her.'

'No. If she had not had other children by that dolt, there might have been a chance of annulment. As it was, nothing short of murder would have released her from that contract. But I would have taken care of her. No-one would ever have known.' He shook his head. 'An old man speaks too much. You think I am immoral?'

There was no answering smile in her eyes. Instead she said: *'Let he that is without sin cast the first stone.'*

He understood then. There was a sudden awkward silence. 'What are you saying, Lúcia?' he asked quietly.

Now the moment had come, she could not tell him. Wordlessly she shook her head.

He studied her closely. She had come to fear his scrutiny, for it was as though he could read her thoughts when he chose. He chose now. 'It is the English pirate.'

'I wanted to tell you, but I could not find the words. He—he treated me with nothing but kindness and consideration. As though I were a guest, not a prisoner at all.'

'And what price did he demand for this consideration, I wonder?'

She said carefully: 'He demanded nothing.'

'You gave of your own free will, then.' When she did not answer he drew his own conclusion, and shook his head. 'Oh, Lúcia, I thought better of you. How can I give you to any man as wife now?'

She stared resolutely out to sea, but her lip trembled. 'I do not wish to marry anyone—else.'

'Lúcia?'

He hated it when women cried. He put his thin hand on hers, willing her to fight back the tears.

To his horror a large tear welled up in her eye and rolled down her cheek. 'I miss him so much, *Pápa*,' she whispered. 'More than anything I wish I had not left him.'

'But you did the right thing,' he assured her.

She shook her head. 'No. I know I did not.'

'But of course you did! You are upsetting yourself. Soon you will be married to Césario. He doesn't need to know ...'

'*No!*'

Taken aback at the vehemence in her voice, Pietro stared at her with rounded eyes. 'No?'

'No. I cannot do it, *Pápa*. You must write to *Senhor* Guerreiro, and inform him that I am spoken for.'

'I can't do that!' he cried aghast, seeing all his plans vanishing. 'Lúcia, be reasonable. It is your only opportunity to marry well.' He changed tack. 'But I blame myself. I should never have allowed you to come with me.'

She did not pick him up on it,. 'Please write to him, Papa. For I will *not* go to Lisbon, and I will *not* marry him!'

'Then what do you propose to do with your life?'

'I will stay with you.'

'And when I am dead?'

'Do not speak of such things. You will not die.'

'We all die, Lúcia,' he reminded her. He took a deep steadying breath. 'Why are you so *difficult*? Why can't you be meek and biddable like other girls, marry where your poor father tells you, do your duty? But no, it is always *I will not!* You are so rebellious.'

A laugh sprang into her eyes. 'But I am your daughter, *Pápa*.'

'Lúcia,' he said with studied patience, 'I have told you and told you my reasons why I wish to see you suitably married before I die. I will not repeat myself again. You must do as I have arranged.'

She faced him then. 'I will not.'

'You will!'

She stamped her foot. 'I will not! And if you do not write to him, I shall, and I shall tell him all that has happened to me.'

'You can't do that!' He was horrified.

'Oh yes I can,' she said and turned away in a rustle of black silk, and went below, leaving him furiously pacing the deck declaring that if she had been a little younger she would have known what it meant to defy her father!

At that moment the lookout cried out. They had arrived at Madeira.

TWENTY-THREE

Captain Bartholomew Roberts raised the glass to his eye, and peered at the distant green hill with its top in the clouds which had appeared on the horizon. No stranger to the island of St. Kitts, he recognised Brimstone Hill immediately, and knew that somewhere in the cloud was a fort with forty-nine guns, although such poor visibility would minimise their effectiveness.

To the south-east, and closer to the approaching ships a thin strip of buildings along the shore-line proclaimed the town of Basseterre, while in Basseterre Road itself half a dozen ships lay quietly—and for now unsuspectingly—at anchor.

David Symson joined him at the gunwale, leaning his hands on the rail. 'Won't find much worth the taking here,' he said and Roberts couldn't help smiling. Ever the pessimist, was Symson. But then they had not come here for gold, but for a spot of sheep rustling, and through the glass he could see the little fluffy balls of wool dotting the stark barren hillsides. Not that sheep rustling was usually in his line.

'It's the sheep we're after,' Roberts said. 'Remember? Belly-timber.'

'Course I remember. I might have had a skin full last night, but I ain't pickled yet!'

'Who will you send?'

'Fernon, Nossiter, Williams. They've already volunteered.'

Roberts raised the glass to take another look at the island. They were much closer now. He gave a message to be passed to the *Fortune* sloop, and then snapped out his orders:

'Call all hands!'

They had anticipated the order, armed with pistols and cutlasses and dirks, and the gun crews took up their positions. At the order, men sanded the decks, distributed water and powder and shot to the gun crews and then waited. Henry Dennis was the gunnery officer on the *Royal Fortune* and Valentine Ashplant on the sloop.

Roberts gave his orders to Harry Glasby, his sailing master, ordered the black flag run up on both ships, and the drummers and trumpeters to their posts.

He was optimistic. He expected a decent haul in goods, and sheep, to keep them fed for a while and to bring in some prize money. The holds on both ships were half full. When they were full,

Roberts planned to sail once more for Africa and exchange some of those goods for good African gold.

They sailed straight into Basseterre road, and he ordered the drums first, the slow rhythmic beat that he knew from experience would do more to demoralise the victims than a barrage from the guns. Closer in, he ordered the trumpets to blare forth defiance, and his men roused themselves on the decks of both ships, waving cutlasses in the air, and screaming their war cry.

The display was truly impressive, the noise appalling, and he grinned. He could imagine the panic this display would inspire in the anchored ships. He doubted if the stoutest captain could persuade a single man in his crew to stand to arms.

'Cap'n, have you seen over there?' Henry Dennis beside him pointed to a shape in the water and Roberts trained the telescope on a charred, half-submerged ruin of a ship with the waves washing forlornly over her blackened sides to drain down into her depths. The masts had disappeared in the flames, but there was something familiar about the cut of her keel and the flush decks. She had been home for nearly a year. There was no mistaking the *Royal Rover*, his first command.

He felt a great sadness that such a beautiful ship should have been so wantonly destroyed. Damn Walter Kennedy! He had brought her here to die. His mood changed abruptly from optimism to anger. They had fired the *Royal Rover*. Kennedy, that blood-thirsty, traitorous, murderous son of a dog. But what could have happened to him and the men with him?

Coldly shouting to be heard above the noise, he ordered the bow-chasers to fire, adding the shock of explosion to the rumpus, although out of range to achieve any damage, but as they sailed past the wreck, his eyes were on the dead *Royal Rover*, the proud frigate Howell Davis had captured from the Dutch and which had served him once so well.

They were close in now, sailing right into the road. With a snarl of satisfaction, Roberts saw the flags of the anchored ships slide ignominiously down the masts, one after the other.

Immediately Roberts set his men to work. Symson divided them into companies, and they boarded and terrorised the ships' crews, relieving the holds of anything of value, including cables and hawsers and spare sails, ferrying it all back to the two pirate ships, while Roberts held their captains under guard on the *Royal Fortune*.

Roberts met them all on his flush deck, bowing to them grandly and extending his hand in greeting. 'Captain Bartholomew Roberts,' he introduced himself. 'Welcome to the *Royal Fortune*, gentlemen. We don't intend to detain you for very long, but we hope you will be patient with us. I trust you will join me for supper in the great cabin at six.'

'You'll expect us to thank you for your hospitality next, sir,' Captain Fowles remarked. 'Or are we to thank you for robbing us?'

Roberts' dark eyes glittered like granite. 'Do you treat my hospitality with disdain, sir?' he demanded quietly.

His men fell silent, expectant. They knew that tone.

Captain Fowles drew himself up to his full height. 'What are you, sir, but a common thief like the man held at Sandy Point?'

Roberts stared at him. 'What man?'

'Why, Captain Roberts, I am surprised you do not know. A man called John Adams. One of your own, once, I hear. Found on the *Royal Rover* which the governor, Lieutenant-General Matthew had burned. He will hang. And so will you.'

Roberts' hand automatically went to his sword hilt, but he caught Symson's warning eye.

Captain Hingston of the *Lloyd* said: 'What do you want with us, Captain?'

'Your co-operation,' Roberts replied smoothly.

'You will never have that from me, sir,' Hingston told him. 'You capture my ship, steal my goods, impress my men, and you expect me to give you co-operation in such villainy.'

Roberts' voice grew dangerously quiet. 'We are civilised men, Captain.'

Hingston growled. 'Civilised, eh? You call this the work of civilised men? And I have heard of you, Captain Roberts, and how you attacked ships in Dominica and how your men treated their prisoners badly, whipping some to death, cutting off the ears of others, and tying some to the masts to use as target practice.'

Roberts looked at him a good deal surprised. True, at Dominica his men had got a little out of hand, for the prize had resisted them. However, as far as he was aware, no such atrocities had taken place. How rumours grew! But it suited his purpose for it to be believed. A little fear made his job easier and his prey would fall into his hands with less opposition. So he smiled and said: 'Is that so?'

Captain Hingston was either a brave or extremely foolish man. 'I do not call that the work of civilised men. Taking what does not belong to them. I call that the work of hyenas and jackals, scavengers of the seas. I demand you let us go immediately!'

'You demand, do you, Captain Hingston?'

'You are a villain, sir,' Hingston repeated. 'A rascally rogue. I shall see you hanged, damn me if I won't!'

'You think so?' Roberts challenged, and his dark eyes glittered with rising anger. 'You stand as a prisoner on my ship and threaten me?'

'I repeat, sir, that you are a villain, and I will live to see you hang!'

The anger surged into Roberts' throat. 'Mr. Symson!'

'Cap'n!'

'The ships belonging to Captain Hingston—choose one and *burn it!*'

Symson grinned. It would be suitable repayment for the death of the *Royal Rover*. 'Aye, aye, Cap'n.'

Symson's boarders gleefully hauled everyone off Hingston's ship, and brought them to the *Royal Fortune*. Then two men ignited the oiled ropes and cordage left on the deck.

Quickly the flames spread, flickering over the decks, and, as the fire took a hold, racing up the sun-dried tallow and tar-coated cordage to the yards, flitting like a swarm of insects along the furled sails, which burst into flame. It was like a live thing, a spitting hissing animal, devouring all in its path. As sails burned they disintegrated, showering the deck with drifting fire, and setting off new fires at every point on the deck.

Smoke poured from her, choking the air. Watching from the *Royal Fortune* as the stricken ship's crew came aboard, Roberts found his view often obscured completely by the thick grey fog, until a little blow of wind wafted it away for a fleeting moment allowing him the privilege of a grand view of flaming decks and towering flaming masts.

But David Symson's thirst for violence was not slated. With John Walden he took his men to windward, for there was another vessel, flying the English flag.

They had a clear field, for the governor of St. Kitt's, Lieutenant-General William Matthew, had no defence. There were four forts built all along the coast, but they were neither manned nor did they have guns, for since the end of the war with the Spanish there seemed to have been little reason to spend money on the upkeep of something which was not needed. St. Kitt's had basked in sleepy security—or so they thought.

However, as darkness began to fall, after a whole day of exquisite mayhem, the governor must have finally got his men organised.

The first inkling was a flash on the skyline, and a second or two later, the crash of a gun echoing across the water.

For a moment Roberts was stunned, then he laughed. 'So Matthew's got his guns to work at last!'

''Tain't nothing to laugh about,' James Phillips growled morosely.

'We are out of range, Mr. Phillips, out of range.'

'Well, and I am mighty pleased to hear it,' Phillips retorted and took himself off.

Roberts caught Anstis's eye on the *Fortune* sloop and made a signal for him to retreat. Then he gave his orders and co-ordinates to Harry Glasby. And in a very sedate manner, the pirate ships slid out of Basseterre Road and stood off away from the island for the night.

But for all Roberts *sang-froid* he was incensed. He had hoped for better treatment from Lieutenant-General Matthew. He had expected him to sue for peace the moment the pirates sailed into Basseterre. He needed provisions and also to trade the goods in the hold. And he was rattled by Fowles and Hingston. So as the men sat drinking and singing topside, he sat down at the bureau and wrote to the governor:

Royal Fortune, September 27th 1720.
Gentlemen,
This comes expressly from me to let you know that had you come off as you ought to a done and drank a glass of wine with me and my Company, I should not harmed the least vessel in your harbour. Farther it is not your guns you fired that affrighted me or hindered our coming on shore, but the wind not proving to our expectation that hindered it. The Royal Rover *you have already burnt and barbarously used some of our men, but we have now a ship as good as her, and for revenge you may assure yourselves here and hereafter not to*

expect anything from our hands but what belongs to a pirate, as farther, Gentlemen, that poor fellow you now have in prison at Sandy Point is entirely ignorant and what he hath was gave him and so pray make conscience for once let me beg you and use that man as an honest man and not as a criminal. If we hear any otherwise, you may expect not to have quarters to any of your island.
Yours, Bartholomew Roberts.

Lieutenant-General Mathew.

Satisfied, he sanded it, and folded it, melted a stick of red wax in the flame of the lamp, and dripped it over the edge to hold it together. He had no signet ring. It did not matter.

Leaving it in the drawer, and snuffing out the lamps, he retired to his own cabin, where he fell into a deep sleep in less than ten seconds.

The night gave Lieutenant-General Matthew the opportunity to reorganise his shore battery. Now he had some powder, and decent shot for his guns, and men who knew how to use them. When that great pirate Roberts came back, he would get a surprise. *If* he came back.

Reports about Roberts from outraged governors had reached him. In the Caribbean, Bartholomew Roberts had assumed the character of Satan himself, a superman that no man could overcome. He had spread fear and terror throughout the region with his exploits. It would be a feather in Matthew's cap to bring him down. Oh, how he wanted him to fall into his trap!

The sun rose behind him, casting long shadows of the island on the dark sea, and then climbed swiftly, warming the air and illuminating the vegetation as it slid away below him. Today there was cloud on top of the hill, and visibility was poor, but in the gaps in the cloud he searched the sea all around him for a sight of the pirates. Then he spotted them hove to towards the south, and he knew then that they would be back.

He looked around him at the fortress on Brimstone Hill which had stood at the summit of the hill for thirty years and had forty-nine long-range cannons. Not that they would be of any use in this cloud. He made a decision. After breakfast he would ride down to the fort at Palmetto point.

Matthew left the fort in a state of readiness, just in case, and took the coast road towards Palmetto point. Keeping his eyes on the pirate ships he saw one of them, the smaller sloop, set sail and turn her bow to the island. Cursing, heaven, hell and that devil Roberts, he urged his mount to further speed.

He had a feeling of terrible foreboding that the sloop would get away before he had time to organise the shore battery at Palmetto Point. He pushed the horse hard.

With his eyes still fixed on the sloop he brought his horse, lathered and sweating and struggling for breath, up the hill into the fort. He slid from the saddle, hot and agitated, and leaving his horse to a young slave boy, he bellowed for his captain of the militia.

Captain Follet had already spotted the sloop and the gun crews were at their stations. Matthew snatched the telescope and stared over the battlements at the incoming vessel. The sloop was small-fry, he knew, a third of the size of the brigantine, and with half the men. With just ten guns she was vulnerable indeed. And she sailed nicely into his line of fire towards Basseterre Road.

'Well, fire then, damn you!' Matthew ordered impatiently.

Overcome by feelings of importance, Captain Follet drew his sword, raised it above his head, and gravely gave the order to fire.

The gun crews put the lighted torches to the fuses, but then there was a nerve-stretching silence as the fuses burnt down. The pirate sloop was sitting perfectly in the line of fire, but each second took her further out of their aim, while the time it took for the fuses to burn down seemed to last a lifetime.

'Fire!' Matthew whispered to himself. 'Fire! *Now!*'

Then suddenly the first gun bellowed, spewing out smoke and shot and wadding with a roar that seemed to come from the pit of hell itself. The ground shook beneath his feet, and the gun recoiled, but Matthew peered at the sloop through the telescope and whooped with glee. The *Fortune* sloop had been hit.

Roberts heard the blast from the *Royal Fortune,* and came on deck at a run, snapping out the telescope. In its single eye he could see the *Fortune* sloop alone in the road, the tell-tale plumes of water around her where the cannon shot fell. At the bow, the jib boom was broken, the white sail trailing in the sea. The main boom too was smashed, so that the mainsail fluttered to the deck with a tangle of ropes and broken spars following it. On her decks, men scurried in all directions, like ants from a disturbed nest to make temporary repairs.

'Get her out!' Roberts whispered, watching anxiously. 'Damn you, Anstis, bring her about and get her out!'

But the damage had made the sloop uncooperative and although Anstis sent men to re-set the sails and to haul them round, the sloop didn't respond.

Roberts watched with sick dread clutching at his belly. The sloop was in a good deal of trouble. The constant fire, not only from cannon, but now from muskets, prevented her crew making repairs. She was hit again, and again. She had only ten guns, too little to make an impression, the size too small to reach the shore.

Roberts made a decision. Snapping the telescope shut he strode imperiously aft, shouting his orders as he went.

'Mr. Moody, clear for action, beat to quarters! Call all hands! Mr. Glasby, make all sail and bring us about! Mr. Dennis, Mr. Sutton, make ready the guns! Weigh the anchor!'

As the drummers beat to quarters, his officers relayed the orders, men ran up the rigging to the yards and the gun crews ran to their posts, hastily stuffing wadding in their ears and tying it in place with kerchiefs, while others hauled up the anchor with the windlass.

The sails were let go and sheeted home, and the wind caught them so that the *Royal Fortune* jerked and then began to move, sliding easily through the slight sea.

Harry Glasby brought her about while Roberts anxiously continued to watch the frantic efforts of the sloop's master, Thomas Anstis, to bring the *Fortune* out of danger. He succeeded in bringing the sloop about in a wide arc that brought her even closer to the guns, and Roberts winced as another ball smashed through her rigging.

Now the cold anger of revenge soared into Roberts' chest. He didn't recognise Matthew's right to protect the island. He saw it only as a hostile act against his men, his ships, and he was determined that Matthew and the island would pay.

While the sloop struggled to get out of range, Roberts brought the *Royal Fortune* into the road. Now the excitement sizzled in his veins, the rush that action sent through his blood.

'Prepare a broadside, Mr. Dennis! Run out the guns!' he cried and Henry Dennis immediately repeated the order: 'Run out! Run out!'

Two tiers of guns emerged on the larboard side, two rows of black menacing teeth. Roberts directed, and Harry Glasby deftly brought the *Royal Fortune* about again. Slowly the *Royal Fortune* slid between the shore and the *Fortune* sloop, right in the line of fire, as a shield between the shore battery and the sloop, parallel to the shore.

Never in his life had Roberts felt so vulnerable, nor so desperate. He had deliberately put himself, his ship, his men in the line of fire to protect the sloop.

The battery on the hill bellowed, and balls splashed into the sea all around them sending plumes of water several feet into the hot sultry air, soaking every man on board. They were uncomfortably close.

As Glasby brought the larboard side to face the fort Roberts, standing by the helm, raised his sword arm. He waited only until the *Royal Fortune* was broadside on to the fort at Palmetto Point and then he brought the sword down swiftly. '*Fire!*'

The agonising two-second delay and then the *Royal Fortune*'s guns bellowed from bow to stern one after the other in a continuous salvo, shaking the decks, tearing the air with deafening noise, and briefly obliterating everything in a pall of smoke.

He didn't expect to do much damage, but he did hope to keep their heads down so that Anstis could get the sloop out.

'Fire as your guns bear!' Roberts bellowed.

They sailed slowly past the fort, the *Royal Fortune*'s guns pounding continually among the cries of: 'Sponge out! Re-load!'

The *Fortune* sloop struggled north-westwards ahead of the wind, unable to manoeuvre away from the island, and Roberts kept the *Royal Fortune* between it and the island. They had to run the gauntlet of the batteries, all the way up the coast, Old Road, Charles Fort, Brimstone Hill and finally Sandy Point, while seventy horse and dragoons kept them company on horseback, presumably to stop them coming ashore.

The *Royal Fortune* kept up the pounding of her guns for two hours as they ran up the coast, until her crews were dog-weary from the work and the noise, their eyes stinging from burning gunpowder fumes.

When at last Roberts ordered them to cease firing, they had left Sandy Point far behind. And as soon as they were out or range of the muskets, the whole company broke into wild cheering. The victory was theirs.

They had not been hit, and they had protected the sloop, and Roberts was satisfied to have come away safely. The sloop, too, it transpired, was not so badly damaged that the carpenter with his team could not repair it. Meantime her men had patched her up and she sailed on, although without her jib and mainsail.

They skirted the island of Saba and then at a safe distance from St. Kitt's he ordered them to heave-to to allow the sloop to make repairs and to allow the prize ship, belonging to Captain Fowles, with a prize crew on board, to catch up.

Then it was time to let the captives go.

Captain Hingston held out his hand to Roberts. 'For your hospitality, I thank you, Captain Roberts. We have been most civilly treated.'

Roberts' eyes narrowed. So the prisoners had decided that they could have come off worse, had they? He took the proffered hand. 'Believe me, it was my pleasure, Captain Hingston. But I would ask a small favour.' He pulled the letter he had written to Lieutenant-General Matthew from his inner pocket. 'I would be grateful if you would convey this letter to the governor when you make your report.'

Captain Hingston took it and turned it over to see the addressee and then bowed stiffly, accepting the charge. 'Very well. I trust we never meet again, Captain.'

Roberts also bowed, but removed his hat, brushing the deck with the decorative ostrich feather, mocking in the courtesy, and then grinned insolently. 'You never know, Captain.'

Because he was happy to be leaving, Captain Hingston let it go. He bowed formally, as did Captain Fowles, and then he followed Fowles to the entry-port.

John Walden folded his arms across his great chest. 'Why all the bowing and scraping?' he demanded insolently.

Roberts met his eyes, considering the man. He was a rebel, was Walden. A law unto no man, unless he chose it. He said: 'Because they think we are barbarians. Because they think they alone are gentlemen. Because it costs nothing to be civil. But more than anything, because it makes it difficult for them to be aggressive towards us if we are civil towards them. In short, it disarms them.'

He turned to his sailing master. 'Mr. Glasby—make all sail, if you please. Set a course for St. Bartholomew's.'

*****

The islanders of St. Bartholomew's received them well, but before long, Roberts turned towards St. Lucia. In three days they seized fifteen French and English ships, and from them increased their numbers dramatically. Among the new recruits was stocky James Skyrme, another Welshman, who had been the mate of the *Greyhound*. They also captured a brigantine, the *Sea King* and, after a long battle which cost many lives on both sides, a Dutch interloper *El Puerto Del Principe* with a hold full of slaves. Roberts signed up some of the slaves, and released the rest on St. Lucia to take their chances as best they may.

The interloper was a fine ship built like a naval rig, which gave Roberts an idea. For, just to the north of St. Lucia was the island of Martinique whose governor, had dared to send out two ships to capture Roberts, just missing him at Carriacou. As he thought about it, his eyes glowed with that unholy look of sweet vengeance, and a small demonic smile played about his mouth. So, the Martinicans had sent ships to capture Bartholomew Roberts, had they?

He had the interloper repaired, fitted her with thirty-six guns, and temporarily moved his command to her. Then, leaving the *Fortune* sloop and the *Royal Fortune* and the *Sea King* at St. Lucia, Roberts sailed past the town of Fort de France in Martinique with the Dutch flag flying. It was a recognised signal for the traders to come out to the ship in the hope of purchasing slaves.

Roberts hove to and waited.

It took time for the Martinicans to man and equip their vessels, but then, one by one they came out to him.

Wearing a dark blue coat, and the opulent gold braid, Roberts watched them come. With his hair tied neatly back beneath a black hat, and fawn breeches and white stockings, he looked as they would expect him to look, like every captain he had ever served under. Yet in his deep capacious pockets he had stowed a brace of loaded pistols, and his sword hung in the baldric on his left hip.

The smile broadened as the first merchant, a Frenchman in a white wig and red coat with fine lace at his wrists and throat appeared at the entry-port.

Roberts bowed, sweeping the deck with his hat. '*Monsieur*, I welcome you to the *Royal Fortune*. I am Captain Bartholomew Roberts, at your service.'

The merchant paused in the act of bowing and straightened

unceremoniously, the smile vanishing from his fat face. 'Roberts? The pirate?'

'I see my fame goes before me,' Roberts said sweetly. Then his voice changed to the business-like accents of a man in control. 'Mr. Symson!'

David Symson knew what he should do. He secured the prisoner, and relieved him of his purse, and brought his boat crew aboard.

It was so easy, childishly simple. One by one all the merchants were taken prisoner, so that there was soon a small armada of boats and sloops gathered about the interloper. Roberts could not hide his glee.

They were a sorry-looking lot, some of them quite humble in workday clothes, others evidently rich merchants in their finery, but all of them hung their heads in frightened misery, not wishing to be picked out by the pirates for special attention.

When he had secured them all, Roberts had them all brought again on deck where he paced slowly in front of them, lord of his domain.

'Gentlemen,' and the voice was mellifluous, snake-like. He saw them shift uneasily, shuffling feet and guessed they were praying to be anywhere else in the world. It amused him to see their discomfort. 'I would not like it said that you came out here for nothing. So you may leave your money behind when you go. You can be sure we shall take good care of it for you.'

His crew laughed, but the unhappy prisoners cast fearful glances at him. He wiped the smile from his face, and instead set an expression of such cold malevolence that they all took a step backwards.

He had no pity on them, as they would have had no pity on him had they caught him. He remembered the ambush that had murdered Howell Davis, and had no illusions. They would see him hang if they could.

'Some few months past your governor armed and equipped two ships to apprehend us,' he told them. 'Did you think it so easy to capture Bartholomew Roberts, eh? You are all a parcel of rogues, damn you! And I hope you always meet with Dutch trade such as this! Mr. Symson—take their gold and their fine clothes, and send them on their way in as few boats as will carry them. Fire all the other boats, and all the other ships.'

'*Mon Dieu!*' someone cried. 'Have mercy, *Capitaine*. Our ships are all we own.'

Roberts' cold dark eyes looked straight at him. 'I give you your lives, *monsieur*, and I am well aware that these ships are not all you possess. Besides, you think I will leave vessels for you to arm and send after us again? Believe me, *monsieurs*, I learn from experience, and I think you will find I am not stupid. Martinicans are not to be trusted. Carry on, Mr. Symson!'

Then he turned on his heel and went below.

He knew his men mistreated the prisoners. He heard yelps and cries, and even shots.

He had a very large company now, men who were new, men who did not know him well, who did not understand his ideas on chivalry. It was going to be more difficult to keep these newer recruits under some kind of control. Sailors generally were rough, mutinous, hard and undisciplined, which was why most merchant and naval captains came down harshly on disorderly ones, of course. How else could you keep control of a crew of beefy sailors?

Roberts swore and went on deck again.

The sight that met him made his blood run cold. A man was tied to a grating, his shirt ripped from his back, his back a bloody mess. Another clutched a blood-drenched hand to his ear. Other men were tied to the mast.

His voice rang across the deck. 'Mr. Symson—what goes on here?'

Everyone stopped and looked at him. A murmur went around his own men. Symson joined him. 'The men take their revenge in their own way,' he explained.

'Not on my ship, Mr. Symson,' Roberts said, his eyes hard like granite. 'We have punished these people enough. I thought I ordered them ashore and the rest of their vessels fired?'

'Aye, aye, Cap'n.'

'Mr. Glasby, get us under weigh.'

TWENTY-FOUR

February 1721, Spithead

Captain Chaloner Ogle warmed himself by the fire. Outside the freezing fog had blown away on a stiff breeze, but the road was solid under foot, frozen into ruts by the intense cold. He hated the cold, and the damp, and the eternal grey of an English winter. He had hoped by now to be frequenting the warmer climate of the tropics, but it had been delay upon delay. First there had been the hold up over the cleaning of the *Weymouth,* then provisions had to be made, rather literally as beef and pork had to be salted down, and hard-tack, the ship's biscuit had to be baked and the ale had to be brewed, for no-one seemed to have enough stock of these necessities to purchase. It all took time. On top of that a crew had to be pressed into service, and when all was done, the weather turned bad, so that the *Whydah* and the *Martha*, two of the ships which were to sail in the convoy, had not arrived at Spithead until last week.

Captain Mungo Heardman sipped the rum from his glass, and shot an anxious look at Captain Ogle who had command of the squadron. The other ships were ready, waiting in the harbour, victualled, and manned, and loaded with goods and passengers. All they waited for now was the First Lord of the Admiralty, who had sent orders that they were not to embark without seeing him.

'He will be here,' Heardman said.

Ogle raised cynical eyebrows at him. 'You think so?'

'He knows we have to set sail or we'll miss the tide.'

'Again.' Ogle glowered at the embers in the grate. Even in this small private room of the inn, the cold penetrated into his bones. It would be worse on the *Swallow*. There was no heating on any ship, save from the galley fire, and the cold could be bone cracking at times.

He looked at Heardman. 'I wish I had your faith in their lordships of the Admiralty,' he said. 'But it seems to me that we have suffered so many delays since we were summoned to Trinity House that they care not whether this Roberts is caught or not!'

'They must want him caught,' Heardman said. 'Why go to the trouble of manning and equipping ships . . .'

'To shut the mouths of those governors who complain, that's why. And besides, what else is there for us to do in times of peace, eh?' He paused, struggling with his own anger. 'The company will have eaten all the provisions ere we set sail,' he said.

'And Roberts be gone back to the Americas, I'll wager.'

'Roberts! As if he is likely to be where we want him to be. There is more chance of finding a particular flea on the back of a lousy dog than there is of finding Roberts! But I tell you, Captain Heardman, if he is there, I will find him.'

Mungo Heardman nodded. He could well believe it. This was his first command, and he was uneasily aware of his own inexperience, whereas Ogle's considerable experience terrified him. In fact Ogle's whole being, his determination, the innate authority in his voice, even the way he looked at Heardman, terrified him. Heardman was frankly relieved that Ogle would be sailing on a different ship.

'Ah!' A glossy carriage pulled by four white horses, and with a shield emblazoned on the door stopped outside the inn, and the First Lord emerged, all plump and splendid in a coat of red decorated with gold braid, and with a huge feather in his hat.

'I suppose we had better go to meet him,' Ogle said with resignation. Whilst he recognised the superiority of those who commanded him, he did not like the toadying that must, of necessity, accompany it.

The First Lord was quick to warm himself by the fire, and Ogle reluctantly yielded his place to him.

'I wished to see you before you sailed,' he said to Ogle. 'Here are your signed orders.' He handed them over, one packet to each man. 'England is relying on you.'

Chaloner Ogle bowed politely. Of course England relied on its navy. It always had and it always would. 'We will do our best to rid the coast of Africa of these parasites.'

The first Lord sat himself down in a chair and puffed wheezily. 'Damned English weather. I wish I were going with you, Ogle, damn me if I don't.'

Ogle said politely: 'Of course, my lord, if you wish to join us—?'

There was no danger of that. His lordship waved a fat white hand dismissively. 'My dear Captain Ogle, if I were ten years younger, it would have been me commanding this squadron, believe me. As it is . . .'

Mungo Heardman inclined his head. 'The British navy has lost a great commander, my lord.'

His lordship studied him for a moment, and a wry smile curled his fat lips. 'And what would you know about it, eh? I retired before you signed on as a midshipman.'

Heardman's translucent white skin reddened. But he said: 'There have been tales about you, sir.'

'Hrmph!' His lordship turned to Ogle again. 'Get this fellow Roberts, Captain. We can't afford to let this scoundrel escape to cause more havoc. He is costing England a fortune in lost revenue and lost goods. Faith! They even tell tales about him in the taverns!'

Ogle said: 'Rest assured, my lord, we shall find Bartholomew Roberts.'

The First Lord of the Admiralty intended to spend the night in the inn. Chaloner Ogle did not wish to waste any more time.

As he left the inn with Mungo Heardman he said: 'We will catch the morning tide.'

Heardman said: 'Do you think we will find this Roberts?' he asked again.

Ogle's piercing brown eyes looked into his. 'If Roberts is on the African coast, we will find him. If not, we will search for him in the Caribbean.' He looked up at the grey blanket which had settled over the hills, and then at the cold grey English sea. 'And I hope the Good Lord sends us a fair wind.'

Heardman nodded. 'Amen.'

They shook hands, and separated, Ogle to the *Swallow*, Heardman to the *Weymouth*.

The *Swallow* was ready to sail, and had been ready for several weeks. She had a full complement of men, new recruits some of them who had spent the long weeks of waiting learning the ropes, rather literally.

Lieutenant Isaac Sun met him on the deck as Ogle, cloaked against the cold, came aboard.

Ogle liked Lieutenant Sun. He was a talented sailor, fine navigator, and an experienced man. They had sailed together before, and Ogle had particularly asked for Sun on this occasion. If he were to go hunting pirates, he wanted his second in command to be a man he could trust to give the right kind of discipline to the men, not too harsh, certainly not too lenient, a man he could exchange ideas with, a man who understood him. Lieutenant Sun fitted the criteria.

Sun was a thin man, the youngest son of five from a noble

family, and he had an aristocratic bearing which sometimes irritated. He had a hooked nose in a thin face and he never wore a wig, but wore his own shiny black hair tied in a black ribbon. It somehow epitomised the no-nonsense attitude of the man.

Beside Lieutenant Sun was John Atkins, the young surgeon. John Atkins was a younger man, not long out of University, but he came with good references as a surgeon. Ogle had already decided that while Atkins knew his business, he was certainly no mariner, and he had a slovenly absent-minded attitude to life, as though his brains were too crammed with book learning to remember mundane things such as a clean neck cloth. He too was a nobleman and counted in with the officers. He even had his own cabin.

'What's that?' Ogle asked glancing meaningfully at the book Atkins had tucked under his arm.

'I intend to write a journal of our voyage,' Atkins said cheerfully.

Ogle nodded. 'An excellent idea. Mr. Sun, do me the honour of joining me in the great cabin, if you please.'

Lieutenant Sun bowed his head. Now he would find out what their orders were.

The following day, 5th February 1721 the convoy of eight ships sailed out of Spithead on the first leg of their voyage, bound for Madeira.

TWENTY-FIVE

Commander Roberts leaned against the gunwale and frowned at the impossibly blue sea. 'When will we be ready to sail, Mr. Moody?' he asked the boatswain.

Christopher Moody cast his eyes over the busy decks. They were anchored off Deseada, taking in provisions and water, ready for another attempt to cross the Atlantic to the Guinea coast, and the deck was the usual turmoil of crates and barrels and rope.

'Tomorrow.'

Roberts nodded, satisfied. For a year he had ranged freely over the Caribbean, but he knew it was time to move on. He had earned himself a fierce reputation, and he knew what they called him: *The Great Pirate Roberts,* and *Black Bart.* He liked it. It made him equal to no other, not even Blackbeard, or Kidd, or any of them. Perhaps future generations would speak of him the way they spoke of Drake or Hawkins, for he had a fighting force as good as they once had, and two excellent new ships.

The new *Royal Fortune* he had taken at Hispaniola, a fine French ship, mounted with forty-nine guns and two swivels in the mizzen mast and manned by two hundred and twenty-eight men, forty-eight of whom were black Africans, freed slaves. The smaller *Sea King* which he had acquired at St. Lucia he had renamed the *Good Fortune,* refitted her and armed her with twelve guns and manned by a hundred and forty men, forty of whom were black Africans. Thomas Anstis was her master, and she was to be consort to the *Royal Fortune.* To her former master he had given the Dutch Interloper he had used to pull the trick on the Martinicans, and sent all the other prisoners from all the other ships he had taken with him. They fired all the other ships, including the old *Royal Fortune* and the *Fortune* sloop which had served them so well.

As reports about him spread, he struck fear in the hearts of everyone in the Caribbean. But the drawback was that he was now hunted, and in addition to the attempts already made to apprehend him from Barbados and Martinique, Governor Hamilton of Antigua had sent out Captain Whitney in *H.M.S Rose.*

He smiled to himself with delighted satisfaction. Certainly he had got his revenge on the Martinicans. He had had a new black jack made to commemorate the event with the figure of Roberts himself holding an hour-glass in one hand and a flaming sword in the other, while beneath each foot was a skull, one with the letters ABH beneath it and the other with AMH, for *A Barbadian's Head* and *A Martinican's Head*. He used this jack at the mainmast head while from the mizzen he flew the old black jack with a figure of himself linking hands with a skeleton holding an hour-glass and beneath it a heart dripping blood. He also flew the favoured *Jolly Roger* a skeleton representing Death.

However he might crow over his accomplishments and congratulate himself on his fame, it did mean that the usual markets were closed to him. He had a hold full of plunder and no way of realising the money from it. So they decided to try once more for West Africa.

He looked up at the noon sky. No need to take a reading today. He knew exactly where they were, and he had already worked out by dead reckoning when he expected to make landfall in Senegal.

Damn, but it was hot! Roberts turned to go below.

'Look at him, strutting like some damned peacock!' The voice stood out from the general hubbub and wafted to him on the hot air. Roberts froze. Were they talking about him?

'Easy Elias,' John Fernon cautioned.

But the words had stung. The company had grown so quickly of late. Over three hundred men, over half of them new men, young men, men ready for trouble. Men who took literally the law which stated that all had a free access to the liquor a right they exercised diligently. Men who, having left the merchant navy to go on the account viewed themselves as good as any other man—as good even as their captain. Fights had become a frequent occurrence. Insolence even more so. And Roberts had reacted by coming down harder on them. It wasn't popular.

'Well, I won't be easy,' John Elias insisted. 'He thinks he's better than anyone, strutting around like he does in his fancy clothes.'

'Elias!' Tom Sutton snapped at him from across the ship.

Roberts turned round to face the man. 'You have something to say, Mr. Elias?'

John Elias, no more than nineteen, lean, hard and arrogant, came forward and stood in front of Roberts on his own, legs apart, arms folded across his chest.

'Aye, I got something to say—*commander*.' He stressed the last word and the lack of respect acted on Roberts like the stab of an ox goad. He felt the anger bubbling up in him. His voice became dangerously quiet. 'Then let's hear it.'

Elias looked to his right and to his left to see who stood with him. Then he put his chin up. 'We done nothing but slave for what is soon spent—victuals and rum. We ain't got no gold! We ain't even sold the things we got in the hold. Call yourself a captain? Lord, you couldn't lead a pack of dogs!' He grinned as he said this last and looked around for corroboration. The men near him murmured in a way which might have been agreement.

Fury ignited in Roberts starting in his belly, and flashing in his eyes. 'Is that so?' His eyes took in all of them and he raised his voice for all to hear. 'I don't value or fear any of you! You can come ashore and take satisfaction of me with sword or pistol if you've the guts!'

Elias was not silenced. 'Oh, so high and mighty, the great Bart Roberts. You've made a great name for yourself in these parts, but I say who captured them ships? Who worked on the yards, fired the guns? We did. You didn't do nothing but stand and wave yer arms about!'

'Are you calling me a coward?' Roberts demanded dangerously.

Seeing the situation rapidly escalating, David Symson together with Henry Dennis and Valentine Ashplant pushed their way through the watching men and tried to intervene. 'Mind your tongue, Elias!' Symson snapped.

Elias ignored him. 'I am calling you a coward. You're a damned coward, Bart Roberts! Ain't a man here who'll disagree.' He paused for effect. Then he said: 'You going to get us all dead on the Guinea coast from thirst like you did them others before us?'

Something exploded deep in Roberts' soul, pushing conscious thought out. He knew a blind terrible urge to shut the man's mouth. Wittingly or unwittingly Elias had touched an open sore, for Roberts had every one of those dead men on his conscience.

In a flash his sword was out of the scabbard at his hip. Before John Elias had time to move, it slid with incredible ease into his chest.

The man's insolent face changed shape, the eyes widening in silent surprise which turned slowly to anguish as he sank to his knees.

Roberts pulled the sword from his body, and it came

reluctantly, with a gruesome sucking noise, pulling the body forward, the lifeblood spurting from the wound, staining the white shirt, spilling onto the deck. There was no sound, no cry, only a small hiss of air, and John Elias's face crashed onto the deck.

Roberts stood still, his feet at the man's head, his breath coming in gasps as though he had just climbed to the topgallant. For several shocked moments, no-one moved, and no-one spoke, but they all stared at the dead man as though expecting him to get up while a puddle of thick crimson crept over the deck planking, congealing in the hot Caribbean sun.

Roberts turned away and they parted in shocked silence for him to pass.

In the sanctuary of the great cabin he threw the still bloodied sword onto the table in disgust and it slid the whole length, just stopping before it fell off the end. Gripping the back of the chair nearest to him he ground his teeth until the killing madness subsided and reaction took over. Then his whole body began to tremble, as though with palsy. Faith! What had he come to? He had become like them, a murderer.

David Symson came in. 'Is he dead?' Roberts asked.

Symson stood still, his legs slightly apart, braced against the slight roll of the ship. 'Aye.' He watched the captain carefully. 'The man was trouble from the time he came aboard. He's bin asking fer it.'

'I know it.' Roberts' voice was tight.

'Still, you didn't have to kill him.'

Roberts rounded on him. 'Dammit man, shut your mouth! I don't want to hear it.'

Symson stood his ground. 'This ain't the end of it, you know. Elias's got friends.'

'Damn them! Damn them all to hell!' Roberts cried bitterly.

'I dare say,' Symson agreed in his laconic way, and left him.

Turning to the large stern window, open to the gallery, Roberts fought the frustration that welled up from the depths of his soul. He was angry and sickened and remorseful all at once. He was tired of the constant antagonism, the bickering, the murmuring, the downright anarchy of the men. For this he had given up Lúcia.

Lúcia. He hadn't thought of her in a long time, but now he allowed himself to remember her, savouring the sharp pain which gave focus to his present grief. If he ever found her again he promised himself he would give up this life. He would never let her go a second time.

He moved irritably away from the window. He was angry now—angry at Elias for driving him to murder, angry at himself for allowing it to happen. He could feel the tension in him, as though some invisible force stretched his nerves tight.

He took up his sword from the table and wiped the blood off on a piece of cloth he used as a towel, discarding it in the corner, and then slid the deadly blade back into the scabbard on his hip. He took a breath to steady himself and went back on deck.

The company fell silent as he appeared. The water party had returned and were evidently being regaled with an account of recent events. The men were in little huddles, two or three here, a couple there, half a dozen by the foremast. Even his officers had congregated together to discuss this event. Every eye was on him.

He could taste the menace in the air, feel their disapproval, and he felt his skin prickle. It didn't help that the dead man was being sewn into his hammock on the open deck.

Roberts did not look at the body, nor did he make eye contact with anyone. He continued his deliberate walk to the helm.

Suddenly the voice of the boatswain, Christopher Moody, cut across the silence. 'You lazy sogers! Get yer backsides moving! Bring that water aboard!'

Slowly, reluctantly, men began to move, and it was with relief that Roberts reached the helm where Harry Glasby waited for his orders.

He began to give the co-ordinates to Glasby, but felt the atmosphere change again, the men falling still once more, and he knew someone was behind him.

Roberts felt the slide in his insides, the sudden blood rush, this time of impending danger, and he turned around.

Thomas Jones, the friend of the dead man, stood on the quarterdeck where only officers were allowed to take their ease, his eyes fixed on the captain, outraged fury suffusing his face. 'Damn you! Damn you to hell you murdering son of a whore! Devil damn you, you deserve the same yourself!'

He rushed at Roberts then, his hands up ready to grab or assault him, but the sword flashed once more in Roberts' hand and he lunged.

Jones side-stepped, but the blade caught him a blow between

his ribs and pelvis at his side. He seemed not to notice any pain. Instead, he bellowed and flung himself forwards, knocking the sword from Roberts' grasp with his left hand and swinging his right fist.

Roberts' head seemed to explode into his eyes, blotting out everything around him. He had gone down, but it took a moment to realise it. He shook his head to clear his vision, and saw Jones towering above him. Roberts may have lost his sword but he was not defenceless. Hooking his leg around the man's knees he caught him off-balance and Jones fell to the deck.

Roberts was upon him in an instant, hitting out with alternate fists, while the crew who had gathered about them roared encouragement, taking sides. Jones came back, kicking out with his foot and sending Roberts reeling backwards, hitting his head with a resounding crack against the mast. The pain was intense and sudden, and he was dazed with the shock of it. The breath had been knocked out of him too, and his knees sagged, but he struggled to fight the fog.

Not waiting for him to recover, Jones laid into him with his fists. He had youth and the hardening power of constant hard work on his side. He was quicker and physically more powerful than Roberts who was winded and hurting.

Roberts had a vision of Jones' face very close to his own, his eyes wide with the killing madness, his teeth gritted.

Another blow and Roberts' saw showering lights and the metallic salty taste of blood filled his mouth. Blindly he grabbed Jones' throat, and the two men went down together.

Once more the watching men roared, some on Roberts' side, others on Jones' as they rolled about the deck together, but Roberts knew he was finished.

Then Jones was free and came to his feet, and Roberts felt himself hauled up by his throat as if he were no weight at all.

Jones hit him again, and he could feel himself going backwards over one of the guns, the barrel in the small of his back.

Blows rained down upon him. The shouting men were now arguing with each other, and dimly Roberts was aware of a fight among them. But everything seemed so far away.

A pistol shot silenced the uproar. 'That's enough!' David Symson cried and hauled Jones bodily from the captain.

Hands helped him off the gun so that he stood upright, but his eyes were swollen almost shut, and blood ran into them so that he could see nothing at all, and his legs wouldn't hold him. Someone—he realised later that it was Ashplant—held him up bodily, holding a cloth to his streaming nose.

David Symson addressed the company, but Roberts could only hear him through a roaring in his ears, and the words didn't seem to make any sense.

'The captain is captain because we voted him into that office,' he cried. 'It's a position of honour, and therefore, it stands to reason the person of the captain didn't ought to be violated by anyone. He is our captain, and the dignity of the captain ought to be supported by all!'

Roberts managed to open one eye. He had a terrible headache, and he ached everywhere else too. His stomach had taken several blows, but it was his head that caused him the most distress.

'As for you, Tom Jones,' Symson went on relentlessly, 'you have violated the captain's person and dignity and it is the will of the company that when your wound has healed you be flogged by two lashes from each member of this company.'

Jones stood in front of Symson, his eyes blazing with injustice.

'Take him below,' Symson ordered, dismissing the company.

He came over to the captain, and looked him over. 'I'll send George Hunter to you, Commander,' he said. 'Ash, take him to his cabin.'

They sailed for Guinea the same day, but it was a week later when punishment was carried out on Thomas Jones. Symson ordered a grating to be upended, naval style. Jones didn't struggle, nor did he protest as they secured wrists and ankles. It wouldn't do for the rest of the company to see him afraid. How they despised cowards! His bronzed muscular body glistened in the equatorial sun, his muscles taught against the anticipated pain.

The entire crew of the *Royal Fortune* had assembled on deck, silent and tense, lined up to inflict punishment. Two lashes from each man, and there were two hundred and twenty eight men on the ship including officers. It would kill him.

As they fell silent, Symson related the charges, reading from a sheet written in Henry Dennis's hand.

'The decision of this company is that you, Thomas Jones, did violate the person of the captain, and did not uphold his dignity. The sentence is two lashes from every man on board.'

Folding the paper he nodded to Christopher Moody who took up the box containing the cat o'nine tails and opened it before the captain.

As the one sinned against, Roberts had the right to inflict the first blows. It was not a task he relished. He had not forgiven Jones the indignity he had inflicted upon his person, but he hated flogging. He had suffered it himself in days gone by at the hands of an autocratic captain. He remembered all too clearly the agony, the indignity, the determination not to cry out. He had promised himself he would not be an autocrat, that he would treat his men fairly, yet here he was to be the first to inflict this punishment on another.

He walked the few paces forward took the cat from the bucket of water where it had been placed, and shook it out, combing its tentacles straight with his fingers. At least it did not have lead or bone in the ends. Even so, it had the ability to lay a man's back open to the bone.

He came ready behind the man. Jones tensed, his muscles knotting across his tanned back and someone shoved a piece of wood between his teeth. He turned his head as Roberts approached, and there was a mixture of fear and defiance in the eyes that met the captain's.

Roberts took a breath. Every eye was upon him. To turn away now would cost him his credibility; he would be seen as weak.

He drew back his arm and then the lash sang through the air, and landed on the man's back, wrapping its tentacles around his body.

It knocked the breath from him and he gasped, but he did not cry out. When Roberts pulled the cat back, the skin looked as though it hadn't been struck, but as he raised his arm again, blood began to seep through in fine hair-like crimson lines across his back.

'One!' the whole crew chanted in unison, and Roberts dipped the cat in the bucket of salt water and combed the strips with his fingers. A knotted whip would kill a man.

Once more those tentacles embraced the bronzed flesh, and Jones shuddered.

Without a word, Roberts turned and put the cat back into the bucket, then he walked off to the helm where he nodded to Thomas Owen at the wheel and took his place there, thankful to leave the frightful scene on the main deck.

Jones held out a long time, longer than most, unable to hold back the cries of pain, until he passed out. On a naval ship it would have been the signal for someone to sling a bucket of water over him to wake him up. However, relinquishing his place at the helm Roberts marched smartly across the main deck.

Jones hung limply unconscious on the grating, his back a raw bleeding mess.

'Enough!' Roberts said.

Symson met his eyes, as if to challenge him, but the captain was the one sinned against. ''Tain't no need to flog a man to death for injured pride,' he added.

Symson looked at Henry Dennis who turned away from him as though this were none of his business, and then at Ashplant.

Ashplant rubbed his bristly chin. 'Can't say that Jones ought to die,' he said. 'It be enough punishment I reckon.'

David Symson relented. 'Very well. Take him below to the surgeon.'

'So what do you think, then?'

Thomas Jones looked across at the *Good Fortune*'s master Thomas Anstis, eager for the answer. In the three weeks since the punishment he had made a remarkable recovery for he was young and healthy, but he seethed with a sense of injustice. Unaware, or perhaps uncaring, that it was Roberts himself who had saved his life by calling a halt, he nursed a murderous grudge against him. If only he had the opportunity . . .

Dismissing a very agreeable mental vision of Roberts with his throat cut, he had formed a different plan. It wanted only the chance to go aboard the *Good Fortune* and speak to her master.

Thomas Anstis removed his hat to scratch his cannonball head through the green kerchief and considered him. 'What you say, Mr. Jones, is mutiny.'

Jones was well aware of it. But he knew Anstis, knew he harboured a grudge almost as big as his own. For Anstis smarted under the leadership of a man who, in his opinion, treated him little better than a lackey. While Roberts swanked about in fancy brocade suits and red damask waistcoat, lord of his domain, Anstis, who commanded the *Good Fortune* was not part of Roberts' intimate circle, nor was he even dignified with the title of captain. Jones had chosen his target well.

He said: 'So you don't mind the way he treats you, eh? I seen it. I seen the way he treats them blacks better'n he does you, Cap'n.' He referred to the erstwhile slaves who were treated by the captain the same way he treated everyone else. To insinuate that the captain treated Anstis worse heaped insult on injury.

Jones saw immediately that he had struck home, for Anstis's eyes flashed. 'Damn me, I value Roberts' opinion no more'n I do a ballad-singer!'

The *Good Fortune*'s boatswain said: 'Aye, it proper eats me liver the way 'e struts like some cock hen, and how we gets just the leftovers from any prize, while the commander's crew gets all the booty. We ain't even got sugar to make punch with!'

Anstis held up his hand to silence him, but those around the table nodded in agreement. The boatswain was right. They had been unfairly treated. And it rankled that Roberts should be made commander when he had been no pirate at all before Davis. Furthermore, Anstis had gone on the account with Davis from the *Buck*.

Anstis rubbed his cannonball head in thought, and toyed with the large gold hoop dangling from his earlobe, a trinket from the *Sagrada Familia*. 'We could do better on our own,' he said. 'At least we could do as well as Roberts. And keep all the booty.'

A large grin lit Jones' face. 'Aye. Easy.'

'And I can navigate,' Anstis added, but didn't add that his navigation skills were quite elementary. 'And I'd be captain. And if anyone wants to say me nay, I'll blow his blasted brains out!'

Jones nodded in vigorous agreement, pleased. 'That sounds good to me.'

Anstis grinned as well. 'What say all of you?'

So during the night of the eighteenth day of April 1721, Thomas Anstis and a crew of seventy men sailed off in the *Good Fortune,* back to the Caribbean.

TWENTY-SIX

April 172, Funchal, Madeira

Situated off the northern coast of Africa, Madeira was a convenient staging post for shipping between Africa or the Americas and England and Europe, for not only did it have a sheltered harbour, and fresh water and provisions, but the Portuguese overlords also carried on a brisk trade in hats, wigs, shirts, stockings and various cloths.

In the six months since the Andrades had arrived in Funchal, Pietro Andrade had found opportunity to increase his income a little by speculating, thus allowing him to hire a modest house outside the town on a hill overlooking the harbour which caught the sea breezes and took the worst out of the heat. His health had improved steadily, and the yellowness of his skin seemed less.

Lúcia too, liked Madeira. Where Guinea and even Brazil were largely untamed backwaters, Funchal was civilised and had its own society that readily accepted her, with no questions asked. She enjoyed the freedom the island afforded her, and she felt she could settle here, among people who were her own kind.

If only she were not still engaged to marry the odious Césario Guerreiro. And if only the King would not send her father off on yet another mission.

'You wished to see me, *Pápa*?'

Pietro Andrade smiled at her in welcome, and offered his cheek for her to kiss dutifully. 'Ah, my daughter, I confess you look more beautiful every day. Just like your mother!'

When he flattered her, she knew he was sweetening her for something she would not like, so she watched him suspiciously, waiting for some clue as to his motive for summoning her to his own private chamber. Knowing it, he raised his brows in mock innocence. 'Do sit down, *filha.*'

Filha! Daughter! Oh yes, he was up to something.

Obediently Lúcia sat down on the stool at his feet, folded her hands primly in her lap and waited, her face a mask of polite interest.

'My child,' he began, 'pleasant though our stay has been here in Funchal, and much as it grieves me to say so, we always knew it would be temporary. The time has come for us to take our leave.'

She felt her heart plummet to somewhere in the region of her knees. 'Oh?'

He frowned. 'The King does not forgive yet, my dear. I have a commission to go on to Guinea—to Whydah.'

Immediately cross, Lúcia stood up. 'And of course it does not occur to the King's Emissary to refuse?'

Pietro had been dreading this. 'Lúcia, my dear child, *filha,* you knew it would happen.'

'I would have thought it obvious that you cannot go. It will kill you to go back to Guinea! *Pápa*, write to the king, and tell him!'

'You forget yourself, daughter!'

Her eyes flashed dangerously. 'I do not think I do. Surely it is a daughter's responsibility to see to it that her ailing father is not put at further risk? You are sick, *Pápa* and another week in Africa will kill you! Did you tell the King that when you reported to him?'

He tried to be the heavy-handed offended father. 'I will not be spoken to like this! I have always done the bidding of King João. You know I am a loyal subject, and where I am sent is where I go.'

'But to give your life to the king's service? *Pápa*, surely he does not demand that much.'

'I daresay his majesty does not understand the rigors of life in Guinea.'

'And neither does he care.'

'Lúcia, you speak treason.'

She pursed her lips in determination. 'I see you are intent on going. Then I will go with you.'

He sighed dramatically. 'Lúcia, Lúcia! Your destiny is different. You have to go back to Lisbon to your mother. We have discussed all this,' he added wearily. 'You need to prepare for your marriage. Your mother was most insistent that I do not delay in sending you back to her.'

'*Pápa*,' she cried exasperated. 'I told you, I am not going to Lisbon! And I will not marry that man.' She compressed her lips. 'I will go with you!'

'Lúcia . . .' He put his head in his hands.

She changed tack abruptly, suddenly becoming soft, and feminine and wheedling. 'Oh *Pápa*, you keep telling me how ill you are, and how you are not long for this world.'

'And this is true,' he acknowledged with satisfaction, but not entirely convinced she saw it his way.

She produced her trump card. 'If I go to Lisbon we will never see each other again. I wish to spend what time you have left with you.'

Even though he knew he was being manipulated, he could not help but be touched. She was so dear to him, this beautiful difficult daughter. A tear came into his eyes. 'Oh, Lúcia, *filha*! My dearest daughter!'

'Your *only* daughter,' she corrected him.

A thought occurred to him. 'And if you go with me, what will happen to you when I die?'

'*If* you should die, Rodrigues will take care of me and see me safely back to Lisbon. Then I will do whatever my mother thinks would be for the best.'

She had it all worked out then. And he had no argument left, for he knew Rodrigues could be trusted to take very good care of her. That was the trouble with arguing with one's own offspring: it was like arguing with oneself!

Pietro Andrade waved both hands in the air in capitulation. 'Very well. Have it your own way. But what I shall write to your mother I do not know! She will not like this.'

She threw her arms around his neck and kissed him. 'I will write to mother myself,' she told him.

He shook his head. 'I know this is not the right thing to be doing.' He sighed resignedly, then brightened. 'There is an English man-of-war in Funchal harbour bound for the Guinea coast. We might buy passage on it.'

Captain Chaloner Ogle looked up from the charts he had been discussing with Captain Heardman and Lieutenant Sun as John Atkins, the surgeon, entered the cabin. 'Yes?'

John Atkins inclined his head politely. 'There is a *senhor* Pietro Andrade and his daughter alongside, demanding an audience, Captain.'

Ogle frowned. 'What the devil do they want?' he snapped.

John Atkins hesitated, for clearly the moment was not right. 'The man is a Portuguese Emissary,' he said carefully. 'I believe he desires passage to Guinea.'

'The devil he does. Let him ask one of the other ships if he wants passage. This is a warship, not a passenger ship!'

Lieutenant Sun cleared his throat. 'If I might explain, Captain?'

Ogle turned his attention to him a good deal surprised. 'You know about this?'

Lieutenant Sun pursed his thin lips thoughtfully. 'I suggested the *senhor* should apply to you for passage. I have been waiting to tell you about it. I met the gentleman yesterday at the governor's residence. I think you might be interested to know that the gentleman and his daughter are acquainted with the pirate Roberts.'

For a long minute Ogle stared at him. 'So when did you intend to tell me about this?' he demanded. 'And what do you mean by 'acquainted'? Did they meet him in passing?'

Lieutenant Sun had reddened at the reprimand, but he shook his head. 'I took the liberty of making enquiries and discovered that the taverns are ripe with gossip that the lady is the same who was kidnapped by Roberts from Brazil. It is rumoured she is or was his mistress.'

'The Devil!' He thought about it for a moment. 'It would seem, gentlemen, that Providence has given me an ace card.'

Mungo Heardman said: 'If that is the case, how will you play that card, Captain?'

'I am not sure. But the lady must have information that may be of use. What kind of woman is she?'

'I have never seen her,' Lieutenant Sun answered. 'But her father is nobility.'

John Atkins said: 'I saw her in the boat just now. Beautiful!'

'Spare me the eulogies,' Ogle said dryly.

He tapped his front tooth with his fingernail thoughtfully. The woman might have information—or she might not. It would not be a good idea, though, to pass up the opportunity. As nobility, he need have no qualms at seating them around his dinner table, where the conversation might just lead to something interesting. Or failing that, outright questioning might be productive of results. Either way it was too good a chance to miss. He said: 'Mr. Sun—can we find space for the lady and her father and their servants?'

'I reckon so, Captain.'

'Very Good. Mr. Atkins, be so good as to welcome them aboard, if you please.'

'Very good, captain.'

Lúcia sat down on the chair in the great cabin. As custom dictated, she had been invited to dine at the Captain's table, along with her father, although he had professed being too ill to take up the invitation. Unlike the pirates in whose company she had taken so many meals, Captain Ogle, Lieutenant Sun and John Atkins had impeccable manners, not belching or make other rude noises in front of her, and not swearing or telling warm stories to embarrass her. But for the food she might have been in an English dining room.

His Majesty's Ship *Swallow* could not boast the luxuries of the *Royal Rover*, or the *Sagrada Familia*, and certainly didn't have the fancy food. She looked at the greasy bacon sliding about on her plate with the movement of the ship and felt her stomach begin its customary revolt. They had strange food, these English, with a never-ending diet of salt pork, salt beef and ship's biscuit washed down with rum, or wine for the captain and officers. Occasionally the diet varied when the cook made a boiled pudding, so thick and solid it formed an indigestible lump in one's inside. The officers—and passengers—ate as their men ate. To Lúcia it was unpalatable, and she started losing weight at an alarming rate. Her father, already ill, worsened before her eyes.

Captain Ogle tucked into his bacon with relish. 'So, *Senhora* Andrade, you accompany your father on his travels,' he opened politely.

Lúcia smiled. She had learnt from the pirates enough English to cope with this new situation. 'Yes, *capitão,* that is so.'

'There is no husband to claim your attention then?'

'No.'

Ogle lapsed into silence. He had reached the limit of his repertoire of small-talk. He was not a man given to polite chatter, she thought. Rather he struck her as rather stern, daunting, a man whose mind was set on his business. John Atkins was different. He sat opposite her, and his pale translucent skin coloured up every time she looked in his direction. He was probably younger than she was, by a year or two, and for all his qualifications, a mere innocent. But he had more of the social graces than Captain Ogle had, and his boyish innocence appealed.

'Where have your travels taken you, *senhora*?' he asked.

'I come the second time to Africa,' she said haltingly, and lisped her 's' charmingly. 'I—we go also to Brazil.'

'Brazil?'

'*Bahia de Todos os Santos,* how do you say?'

'All Saints Bay,' Ogle supplied.

'We are going to Brazil after Africa,' John Atkins said.

She met his eyes directly, and was intrigued by the flush which crept up his neck and suffused his cheeks. She said: 'Why?'

Ogle said abruptly: 'We go in search of pirates, madam.'

Her eyes flew to his face. 'Pirates?'

Ogle pretended not to notice her reaction. 'That is our commission. To search out and apprehend any pirates we may hear of in Africa or in Brazil.'

She smiled. 'And I am sure God will bless your efforts, *capitão*.'

His light brown eyes looked seriously into hers. 'No doubt.' He poured her more wine from a squat green bottle. 'Have you come across any pirates on your travels, madam?'

It was casually said, but her lips had gone dry, and her heart began to pound in her breast. Suddenly she wished her father were present, for something warned her that she was being led into a trap. Should she lie? What had he heard?

The shock in her eyes told Ogle what he wanted to know. He pretended not to notice, but bent his head over his salt pork. 'We were attacked by pirates, off Bahia,' she said at last.

'Oh?'

'A fierce band.'

'Who was their captain?'

'I do not know.'

'Were they English?'

'French perhaps. There was a—fight—with swords—many dead. But they let us go and took the ship.'

'French, you say?'

'Perhaps.'

'I see. Have you heard of a man called Bartholomew Roberts?'

The colour drained from her face. 'N-no, *senhor*.'

'The very devil of a man,' Ogle said smoothly, watching her closely from over the top of his wine glass. 'We hear of him from all over the Atlantic. We understand him to be in Guinea now.'

Her mind raced. *Bartolomeo in Africa*? And these men were hunting him down. And she had walked of her own free will onto their ship. In the name of all that was sacred, how could fate which had brought her twice to Bartolomeo now play such a cruel trick?

'Since I do not know this man, I cannot say.'

'I think the pirates who attacked your ship at Bahia were not French but English.'

She felt cold with fear, and she began to tremble. She tried to hide it. 'I do not know.'

'And I think Bartholomew Roberts was their leader.'

'I do not know.'

Ogle put his wine glass down on the white table cloth, and grabbed her wrist in a grip so tight she thought he would crush the bones. She cried out and John Atkins came to his feet in protest. 'Captain!'

'Sit down Mr. Atkins,' Lieutenant Sun said smoothly.

Ogle ignored them both. 'I think, madam, that you know this Bartholomew Roberts.'

'I do not. You hurt me.'

'Oh but you do. I think he took you prisoner, and took you away with him on his ship.'

How could he know? 'You are mad. I do not know him.'

'And I think you became his mistress.'

'I do not know what you speak of.'

'His lover, then.'

'No!' She summoned up every ounce of outrage she could muster. 'How dare you speak of me in such terms!' She tried to stand up, but he held her wrist tightly on the table and she was forced to sit down again. 'Let me go! I will not listen to this. I thought the captain was a gentleman. I was wrong!'

His eyes were penetrating, unforgiving. 'Oh, I know it to be true. And when we get to Cape Corso, my dear, so will the governor. I am sure he will wish to speak with you, too.'

He let her wrist go then, flinging it away from him as though it were a loathsome thing, so that it hit the table with a crack.

'I do not know what you speak of,' she said again, massaging her wrist. 'I will not be treated like this,' and she did stand up.

Ogle pretended not to notice. 'Eat up your dinner my dear,' he said almost kindly.

'I will not stay here with such a brute!' she cried with a toss of her head, and swept from the cabin.

'What do you make of that?' Ogle asked not without satisfaction as the door snapped shut behind her.

Lieutenant Isaac Sun shook his head. 'Lied through her teeth. She knows Roberts alright.'

'Indeed she does. It seems your information was correct, Mr. Sun.'

John Atkins was moved to protest. 'The *senhora* is a lady. Should we not believe the word of a lady?'

Captain Ogle raised a sardonic eyebrow at him. 'The lady is not English, and remember, women are not to be trusted.'

John Atkins was taken aback. 'Well, I don't think I agree with that, Captain.'

Ogle exchanged amused glances with Lieutenant Sun. Clearly they thought the learned doctor was naïve and had much to learn about life in general and women in particular. 'Well, you are entitled to your opinion, doctor, but we have a commission from the King to carry out, and we must use everything at our disposal to do it.'

Sun said: 'You will take her to Corso?'

'Naturally. I am sure the governor has his own way of dealing with lying foreigners.

'Sir, I must protest!' John Atkins said.

Ogle smiled at him from over the rim of his wineglass. 'Protest all you like, doctor,' he invited mildly.

As soon as she escaped from the great cabin, Lúcia went to her father's cabin where he was lying prostrate on the bunk. Seasickness did not help his agony. She wanted to tell him what had happened, to put her worries on the shoulders of the man whose task it was to protect her, but she knew when she saw how ill he looked that she could not. Instead she soothed him, and held his hand while her mind raced.

So, they were in search of pirates, and Bartolomeo was in Guinea where they intended to search. He was going to sail right into them, and she could not stop him. Now she knew why Ogle had been so quick to allow them to sail with him, but she could not think what he wanted from her. Even if she admitted knowing Roberts, how could it help Ogle? What could she possibly tell him that he wanted to know? It had been a year since Devil's Island, and anything she had known might well have changed in that time.

Even so, she had an overwhelming urge to get away from what had suddenly become to her a dangerous situation. However, with her father so sick, how could she? Furthermore, when they stopped at Cape Verde Islands on 27th March, some nine days out of Madeira, her father was too ill to even think about jumping ship and just to make sure, Captain Ogle confined her to her cabin, while the crew watered the ship. It wasn't until 7th April 1721 when the

Swallow arrived at Sierra Leone that Captain Ogle relented a little, allowing her the freedom to accompany him and his officers ashore.

By this time her father was so ill that he had to stay on the ship in the care of Rodrigues, and Ogle knew she would not try to escape and leave him behind.

TWENTY-SEVEN

June 1721, Guinea Coast, West Africa

Thick blood-warm droplets fell hard as pebbles out of a leaden sky beating the men working the *Royal Fortune* and creating a thick blue mist which hid the land from Roberts' view.

He cursed softly. He had no wish to run aground on land he couldn't see, and he knew it was close, for even in the driving rain he could smell the slave corrals of Bence Island just off Sierra Leone.

'We must heave to,' he said to Glasby, and as he said it, the rain stopped, the curtain of mist vanished, and the land appeared. It was still some distance away, shrouded in the thick green vegetation of the mangrove forests, with a single tall sentinel tree. And there, quite clearly in the telescope, he could see the wide mouth of the river.

Roberts and Symson exchanged grins. Here they could expect a welcome from men who were like themselves, retired pirates who would not turn down the opportunity of buying some of the goods they had in the *Royal Fortune*'s hold. For their part they could rest awhile, enjoy the delights of the local women and clean the ships.

Roberts smiled in satisfaction. The loss of Thomas Anstis and the *Good Fortune* had been a blow, but he had recovered from that now. On their arrival on the Guinea coast at Senegal they had captured two French interlopers. The larger one, the *St. Agnes* they made consort to the *Royal Fortune* and called her the *Great Ranger* or just plain *Ranger,* while the smaller one they turned into a supply ship and renamed the *Little Ranger.* Wanting no repeat of Anstis's betrayal, Roberts put officers on the *Ranger* he could trust: Dennis, and Ashplant, Richard Hardy and Robert Birdson. He made stocky James Skyrme another Welshman her master. He had joined them from the *Greyhound* at St. Kitts, and like Anstis, Roberts did not dignify him with the title of Captain. On the *Little Ranger* he had assigned William Williams, George Smith and the big Belgian Michael Maer. And Roberts, because he had three ships under his command, accepted the courtesy title *Commodore.*

As the *Royal Fortune* and her consorts and another captured ship sailed into the river estuary, three guns fired from the settlement.

'Are they firing on us?' Symson demanded.

Roberts peered through the telescope and frowned. In the distance against the green of the hills, little puffs of cloud announced the position of the cannon, but no cannonballs splashed into the sea near them. 'A salute, I think,' he said. 'We are being welcomed!' It added to his sense of satisfaction.

The Portuguese explorer who had discovered Sierra Leone had named it for the thunderclouds which even now sat on the hills surrounding the estuary at the cape. Lion Mountains, it meant. It earned its name.

At first sight it wasn't a place Roberts liked. The banks of mangrove swamps which lined the river emitted an unpleasant odour, a musty smell of rotting vegetation. In the water gentle manatees could be seen swimming near the ship. The locals used them for food and leather. Hippopotamus lolled lazily in the water, looking for all the world like half-submerged rocks. With the English propensity for misnomers, the sailors called them sea-horses, although any resemblance to a horse must have been in someone's drunken imagination. They were fearsome creatures, and for all their comical looks they were as dangerous as the crocodiles. Their teeth, while not as prized as the elephant tusk, were exported as inferior quality ivory.

And then, of course, there were the crocodiles lurking in the waters, viewed by the sailors with exaggerated horror, for who had not heard the tales of men who had been eaten by such fearsome beasts?

Sierra Leone was a labyrinth of rivers, a swampland with inlets and creeks where a ship could be lost for weeks, if not years. In Frenchman's Creek the pirates took another ship which lay at anchor and all five ships subsequently anchored in another creek which came to be called Pirates' Bay because of them.

Here they were among friends. Those who had sailed with Howell Davis, Symson, Ashplant, Dennis, Hardy, had been here already and assured Roberts that pirates were welcome here. They could relax a little, take some furlough, enjoy the comforts of the local women. But first it was time to make the acquaintance of the locals.

After the sea breezes, the air on land was hot and heavy and seemed very still. Flies and mosquitoes hovered in clouds and buzzed around their ears. They had come in the rainy season, and thick clouds rolled down from the mountains dumping impossibly huge amounts of water on the land in short sharp bursts of stinking warm rain, before opening to let the sun come through and turn the jungle into steam.

As they approached the town the tribespeople came out to stare at the visitors. Tight-breasted girls, dressed only in a bright blue cloth about their brown hips, and with bangles of copper about wrist and ankle, giggled together at the tall overdressed and sweating Englishmen. The older women, with fat little children strapped to their backs stared silently, while the men, sitting together in a group in the shade of the large tree, and smoking and drinking from large earthen pots, watched their progress from suspicious eyes.

The pirates swaggered on, as some of the women, becoming braver, came forward and began to crowd round the visitors in a noisy jabbering mob. A girl reached out with a thin brown hand to touch Roberts' face and then his arm through his shirt, as though feeling the strength of his muscles. He found himself looking into a handsome dark face with huge brown eyes and grinning white teeth. The rest of the crew needed no further encouragement. With whoops of delight they grabbed the giggling shrieking women and took full advantage of the hospitality while the husbands looked on.

'It is considered a great privilege to bear a white man's child.'

The speaker was a large man with skin as black and shiny as newly-cut coal, thick lips a dark purple colour, and a wide flat nose. He bowed respectfully. 'You are welcome,' he said. 'My master bids you come and eat at his own house.'

'How is your master?' David Symson asked.

'He is well,' the servant said solemnly. 'Please to come this way.'

He led them through the forest path and up the hill to a large stilted colonial house with three cannons stationed on the front lawn—the same three which had fired in welcome no doubt.

'Gentlemen! Welcome, welcome!' Roberts turned to see a white man of perhaps sixty or more, coming towards them. 'This is Captain John Leadstine,' Symson whispered to Roberts. 'Old Crackers—I told you about him.'

John Leadstine had certainly earned himself the nickname. He looked wild, or mad, with a shock of long white hair sticking upwards from his head like a halo and a beard and moustache to match, reminding Roberts of a lion with an albino mane. He peered with startlingly blue eyes at David Symson. 'Didn't you come here with Cap'n Davis a year or two back?'

'Aye,' Symson laughed. 'Nothing wrong with yer memory!' Then his face clouded. 'Cap'n Davis was killed at Princes along with Stephens. You remember Stephens, the surgeon?'

'Aye, I remember,' Crackers replied grimly. 'Killed, eh?'

''Twere a bad business.' Then he brightened and belatedly remembered the commodore waiting patiently beside him. 'This is Cap'n Bartholomew Roberts. William Magnes, quartermaster, and Harry Glasby our sailing master.' Magnes had replaced Symson as quartermaster as they arrived on the coast.

Crackers grinned broadly and he had no teeth at all. He viewed every newcomer as a prospective customer in provisions at least, but pirates were particularly welcome. 'Well, and it's pleased I am to meet ye, Cap'n Roberts.' His ice blue eyes studied Roberts keenly. 'I heard about ye.'

'You've heard about me?' Roberts asked a good deal surprised, as Crackers showed them into his neat, clean house.

'Oh aye.' Crackers, bent as he was, turned to peer up at Roberts. 'You've affrighted the world, by what I hear.'

Roberts was pleased. So his reputation had gone before him.

'Navy's bin asking after ye,' Crackers added, 'so I bin sort of expecting ye. Come in, come in.'

He showed them into his withdrawing room. It was crammed full of furniture and odd items taken from different ships and used as decoration. Roberts gave it cursory inspection. 'The navy?'

Crackers peered up at him. 'Aye, Chaloner Ogle to be precise. And a man called Heardman. In the *Swallow* and the *Weymouth*.'

Roberts became uneasy. 'How could they know about us?' He sought his memory. 'Don't we have a man from the *Swallow* with us? Or am I remembering wrongly?'

'Yes we do,' William Magnes said. 'Thomas Robert Armstrong. Deserted from the *Swallow* in Madeira. We picked him up from a Dutch galley.'

'Did he say anything about this Ogle looking for us?'

William Magnes shrugged. 'Don't reckon he knew. If he'd a said so, you'd have known.'

Roberts frowned intending to have a word with Armstrong at the first opportunity. 'When were they here?' he asked Crackers.

Crackers considered, his bushy white eyebrows meeting over

his huge nose. 'I dunno. Two months maybe. I dunno. 'Twere before the rainy season got under weigh proper.'

'About the time we left the Carib, then,' Symson said.

'And how could they know we were coming here? We didn't know ourselves!'

Crackers shrugged. 'They didn't say. But they were pretty sure you were here already.'

Roberts frowned. Had they intercepted Anstis, then? He was the only one who knew where they were heading.

As he considered it, the door opened to admit a native woman carrying a laden silver salver and Crackers' blue eyes lit up. He licked his lips with the tip of a pink tongue unconsciously, and Roberts smiled to himself.

The woman was plump with skin like mahogany silk, and a large round moon-face. Like all the natives she wore only a blue cloth about her hips, just enough to cover half way down her short plump thighs and her large heavy breasts hung free, swinging pendulously.

They were used to seeing natives on both sides of the Atlantic in various states of undress, but they had been at sea sometime, and the woman was both shocking and erotic.

Even David Symson, whose exploits with women were legendary among the company, looked away.

'This is Mary,' Crackers told them, 'my chief woman. You like her?' He was looking at Roberts who didn't answer. Crackers said something in the native language to the woman who giggled girlishly.

She set the tray down on the card-table, and served each of the guests—elaborate cut glass goblets for the rum, and a delicate blue-and-white china cup and small matching pot for the tea. Then she left the men as silently as she had come in.

With a huge effort, Roberts brought his mind back to the present. 'Where is the *Swallow* now?' he asked.

'South,' Crackers told him. 'Not due back 'til Christmas.'

Roberts smiled. 'That leaves us clear, then. If we also follow him south, we can get word as we go.'

'You're leaving straight away?' Crackers asked, unable to hide his dismay.

Roberts shook his head and grinned. 'Nope. We've earned ourselves some time ashore, I reckon.'

'Then I got women for you,' Crackers said, pleased.

Robert Glynn was one of the few respectable traders of the settlement, having once been employed by the Royal African Company in Gambia, and then gone into business with a man called Richard Warren and another known only as Norton, in the ownership of two long-boats and two small boats. He had already purchased a large quantity of goods from the *Royal Fortune*, and now he and several of the other traders sat round the fires with the pirates who had set up camp ashore while they careened the up-ended *Royal Fortune*. A protective thicket of thorns together with fires and armed men constantly on the watch around the camp kept leopards and crocodiles at bay.

Night had come with the suddenness of the tropics and with it a short but very fierce rainstorm, so that the sails pressed into service as tents were of little value in keeping out the wet. But sailors were used to all sorts of weather and being constantly wet anyway, so that the discomfort went mostly unnoticed. A decent fire, a bottle of rum and soft warm women were all a man needed to restore that sense of well-being that the weather tried hard to dispel.

'The King's men were here looking for you,' Robert Glynn said chewing on his pipe and stretching his feet to the fire. He had the cultured accent of the educated.

'So Crackers said.'

'Crackers, huh!' Glynn spat disparagingly into the fire. 'Reckons he's king here.' Roberts smiled to himself. 'Anyway,' Glynn went on, 'he was quick about entertaining the King's navy.'

'That were because of the woman,' Richard Warren put in and he had a surly voice.

'Oh aye, the woman,' Robert Glynn smiled in the firelight at the memory. Somewhere along the beach, the scrape of fiddles and the shriek of pipes accompanied a song which was chorused by a hundred drunken voices. 'Listen to that racket!'

'What woman?' David Symson asked the question all of them wanted to know.

'A passenger. It's the first time I've heard of the navy taking passengers.'

'And what a woman!' Richard Warren put in a voice of awe. 'One of them quality pieces. Portuguese. An ambassador's daughter.'

Roberts' heart stopped and then lurched onwards. Symson met his eyes across the fire.

'Not an ambassador's daughter,' Glynn corrected Warren. 'Emissary. That's a messenger.'

'*Senhor* Pietro Andrade and his daughter,' Roberts said quietly, not looking at either man.

She is here! On this coast!

'You know them?' Glynn asked staring at Roberts.

David Symson shifted uneasily and exchanged glances with Henry Dennis who had wandered to the edge of the group and sat down on the soft sand.

'We've occasioned across 'em a time or two,' Roberts said casually. 'Do you know where they're going?'

'With the *Swallow*. That is to say they left with the *Swallow*. Captain Ogle announced his intention to go south.'

'I tell you, I ain't never seen such a beauty,' Warren put in. ''Tis a long time since I met such a woman. Hair like black silk. Skin like pearl.'

There was a look in Roberts' eyes that prompted Glynn to say: 'Don't mind him. The ravings of a desperate man! She would no more notice him than a fly on the wall. She was a lady, proud, and more concerned with her sick father than with anything else.'

So where is she going? Where is she now? On this coast somewhere.

Roberts said: 'What about her husband?'

'There was no husband,' Robert Glynn said. 'Just her father and two servants.'

So, she had not married. Roberts stared into the embers of the fire yet did not see them. Instead he could see Lúcia with her luxuriant hair, and black expressive eyes, and he longed to reach out and touch her. The need was deep, physical, and intense.

Further along the beach someone fell over and caught his hand in the edge of one of the fires, and shrieked with pain. It brought raucous laughter from the rest, but Roberts paid it no heed. Another time their drunken antics would have made him laugh or would have drawn censure. Now he hardly noticed.

With an effort he brought his mind back to Robert Glynn. 'What is Captain Ogle like?' he asked.

Glynn thought for a moment. 'Ordinary. Plump, but not yet fat. Double chin. Wears an expensive wig.'

'As a man?'

'Oh! Clever. Sharp. Not a fool. His men don't cross him, I can tell you. I'd say he was dangerous. I didn't like him. Too lofty by far. And that Lieutenant Sun of his, well a real aristo, and no mistake.'

'He don't miss anything,' Warren put in.

'Oh, he's a dangerous man, Captain Roberts. And I would suggest you be wary of him.'

'He were asking about you, Captain,' Warren added.

'So I heard.'

'He wants to stretch your neck.'

'He'll have a long wait.'

Glynn said: 'He thinks you're here before him, but further south. That's where he'll be.'

'Then we have nothing to fear,' Roberts said.

The conversation turned. Glynn asked about Howell Davis, and Roberts left it to Symson and Dennis and Ashplant to tell him what had happened while he ate some of the roast chicken. He found, though, that he wasn't hungry. He had to fight the urge to right the ship immediately and sail out before the dawn in search of Lúcia. He couldn't, of course. The men had been at sea for too long and had worked hard. They deserved time off. To cancel their furlough would be to incite mutiny, and while he might be *pistol proof* he was not bullet-proof. But oh, how he longed to find Lúcia! And when he did, he would not let her go a second time.

TWENTY-EIGHT

June 1721, Guinea Coast

H.M.S. *Swallow* and H.M.S. *Weymouth* made leisurely progress down the western coast of Africa, stopping at Cestos and Cape Appolonia and arriving at Cape Corso in mid-June.

From the deck of the *Swallow,* Lúcia had her first glimpse of the English capital of the Gold Coast. It was an immense, forbidding castellated grey stone fort jutting out into the Atlantic on a rocky ledge, and surrounded by barren hills and a ramshackle native town sprawling to the east. Lúcia thought it a supremely ugly edifice, giving the lie to picturesque palm-edged sandy beaches which flanked it.

The squadron under Ogle's command hove-to and dropped anchor off-shore.

John Atkins, joined her at the guard rail. '*Senhora* the captain has asked me to advise you to get your things together. You and your father are going ashore.'

She studied him for a moment, searching for clues. 'What do they want from us, *senhor?*'

He avoided her gaze. In the months since they left Madeira she had found herself drawn to him, sensing that he was the only man on board she could trust and it fascinated her that he kept a journal of his travels. For his part, John Atkins spent a good deal of time tending her father in his sickness, which brought them together quite often. He made it plain that he would have liked to take the friendship further.

'They want the pirate, that's all.'

'Are we in danger, *senhor* Atkins?'

He smiled. 'I shouldn't think so.'

She looked at the castle walls and shivered. 'I do not like this place.'

An hour later they were being admitted into the castle gates.

It was built around a quadrangle, or more precisely, a triangle, and contained a smithy, a cooperage, storehouses, a chapel and houses for the officers and servants. There were four dungeons at ground-level, built like tunnels with arched ceilings fifteen feet high, no windows save for the iron-grilled door at the front. These were the holding cells for the slaves, where the poor wretches were held for ninety days in a deliberate attempt to weed out the weakest. There were slaves in them now, silent and abused and stinking. Lúcia found herself remembering what Bartolomeo had said of the slave trade, how he had despised the brutality, the cruelty, the treating of people as less than a man would treat his dog or his horse, and she thought of the poor wretches who suffered there. He had called it a crime against God and man.

Without thought for the contradiction, the chapel had been built on top of the dungeons. Did they think to make it right by bringing God into it? The hypocrisy of it struck her, and at the same time she realised how her own thinking had changed. A year ago she was convinced that the civilised world needed slaves. Now she knew it for what it was—an abomination. And her heart went out to the wretches she could just see in the shadows as they passed.

Near the dungeons were the large holding tanks built into the ground which collected the rain running off from the pavements sloping towards them, for there was no ground water nearby except for a stagnant pool outside the castle. The tanks were for the castle itself; visiting ships had to use the stinking water from the pool.

She had heard of Cape Corso's grim reputation. For not only were the native Africans slaves here but, in effect, so were the white men. Merchants, company agents, writers, miners, craftsmen and soldiers came out to the coast to make their fortune, only to find that their salaries were barely sufficient to buy 'canky', the peculiar bread of the region, and fish and palm-oil, the subsistence diet of both black and white people. In London these same artisans might well have earned fifty to a hundred pounds a year and been well off. Worse, they were paid in 'crackra', the token money of the castle, so that they could not buy goods or food from visiting ships, for no captain would accept money which was valueless elsewhere. Neither could they leave, for the law stated that a man's debts had to be paid in full before he could leave—and even in those rare occurrences where by careful management and near starvation a man kept himself out of debt, there were devious ways of ensuring that there was always something outstanding. In short, once the director-general had a man in his clutches, he was not going to let him go.

Meanwhile, the director-general James Phipps ensured that he was king supreme, granting himself two thousand pounds a year. He had a native 'wife', and six children, good food, a garden that provided all his wants, and a great deal besides. He had an apartment which adjoined the chapel which place of worship was a large vaulted hall serving many purposes besides worship—namely to dine in, to drink in, and to discuss trade. Next to that a bastion looked out to sea, so that with a telescope he could personally observe every ship which sailed into the road, and even the ships anchored at Del Mina further along the coast.

It was to this vaulted chapel that Captains Ogle and Heardman, Lieutenant Sun and John Atkins and Lúcia and Pietro Andrade were brought by a depressed pale-faced half-starved soldier who spoke with the secretary.

Lúcia glanced at her father. He had aged considerably since Madeira, his frame bent almost double, his face a mask of pain. The yellow tinge had become a permanent feature of his skin. The voyage, the seasickness, the bad food, the cramped unhealthy conditions had all taken their toll. She glanced at John Atkins who looked steadily back at her with his light eyes mirroring his concern. He had already told her that, in his opinion, Pietro had no more than six months left.

'The Director-General will see you now,' the secretary said, bending himself in a bow.

The two captains, Lieutenant Sun and surgeon Atkins went into the office, but when Lúcia and her father made to follow them, the soldier prevented them, and indicated that they should sit down on the wooden benches which served as pews, to wait.

For an hour they waited in virtual silence. It was strangely quiet inside the chapel, the noise outside of people in the quadrangle, the shouts and orders of the soldiers, the groans and screams of some poor wretches in the dungeons, as well as the wash and hammering of the sea against the walls seemed as if part of another world. Lúcia's thoughts were with the men in the office. What were they saying about her?

The huge arched door opened again, and the secretary said: 'Director-General Phipps will see you now, *senhor*.' He waited stiffly while Pietro Andrade struggled to his feet, and he and Lúcia entered the Director-General's office.

The room was fairly small, the lime-washed walls lined with bookshelves and many volumes. There were two large desks, one for Director-General James Phipps who sat behind it, the other for his secretary. The four naval men had chairs in front of the main desk, but were standing in front of them out of politeness for Lúcia and her father's entrance, and two more empty chairs were added.

That Phipps did not suffer the same want as those underlings in the castle was evident from the enormous bulk of his person behind the desk. He had a fat round face, pink with an unhealthy flush, a double chin, and tiny little eyes almost swallowed by the surrounding flesh.

His expression changed from grim business to surprised pleasure as his eyes rested on Lúcia. '*Senhora!* Enchanted!'

She dropped a quick polite curtsey. Pietro Andrade bowed.

Phipps invited them to sit down, and Ogle, Heardman, Sun and Atkins also sat.

'I am delighted to make your acquaintance, sir,' Phipps said in English to Pietro Andrade, and Lúcia had to translate.

'Tell this son of an English whore that he stinks!' Andrade said tetchily.

Lúcia said diplomatically: 'My father is pleased to meet you too.'

Phipps suspected that she had not made a true translation, but she met his enquiring look with wide blankly innocent eyes.

'And what is your business on this coast, sir?' Phipps demanded.

Again Lúcia translated.

'Tell that English pig that I go to Whydah to the Portuguese fort there, at the orders of the most sovereign King João of Portugal,' Pietro Andrade said.

Lúcia translated.

Phipps focused on Lúcia. 'And you, madam?'

'I go with my father,' Lúcia explained.

Phipps studied her with small piggy eyes. She could see in the slight smirk on his fat lips and the glint in those eyes what he thought of her, and she decided in that moment that she did not like this man at all. She knew his sort, a lecherous old man who thought that his wealth and position would entice any female he liked the look of into his bed.

Phipps, his voice oily smooth, said: 'I understand, *senhora* Andrade that you are the mistress of the great pirate Roberts?'

Lúcia put her chin up, looked him straight in the eye and said: 'No.'

'What are they saying, Lúcia?' her father asked.

'They are talking to me, *Pápa*. It need not concern you.'

Phipps glanced at Andrade, then raised a questioning eyebrow at Captain Ogle. Ogle said nothing, but sat quite still, his face impassive.

'Captain Ogle says that you were abducted by Captain Roberts, *senhora*.'

'Abducted? I do not understand.'

'Taken away.' He replied irritably. 'The pirate took you away.' He raised his voice and spoke much more slowly now as though he spoke to an idiot. She had noticed this habit among the English when speaking to foreigners.

'Captain Ogle has asked me if that is so. I told him as I tell you, that it is not.'

'But you have met this Roberts?'

'My maid and I waited on a Portuguese ship anchored off Bahia bound for Lisbon when pirates attacked and took the ship. As to whom the pirates were, I have not the slightest idea. We thought they were French, or perhaps Dutch.'

Ogle cut in. 'So how is it, madam, that the report reached London of a woman abducted by the pirate?'

Lúcia shrugged carelessly, but her heart was beating quickly. 'I do not know how these stories start.'

Ogle turned to Phipps. 'The Admiralty has a report of this case, a complaint from the Emissary himself, *senhor* Andrade.'

Lúcia said with aplomb: 'My father was not on the ship with me and the first reports were wrong, as he was pleased to learn.'

The smile on Phipps' fat lips widened, but the eyes hardened. 'You must think me very stupid, my dear.'

'Yes I do,' she said sweetly, 'if you believe such tales. I, Lúcia Margarida Carvalho Andrade would never deal with a common pirate!'

Phipps considered her, pursing his fat wet lips. 'We shall see. I think we will be able to find lodgings for you here in the castle.'

She stood up. 'You cannot keep us here.'

'Can I not?'

'My father has a commission from the King of Portugal! The King shall hear of this.'

'No doubt,' Phipps agreed dryly.

Pietro Andrade also stood up. 'What is happening, Lúcia?'

She gave him a brief outline.

'Tell that son of an English whore that I have to go on to

Whydah, and that if he does not let us go he will have the Portuguese navy about his ears!'

Lúcia translated, but John Atkins cut across her, also coming to his feet. 'I must protest, sir,' he said, 'the *senhor* is sick. This place will see him in his grave.'

'This place sees a lot of men much younger than the *senhor* in their graves,' Phipps said coldly. 'It is of no consequence.'

Lúcia appealed to Captain Ogle. 'You will let him do this to us, *capitão?*'

Captain Ogle looked at her. 'You mistake the matter, madam, if you think I have any jurisdiction here. Director-General Phipps must do as he sees fit. I am sure you will be well-treated.'

Lúcia glared at him. 'How can you do this, how can you let this happen?'

But Captain Ogle had turned away from her, his face a blank mask.

As Phipps gave the order, a soldier took hold of Lúcia's arm, and she and her father were led, protesting, from the office.

'What do you think?' Ogle asked Phipps when they had gone.

'She is lying,' Phipps said easily. 'If Roberts were any sort of a man and he set eyes on that woman, he would not have let her off lightly. But I cannot see at the moment how that will serve us, even if she admitted it. In any case there is no report of Roberts on this coast. I think you are mistaken that he is here.'

Ogle clamped his lips together, considering his options. 'I see no reason to keep the woman and her father prisoner here. If Roberts is not here, and it seems that is the case, then they are of no use to us anyway. They wish to go to Whydah, and I intend to go down the coast myself, we shall take them with us.'

'I want to keep them a little longer.'

Ogle knew what he wanted. He said diplomatically, 'They will be a drain on your purse. I see no reason to do so.'

Phipps sucked air in through his teeth. 'Very well. I hope we don't regret this day's work.'

To Lúcia Whydah was a dank, dark, mosquito-infested hell-hole no better than Cape Corso, a fearsome place where a small knot of civilisation sat in the middle of local tribes with their voodoo witchdoctors. There were three forts there, built by the English, the Dutch and the Portuguese to protect their trading interests. Here

Pietro Andrade and his daughter were greeted by the Portuguese governor, and housed in his palace.

Looking about her Lúcia wished she had never come. While she could have no complaints about the new fort and palace she felt like a prisoner unable to venture into the fearfulness outside.

Captain Ogle's company had no such qualms. For two weeks in July they enjoyed themselves mightily with the local women. At all the places they stopped as they travelled along the coast they had enquired of Roberts, or indeed any pirates, and always received the same answer. No-one knew anything of them. It seemed they had come to Africa to no purpose, and Ogle had no second thoughts about leaving the Andrades at Whydah.

On 20th July the *Swallow* and the *Weymouth* left Whydah, still intent on travelling south, and arrived at Príncipe or Prince's Island on 28th July, where they cleaned ship and enjoyed the accommodating women the pirates had enjoyed over a year earlier.

Surveying the huge *Swallow* tipped over on her side, Captain Ogle shook his head. He was eager to be going, but the careening would keep him here at least two weeks, a necessary but frustrating business. The sooner he confirmed that there were no pirates at present operating on this coast, the sooner he could be off to Brazil or the Caribbean. He might find Roberts there. Certainly he would find other pirates there.

But it was Roberts he wanted. No other pirate company matched his calibre. It was estimated now that he had plundered three hundred ships. That was a terrible number of ships in just two years. No wonder he was a legend! It was as though he had a special mission not to let any ship go without attack. However, it was his ability to evade capture which most fascinated Ogle. Despite repeated attempts by various agencies he seemed to have the Devil's own luck. Which made him a fitting adversary for Ogle's skills.

John Atkins, the surgeon, crossed his line of vision, and brought Ogle out of his reverie. Atkins seemed to be making his way directly to Captain Ogle's tent with long purposeful strides. He was not wearing his coat, but was in rolled-up shirt-sleeves, a circumstance that would ordinarily have earned a remark from the captain; he deplored slovenly dress.

However, something in the way Atkins approached warned Ogle of trouble. As he came nearer, Ogle saw that his face was set, his expression grim, and Ogle knew that slide in his belly which told him to expect the worst.

As John Atkins came into the shade of the tent, Ogle set aside his pen. 'Mr. Atkins?'

John Atkins leaned forward across the captain's table, his sun-reddened face beaded with sweat, his pale eyebrows drawn together across the bridge of his nose with alarm. 'Captain, we have fever among the crew.'

Ogle felt the sudden lurch of dread in his belly, but outwardly he remained completely imperturbable. 'What kind of fever, Mr. Atkins?'

'Yellow fever.'

Ogle took a breath to give himself time to think. Yellow fever was the most feared of all the ailments which assailed Englishmen in the tropics. Once a man had it, his agonising demise was a foregone conclusion. None survived. 'Yellow fever? You are sure of this?'

'William Metcalf collapsed this morning, and was brought to me with all the symptoms: violent headache, backache, nausea, high fever.'

Ogle struggled to hope for the best. 'Forgive me, doctor, but do not those symptoms cover many ailments?'

'Aye. But just now, before I came to you, he vomited blood. It is the classic sign. As the fever progresses his skin and the whites of his eyes will turn yellow, and then there will be no more doubt.'

Captain Ogle could not argue with John Atkins. He was all too familiar with the symptoms of yellow fever. 'Damn it to hell! Are others sick?'

'Not yet, sir.' But they both knew that if one man had yellow fever, everyone would get it.

Ogle felt the coils of dread in his insides. Pacing the deck in his agitation he saw disaster on a grand scale looming, and he was powerless to do anything about it. A large number of his company were going to die.

Not understanding that yellow fever was transmitted by mosquitoes, and likely contracted at Whydah, he blamed the outbreak on the men's freeness with the local women who were obviously poisonous. Men fresh out from England were always the first to succumb to tropical diseases, not like the seasoned sailors, and those who had lived all their lives in the tropics. And nearly all the men aboard the *Swallow* and *Weymouth* were pressed men who had never before stepped out of their own villages, let alone visited the tropics. They had no immunity.

'You have him in isolation?' he demanded of Atkins.

'Naturally. But I doubt it will prevent an outbreak. They have contracted the fevers from the women. In my experience, if one man has it, they will all have it. I am doing all I can.' He went on to tell of the arrangements he had made for nursing the sick, but Ogle wasn't listening. The coming disaster occupied the whole of his thoughts. They ought to leave Prince's now, but with the ships hauled over on their sides for cleaning they were trapped, and it would be at least two weeks before they were ready to sail. By that time the plague would have raced through the company like an Old Testament angel of death.

He left Atkins and went out of the tent bellowing for Lieutenant Sun and Captain Heardman at the top of his voice. Then, remembering Atkins he turned round and said: 'Thank you, Mr. Atkins. Carry on.'

As Atkins left, Lieutenant Sun arrived, also in his shirt-sleeves, making an effort to put on his coat.

Ogle disregarded it. 'How soon before we can right the ships?' he demanded.

Lieutenant Sun blinked at him. 'Two weeks at the earliest,' he said.

'I want it done sooner. Less than a week.'

'But Captain—'

Ogle said shortly: 'We have a case of yellow fever. I don't need to tell you what that means. I want all shore leave cancelled. No man is to consort with the local women.'

Lieutenant Sun's heart sank. How could he cancel shore leave when they were already on the shore? And as for stopping the women, well, he knew that while they were ashore it was impossible to prevent the men straying. Besides, they had earned it! But he knew better than to argue. He said: 'Very good Captain.'

It wasn't that Captain Ogle distrusted John Atkins' judgement that made him decide to see for himself, rather, he was clutching at a thread of hope that perhaps Atkins, himself no seasoned sailor, had made a mistake.

But the sick man, William Metcalf had been joined by three others.

Ogle was appalled at what he saw. Metcalf had turned a terrible yellow colour. He bled from his eyes, nose, mouth, rectum and open abrasions on his skin and he vomited black blood. He screamed out and thrashed about in his pain and delirium. It would have been kinder to put a pistol to his head and pull the trigger.

As they came out of the sick tent, Atkins said: 'Seen enough, Captain?'

Ogle looked at him. 'Is there nothing you can do?'

Atkins said: 'If there were something, I would do it.'

By the end of the week they were burying three and four men a day from each ship, and the ships still had not been careened. They had not the manpower to do it. At the end of six weeks the *Weymouth* had two hundred and eighty men dead on her books, having sailed from England with two hundred and forty, and pressing men from other ships. The *Swallow* fared just a little better.

Ogle was desperate. He summoned John Atkins to a meeting in the *Swallow*'s great cabin with Captain Heardman.

''Tis impossible to keep the men from the women,' Lieutenant Sun explained. 'And that must be the reason for the continuing plague.'

'You were given an order, Mr. Sun, to stop these liaisons.'

Sun said nothing.

John Atkins said: 'I fear Captain that if we do not weigh anchor from these parts, we will lose the whole company.'

Captain Ogle ground his teeth. 'What do you think, Captain Heardman?'

Mungo Heardman frowned in perplexity. 'I do not have enough men to get the *Weymouth* under sail.'

Captain Ogle looked up at the deckhead beam in despair. His own company would have difficulty getting off the island.

John Atkins insisted: 'I think it to be of the utmost importance to leave, Captain, to find some fresh provisions, fresh air, keep the men away from the women.'

Lieutenant Sun offered: 'If we had the assistance of the Dutch ship anchored in the bay, we could do it.'

Mungo Heardman agreed. 'Aye.'

Captain Ogle said: 'Very well gentlemen. We sail on the morning tide.'

TWENTY-NINE

May 1721, Cestos

Roberts looked about him, at the havoc his men had managed to create, at the unwanted things floating in the water drifting off with the current, and then at the captured passengers and crew. There were a good number of them. The sailors were fifteen in number, but there were also soldiers in their scarlet uniforms, about thirty of them, a few civilians, and a woman standing nervously at the rear.

Roberts swept his hat in front of him in a bow, smiled and addressed them all: 'Gentlemen—and lady! As you probably know, I am Bartholomew Roberts and this is my company. We are gentlemen of fortune.' A gratifying murmur suggested they had heard of him. 'Where is your captain?'

'Ashore.' A man at the front of the prisoners stood with his legs apart, and his muscled arms folded arrogantly across his chest.

'And you are?'

'Philip Bill.'

'And why, Mr. Bill, would the *Onslow*'s captain go ashore here at Cestos if not for some illegal private trading?'

'Can't say.'

'Whither are you bound?'

'Cape Corso.'

Roberts raised a brow and his gaze took in them all. 'Cape Corso, eh?' *Poor fools!*

'I must protest!' The voice came from the ranks of the passengers, and Roberts found himself looking at a man in a clerical collar who seemed to be half his size both in height and in width.

'And who are you, sir?'

'I am the Reverend Roger Price, sir, bound for Whydah. And I must say, sir, that we have been roughly treated by your men.'

Roberts' men made a derisory sound behind him. He raised his hand, and asked Mr. Price: 'In what way, sir?' He knew in what way; the evidence was in all the destruction around him.

'Well, look at it, sir!' Price said, understandably affronted.

'What do you expect of pirates, sir?'

'We expected your men to take the things of value to them, but not destroy the things they do not want. We have lost personal possessions, and the Lord knows we have very little chance of replacing them on this coast! And it is not what we expect of Englishmen.'

Roberts cast his eyes over the rest of the passengers, three gentlemen and the woman. One of the men spoke up as Roberts looked at him. 'I am Edward Crispe and this is Thomas Castell, agents for the Royal African Company. The behaviour of your men, Captain is a blight to all right-minded Englishmen. Do you have no control over your company, sir, or are you Captain in name only?'

Edward Crispe himself seemed to Roberts to be the kind of despot he and his men had sought to escape, with his fine coat and snowy lace cravat and the long white curls of an expensive wig. He had the air of a man who thought himself superior to the rabble. Even so, the jibe found its mark, and Roberts' dark eyes hardened. He said smoothly: 'You mistake the matter, Mr. Crispe. We are gentlemen of fortune and under no man's rule. We are free men.'

'Then I do not envy your freedom, sir.'

Roberts ignored this last remark and his gaze moved onwards to a man with no wig, but whose brown coat had been well-cut. 'And who are you, sir?'

'The name is Trengrove, and I am a mine captain.'

'And this?' He indicated the woman.

'My wife Elizabeth.'

Elizabeth Trengrove was uncommonly pretty, a woman with pale hair and pale blue eyes, and a neat trim body. She stood quietly by her husband. After a moment's appreciation of this beauty, Roberts addressed them all. 'We are in need of men. Any man who wishes to sign up, see my quartermaster, Mr. Magnes.' Magnes bowed. 'You will find the pay good, and the conditions better than you are used to. So, who will go?'

No-one moved, but the sailors exchanged glances with each other.

Watching their faces, it occurred to Roberts that some might join but were afraid to declare it openly in case they were denounced later. After all if they were caught as pirates they would stand trial at Corso and everyone else on board would be witnesses for the prosecution. Roberts turned to William Magnes. 'I must oblige these fellows with a show of force,' he said. 'Carry on, Mr. Magnes.'

Magnes said: 'Very good, cap'n.'

As his men began rounding up the sailors, many willingly signed the articles, and not a few of the soldiers desired to do so.

'We don't want landlubbers!' John Walden said in disgust. Roberts smiled. Life on the account must be infinitely preferable to life as a soldier at Cape Corso castle.

David Symson tipped the bottle and drank the rum directly from it in several gulps. He savoured the burning at the back of his throat, the rich aroma in his nose, and then the punch as the alcohol hit his bloodstream.

'Damn, that's mighty fine rum,' he said hoarsely.

Tom Sutton held his hand out. 'Thank 'ee!'

David Symson handed him the bottle. 'Did ye see the woman?' he asked the others.

Ashplant looked up from polishing his pistol. 'Aye. Trouble if you ask me. Women be always trouble on a ship!'

'Husband's no sort of man,' Henry Dennis put in. 'I'll wager it was an arranged marriage.'

'You reckon?'

'Well, he's a deal older than she is, and wealthy to boot. I reckon so.'

'She's a good-looking woman,' Symson said.

'And the Captain expects the prisoners, especially women to be treated with respect.' Henry Dennis inspected his own pistol, peering down the barrel to see if it were clean.

Tom Sutton tried on a wig he had found in one of the lockers. It was white and had curls which fell past his shoulders. 'How do I look?'

'Like some fancy woman,' Ashplant growled. 'Give us a kiss!' He made to catch him, but Sutton was too quick for him, and the others howled with laughter as he ran off around the gunroom, prancing in an exaggerated feminine way.

David Symson saw the woman first. She stood in the doorway, looking at them uncertainly, her hair in disarray, her cheeks glowing crimson, even in this half-light. She had pretty pale hair, and where it had escaped from the lace cap, it formed soft curls around her face and a stray golden curl tumbled over one shoulder. My, she was a pretty little thing!

John Mitchell stood behind her. 'Mistress Trengrove has come to beg protection, gentlemen,' he said.

'Oh?' David Symson did his best to sound suitably unconcerned.

She gave a toss of her head. 'One of your men was very rude to me,' she complained.

'Can't think why,' Henry Dennis remarked under his breath. 'Wouldn't mind being very rude to her myself!'

For some reason the remark, which was tame by usual standards, angered Symson. He said: 'What Mistress Trengrove needs is a sentinel. Upon my soul, I'll guard her honour.'

'I bet you will!' Sutton said, laughing.

He ignored him, and bowed to the lady. 'Madam, if you will permit me, I will see to it that you are safe.'

She looked up at him with her trusting pale eyes. And in that moment David Symson was smitten. She smiled. 'Thank you, sir, I would be very grateful.'

'Then I shall conduct you to your cabin!' he said, and ignored the ribald comments that followed them as they left the gunroom.

Elizabeth was under no illusions. She had seen the look in Symson's eyes when they rested on her, and knew the look well. She guessed the price she would have to pay for his sentinel duty.

Not that the man was unattractive. True, he did not have the looks of the captain—his nose was too long and hooked, and a scar ran across his cheek from the corner of his eye. Neither did he have the middle-class breeding of her husband. No, David Symson was a rough man, a man used to hard work and hard living. But there was a sensuality about him, in his hard muscles, in the way he walked, in the look in those vivid blue eyes when they rested on her, which made her catch her breath.

'Chess?' he asked, producing a fine chessboard and a box of chessmen from the chest in the small cabin.

She blinked at him. 'Chess?'

He sat down next to her on the bunk. There was no room for a chair in the cabin. 'You expected something else?' he asked mocking her.

Well yes, she had, actually. 'You know you have me in your power, sir.'

'Aye, I do that.'

She studied him uncertainly. Then she smiled, and the warmth reached her eyes. 'Then chess it is.'

He could have forced himself on her, of course. And it had crossed his mind, for she was a very taking little thing. But there was a vulnerability about her that awoke a protective urge in him which he hadn't realised existed. That was certainly a new experience.

He set up the chessboard, and the pieces on her travelling chest. 'Black or white?'

'White.' Her voice was breathless, small, like she was.

'Then you can go first.'

She moved a knight, he a pawn.

'So why are you going to Corso?' he asked.

She did not answer immediately, concentrating on moving her knight further and taking one of his pawns. 'My husband is a mine captain. They need him.'

He frowned at the chessboard. He had not expected her to be an accomplished player! 'You know it is a terrible place.'

'Is it? My husband thought he would make his fortune here in Africa.'

'If he does, it won't be in Corso.' He looked at her seriously. 'There is corruption in Corso, on a grand scale. The governor keeps even white men as slaves, you know. Your husband will be paid in crackra, the money of the Castle, and it will buy you barely enough to eat. And you will not escape.'

'You make it sound like some kind of prison, Mr. Symson.'

'It is.'

The thought troubled her. 'We have come a long way for this.'

'Then I'm sorry for it.'

She moved a pawn. 'Your turn I think.'

She played a good game, pushed him hard, and gradually she began to lose her reserve, clapping her little hands with glee when she took one of his pieces.

'Check—and mate, I think!' she cried at last.

He stared at the board in disbelief. 'Well I don't know!'

She put her head on one side and looked at him, a big grin across her face. 'Beaten by a woman, by gad!'

'Aye. But don't tell the others.' He smiled ruefully.

She laughed. Then she said: 'Tell me, Mr. Symson, where is it you are from?'

'Berwick.'

'You have an accent. Scotland, is it?'

'Almost. Berwick can't make up its mind, I reckon, whether to be in Scotland or England.'

'I have lived all my life in Truro, Cornwall. I was pledged to my husband when we were children.'

"Tain't a love match, then?'

'No. These things seldom are. We deal well enough together, though. Are you married?'

'Me?' He laughed. 'Lord, no! Ain't no woman would have me.'

'Wouldn't they? But you are a kind man.'

Nobody, not in their wildest moments had ever called him kind before. His heart seemed to miss a beat. He said for something to say: 'Am I?'

'I think so,' she said gently. 'You know I was afraid of you. But I'm not now.'

He thought: *If you knew what I wanted to do to you, you would be!*

She changed the subject. 'What made you turn pirate?'

He thought about it. 'I signed up. Better pay. Better conditions. Better food. Mistress Trengrove . . .'

She looked at him, her eyes wide and clear and grey. 'Yes?'

He stopped, unable to say more.

'Yes, Mr. Symson?' she prompted gently.

It was a strange situation. He had never been shy with a woman before, never been backward, but then the women he had known had been very willing prostitutes, whose good opinion of him didn't matter. This was quite different. If ever the others discovered that he had spent the afternoon alone with a beautiful woman merely playing chess he would never live it down!

'Mistress Trengrove—would you like another game of chess?'

Roberts had decided that he wanted to keep the *Onslow*, which was a fine frigate-built ship of four hundred and ten tons burden and twenty-six guns, and he ordered his men to make her flush and give her forty guns. It would take a few days, but there was no rush. With the *Swallow* presumably much further south, they were quite safe here at Cestos.

So David Symson found himself on duty as sentinel for longer than he had anticipated. He found himself to be the lady's shadow—walking with her on deck, and eating with her in the *Onslow*'s great cabin with the captain and the others. Her husband, meanwhile, had been taken aboard the *Royal Fortune* with the other prisoners.

She talked of her life in Truro, he of his life at sea, of battles and of the excitement of being on the account.

She asked him: 'Would you ever leave the sea, David?'

He leaned on the gunwale and looked out at the sea, the vivid blue of the ocean reflecting in his eyes, and she knew the true answer, even though he said: 'One day. When I find me a good woman.'

'You would leave the sea for a woman?'

He continued watching the sea, and it was some moments before he spoke. 'I would leave the sea for you.'

The blood shot up into her cheeks. 'Would you?' His eyes rested on her.

'Mr. Symson!' With difficulty Symson tore his eyes away from her to William Williams who crossed the deck to him. 'Mr. Symson, how many guns does the Commodore want to put on her?'

'Forty, I think. Best ask Tom Sutton.'

'Can't find him.'

'Last I seen he was looking over the stores.'

'Very good.' Williams glanced at Elizabeth. 'Ma'am,' and took himself off.

Elizabeth said: 'It is chilly.'

It wasn't cold. If anything it was steaming hot, but she shivered so he said: 'I'll take you below.'

She nodded, and pulled her shawl around her. 'Thank you. I must be a sad trial to you. I doubt you knew what you were taking on when you volunteered to guard me.'

He didn't answer her, but followed her to the hatch. 'I will go first,' he said for the ladder was vertical, and she found the steps difficult to manage with her petticoats.

It was a tricky manoeuvre. He went a few steps down and waited, she turned at the top and had to kneel on the deck, at the same time trying to keep her skirts from displaying anything unseemly. Because he was taller than she, he was able to put his arm around her waist and lift her to the lower deck using it as a good excuse to touch her. She turned within his arms to face him.

His heart crashed against his ribs. She was so close, her face so near, and just here, screened from everyone above or below, they were alone. His arms tightened around her. 'Elizabeth . . .'

She trembled in his grasp. 'I'm a married woman,' she reminded him breathlessly.

'Married to a man you do not love.'

'But I am still married.'

She pulled away from him, and he let her go, following her to the small cabin which was hers. She went in, and made to shut the door but he followed her into the gloom, closing and bolting the door behind him.

She turned and looked at him, but not afraid. 'David, please!'

He paid her no heed, but pulled her into the circle of his arms. Her pretty face turned up towards him, and her breath came in short gasps causing her breasts to rise and fall in rhythm. 'Elizabeth . . .'

He kissed her, and all at once she was kissing him, clinging to him, whispering his name.

'What happened to the woman?' Roberts asked William Magnes who, as quartermaster, had responsibility for all the prisoners.

'Little Davy is standing sentinel.' Magnes helped himself to a banana and peeled it. He was short and stocky, thickset. As quartermaster he was good with the men, although less decisive, and less of a rogue than David Symson had been. In Roberts' opinion, Symson made a better quartermaster, and it was a pity he had conceded his post to Magnes.

Henry Dennis sucked on his clay pipe. 'Davy Symson! Faith, we'll have her husband round our necks next!'

William Magnes shot him a look. 'I doubt it. The woman ain't complained, and I did speak to her.' He bit off half the banana and chewed with his mouth open. 'Seems Davy told her about Harry Glasby.'

Roberts frowned. 'Now why would he do that?'

'I dunno. Seems she were curious, like. Wanted to see Glasby on account he was married with a child. But I said as how we didn't let Glasby off the *Fortune* on account of we couldn't trust him not to leave.'

'And she didn't complain about Davy?'

'Nope. Seems to me she and Davy were getting on just fine.'

Roberts knew a stab of envy. He changed the subject. 'What about those soldiers? Are you signing them up?'

'The men seem keen. And the soldiers are begging to join us. After all, who can condemn men to work for that good-for-nothing fellow at Corso? All they'll get is a little canky and thirteen pounds a year in *crackra* money. I say we should give 'em a chance.'

'Well, you're the quartermaster. But bear in mind they are

landsmen, and will need to be taught to work a ship.'

'If the blacks can learn, so can a few English soldiers.'

Roberts glanced at Dennis. 'How's the *Onslow* progressing?'

'Well enough.'

'Good. The sooner Captain Gee takes his men and departs, the happier I'll be.'

Dennis peered at the bowl end of his pipe and tapped it on his hand. 'There's a chaplain with the prisoners,' he said.

'Yes,' Roberts said.

'The Reverend Roger Price. On his way to Whydah where he is appointed chaplain at the fort there.'

'What of it?'

'The men want to keep him.'

Roberts looked up from the papers in front of him and stared at Dennis. 'They want to keep him? Hell's teeth, this is a pirate company!'

'Well, that's as maybe. But there's no denying a little insurance don't go amiss, like.'

'What'd we do with a priest? Faith, don't they know we're all consigned to hell anyway?'

Dennis shrugged. In his opinion those who did not make it to the House of Lords—and some of those who did—were far beneath him intellectually, and as such were incomprehensible.

Roberts said: 'Well, you can ask him if he wants to join us, though what good a priest will do I don't know! But I'll not have a priest forced, that I won't!'

David Symson paused on the threshold and looked at the woman and the ready smile in her pale eyes faltered. 'David—what is it?'

He said: 'You've been ordered aboard the old *Royal Fortune*.'

'Oh.' He saw something like shutters come down behind her eyes. She knew what it meant.

He took a breath. 'Elizabeth . . .' He stopped, for the first time in his life uncertain. In all his thirty-six years he had never thought such a woman would come his way. He thought it would kill him to lose her now.

She widened her eyes, and he felt the breath catch in his throat. His belly churned within him, and his hands were shaking.

'Elizabeth—don't go. Stay with me.'

She turned away from him so that he could not see her lip

tremble, her eyes fill with tears. Forcing a lightness into her voice she said: 'Why should I stay with you? What could you possibly offer me?'

He was shocked into a brief silence. Then: 'What do you mean?'

When she didn't answer, he grabbed her arm and spun her round to face him. 'What do you mean?' he thundered.

She couldn't look up at him. 'Just what I said. What kind of life can you offer me David? A life in hiding, away from society, away from my peers? I would get you hanged because I would tie you down. Or you would be yearning for this life, and tire of being shackled to me. I don't want that.'

It went against everything he believed to lay himself wide open, yet he had only one card to play. 'But I love you,' he said helplessly.

'David, you can't give me what I want.'

'Then what do you want?' His voice rose angrily.

'I want the kind of life my husband will provide.'

'Tea parties, and dinner parties and a nice house in London, I suppose,' he said derisively. 'At Corso.'

'Yes.'

'You sell yourself to the highest bidder.'

Perhaps he was right. But it hurt to hear him say it. Was this what he really thought of her?

'And you, David Symson are a pirate, a thief, a sea-robber, a rogue. And you'll never change. It was temporary, David. A brief affair. I thought you knew that.'

He felt as though he had been kicked in the belly. What was this? Had she not given herself willingly to him? Had she not whispered words of love in his ears? Did she not come up to him when they were alone, and slip her arms around him, and hold herself against him until he thought that his heart would burst with love for her?

Her lip trembled. 'It was fun, David. You got what you wanted. Now it is over.'

He reacted angrily. 'Then madam, I wonder that you play the trollop with me!'

She had turned away again, and he could not see her face. 'Oh come now, David. I had no choice! You defended my 'honour' did you not? I knew what the price was. It was a pleasant interlude, passing away what would have been a boring three days. I am not entirely stupid, you know.'

His insides churned, and his heart pounded. 'No, but you must think I am!'

'Well I suppose you must be,' she retorted. 'For I thought you knew the rules as well. You took the job of sentinel in the hope of forcing yourself upon me, did you not? Isn't it one of the rewards of the job?'

He struggled to understand. 'You said . . .' As he remembered what she had said he felt a wound opening up inside him.

'I know what I said.'

He didn't understand it. Why was she so callous? He said stiffly: 'I mislike your games, madam.'

'Do you now? But I thought that was what you had in mind. Now I go back to my husband.'

He said with difficulty: 'I would marry you.' He had never said that to any woman, and thought he never would!

She shrugged with seeming indifference. 'I am already married.'

'Elizabeth, do not do this to me.' He was begging. 'There are places—Madagascar, Sierra Leone—where no-one will ever find us. I have gold, much gold, to set myself up as a trader. I can take care of you.'

'You are a pirate, David.'

Anger glowed white hot then in his chest. 'And you, madam, you are nothing but a high-class whore,' he cried, and had the satisfaction of seeing her flinch. At last he had hurt her the way she hurt him. 'If your husband knew what you had done with me . . .'

She spun round and fear leapt into her eyes. 'You must not tell him! David you promised me you would never tell.'

'Why should I not?' He looked at her, but he was cold inside, trembling, and angry. 'Dammit, you're not worth it.'

And he turned and left her, stalking angrily up the companionway.

Left alone, Elizabeth Trengrove closed the door on him, and, leaning against it let the tears which she had managed to hold off, come.

On the deck, the pirate company were arguing with the priest. Symson had a desperate urge to be by himself. No chance of that!

The enclosed world of a ship did not allow for solitude unless you were the captain, and often not then.

He went to the gunwale, and leaned on it, struggling to overcome the emotion that boiled within him. From here he had a view of the shore line of Cestos with the vivid green vegetation almost down to the water's edge. He hardly saw it. Inside the pain was severe, a gut-wrenching agony, and with it a fierce anger. He had offered that woman his love. He had never done that before to any woman, for he had never fallen in love before. It was an alien emotion to him, frightening in its power. Was this what the captain had gone through with the Portuguese woman? No wonder he'd not been able to think straight, and had been in such a bad temper! How did one get over it?

'If you stay you'll get a share of the prize money,' someone said to the chaplain.

'I thank you for the honour, gentlemen, but really I do not think I would like life at sea.'

'All you have to do is say prayers and mix up rum punch!' someone else offered hopefully.

'No, I thank you.'

David Symson went over to them, pushing his way through, and stood looking down at the little man. 'Leave him be!' Symson bellowed at the others. 'Can't you see the man's a Christian, and ain't interested in a parcel of rogues destined for hell fire!'

'Well, I w-wouldn't go so far as to say that . . .' Price began.

'Wouldn't you?' Symson demanded with such awfulness that the man shrank before them.

'Leave be, Davy,' Ashplant growled at him. 'He ain't done nuthin' to you.'

No, but the woman had.

William Magnes stepped in. 'Mr. Price, you are free to go. Give him back his things, gentlemen.'

David Symson turned away in search of the rum. Perhaps if he got stinking drunk the pain might go away.

Magnes said to Price: 'Tell them what things are yours, and you can keep them.'

The chaplain thanked them. He told them all the things that were his, including some things which belonged to others on the ship, but they kept four things belonging to him: four prayer books and a corkscrew.

'Damned if I know what they want prayer books for,' David Symson said to Roberts later, as they made themselves at home in the new *Royal Fortune*, formerly the *Onslow*.

'You're drunk,' Roberts accused.

Symson studied him with unfocussed eyes. 'So what if I am!' he demanded defiantly.

Roberts understood then, felt the ready sympathy of one who had similarly suffered.

He turned to Harry Glasby. 'Make ready to sail!'

David Symson went to the gunwale. He could see Elizabeth Trengrove standing on the old *Royal Fortune*'s deck, her little hands on the taffrail looking straight at him, and he thought he wouldn't survive it. 'Damn women,' he said. 'Damn them all.'

THIRTY

October 1721, Whydah

Lúcia looked up as her father came in. He walked with sticks now, and Rodrigues supported him. A bout of malaria had worsened his condition, and he seemed now a shadow of the man he once was.

Putting her stitchery aside she stood up and shook out her skirts. To fuss round him would make him crotchety. So she waited by the window for some sign from him as to what he wanted her to do.

'Ah—*filha*—my child, there you are! I hoped I might find you here. A nice room this, do you not think?'

'Yes *Pápa*, I do think so.' And so it was, with its vaulted ceiling embellished with whitewashed plaster mouldings, and whitewashed walls. It was cool in here, and the doors and windows opened onto a low overhanging roof which offered shade from the fierce African sun. In the distance, below them, the rough sea battered the smooth white shoreline, picturesque from this distance; anything but to the ships struggling to avoid the sandbar which guarded the entrance to the Whydah 'road'.

Rodrigues saw to it that Pietro Andrade was seated in a comfortable chair, a blanket wrapped around his thin legs. 'Alright, Rodrigues, don't fuss! That will be all!'

Lúcia sat down also, and picked up her needlework. It was an elaborate piece of embroidery, of peacocks and elephants in the Indian style, but she wasn't yet sure what she would use it for. She would see when she had completed it what she thought it suited best.

'I hoped I would find you, *filha*,' Pietro said. 'I need to speak with you.'

She looked at him sharply, for his breathing was laboured, difficult. '*Pápa*, are you ill again?'

He shook his head. 'My child, I am a dying man.'

She had heard it so many times before, but this time she knew it to be true. Setting her needlework aside again she jumped up to go to him, sinking to her knees beside him. '*Pápa*, do not say so. I cannot bear it when you say that!'

'You know, Lúcia, I think I like it better when you rip up at me! I know what I am about then! When you are concerned, I think I hardly know you!'

She laughed in spite of herself. 'It is true. But, *Pápa*, you are always saying that and it frightens me.'

'Death should not frighten you, my child. Go sit down over there where I can see you.' She obeyed, and he continued: 'All of us have to die sometime. It is just my turn, that's all. And I am not too upset over it. I have had a good life. I have been blessed with wealth and position, and excitement in my life. I have found a beautiful daughter, and I have known love. I am nearly sixty, Lúcia, and in this climate I ask how much more can a man expect to live? My only regret is that you will be alone in the world. If that dolt of a husband of your mother's were to die then I could be easy, for I know your mother would take care of you. But I think he will outlast me. In fact I reckon he will outlast Methuselah, that one! So it is with tiresome people! They go on forever!'

'I am able to take care of myself, *Pápa*.'

'No. Much as you would like to, you are not able to. Which is why I most particularly wanted to talk with you today. I have left you a little something in my will, Lúcia. It is not a fortune, for indeed the King has given my fortune to your cousin. But I am not entirely destitute. I have left the will in Madeira with the Monteiras. It is not a fortune, Lúcia, but it will be enough to buy you a husband.'

'Oh *Pápa*!'

'It will be yours. But Lúcia, you must promise me to marry wisely. Even this modest sum will attract those who look for fortune.'

'Oh, *Pápa*, I wish you will not talk so!'

'Lúcia, Lúcia, I know I have reached the end. I am sorry I could not have found a husband for you. Ah, but you were ever the stubborn one!'

'If you mean I would not marry Césario Guerreiro then you are right! I think I am worth more than that.'

'It is a pity you did not marry him. Just think of the estates your son would have inherited!'

'What son?'

'Why, the son you would have borne your husband.'

'*Pápa*!'

He grinned, for a moment his old self. 'Well and these things happen.' He became serious again. 'Lúcia, when I am gone, I want you to go back to Lisbon and let your mother find you a husband.'

'You forget, *Pápa*, that I am not legitimate.'

'Money talks, my dear.'

She sighed and looked out of the window at the white rolling waves on the iridescent sea. He watched her for a while, then he said: 'You think of the English pirate, do you not?'

She turned to face him. 'It is difficult to forget him, yes.' How could she forget such a man? 'Captain Ogle thought he was here on the African coast, yet we hear nothing of him here. Perhaps Captain Ogle was wrong.'

'Perhaps. You must forget him, Lúcia.'

'I know.' She forced a smile. 'And you are tired. Shall I call Rodrigues?'

'Yes, you can call Rodrigues.' He caught her hand as she went past. 'But Lúcia, I mean it. Forget this Englishman.'

'I will never forget him,' she said. 'But I will do as you say, *Pápa*. I will marry wherever my mother arranges for me.'

He touched her face, her silky hair. 'I love your mother,' he said simply.

Lúcia entered her father's chamber clutching a candle-lamp in her hands, and knew immediately that the stench in that room was of death.

Her father lay on the bed surrounded by glorious hangings, and he looked smaller and frailer than she had ever seen him. In the candlelight his skin was no longer yellow but grey and his eyeballs seemed to have disappeared into his head, so that she could only see the whites of his eyes.

She looked questioningly at Rodrigues, and he shook his head. Biting her lip she sat down on the stool beside the bed, and took the frail hand in hers. The veins stood out beneath the skin like blue ropes and his skin was cold and clammy.

Anxiously she looked for signs of life, and his chest moved very slightly.

'*Pápa*?' She tried to wake him. '*Pápa*?' But there was no indication that he heard her.

A tight knot formed in her stomach. No-one needed to tell her that he was dying. She looked up at Rodrigues. 'He is unshriven.'

'The priest came this afternoon while the *senhora* was sleeping.'

She was grateful. 'Oh *Pápa*,' she whispered, 'I should not have brought you here.'

Rodrigues said gently: 'He came of his own will, *senhora*.'

Lúcia nodded. She sat quietly, keeping vigil. And gradually, before dawn, Pietro Andrade died.

'Perhaps you have heard, Captain Ogle, that Bartholomew Roberts is on this coast?' Captain Bird asked, raising a glass of wine to his lips and drinking greedily.

Mungo Heardman's eyes flew to Ogle's face, but he remained impassive, merely pouring another glass of wine for the good captain. This was what Ogle had hoped for. He had watered and provisioned his ships at São Tomé but now in need of new recruits to make up for the men who had died, he had turned Northwest intending to reach as far along the coast as possible so that if pirates were on the coast he would find himself behind them. Now here at Cape Appollonia, Captain Bird had told him what he had been hoping to hear for months.

'Is that a fact?'

'I encountered him myself,' Bird said. 'Took the goods from my hold, and some of my blacks he pressed into service, and, damn him, set the rest free. Free! I ask you, Captain Ogle, is that the action of a rational man?'

Ogle ignored the question. 'How many ships does he have?'

'Three at the last count. A frigate-built with upwards of forty guns, and a galley, and a smaller ship. I tell you, Captain, we were pleased to escape with our lives. The frigate was once the *Onslow* I have been told, belonging to Captain Gee. Roberts took her at Cestos, and misused her people terribly.'

'We have to find this Roberts,' Captain Ogle said to Mungo Heardman later.

'Now we know he is here, we can find him. He must have been to windward of us.'

'Aye. Behind not in front. And while we languished at Príncipe, he has virtually put a stop to trading in these waters!'

Director General Phipps at Cape Corso confirmed it. 'I have had so many reports about him. He is taking three or four ships a day. Dammit, I thought you would have caught him before this, Ogle.'

Captain Ogle's eyes narrowed. Faith, how he hated this man! If it were not for his orders from the Admiralty that he was to do

Phipps' bidding he'd have told him what he thought of him. He said tightly: 'We have had severe misfortune, sir. We have lost over three hundred men to yellow fever and malaria since we last saw you, and we have been held up at Prince's for six weeks together.'

Phipps was unconcerned about the tragedy. Such men as common sailors were expendable. 'And since then?' he asked.

With visions of the horror still fresh in his mind, it took superhuman effort to stifle the desire to plant his fist in the middle of the fat shiny face. He said with studied control: 'We cannot continue without more men. We must impress men from the ships in the road.'

Phipps clicked his tongue. The men on every ship were needed and it would leave many captains short-handed. He didn't need to say so, of course. Ogle knew that. Besides, he was not much interested in others' misfortunes himself. Instead Phipps came back to the subject that interested him most. 'And that fellow Roberts?'

Ogle could read the man, knew what he was thinking, and was incensed at his lack of humanity. Mungo Heardman stepped into the silence. 'Everywhere along the coast we hear of his attacks, sir. Scarce a ship escapes his notice.'

'Damn the man!' Phipps exploded, 'I have a letter from Mr. Robert Plunket in Sierra Leone informing me that Roberts was there in July. He attacked the fort at Bence Island and did considerable damage so that Plunket was in fear of his life. And you heard about the *Onslow*? Roberts signed up half her men! Even some who were soldiers destined to guard this post. Roberts took the ship and left captain Gee his old ship, which was leaking I tell you. That's it there in the road, hardly sea-worthy!'

Ogle looked out at the old *Royal Fortune* with interest. From this distance she was a ship, like any other, three-masted, but with flush decks. He said: 'Where is Captain Gee? I would like to speak with him.'

'That can be arranged. And what next, Captain Ogle?'

Ogle said: 'I will leave the *Weymouth* here with Captain Heardman until he can press enough men to man her, and I shall continue the search for Roberts alone.'

Phipps stood up, and his face was set. 'Get this Roberts, Captain Ogle,' he said.

Ogle met his eyes squarely. 'If Roberts is on this coast, I swear before God that I shall find him.'

Even so, finding Roberts was easier said than done. Later Captain Heardman asked: 'Where will you look, Captain?'

Ogle shook his head. 'He has been operating around Appollonia, Cape Three Points, Dixcove, Axim, so that seems the place to look.' That meant travelling west, back from where they had come.

Heardman pursed his lips thoughtfully. 'You think he is still there, sir?'

'Phipps mentioned that Roberts was in Sierra Leone back in July two months after we left. You can wager that that old man Leadstine, the one they call Old Crackers, will have told him about us being there, and that we planned to sail south. Roberts will be betting that we are as far south as the Cape, and not due back for another two months. He thinks he is safe.'

'And if I were Roberts, I would hunt for ships around the trading forts.'

'And that is what he will do. So that is where he will be.'

'But you are just one ship, sir.'

'Well, we shall see what happens.'

'I would we were going with you.'

'Impossible. But later when you are manned, you shall join us. We'll come back for you.'

Heardman didn't like it, but he knew he had no choice. 'Very good, sir.'

In fact Roberts was not where Ogle thought him to be, but nearly a thousand miles to the east of Cape Corso.

THIRTY-ONE

October 1721, Old Calabar

The river at Old Calabar reminded Roberts of Sierra Leone, with the same leggy mangrove swamps on either side alive with noise and movement, the flash of colour as birds, perhaps startled by the ships, took off into panic-stricken flight, and, above the constant screech and chatter of monkeys high in the trees, the constant buzz, whine and hum of insects. A floating log turned into the pink and terrifyingly gaping jaws of a crocodile and humps in the river became the sea-horse or hippopotamus.

The further inland they travelled the hotter it seemed to become, the comparative coolness of the sea-breezes vanishing in the heavy insect-laden air.

'God-forsaken place,' Symson cursed irritably. Roberts cast him a sideways glance. Symson's usually long thin face seemed somehow thinner, and there was a broodiness about his eyes. Roberts knew the cause of the trouble.

'What's bothering you?' he invited.

Symson took a breath. 'Nothing,' he snapped.

Roberts nodded. Alright, he would respect his privacy.

Symson was silent for a while. Roberts could sense the anger seething through him. It had erupted in more than one drunken brawl, and he had even called a man out with pistols, only Magnes had intervened.

'Damned bitch!' Symson swore at last.

'Want to talk about it?'

Symson shook his head. What was the point? Nothing could take away the terrible sense of loss that gnawed at him like an open sore. How could he explain that he just wasn't good enough for her? She was, after all, a lady, while he was just a common sailor—a pirate. He would never forgive her for it. Never. He glanced at Roberts. But then he knew, didn't he? Hadn't that happened to him too?

Symson slapped his neck suddenly as something sunk a proboscis into his weather-tanned skin, and he cursed again irritably.

Roberts lifted his hat and wiped the sweat from his forehead on the sleeve of his shirt, and then combed his black hair out of his eyes with his fingers before replacing it. 'Want to be in England, do you

Davy?' he asked, giving Symson a different turn of thought. ''Tis October, and according to my recollection, it should be cold and wet and perhaps windy.'

Symson shuddered. 'No, not at all! Give me hot steamy jungle any day!' He managed a smile.

Roberts, not knowing the shallows of the river himself, had pressed Captain Loane into service as a pilot, and now he brought the three ships to the left bank at Old Calabar which could take vessels of nineteen and a half feet draught, anchoring them alongside two other ships.

Roberts paid Captain Loane for his services, dismissed him and turned his attention to urgent matters. He had three ships full of goods that he was eager to sell and was in dire need of provisions.

'Joseph—is there not a man on board who hails from this part of Africa?' Roberts asked when he went below.

'Aye, Captain, a man we call Samuel. Do you want to see him?'

'Yes, if you please.'

Samuel, one of the liberated slaves, was a native of Calabar of the Efik tribe. Typical of his people, he was tall, with a long noble face, flat-nosed, and thick lipped and with a long hole in his earlobes. Across his forehead he bore the tribal marks of a respected man, the scar of a knife cut drawn downwards by thumbs at the corners.

'You sent for me, Captain?'

Roberts looked up from the journal he was writing. 'Yes. I understand you come from these parts.'

'Yes, Captain.'

'We need an interpreter with the people. Will you help us?'

Samuel nodded. 'But I ask something in return, Captain.'

'Yes?'

'My freedom.'

Roberts considered him. 'You know I have given many men their freedom. You have served us well, and I hope you have not disliked your time with us.'

'Not at all, Captain. But here is where I have family—wives and children and brothers and sisters who I thought never to see again. Do you take me away from them again, Captain?'

'No, Samuel. I shall give you your freedom. And the clothes and gold that belong to you. But in return I need you to act as interpreter for us when we trade with the people.'

'Very good, Captain.'

Old Calabar was a rich town, having built its wealth on the trade that came up the river, selling mostly provisions: fish, cassava, bananas, palm oil and kernels as well as cattle goats and fowl. But their main income came from selling the slaves captured in wars with neighbouring tribes, or those convicted of crimes against the community—anything from adultery to theft to kidnapping—and the evidence of their wealth was everywhere, in the richly patterned silks and metal bowls and dishes, knives and even guns.

The Efik people, a branch of the Ibo, had a finely stockaded town made up of small family hamlets of mud and thatched huts, with a larger hut with many rooms for the head of the community and his wives and children, and several small huts for his slaves, all enclosed within a wall. There was also a marketplace and a meeting place.

It was to this meeting place that Samuel led the pirates, watched by the stately handsome people who paused in their daily chores to watch this procession. They waited some minutes, as the people gathered, the women bare-breasted with jars on their heads, children tied to their backs, the men large and muscular, all of them watching the newcomers with wide-eyed interest. Then the elders appeared.

There were nine of them of differing ages—some with balding pates the woolly hair touched with white, others with white crowns, and still others men with their hair black, in their prime, but all wearing feather headdresses. Each of them had a scar across his forehead like Samuel's, a thick welt which was the sign of a proud lineage, and each man carried a spear in his hand and a dagger in the belt which held a toga-like garment in place topped by a cloth cloak of blue. They sat down on mats to hear what the English had to say, and invited the English to sit down too.

One of them spoke to Samuel in their peculiar language, and to his relief Samuel understood and answered. They questioned Samuel carefully, perhaps finding out where he was from and how he came to be with the English, for Samuel had said they would ask him these things, and then Roberts heard his name mentioned and the eyes of all nine elders slid in his direction.

Roberts inclined his head towards the man who was speaking, and said: 'Give them my best wishes, Samuel, and those of King

George of England.' He knew African people were impressed by talk of white kings, and he saw their interest aroused still further as Samuel translated. 'Tell them that we bring goods for the Efik people,' Roberts continued, and spread his hand towards the sample goods displayed on the sand. 'Tell them that we have three ships full of such goods, and that the elders may inspect them if they wish.'

An interlude of unintelligible conversation ensued, and then Samuel said: 'They want to know what you desire in return.'

'Provisions,' Roberts said. 'And water.'

There was another long interlude while the men discussed this together, every so often stopping to look at the English. Roberts grew uneasy. It occurred to him that they were surrounded by the people of the town and that if the locals took a dislike to them, it would go ill with them indeed. Worse, he sensed from the conversation conducted in front of him that the elders were not sure of them.

David Symson sensed it too. 'I don't like it,' he said beside Roberts.

'Hold your peace,' Roberts warned sharply. 'They speak some English and can understand you.'

Symson looked at him and raised his brows. Roberts nodded, and whispered: 'It is sheer idleness that stops them speaking English to us. They are excluding us by using their own language.'

At length Samuel said: 'They want you to come back tomorrow, Captain, and they will keep the samples.'

'Keep the silk?' Roberts was not happy. 'No.'

The elders all looked at him. They understood alright.

Samuel said hastily: 'You have no choice, Captain. Unless you intend to take it from them by force?'

Roberts looked at the elders and then at the black faces surrounding him, and gave in gracefully. 'Tell them they may keep the samples as a gift of goodwill,' he said and forced a smile.'

'Then you shall have their answer tomorrow,' Samuel told him.

With the uncomfortable feeling that he had been out-manoeuvred, Roberts could do no more than agree.

The elders rose, and correctly interpreting that the meeting was at an end, the English rose too. The two camps bowed to each other, then the elders returned in stately dignity to the meeting house. Losing interest in the white men the rest of the people drifted back to their work, leaving just a group of children.

Roberts turned to Samuel. 'Do you come back with us?'

'I will stay here with my people, and I will search for my family.'

Roberts put his hand on the man's shoulder. 'Very well. I promised you freedom. You have done well for yourself, Samuel. You have gold enough to buy many wives.'

Samuel grinned happily. 'I shall be a rich man among my people.'

'And may God go with you.'

And in the next moment he had vanished among the throng.

'Well, if it ain't Israel Hynde!'

James Phillips came forward and gripped a man by the hand. 'Israel Hynde, as I live and die!'

'Don't tell me, he sailed under Blackbeard,' David Symson said dryly.

'I did that, sir,' Hynde told him. 'Got shot in the knee for my pains, and so I walk with a limp, sir.'

'Do you join us, Mr. Hynde?' William Magnes asked.

They signed up also from the *Mercy* surgeon William Child, and the surgeon from the *Cornwall* Peter Scudamore.

Captain Rolls of the *Cornwall,* anchored alongside the *Royal Fortune* at Calabar was scathing about Scudamore. 'And you can keep him,' he said to Roberts. 'A greater rogue I never met.'

'Aye?'

'A knave, by all that is dear,' Captain Rolls declared roundly. 'Always drunk, and a bad surgeon to boot. I think he learned his trade in the butcher's yard. He kills more men than he saves, that I swear. If I ever get him back to England I swear I will see him hang.'

'Bad as that, eh?' Roberts said quietly.

Captain Rolls waved a lump of goat's meat in the air. 'I tell you Captain Roberts, you take him at your peril.'

'I thank you for the warning, Captain Rolls, but I have to tell you that a bad surgeon is better than no surgeon at all, and that is where we stand at present.' For having left George Hunter at Sierra Leone where he settled down with one of the native women, they were in desperate need of a medical man.

Captain Rolls tossed back the last of the wine, and Roberts waited until he had finished before asking: 'Tell me, Captain Rolls, have you heard anything of a Portuguese Emissary and his daughter on this coast?'

Captain Rolls frowned. 'Aye, come to think of it, I have.' And as Roberts' heart began to thud in his chest, he added: 'A small man, yellow, like he's got some illness, and a young woman. His daughter you say?'

'That's them.'

'They're at Cape Corso last I saw.'

'Corso.' Roberts mulled it over. What were they doing at Corso? He said: 'And the navy ships, the *Swallow* or *Weymouth*?'

'Both at Corso. But that was some months ago.'

Roberts nodded, satisfied. Both ships should be south. He thought of Lúcia and her father. Surely Phipps would not keep them at Corso for long.

After a moment's thought, Captain Rolls said: 'You know Phipps is after you, don't you? He knows you are on this coast.' Rolls hesitated. ''Tis said that the Portuguese woman is your . . .' He waved his hand in the air expansively.

Roberts' eyes narrowed dangerously. 'Go on, captain. This is most interesting.'

Captain Rolls' eyes met Roberts' without flinching. ''Tis said they hope you will try to rescue her from Corso.'

Roberts continued to subject captain Rolls to close scrutiny. 'Indeed?'

Rolls looked down at his plate. 'Well, that's the gossip anyway.'

Roberts' mind raced. So they had laid a trap for him using Lúcia. How the devil did they know? Did she tell them? He didn't think she would. But to leave her there in the hell-pit of Corso Castle, so close but unreachable, suffering the privations common to all in the castle, was unthinkable. He began formulating plans in his head, only for him to dismiss them immediately for he realised he could not take the company to Corso. To risk his men's lives to take them where he knew danger would be waiting for them for his own personal business would be 'far exceeding his prescription' and they would never agree. The only way to do it would be for him to go by himself using stealth but he could not leave the company to do it. *Damn Phipps! Damn Ogle! Damn them all!*

Dinner over, Roberts escorted Captain Rolls from the *Royal Fortune*, offering a friendly hand. 'I wish you good speed, Captain

Rolls.'

Rolls took the hand and shook it. 'And you, Captain Roberts, I do not know what I wish you!'

Roberts laughed as from behind him the new man, Peter Scudamore called: 'Goodbye, Captain Rolls.'

Roberts glanced at him.

Scudamore's eyes were hard, like ice, as he approached Captain Rolls, and he added sarcastically: 'When you get home, sir, perhaps you will be so kind as to put a notice about me in the Gazette as to how I became a pirate against your good offices?'

Captain Rolls glared at him with open dislike. 'Your sarcasm, sir, does you no honour.' He climbed over the side.

'Don't you wish to go with them, sir?' William Main, the boatswain asked Scudamore in a last attempt to be rid of one who came with such a bad reference.

Peter Scudamore smiled coldly. 'Me? No. And I wish the rascal may be drowned, for he is a great rogue and has endeavoured to do me all the ill-offices he could among these gentlemen.' His glance took them all in.

Christopher Moody summed up for them all, growling: 'Well, then, surgeon, you'll have to prove you ain't no butcher, won't you!'

In fact Peter Scudamore was pleased to be the first surgeon to actually sign the pirates' articles, swearing on the Bible that he would honour the laws, and bragging that although he was the first, he hoped others would benefit. 'And I hope I'm as great a rogue as any of you,' he added laughing.

'Samuel's back, Cap'n,' Sutton announced, poking his head round the cabin door.

Roberts paused in the act of allowing Joseph to shrug him into his favourite red coat. 'Send him down, if you please, Mr. Sutton,' he said and Sutton's head disappeared again.

Joseph finished arranging the coat and stood back to allow Roberts to study his reflection in the mirror.

As ever, Roberts dressed to impress, in this case the natives with whom he expected to do some hard bargaining. 'The cross, please Joseph.'

While Joseph retrieved it from a drawer, Roberts smoothed his unruly black curls down with a brush, and Joseph produced a black ribbon to confine them at the nape of his neck. Then Joseph put the chain over his head, and the heavy six inch cross, studded with diamonds fell to his waist. It was one of the few remaining things from the *Sagrada Familia*'s booty, the cross, the chain, and a heavy ring with a large blood red ruby set in it which he wore on his right hand third finger. Putting his hat in place he grinned with satisfaction, his teeth glowing white in his dark skin but he noticed too how in this better mirror, purloined from the *Mercy*, little lines had appeared just below his eyes. Well, he told himself, he was nearly thirty-eight, so he couldn't complain. Tropical sun was known to age white skin. At least his hair, was still black.

Sutton returned.

'Where's Samuel, Mr. Sutton?' Roberts asked.

Looking him up and down appreciatively, Sutton said: 'Won't come aboard, Cap'n. Says he has a message for you from the town elders.'

Roberts frowned, irritated, his careful preparations forgotten. 'Very well.'

As soon as Samuel saw him, he bowed his head. At first Roberts didn't recognise him, for he now wore the loin cloth of the natives instead of slops and shirt, and there were feathers in his newly-plaited hair.

'Captain, I have a message for you.'

'Very well,' Roberts said. 'You may come aboard.'

'Begging your pardon, Captain, but I must hesitate to do so.'

Roberts was not pleased. 'In the name of all that is sacred, why?'

'The message that I bear is not to your desiring, Captain.'

Roberts' irritation was becoming anger. 'How so?'

Samuel bowed again in a placatory way. 'Captain, the elders say they will not trade with you. They say that you have robbed other white men's ships. They say they cannot trust men who rob their own kind. They will have no dealings with pirates.'

'*What!*' Roberts roared, and his voice was drowned by a hundred crewmen. 'May they be damned! I swear I'll teach them a lesson they'll never forget. Accursed double-crossing . . .'

'Shall I kill him, Cap'n?' Sutton suggested helpfully, waving his pistol in the general direction of the unfortunate messenger.

Samuel threw himself spread-eagle on the ground, just in case.

Roberts was so angry that he actually hesitated, tempted, and then, ashamed of the murderous rage that had already cost one man his life and nearly another, he forced it down by sheer effort of will and put his hand on Sutton's outstretched wrist. He himself had given Samuel his freedom, and he knew how he had longed to be home with his loved ones. It was not his fault the elders had selected him to be the bearer of bad tidings. 'Stay your hand,' he growled.

Samuel's eyes rolled with terror in his black face, but he saw the pistol lowered and in a moment he was up on his feet, vanishing into the mangrove forest as elusive as the early morning mist.

Around Roberts his men murmured angrily at the seeming injustice. For several days food had been severely rationed between the three ships save for brief moments of plenty on raiding the *Mercy* and the *Cornwall*, and they had looked to Calabar for fresh provisions.

He chose his officers. 'Mr. Ashplant, Mr. Symson, Mr. Sutton, Mr. Maer, Mr. Main—take forty men and force them to trade. If they will not, then teach them a lesson!'

'Aye, aye, Cap'n!'

'Oh—and gentlemen! Not the women and children.'

But the town was deserted.

'Cap'n—you'd better come and see.'

Roberts looked up from the charts he had been studying, struck by the urgency in Richard Hardy's voice. Leaving the charts, he followed him.

'What is it?' he demanded as Hardy scooted up the companionway ladder before him.

'The blacks have come for us!'

As he came out onto the open deck, the glare of the African sun made him blink, and it was several seconds before he could make out people in the forest.

With the telescope he could see more. The Efik men had gathered in the forest, their faces painted with red paste, and they were armed with spears and knives. 'They're only damned foreigners,' Valentine Ashplant growled. And every Englishman had utter contempt for foreigners when it came to skills at warfare and bravado.

Roberts considered the matter. A war with the local people was not what he had in mind. But with the number of men he had at his disposal, and the cannon fire, and the pistols and muskets, he knew he would not have to turn tail and run.

'Very well. Mr. Symson, take a detachment of men and show these blacks that the English do not flee in terror at their threats! Joseph! My sword, pistols and a musket if you please.'

'You're not going?' Henry Dennis was horrified.

Roberts looked at him. 'I haven't deserted my men in battle yet, Mr. Dennis, and I do not intend to do so in the future. But if you are afraid . . .'

Dennis swore profanely, and went in search of his own weapons.

Leaving the three ships to the command of Tom Sutton, the new master gunner, Roberts joined his men in the boat. Under the cover of deafening cannon fire from the ships they rowed ashore and immediately sank into positions along the shore facing the jungle, muskets at the ready.

Silently, ahead of them, the jungle seemed to breathe, a soft rustle of vegetation as the Efik moved forward, and Roberts felt the surge of excitement in his veins. He had heard what the natives could do to a man, how they could take days to torture a man to death as though it were some sport. Somehow it added spice to the danger.

'Ain't no damn black gonna get his filthy hands on me,' Ashplant growled low in his throat not far from where Roberts peered through the undergrowth.

'Nor me neither,' someone else said.

Above the vegetation, a black head appeared, decorated with feathers, and a spear rose up on a disembodied arm.

'Down!' Roberts bellowed. 'Damn you, get your heads down or you'll lose 'em.'

Not needing to be told more than once, the English flattened, and at the same moment the Efik came from the forest in a tide of black bodies, some two thousand of them, with painted cheeks and plumes waving in their close-cropped hair.

'Sweet Jesus!' Benjamin Jeffries exclaimed, and aimed one of the muskets beside him. He had six, which was just about all he could carry.

'Hold your fire!' Roberts cried, and Ashplant and Dennis and Symson and Magnes, the group leaders, repeated the cry. 'Hold your fire! Mark your target!'

Symson raised his sword, and waited as the Efik came forward at a run, with a terrible war cry: '*Hoo-hoo!*'

From the ships the thunder of guns and the whistle and thud of connonballs in little explosions of dust and mud and breaking trees continued unabated. A few painted black men fell.

The Efik hesitated, fell back a little, then gave another '*Hoo-hoo!*' and came towards them at a run.

'*Fire!*' Roberts bellowed, and the others bellowed too, all along the beach. Immediately forty muskets exploded in a volley of sound and lethal lead.

The front row of Efik stopped and fell as if they had hit an invisible wall just a hundred feet in front of them at the edge of the forest. Spears flew through the air towards the English as they grabbed the next musket beside them. Behind them the youngest members of the company fought desperately with powder horns and lint and little lead balls to reload the spent muskets.

'Fire at will!' Symson ordered.

Disobeying orders, James Fielding raised himself up to take a better aim, and paid for it as he took the full shaft of a hurled spear through the chest, and he fell backwards with a rattling cry. His killer was stopped with a shot from Michael Maer's pistol.

More Efik bodies dropped with the second round of fire from the muskets, and still the ships pounded the forest.

The Efik fell back, startled by such slaughter, confused by such firepower, and Roberts saw his chance. Immediately the pirates were on their feet, chasing them, cutlasses waving, and with their own war cry every bit as terrifying as the Efik's.

Fuelled by the excitement of battle, the killing instinct took over in Roberts, the desire for revenge. He surged forward at the head of the others, roaring with the fury, intent on slitting the throats of some of the enemy, hurtling over the bodies of the fallen.

The Efik who had long regarded the forest as their own personal territory saw the oncoming pirates with disbelief. They didn't understand the power of musket or cannon, and saw only the neat little holes in their brothers as they fell dead. The white men had tools that smoked and spewed out death. And with superstitious dread, they fled.

The pirates chased them as far as the town, but the Efik, with better acquaintance of the terrain, had disappeared into the forest.

The town was deserted, as silent as if no-one had ever lived there. The pirates looked about them. Then Roberts and Symson reached the same decision together: 'Burn it!'

THIRTY-TWO

December 1721, Cape Corso Castle

Captain Chaloner Ogle bowed, and Phipps turned and came away from the bastion to take his hand.

'My dear Captain Ogle! Well come.'

Ogle regarded him dourly and wandered to the bastion himself to look out at the ships riding at anchor in the road, bobbing like corks on the turquoise sea. He could pick out his own *Swallow*, but one ship was noticeable by its absence. 'I see, sir, that the *Weymouth* is not riding at anchor in the road.'

'No.' Phipps rubbed his nose uneasily and walked away a little to study the view. 'Two days ago, sir, I commissioned the *Weymouth* to go to the rescue of some of my soldiers held at Del Mina.'

Ogle uttered an oath. It was a risk he had had to take, leaving the *Weymouth* at Corso, for of course, if the ship were needed, Captain Heardman would have to do the bidding of the Director-General. It was frustrating, but Del Mina was such a short distance along the coast, certainly less than a day's sail. Hopefully, the *Weymouth* would put in an appearance before the week was out.

Still, he needed to re-provision and water his ship, although that would mean his men could spend a few days ashore with the native women—which Ogle deplored, and John Atkins condemned as foolhardy, but which he knew to be essential in keeping up the spirits of his men. A happy crew was an efficient crew.

'Any news of Roberts?' Ogle asked.

'I do have news of the blackguard Roberts,' Phipps said. Ogle's heart crashed against his ribs with hope, and his whole attention was on Phipps' fat red face. 'Oh?'

Phipps fumbled in his pocket and pulled out two folded sheets of paper. 'I have this day received two messages from my agents along the coast—from Axim and from Dixcove, both relating the terrible occurrence of a ship—a galley—that was seen chased by three ships, and which fell into their hand.' He unfolded the letters and held them out. Taking them, Ogle looked over them, reading quickly, his forefinger pressed thoughtfully against his lips. After some moments he handed them back.

'We have not long left Cape Three Points, and before that Cape Appollonia,' he said. Cape three Points was only a few miles east of

Axim.

'There are reports of pirate activity all along this coast,' Phipps said dourly. 'I wonder that you missed them.'

Ogle's lips set in a tight line. *The very Devil must be looking after Roberts*, he thought. 'You think it to be Roberts?'

'Of course it's Roberts! He is known to be operating on this coast. We have had reports—from Plunket as I told you in Sierra Leone—but none so close.'

Ogle considered it. 'Roberts will have heard we are here. He will know we are in fine health, and that we are looking for him. He has made a mistake in hugging the coast. But I doubt he'll make the same mistake twice. In his position, I would leave the coast, perhaps going for the Caribbean again. That would mean picking up the trade wind at Gabon or Cape Lopez, and then St. Thomas's or Prince's. But first he will want gold. My guess is he hasn't got it yet. There are no reports from Whydah, are there?'

'Nothing.'

'He's not got that far yet, then. He won't want to leave Africa without the gold. So he will go next to Whydah before leaving for the Caribbean. Besides, the woman is there, and he may try to find her.'

'You think so?' Phipps asked doubtfully.

It was an educated guess but Ogle replied confidently: 'I know so.' His dark eyes glittered at the thought of surprising Roberts at Whydah.

'Well it may do no harm to enquire on the way,' Phipps suggested. 'At Accra, and perhaps Apong.' He raised his brows and Ogle did not miss the inference.

'You mean enquire of Miss Betty?' Miss Betty's establishment at Apong was well-known to sailors, and information might be forthcoming there. But he deplored the morals of the men who frequented such houses. 'It will cost us time to go there,' he objected.

'Well, I think a few hours will hardly make any difference at all,' Phipps said genially. 'And my guess is that Roberts won't keep his men from going ashore to visit Miss Betty's. If he's come this way, Miss Betty will know.'

Ogle nodded. Phipps might be right. 'Very well.' He thought about the *Weymouth*. But Heardman might not be back for another week. Ogle could have sworn in sheer frustration. He really needed the *Weymouth*'s help. Roberts had three ships to his one. But if he waited for Heardman, he'd miss Roberts. And more than anything he wanted Bartholomew Roberts.

He said to Phipps: 'We are nearly provisioned, and we will sail in the morning.'

Pleased, Director-General Phipps held out his hand. 'I wish you good speed, Captain,' he said.

THIRTY-THREE

January 1722

'Upon my soul! George Wilson!'

George Wilson grinned as Roberts clambered aboard the latest prize, the *Elizabeth*. 'Well I never did! Captain Roberts! Well met, Captain!'

'Wherever did you get to?' Roberts demanded, standing on the *Elizabeth's* deck.

Back in August when they had captured the *Stanwich*, George Wilson had come aboard the *Royal Fortune* in lieu of the *Stanwich's* captain who was sick with fever, and promptly volunteered himself to be the chief surgeon of the company. However, Wilson with a typical lack of forethought, had left his surgeon's instruments on the *Stanwich* and requested that he row back to get them. He and six men embarked in a high wind to cross the short distance to the *Stanwich,* only to find themselves blown off course.

'Thought better of his decision to join us, I'll wager,' Symson said dourly.

'Not at all!' George Wilson turned offended eyes upon him. 'You think I would be so—so—*cowardly?*' He appealed to Roberts. 'Captain—I have been to Tartarus and back. Tartarus, I say.' He rolled his eyes theatrically and shook his head. 'Crossing to the *Stanwich*, the wind blew up and we were blown ashore at Cape Montezerade. Indeed we were. My dear sir, you have no idea! The natives. Ugh! Not that they're not jolly decent fellows, you understand. Not cannibals at all. But it ain't the same as civilisation, you know.'

Roberts chuckled. 'We wondered what had happened to you. Do you join us again?'

Wilson nodded. 'That I will, Captain. I'll come aboard immediately. But first, let me get my chest *before* I leave the *Elizabeth!*'

George Wilson ran down the companionway ladder to the surgeon's cabin, and began rifling through the instruments set out in the neat drawers built into the bulkhead. Surgical instruments of all kinds were expensive, and medicines not easily come by, and of course a surgeon could not practise without them. The medical chest was often one of the first things the pirates took when they captured a ship.

'What are you up to, sir?'

Wilson jumped and spun round to see Adam Comry the *Elizabeth*'s other surgeon leaning against the bulkhead watching him.

Adam Comry was the same age as George Wilson, just out of college, enthusiastic, but as green as the new leaves on the May tree, and impressionable. Wilson sized him up. Comry must have realised why Wilson was taking the medical instruments.

Wilson took a breath. 'Come with us, Comry.'

'And be a rogue like you Mr. Wilson?' Adam Comry raised a pale eyebrow questioningly.

'You could do worse than come with us,' Wilson said. He put two syringes into the chest where they fell with a clang of metal upon metal then he came close to Comry, lowering his voice conspiratorially. 'Listen—we can go with these men to Brazil, and in eight or ten months when perchance we have got six or seven hundred pounds, we may leave for pastures new. Just think—that's enough to set you up for life!'

'That's right,' Peter Scudamore agreed from the doorway.

They both looked round. 'Who are you, sir?' Wilson asked.

Scudamore was five years older and had the world-weary way of sizing up every opportunity. 'Scudamore. Surgeon of the *Royal Fortune*. Thought I'd come and relieve the *Elizabeth* of her medical equipment, but I see gentlemen, that you have done it for me.' He smiled at them both, his arms folded across his chest. Wilson did not like him. 'There's little to do but deal with the pox or malaria. Mercury and quinine, my boys, mercury and quinine. Couldn't be easier.'

So Adam Comry allowed himself to be persuaded, and he too signed the pirates' articles.

As did a man called Peter De Vine, who was known to James Phillips and Israel Hynde, having also sailed on the *Revenge* under Captain Stede Bonnet in Blackbeard's company.

'Blown away from the ships,' George Wilson related again over dinner that evening. 'Came ashore at Montezerade.'

Roberts leaned back in his chair, his cheek resting in his hand, listening to the story, and grinned at David Symson who met his eyes briefly with a look of anguish.

'They be cannibals there,' Tom Sutton said knowingly.

'Not at all, sir, not at all. Indeed they were quite jolly fellows, when you got to know them. Those of us who had been in the boat—five of your Frenchmen and an Englishman whose names I forget—such a short acquaintance you understand—settled with the natives—had no choice, you see, had no choice.'

'You lived like a native?' Ashplant paused in the act of conveying a spoonful of spicy stew to his mouth, his bulbous eyes wide with disbelief. 'In a mud hut?' Clearly this was something beyond his understanding.

'My dear sir,' Wilson explained patiently, 'there was nothing else! Or would you have me brave the jungle?' He shuddered. 'No. No indeed! All sorts of unmentionable things in the jungle, you understand.'

'I know,' Ashplant growled with feeling. 'I remember when we was in Calabar.'

Wilson interrupted him without a by your leave. After all, this was his tale. 'I set up a little station and did my best to treat the natives of their various maladies, but I had nothing to work with, you understand. I caught a skin disease from them which looked pretty nasty but which cleared up in a few weeks. Then Captain Thomas Tarlton came along in the *Tarlton.*'

The eyes of everyone swivelled to Captain Thomas Tarlton. Tarlton, and Captain Sharp of the *Elizabeth,* as well as the masters of the *Flushing* and the *Gertruycht* from Holland, the *King Solomon* and the *Diligence,* were presently 'guests' of the pirates while they robbed their ships, and according to Roberts' custom were civilly treated, being invited to eat at the Captain's table. Captain Tarlton did not look up from his plate, but steadfastly ignored them all.

'The brother of the Captain John Tarlton of my old ship, the Stanwich.' He paused to let this sink in. 'The most damnable luck, gentlemen, for as it happened the two captains had met together and Captain Thomas Tarlton knew I had signed your articles. I was in a sorry state by this time, starving sirs, starving. I begged him to take me with him, but he refused, saying that I had signed pirates' articles and could expect nothing from him. So I begged a little biscuit and salt meat. And even these he denied me.'

Captain Thomas Tarlton looked up and scowled at Wilson. 'Damn you for a rogue, George Wilson! I appeal to you, Captain Roberts, would you take a man on board who looked like he was rotting away with some loathsome disease? Lord, I'd have had my whole ship down with some unmentionable plague before I could look round, and I had my slaves to think of.'

'Ah yes, the slaves,' Roberts murmured, his eyes glittering.

'But a little biscuit and salt meat?' Tom Sutton was disgusted by this cavalier attitude.

'I was in short supply myself. I couldn't spare any.'

'I don't like the sound of that,' Tom Sutton said frankly.

Roberts studied Thomas Tarlton. He was one of three brothers from Liverpool his brother John being captain of the *Stanwich* and his younger brother Edward was 'learning the ropes' under his command. They were rich ship-owners, well known in the shipping world, the kind of men the pirates despised, for their wages and profits were tied up in the ships they commanded, and which meant that they cut rations and bought cheap rations to increase those profits at the sailors' expense.

Roberts turned away from him. 'What happened to the boat crew?' he asked Wilson.

Wilson shrugged. 'They died. Leastways they disappeared, one by one.'

'Into the stewpot!' Sutton said with relish.

'No. I told you, sir, they were not cannibals!'

'But you don't know that,' Sutton argued unwilling to let go a good story.

'Never mind that,' Ashplant growled impatiently. 'How did you get off Montezerade?'

'Well, a short time later, a French ship came in and they were more Christian than Tarlton, for they took me off and paid besides a ransom to the natives for me. But I had this skin disease, like I said—happily I am now cured—but they didn't want me on their ship either, so they put me off at Cestos where I again lived with the natives. And that is where Captain Sharp found me, again paying the natives a ransom for me, for which I am greatly obliged. I trust, Captain Roberts, that you will treat Captain Sharp with the greatest civility, for he has been mightily kind to me.'

Captain Sharp, said wryly: 'Pleased to be of service, I am sure. Though if you take my surgeon Comry, I'll not be happy about that.'

Roberts shook his head in wonder. 'You, George Wilson, must have an angel guarding you!'

William Magnes said under his breath: 'More like the Devil.

Come then, Mr. Wilson, Mr. Comry, let's find a place for you in the gunroom.'

Wilson grinned in his endearing way, and tossed off the last of his wine. 'Captain Roberts, I thank you. Lead on, old chap!'

With the departure of the surgeons and the captured captains, Roberts was left with his own men.

Ashplant cleared his throat noisily and rasped at his whiskers with his hand. Roberts looked at him, raising his brows.

'So where do we go now, Cap'n?' Ashplant wanted to know.

'You have reason for asking?' Roberts asked warily.

Ashplant hesitated. 'The articles do say that when we've made a thousand pounds each, we could think of breaking up the company.'

Roberts pursed his lips. 'That ain't quite what it says.'

'Well anyhows, Captain, I bin a-thinking. We bin pretty clever, and we've taken many ships. We have more'n a thousand pounds each, by my reckoning. But also we have shaken up the settlements all along the coast. They even send out ships from the navy after us. The *Swallow* was to be back in Sierra Leone by Christmas. It strikes me that we be hunted men, and I tell you it fair makes me twitch!'

In fact after leaving Calabar, Roberts had taken his company to Cape Lopez, then Annabon, the southernmost island of the São Tomé and Príncipe archipelago. Then on the 6th January he came to Cape Lahou, and then to Cape Appollonia, not realising that just thirteen days previously the *Swallow* had been hunting for him there. Indeed, he thought that if the *Swallow* had indeed gone back to Sierra Leone for Christmas, Captain Ogle was over seven hundred miles behind them to the west-north-west.

What he didn't realise was that the *Swallow* was in the opposite direction, some two hundred and eighty miles to the east of them at Cape Corso.

'So what are you saying, Ash?' David Symson asked.

Ashplant glared at Roberts. 'I think, and some of the men agree with me, that 'tis time we broke up the company.'

Roberts was silent for a long while, aware that he too wanted to leave the pirate round. Had he not already said as much to David Symson? But his retirement depended upon his finding Lúcia. If they broke up the company, he would be free to search for her. His glance darted from Ashplant, to Symson, to Dennis, and even Sutton trying to read their thoughts. They all avoided his gaze and he realised they had discussed this among themselves.

He thought about them, how they had fought side by side, and he would be sorry to lose their comradeship. Yet there was a longing inside him for a settled life, with Lúcia, without risk. A few years ago, retired pirates settled on Madagascar. That had lately fallen out of fashion, but there were other remote places. Oh, how he longed for it.

'What do you all think?' he asked them carefully, not wishing to commit himself.

Symson said straightly: 'If we stay on the account, we'll be caught. The *Swallow*'s on the prowl, and there ain't no sense in risking a hanging.'

'And you, Mr. Dennis?'

Dennis nodded. He sported a new wig these days, a short perruke with a little tail. 'Aye, I think that's the truth of it.'

'I think we're all of the same mind, Cap'n,' Ashplant said. 'I've a fancy for a pretty woman. Our days be done. It be like a man who gambles—to know when to stop.'

It was decided then. Roberts said: 'Very well. However, I suggest we say nothing to the men as yet. We came to Guinea for a reason. For gold. It'd be churlish to leave without it. I suggest we go to Whydah and then put it to the men.'

They nodded solemnly.

William Magnes, the quartermaster put his head round the door. 'Cap'n, 'tis Moody and Harper.'

Roberts uttered an oath. 'Now what?' Always, there was trouble. It was like overseeing a group of dangerous children.

''Twould seem that the problem is Captain Tarlton. Seeing as how Captain Tarlton abandoned the surgeon to the natives at Montezerade, the general opinion of the company is that a rogue like that ought not to live!'

Roberts sighed. 'A little harsh, don't you think, considering Mr. Wilson survived the ordeal?'

'Moody and Harper are searching for him all over the ship. Seems to have disappeared.'

'Good.'

'Leave 'em to it,' Symson recommended. 'If they find him, be ready to intervene.'

As Magnes departed Roberts put his hands over his eyes. He was tired of this, tired of the command. 'Whydah, it is,' he said.

THIRTY-FOUR

January 1722, Whydah

Whydah, with its sloping sandy beach edged by palm trees and rainforest, was one of the chief slaving depots of the Portuguese, second only to Príncipe and São Tomé, and they defended their interests with the fort of São João Batista. However the English also had an interest there as did the French, and both of them had their forts, so that Whydah was perhaps the most heavily defended town on the Guinea coast.

Not that that deterred Bartholomew Roberts. Carefully negotiating the two sand bars that blocked the entrance to the harbour, he brought the *Royal Fortune,* the *Great Ranger* and the *Little Ranger* into the Whydah Road. The *Royal Fortune* had a St. George's ensign flying at the mast head, the black jack with A.B.H. and A.M.H. at the mizzen peak as well as the Jolly Roger at the foremast. They would know who he was.

There were eleven sail riding unsuspectingly at anchor—English, French and Portuguese. And on the shore he could make out the flurry of men as they worked to bring the slaves out to the waiting vessels. The familiar stench of slavery assailed his nostrils, that gut-heaving stench of despair and misery and cruelty that had propelled him out of honest sailing. The smell reminded him sharply of the evil conditions on a slave ship, renewing his resolve never to engage in that abominable trade again.

All the ships were well-armed, the Frenchmen, for example, carrying thirty guns and upwards of a hundred men apiece, yet as Roberts approached and fired a warning shot, all of them struck their colours. His fame had gone before him and no-one dared defy three well-armed and well-manned pirate ships sailing in company.

He sent his men aboard each of them with messages for the captains, demanding eight pounds of gold dust as a ransom for the release of each ship. They demanded time to pay and in the interim Captain Dittwitt of the *Hardey* took it into his head to pay Roberts a visit, bringing with him the ransom demanded carried in two sacks, one in each hand, which he dumped with a loud thud on the polished oak table in the *Royal F*ortune's great cabin.

Surprised, Roberts greeted him with an outstretched hand, invited him to sit down on the red damask-upholstered chair, and offered him wine. The sacks on the table almost certainly contained the gold dust, the ransom Roberts had demanded. But it was only when Captain Dittwitt had a goblet of wine in his long fingers that Roberts, who sat at the head of the table thoughtfully watching him, asked: 'And to what do we owe the honour of this visit, Captain?'

Captain Dittwitt savoured the wine, then swallowed. Then his hazel eyes met those of Roberts across the table.

'You seem like a reasonable man to me, Captain Roberts,' he began.

Subtly, Roberts' face changed, his eyes narrowing slightly, his lips twitching in a slight smile as he waited for the offer he expected Captain Dittwitt to make. 'Go on, Captain.'

Captain Dittwitt glanced at the other men who stood around the table, then back at Roberts. 'I suppose it wouldn't do to offer all my slaves and all my goods to keep the gold?' he asked.

'Nope.'

Dittwitt nodded, not in the least put out. 'I thought not. Well in that case, I come in the name of all the commanders here. Many of us—the Portuguese and Frenchies especially—fear that we may not be believed when we go home. After all, you take the gold and it is not so obvious as slaves. Some of them fear they may be hanged for theft.'

'You want me to discharge you from this, then, Captain Dittwitt? But I think I should tell you that we came here especially for the gold.'

'Then what is to be done, sir? Are we all to be hanged like dogs for theft?'

'No.' Roberts thought about it. 'We shall write you receipts for your gold. And you can tell all the captains that when they pay we shall discharge their ships and give them receipts.'

'I've brought you my ransom, Captain Roberts. Eight pounds of gold dust. That is the agreed price, is it not?'

'It is.'

Captain Dittwitt pursed his lips. 'You are a great rogue, Captain Roberts. But a clever one.'

Roberts inclined his head, acknowledging the compliment. Then he rose from his chair and while Dittwitt finished off his wine retrieved paper from the drawer and the inkstand, and brought all back to the table. There he wrote:

This is to certify whom it may or doth concern, that we GENTLEMEN OF FORTUNE have received eight pounds of Gold-dust for the ransom of the Hardey, *Captain Dittwitt commander, so that we discharge the said ship. Witness our hands this 13th of Jan. 1721-2*
Batt. Roberts
Harry Glasby

Harry Glasby of course signed his own name.

Nine other captains sent or brought their ransom to the *Royal Fortune,* and they too received receipts, some of them signed by David Symson and Thomas Sutton, by now quite 'well to live' with rum punch, who thought it a great joke to sign them:
Aaron Whifflingpin
Simon Tugmutton.

Henry Dennis interrupted Roberts in the writing out of the last receipt, marching so swiftly into the great cabin that Roberts looked up with enquiry. Dennis held out a sheet of paper.

'Found this, Captain,' he said shortly.

Dennis's face warned him of something unusual, and Roberts frowned as he took the letter. It had been unfolded, and the seal broken, but it was addressed to Mr. Baldwin, the Royal Africa Company's agent at Whydah, from Director-General James Phipps at Cape Corso, and as Roberts read it he felt the swoop of alarm in his belly. He kept his face inscrutable, however, for the sake of the Portuguese captain waiting to receive his piece of paper, but he met the eyes of Henry Dennis. 'Where did you find this, Mr. Dennis?'

'On the *Carlton.*'

'Captain Allright?' The *Carlton* had been one of the ships which sailed from Spithead with Captain Ogle in the *Swallow* to Cape Corso although Roberts did not know that.

'Be so good as to call all the company together,' he said quietly, and carefully re-folded the paper.

He saw the question in David Symson's eyes, but Roberts finished the receipt and signed it with a flourish before passing it to Harry Glasby to add his signature, giving no hint of the letter's contents until the captain of this last ship had departed with his receipt. Then they followed him on deck.

The entire company, plus the new recruits, eighteen of whom had signed from one of the French ships at Whydah, crowded onto the *Royal Fortune*'s decks so that there was hardly a space for another man, and at that some hung in the shrouds to listen to the news.

Roberts, resplendent in his red damask waistcoat, looked over them and thought fleetingly that he had come a long way since he joined Davis's crew.

'Gentlemen,' he began, and his voice rang across the ship. 'I am in receipt of a letter to Mr. Baldwin, the Royal Africa Company's agent here at Whydah, from the Director-General of Corso, Mr. Phipps, which speech I shall read to you, gentlemen.

'"Most honourable sir, It is my duty in haste to warn you of the imminent arrival of the ships of the pirate Bartholomew Roberts and his crew, which hath been seen off Cape Three Points and who is expected to be making towards Whydah Road. With this foreknowledge, it hath been my hope, sir, that you will be able to guard against this rogue should they arrive before his Majesty's Ship, the *Swallow* which pursueth him there. I remain, sir, your most obedient servant, James Phipps."'

There was a silence as this information filtered into their rum-fuddled brains and then they all began crying out at once with bravado. 'Let 'em come here! We'll show 'em! We ain't afeard of no navy!'

Roberts put up his hands to quell the riot which seemed about to break forth, and waited until they had quietened enough for him to speak.

'Aye. And we're all known as brave fellows! However, it seems to me that even though we're not affrighted at one ship, yet it would be better to avoid a fight that can lead to no account, which is the best we can expect if we're overtaken. So—we sail with the tide, gentlemen!'

To which they agreed. No-one had any desire to get his head blown off in an unnecessary battle with the *Swallow*.

He turned away and called John Walden to him.

'Cap'n?'

'The *Porcupine* hasn't paid the ransom.'

'No, Cap'n.' Faith, John Walden was an ugly brute!

'Take a party and enough boats to the *Porcupine*, and bring all the slaves aboard our own ships. Get them all off. Then torch her.'

'Aye, aye, Cap'n.'

'Oh, and Mr. Walden! Do not be too long about it!' And he went below, pleased with himself.

Because the captain of the *Porcupine* had chosen not to pay the fine imposed by the pirates, it gave him a good excuse to liberate the slaves. It pleased him that he could make some reparation for all the years he had worked a slaver. He would give them the gift of freedom. No doubt some of them would not wish to join the company, and he would put them ashore somewhere else, where they might have a chance of freedom. Perhaps when God in his infinite mercy looked upon Bartholomew Roberts on Judgement Day, He might remember this good deed.

John Walden took twenty men and two boats with which to transport the slaves.

The *Porcupine* had just a few men on board—some of her own crew, and the pirate prize crew. Walden ordered the captured crew off, and they obeyed with alacrity, hoisting out their own boat. The pirates he ordered to open the hatches.

The ship was slaved, that is full of its cargo of slaves and ready to sail, and the stench from the hold boiled out in a thick fetid cloud, the slave stench that made even hardened sailors struggle to hold onto the contents of their stomachs. It added to his impatience to get the job done, and he was conscious of the need to be under weigh with the tide. He wished the commander had chosen another man for this job and his uncertain temper chafed at the task. What did they want with more blacks in the company?

'Unchain 'em, then!' he bellowed. 'Get 'em into the boats.'

More than a hundred and fifty Africans, mother-naked and chained by twos lay in tiers in the overheated hold of the pitching ship, unable to sit up, or to stand, or even to turn over, lying in urine and their own filth and the results of seasickness. The ones on the bottom tier suffered the worst, for the filth fell through the upper tiers onto them.

The pirates had to undo the chains. There were no keys, the chains were riveted around the ankles, and it took a good sharp blow with a hammer and bolster to free them. It was long hot work, had to be carried out in the stinking hold, and was agonisingly slow. Furthermore, the freed slaves could hardly move, having been lying in one position for several days already, so that it was with difficulty that the first men scrambled up the ladder to the deck, wondering what yet the white devils might have in store for them.

John Walden himself retched at the stench and filth, as they cleared the first tier, then he came on deck again. The tide was rising fast, and he knew that time was limited.

'Come on, get a move on!' he bellowed at his men.

Oh, but they were slow, agonisingly slow. At this rate they would miss the high tide, and with the *Swallow* hard on their heels, they couldn't afford to. 'Come on, damn you, get it done!'

But his men, unused now to working slavers, were retching so much, it rendered them as good as useless.

William Guineys, who had deserted the *Porcupine* himself to join the pirates, had no love for the slaves. 'We'll never get 'em all off at this rate,' he said to Walden. 'We'll miss the tide, and I'll be damned if I'm gonna stay here to be hanged for a bunch of filthy slaves.'

It fuelled Walden's own anxiety. He glanced across at the *Royal Fortune*. Her crew were making ready to sail. High tide would be in less than an hour. And it would take longer than that to empty the ship. They were only blacks after all, he thought. Filthy stinking slaves. What did it matter? They were not even really human. And he had no intention of risking his life for them.

He had released only a quarter of them when he came to a decision.

'Fire the ship!' he commanded.

Guineys looked at him and nodded.

William Davison and Sam Morwell had already smeared the *Porcupine's* decks with tar. They looked at each other in disbelief. 'But they ain't out yet!' Sam Morwell protested.

'I give the orders here!' Walden snarled at him, and pulled his pistol.

Already the rest of the pirates were clambering out of the hold, and piling over the side into the waiting boats. They had already freed some of the slaves, and they too came on deck, looking for a way off the ship.

Reluctantly Sam Morwell threw the lighted oil lantern onto the deck where the glass smashed and sent a sheet of blue flame across the tarred deck. It caught the ropes and then shot upwards onto the furled sails. It was frighteningly swift, for everything on the ship had been baked tinder-dry by the African sun.

The slaves on deck threatened to jump into the pirates' boats, but Walden held them off with his pistol, and ordered his men to shove off as Morwell and Davison slithered down the side of the ship to find their places in the boat.

They pulled on the oars and in a few strokes the boat was away from the burning ship.

The smell of smoke seared the nostrils and lungs and alerted the rest of the slaves still in the hold. In a moment screams and shrieks of panic rose from the bowels of the ship as men tried to scramble out of the burning hulk.

'Pull, damn ye, pull!' Walden ordered the men at the oars. As those on the deck jumped into the water, he could see the possibility of some of them reaching the boat.

Now the furled sails were orange flame, the masts towering pillars of fire, the decks sheets of flame.

Those slaves that could clambered out of the hold, to burn their hands and feet and legs on the deck in a terrifying parody of hell. They cried out in agony and ran for the side. They had no choice but to jump into the water, even though they could not swim, and did their best to aim for the shore. Some, still chained by twos disappeared beneath the water as the weight of their shackles pulled them down. Others were trapped in the hold.

It was panic, and terror, and screams, and the sickly sweet stench of roasting flesh as the *Porcupine* burned, and the sharks came in for the kill.

Roberts gripped the *Royal Fortune*'s guard-rail, clenching his teeth hard until his jaw ached and his knuckles were white where he gripped the rail. His whole body trembled, and he felt cold, chilled despite the heat of the African sun.

'What happened?' he demanded of David Symson, and in his own ears his voice did not sound like his own.

'Walden,' Symson spat the name out. 'Damned murdering son of a bitch!'

'I gave orders for the slaves to be got off first.'

'He ain't got no liking for slaves,' Symson said grimly.

'Damn his blood!' Roberts swore. But it didn't relieve the sheer gut wrenching nausea in his belly. He couldn't bear the agony, the screams, the panic, the stench of roasting flesh, and smoke pall.

Abruptly he turned and pushed his way through the silent

shocked crew, seeking the sanctuary of his own quarters. But even down here, through the hull, through the wash of water against the rudder, through the twang of the lines on the masts, he could hear the screams and the agony.

He leaned against the great cabin door, holding it closed with his shoulders. His was the guilt. As commander he must bear the responsibility for the deaths of these people. His act of mercy had turned into an act of inhuman carnage. He in his misjudgement had sent out John Walden to perform a simple task. John Walden. He should have known better.

Gradually the screams died away, and only the crack and spit of burning timber, the roar of flames reached him.

Helpless rage welled up in him. He struck the deckhead beam directly above him with his clenched fist until his hand was bruised and bleeding. Damn the man! John Walden would pay for this!

And suddenly he turned and went on deck.

'Mr. Main!'

William Main, the boatswain, had been standing with the others at the guard-rail as mesmerised as they were by the horror, but he turned now. 'Cap'n?'

Roberts' face was set like stone, his eyes steely hard. 'Make all sail.'

William Main hesitated only fractionally. There was nothing they could do to help the victims. They were gone. But if they did not get themselves out of Whydah they too would be victims. 'Aye, aye, Cap'n.'

Roberts nodded. Then he said: 'Mr. Main, is Mr. Walden back on board?'

'Yes, Cap'n.'

'Send him to me.'

And he turned on his heel and went below to plot the course.

They stood with haughty self-assurance before him, twenty-one men crowded into the great cabin with John Walden at the front of the band, his arms folded arrogantly across his large chest, his chin up mutinously.

Never before had Roberts been so forcibly reminded that he was a commander in name only, an elected figurehead. If it had been up to him, he would have tied Walden to the mast and shot him dead himself. As it was, he had no such authority, although William

Magnes as the quartermaster had the authority to impose a punishment if he saw fit. Not that Roberts had a lot of faith in Magnes. He was not of the same calibre as David Symson.

'What happened?' Roberts demanded shortly. 'You had orders to free the slaves first.'

Walden shrugged in a couldn't-care-less way. 'They were slaves,' he said as though this were all the explanation necessary.'

'They was all chained together,' Sam Morwell explained indifferently. 'It took too long to free them.'

Indignant at their cold-hearted arrogance, Roberts struggled with his anger. He clenched his teeth in an effort to control it, but his eyes flashed dangerously. 'So you murdered over a hundred men! You disobeyed a direct order given in action, and murdered over a hundred people!'

'They was only blacks,' Walden said derisively, and wrinkled his nose in distaste.

Roberts' indignation fanned quickly into fury, and his fists clenched at his sides. 'Only blacks?' he hissed dangerously. 'There are black men on this ship who fight side by side with you, who watch your backs and die with you, men as brave as any Englishman.'

'What are you going to do about it, then, *Captain*?' He stressed the last word insolently.

Roberts' self-control snapped. Before he realised what he did, his fist flew out and struck Walden squarely in the face, breaking his nose and sending him reeling across the cabin, where he crashed into the bulkhead.

William Magnes grabbed Roberts' arm, forcibly preventing him from following up his advantage, while David Symson came between the protagonists. 'Easy Cap'n.'

Walden came to his feet, disregarding his bloody nose and ready to return the blow, but Symson turned and stopped him too. 'You know the rules,' Symson said. 'Differences to be settled ashore. Pistol or cutlass.'

Roberts glared at Walden. 'Well then? Or is it that only defenceless slaves are suitable opponents for you?'

'I ain't fighting a cove like you, Bart Roberts,' Walden growled. 'Though I ain't afeard of you.'

Roberts let his breath go in a hiss through his teeth. 'You are a coward, John Walden! A hundred innocent men died at your hand.

Yet you won't meet me! Mr. Magnes!'

Magnes hesitated. He was afraid of Walden's temper, as were all the crew and he had no desire to raise his ire by having him flogged. At the same time, he had a good deal of respect for the commander.

David Symson, who had once been quartermaster, but now had no such authority said: 'There should be a trial.'

William Magnes growled low in his throat with unease. 'They ain't actually broke the articles,' he pointed out. 'What law do you intend to try them on?'

The newer recruits shrank visibly. They hadn't signed the articles to be shot for breaking them in the first week.

Magnes made a decision. 'I think the crew of the *Royal Fortune* are unhappy about this. Mr. Walden—gentlemen—some of you will be transferred to the *Ranger* and others of you to the *Little Ranger*.'

It wasn't what Walden wanted at all. He viewed it as a downgrading of his position, a demotion. Every man wanted to be on the flagship.

And it wasn't what Roberts wanted either, for he regarded it as hardly any punishment at all for the lives of a hundred men. But they all accepted what the quartermaster decreed, especially as his decision was supported by the majority of the crew.

Angry that justice had not been done, Roberts retired to his own quarters, sickened by the brutality and weary with the effort of governing the ungovernable. With Symson as quartermaster, they had worked together. But Magnes was different—elected by the crew because they felt Symson was too hard on them, a direct result of an earlier discipline campaign.

Roberts had had enough. It was time to retire.

THIRTY-FIVE

January 1722, Whydah

Lúcia set aside her stitchery and gazed out of the window at the ships in the bay. From where she sat she could see fourteen of them, all lying at anchor. One of them would take her home, if Rodrigues had managed to secure a berth for them.

She had been cocooned here in the fort since her father's death, lost in her mourning, uncaring of the outside world, but now she must make a decision. It was a strange feeling, having to decide for herself instead of merely following what her father decided, one that reminded her painfully of her loss. Even now, three months since his death, the mere thought of him brought tears to her eyes. He had alternately infuriated and amused her but in the short time she had known him she had grown to love him dearly.

Oh, Pápa, how I miss you. How will I ever go on without you?

'Will the *senhora* join the governor and his guests or will you eat here in your room?' María had come in and Rodrigues followed her.

'I am not hungry. Ah, Rodrigues. Did you manage to secure a ship to take us back to Portugal?'

'I am sorry, *senhora,* but no ship is taking passengers at the moment. Pirates are operating out in the road.'

Her heart missed a beat. 'Pirates?'

'It is said they have captured eleven ships, and have three of their own.' He exchanged glances with María which alerted Lúcia immediately.

Even though she had guessed the answer, she asked: 'Do they know which pirate?'

He hesitated then said reluctantly: 'It is the English pirate they call Roberts.'

Lúcia's breath caught in her throat and she clasped her hands tightly in her lap. He was here! He had come for her! He had somehow found out about her and he had come for her!

Rodrigues went to the window and studied the ships. 'They have set one of them alight.' He said.

María ran to the window also, and Lúcia too stood up the better to see. Sure enough, plumes of black smoke billowed from one of the ships, although the sun and the distance made it impossible for her to see flames. Why had they set the ship ablaze? It reminded her of Príncipe, when Roberts had left the island and set two ships alight in the entrance to the harbour there. As she watched figures, people, jumped over the side into the water. There were people on board! Her hand went to her mouth in horror. 'What are they doing?'

'I think it is the slaves, *senhora*, trying to get off the ship.'

'But there are sharks in the water! They will be eaten by the sharks!'

María uttered a small prayer and crossed herself. So did Lúcia.

Rodrigues did not answer, but Lúcia's mind raced. It was not like Bartolomeo to kill men wantonly. 'Perhaps it is not the English Roberto,' she ventured.

'It is his jack on the mast, *senhora*. It has been identified as his.'

Torn between her need to be with Roberts, and what seemed to be wanton cruelty, she began to pace the room, her eyes on the horror unfolding at sea. No, he could not be responsible for killing the slaves, she was sure of it. It was he who had taught her that slaves were men the same as any other man. He had taught her to view them differently. He would not kill them like this. No, she had faith in him.

Watching her Rodrigues said: 'This Roberts is a pirate.'

'He would not, he could not, do this. Something must have gone wrong.'

'He thought nothing of capturing the ships.'

'That is different. That is trade.'

This was murder.

Continuing to pace, and continuing to watch the unfolding drama, she found herself in turmoil. She must go to him. When she saw him he would explain to her that it had been an accident. She had absolute faith in him for love had blinded her. She could not see him as a villain, as a bad man. Yet deep in her heart she knew he was. The English hanged men for piracy.

Suddenly she stopped pacing as something new caught her eye. 'What are they doing now?'

Rodrigues continued to peer at the ships. 'The English pirates are making sail. They are leaving.'

María remarked: 'Perhaps they know the English *capitão* is coming for them.'

Lúcia could see them clearly, the big frigate-built *Royal*

Fortune, and the two smaller consort ships. He was leaving Whydah. He was leaving her behind. As she watched the three ships sail away, she felt her heart turn to lead within her. He had not come for her after all. Perhaps he did not know she was here. But as the ships left, hope left with them.

Defeated, she said: 'As soon as you can Rodrigues, book us passage for Lisbon.'

'So—where is he then?' Chaloner Ogle demanded as he scanned the Whydah road with his telescope.

Lieutenant Sun felt his heart sink. They had been so certain. The decks had been cleared for action and sanded, the guns ready, only to find the Whydah road disappointingly empty.

Ogle swore. He knew they should not have gone to Apong to ask in Miss Betty's establishment. What did Phipps know? More to the point what did Miss Betty or her whores know? Nothing! He should have stayed with his instincts and carried straight on to Whydah himself.

'He's been here,' Ogle said. He pointed to the charred wreck. 'If that isn't the work of Roberts, I don't know what is!'

Sun peered through the telescope. 'It's still smouldering. We must have missed him by a few hours only.'

'Damn him! Damn Phipps! Damn Miss Betty! Damn the whole damned lot of them!' Ogle swore and went below.

Lieutenant Sun met the eyes of the mate and sighed. 'Tell the men to stand down,' he said and followed Ogle below.

Already the captain had the charts out on the table, and leaned over them, peering at them. He did not look up as Sun entered the cabin, but said: 'Where will they have gone?'

'Perhaps, Captain, if we ask the people here we might learn something.'

Ogle looked at him then. 'If you think Roberts will have told his men in advance of his plans you are much mistaken. He knows the value of secrecy, that one.'

Sun pursed his lips. 'Even so, there may be something we can learn to our advantage.'

Ogle sighed resignedly. He had a desperate urge to turn out of Whydah and give chase. It was a gut reaction, not a reasoned response, and he knew he must use his head or lose his quarry. So far he had bided his time, and he had come so close. He would come close again if he did not act without thought. 'Very well. Tell Mr. MacLaughlin to bring us to anchor.'

As it turned out the people in Whydah did indeed have information that would give him a vital clue.

Captain Fletcher, of the *Porcupine*, the ship which had been fired by the pirates, was most informative.

'Held us to ransom,' he told Captain Ogle and Lieutenant Sun over a bottle of rum. 'And I'll be damned, gentlemen, if I will pay a ransom to anyone.'

Ogle met the man's eyes squarely. 'Well, perhaps you ought to have done, Captain. For now you have no ship and no cargo.'

'Killed all my slaves, he did,' Fletcher said, pleased to be able to air his grievances. 'Did you ever hear anything so inhuman? Firing a ship with slaves chained aboard! The man's a devil!'

'Almost as bad as slavery itself,' Lieutenant Sun said quietly.

Captain Ogle's dark eyes flicked to his face, and there was a hint of acknowledgement there, but then back to Fletcher. 'So what was the ransom?'

'Eight pounds of gold dust per ship,' Fletcher said promptly, and took another swig from the bottle. He had already drunk a considerable amount, and his cheeks above an unkempt golden beard were flushed. 'Unreasonable amount, I say.'

'And was your ship and cargo worth that amount?' Ogle asked, drinking wine from a glass.

Fletcher growled low in his throat. 'Worth more'n that.'

'Then would it not have been politic to pay the fine?'

'Didn't think he'd do it,' Fletcher said. 'The others—that is Captain Dittwitt of the *Hardey* said he were a reasonable man. Reasonable men don't fire ships, do they?'

'Captain Roberts is a ruthless man,' Ogle told him. 'As indeed you have found out. What else did he do?'

'Nothing. Took the French ship, and left behind one of his own for the French commander, who was not best pleased with the exchange, for I tell you the ship they left leaked something abominable!'

'Which ship did they take?'

Fletcher struggled to remember. 'The *Count de Thoulouse*. Yes, that was it.' He frowned groggily at the bottle in his hand.

Ogle nodded, tossed off the wine in his glass and jerked his head at Lieutenant Sun, who finished the rum in his own glass and stood up.

Fletcher hardly seemed to notice them going. 'Left in a hurry,' he mumbled.

Ogle put his hand up to stay Lieutenant Sun. 'Oh?'

'Aye. Word is, they knew you were coming here!'

Ogle nodded thoughtfully. 'Thank you, Captain Fletcher.'

Outside in the heat, Ogle thought about what Fletcher had said. 'You were right, Mr. Sun, we have the information we need.'

Sun did not completely understand, but went over the conversation with Fletcher again in his head. He could see nothing there that would tell them where Roberts was heading.

'They took a ship, Mr. Sun,' Ogle explained patiently as he made his way through what was effectively a market, of petty traders with goods to sell, as well as the victuallers and the slavers with their pathetic groups of chained people. Ogle barely saw them. 'A French slaver, Mr. Sun. And what is the first thing they will do with her?'

Now daylight dawned on Sun. 'They will clean her, and refit her to make her flush.'

'And where do you think they will do that, Mr. Sun?'

Sun watched a woman dressed in black coming towards them without really seeing her. 'Deep water. Calabar?'

Ogle was not convinced. 'Roberts knew we were coming. How could he have known that?'

'Did Phipps write to the governor here?'

Ogle uttered an oath. 'Sort of thing he would do!' He ground his teeth, furious at Phipps' stupidity. 'Anyway,' he continued after a moment, 'Roberts knew we were coming, so he will not have gone to Calabar. He won't risk being trapped in the river there. There are better places for cleaning. Prince's Island, for example. Or Annobon.'

Sun thought about it. 'What about the River Gabon? Or Cape Lopez?'

There were not that many places suitable for beaching and cleaning ship on the coast. It wanted deep water close in shore and trees near enough to the beach to use to haul the ship over on her side. 'Aye,' Ogle said thoughtfully. 'It'll be either Prince's, Gabon or Lopez.' It would take Roberts a few weeks to clean ship and give his men furlough. Time enough to search all three possibilities. 'Who is this now?' Ogle stopped walking and doffed his hat. 'Why, *senhora* Andrade, unless I am mistaken.'

She looked at him uncertainly and then inclined her head. 'Captain Ogle, if I am not mistaken!'

'I trust we find you well—and your father?'

'My father died over three months ago, Captain Ogle,' she said.

He was polite concern. 'I am truly sorry to hear of it, madam.'

'He had been ill such a long time. Do you—I mean are you—that is, I need passage to Portugal.'

'Not from us this time, *senhora*,' Lieutenant Sun said. 'We are still searching for the pirate.'

She sighed. 'He was here. But now he is gone. I did not see him.'

Captain Ogle said: 'Our search continues. Alas, *senhora*, we do not go home yet. There will be Portuguese ships come in to Whydah, I am sure.'

'Very few. They are all bound for the Americas or Brazil. That is the market for slaves.'

Lieutenant Sun suggested helpfully: 'If you can get a ship to take you to Prince's Island, you will be bound there to find passage home.'

Prince's. Príncipe. Where she had first set eyes on *him*. She nodded and smiled wanly. 'Yes, of course.'

'May we wish you good speed, madam,' Ogle said bending over her hand.

She thanked them both and continued on her way, her maid trailing behind.

'A beautiful woman, that,' Lieutenant Sun breathed reverently.

Ogle curled his lip disparagingly. 'Aye. A pirate's whore.'

Lieutenant Sun looked at him. 'This Roberts has good taste, I think.'

They had come now to the water's edge where the pinnace awaited them. By the time they climbed aboard the *Swallow*, Ogle had come to a decision. 'Mr. Sun!'

'Captain?'

'Make all sail. For Prince's Island. If our Mr. Roberts is not there, we will try south, and we will look for him as we go.'

'Very good, Captain.' He began to give the orders and Captain Ogle went below, taking the charts and spreading them on the table. He needed to give co-ordinates, but he found himself staring out of the stern window at the vivid blue sea. Bartholomew Roberts was an exasperatingly elusive man, and finding him had become something of an obsession with Ogle. He would find him. He would put a stop to his antics.

Roberts was an extraordinary man, Ogle conceded, no mere pirate of the likes of Blackbeard or Bonnet, or even Howell Davis. This man was in a league of his own. He had devastated shipping up and down the African coast with consummate skill and panache, even as he had in the Americas, bringing trade to a complete standstill. No ship was safe. For the good of England, for the sake of Britain's interests in the slave trade, the most lucrative part of the Royal African Company's interests, Roberts had to be stopped. Roberts was out there somewhere. *I will find you. As God is living, I promise you, you will not escape me!*

He heard the mate, Daniel MacLaughlin's voice bellowing above the waves. 'All ready forward?'

Ogle listened to the replies, and then to MacLaughlin's exultant cry: 'Let go!'

The *Swallow* jerked as the wind found her sails, and the heavy clank and pawl of the rising anchor, and then the banking of the ship as she turned to leave Whydah.

'Now Captain Roberts, we shall see,' Ogle said quietly as the *Swallow* straightened, and turned her bowsprit for the open sea.

'There is an English ship in the road heading for Príncipe,' Rodrigues announced as he came into the cool whitewashed room where Lúcia sat, needlework on her lap.

She looked up. 'And have you spoken to the captain?'

'I have. A captain Thomas Hill, of the *Neptune*, and he is bound first for Cape Lopez and then for Príncipe. Furthermore, he is willing to take us—for a price.'

'We can afford it?'

'We can. Just about. Captain Hill drives a hard bargain.'

'When do we leave?'

'Tomorrow.'

Lúcia nodded resignedly. With Roberts having come and gone without her seeing him, she had lost all hope. Fate was evidently against her. It would be a relief now to go home.

THIRTY-SIX

February 1722, Cape Lopez

Roberts cursed the weather. For days on end they had battled against the storms which seemed to afflict this coast. It was impossible to make for Annobon, the southernmost island of the São Tomé and Príncipe archipelago, and instead the company had voted to hug the coast and turned the bowsprit south for Cape Lopez.

Cape Lopez offered shelter from the storms, as well as trade and provisions and willing, if smelly, women. Most important of all, if offered a place for careening and re-fitting a ship, for the French ship needed desperate attention.

Roberts was acquainted with the Cape. He knew the shallows called Frenchman's bank and skilfully avoided them as he brought the three ships into the shelter of the bay and dropped anchor. More importantly, Roberts was familiar with the Mpongwe tribe which inhabited these parts.

'Mr. Main!'

The boatswain grinned. 'A reception is it, for the chief?' he asked.

'You read my mind, Mr. Main. See to it, would you?'

Accordingly William Main oversaw the preparation of a reception for the King or *chave-pongo* as he was called. Not on the ship—the Mpongwe were, understandably nervous of venturing on any ship lest they be clapped in irons and put in the hold for sale. So, William Main prepared refreshment for his majesty, King Jacobus, on the beach.

Roberts dressed in his finest red coat, and his officers wore their finest clothes. It was prudent to honour the King in this way, and indeed Jacobus appreciated the effort, flashing at the visitors sparkling white teeth which had been filed to points. He was a large man, with a soft round belly, and his plump brown skin glistened with oil. Upon his august head he wore an old white perruke, but back to front, so that the pigtail fell over his face, hanging down his wide black nose. Half a pair of breeches, a jacket and hat completed his toilette, and it was clear he felt as grand as any of the richly dressed English.

He clapped his hands three times, and then said in a kind of Pidgin-Portuguese: 'Welcome English!'

Roberts struggled to keep his eyes on the king's face, and by sheer effort of will managed to ignore the pigtail hanging first over the king's left eye and then over the right, and returned the greeting by solemnly clapping his hands together three times.

'Your majesty will come into my tent?' They had spread sails out on poles to make a covering. 'And partake of some refreshment?'

There was nothing his majesty liked better than to sit and drink with visitors, and he beamed sunnily on Roberts and his officers, and walked ponderously across the sand to where the red damask-upholstered chairs from the *Royal Fortune's* great cabin had been arranged, with Roberts beside him, and closely followed by his aides. Still grinning delightedly he sat his kingly bulk down on one of the chairs and Joseph poured brandy for everyone present into cut glass goblets which the king much admired.

The king held the glass to his lips and paused. Immediately two of his aides solemnly raised a cloth so that his face could not be seen as he drank—as befitted the king's consequence. Symson raised his brows at Roberts who met the query with a blank stare, only the corners of his mouth twitching ever so slightly.

'So, Captain, what do you have for me?' King Jacobus demanded in Pidgin-Portuguese.

A day of tough haggling followed. As the brandy disappeared into the King and his aides at an alarming rate his consequence evidently diminished as a direct result, for after the fourth glass, they forgot to raise the cloth. It occurred to the pirates that it might not go amiss to dilute the brandy a little, for the King and his aides were growing so drunk it was becoming difficult to strike a deal. In fact Roberts began to despair of ever reaching an agreement. But at last a bargain was concluded which satisfied everyone. Roberts and Magnes felt they had come out of it at a profit, while King Jacobus was highly delighted with his bargains.

After a final glass of brandy the King rose unsteadily to his feet, staggered a little, and then with determined effort, hauled himself upright. Then he took both of Roberts' hands and said: '*Palaaver suquebah.*' It was the formal seal of the bargain and Roberts replied in kind: '*Palaaver suquebah.*'

Then the king staggered in drunken satisfaction across the beach and into the jungle.

Roberts and Magnes bought wax cakes and honey for the

company as well as plantains, goats and fowls, while the crewmen traded old hats and clothes for beautiful grey parrots to keep as pets on the ship and with a view to trading them at a later date elsewhere. More impressively, the natives offered ivory and a little gold, which, because they did not understand the value to the white man, Roberts traded for at very cheap rates, giving them linen, calico, pewter spoons, knives, tin and copper bowls and even old nails which the natives could melt down to make weapons or other objects.

But the chief commodity the Mpongwe had to offer, was the sexual favours of their women, every man offering his wives and daughters for as little as an old dagger. However, only a few of the crew took advantage of the offer. Those who, as David Symson remarked wryly, had lost their sense of smell. For the Mpongwe women beautified themselves by smearing upon their almost naked bodies a pungent mixture of elephant or buffalo grease and another red-coloured substance, and the stench was detectable at two hundred paces. While few sailors usually turned down such an offer, on this occasion few were desperate enough to take it up, and the stay at Cape Lopez was enlivened by the unusual sight of the native women chasing the Englishmen.

Finding no sign of the pirates in Príncipe, Captain Ogle gave orders to sail for the Gabon River, just north of Cape Lopez, where he provisioned and watered his ship. An enquiry of another ship suggested Roberts had gone north.

'I don't think so,' he confided to Lieutenant Sun and John Atkins. 'My guess is he is south.'

'Cape Lopez.' Lieutenant Sun was definite.

'Aye, Cape Lopez.'

Accordingly they left Gabon on 3rd February and on 5th February approached Cape Lopez from the south-west to avoid the treacherous sandbank. And there, on the other side of the spit of land that separated the bay from the Atlantic Ocean Captain Ogle saw three ships, one hauled over for cleaning, and an encampment on the shore.

Captain Ogle's heart skipped a beat as he peered at the scene through the telescope. He knew he had found his quarry. For ten frustrating months he had hunted Roberts, and now at last, without any degree of doubt, he had found him.

He passed the telescope to Lieutenant Sun, and when he spoke his voice was calm, betraying none of the excitement which had suddenly flooded his veins. 'I believe, Mr. Sun, that that is the company of Captain Bartholomew Roberts.'

Lieutenant Sun peered at the ships while Ogle considered his options. If he attacked straightaway, he would be hopelessly outnumbered and trapped within the confines of the bay. He cursed again that the *Weymouth* was held up on the Guinea coast. But then a plan formed in his brain. He peered through the telescope again. 'A frigate-built ship of forty-two guns by my count, on her side,' he said. 'Another of, say, thirty guns, at anchor, and a small ship of ten guns, also at anchor.'

'Captain!' Daniel MacLaughlin interrupted him, pointing forward. 'Captain, the Frenchman's bank!'

Captain Ogle swung the telescope forward. The white-crested waves breaking over the shallow sand bank betrayed its position clearly. It gave him an idea.

'Steer off, Mr. MacLaughlin. North by north-west. And make it seem as if we are in haste. Mr. Baldric—lower our colours and raise the Portuguese flag.'

'What is it?' Roberts demanded, coming to his feet and walking the two or three yards to where stocky James Skyrme stood on the shoreline and scanning the stretch of blue foaming water beyond the bay.

James Skyrme, the *Great Ranger*'s master, lowered his telescope and grinned into the distance. The ship had just turned to veer off around the point. 'Portuguese,' he announced with satisfaction. 'Took fright when she saw us.'

Valentine Ashplant rasped his bristly chin with the flat of his hand thoughtfully. 'Portuguese, eh?' He reached for the telescope and Skyrme readily relinquished it to him.

'Aye—and Portuguese means sugar. And sugar means rum punch.'

Ashplant licked his lips. The *Great Ranger*'s company had run out of sugar some days previously, a disaster which meant they could not make their favourite rum punch. It had become a cause of grievance and even fights between the crews of the *Great Ranger* and the *Royal Fortune*, resolved often with pistols at dawn, for the crew of the *Royal Fortune* had plenty of sugar but had refused to give any to their fellows.

Roberts said: 'Well, if there's sugar in the offing, better bring it in and put a stop to the mumbling. Man the *Ranger* and go after her!'

Henry Dennis grinned. The loss of his favourite cordial had come as a severe deprivation, and he was eager to imbibe once more. 'Well, then, let's not tarry! Let's go get her!'

With surprising speed, the *Great Ranger*'s company, plus some enthusiastic volunteers from the *Little Ranger*, and a few from the *Royal Fortune* rowed the short distance from shore to ship, hauled up the anchor and had her under sail before the *Swallow* had disappeared from view.

Roberts grinned with satisfaction, turning back to his own tent, where had had been dozing in its shade. It was all too easy these days. The *Great Ranger* would be back before nightfall.

James Skyrme wasted no time. Once clear of the bay and Frenchman's bank, he piled as much sail on the *Ranger* as she would bear, determined to catch the fleeing ship. The weather had turned stormy yet again, and the sea was rough, the waves high, and green water slid over the bows as the *Ranger* ploughed her way doggedly through the Atlantic, riding one wave, crashing down into the hollows with a jarring thud to rise again with the next.

He heard the mutterings of his men: 'He'll drive her under!' but he paid them no heed. And he saw that his efforts brought satisfaction, for they were gaining on the *Swallow*.

James Skyrme grinned, pleased with himself. He was captain of this ship, and he didn't need the commander to tell him what to do. He was a good seaman, and he would prove he was capable, and worthy of the commander's respect. He would bring back sugar and whatever else lay in the 'Portuguee's' hold.

However, it was not because of James Skyrme's ability as master that the *Ranger* gained on her quarry. Rather it was because of deliberately bad seamanship on the part of the navy. Captain Ogle kept the *Swallow* from out-pacing the *Great Ranger* by keeping her main tacks on board, her main sheets aft and her main yard braced, at the same time keeping her fore tack on board and her top-gallant sails set, but with no steering sails nor spritsail. Under these circumstances the lowliest slowest Portuguese galley would have been swifter than the *Swallow*. Lieutenant Sun also steered her deliberately badly so that her sails spilled the wind out of them. It was therefore no great wonder that the *Great Ranger* gained steadily, although Lieutenant Sun was careful to keep just far enough ahead so that the pirate's bow-chasers were useless.

Captain Ogle smiled to himself as he surveyed the pursuer through the glass and his smile broadened when he saw the Jolly Roger at the masthead with Roberts' arrogant portrayal of himself on the ABH and AMH skulls. *Oh yes, Captain Roberts, now we shall see!* The satisfaction warmed his belly. He had baited the trap and they had fallen for it. All he needed now was to lure them so far away from the Cape that cannon shot would not be heard by the other half of the pirate company, then he could close the trap.

He turned back to Lieutenant Sun. 'I think we might let them catch us, Mr. Sun,' he said.

THIRTY-SEVEN

Standing on the *Royal Fortune*'s quarterdeck, Roberts looked up and frowned. The sky was gloomy grey, and on the western horizon clouds like a thick slate canopy began to build ominously. The wind had increased over the last few hours, whistling and moaning through the *Royal Fortune*'s stays, making the lines slap against the masts. This part of the coastline was known for its savage storms, its hurricanes and whirlwinds which could smash ships to matchwood, and Roberts was pleased to have got the *Royal Fortune* righted before the storm struck. It was certainly not sailing weather, and any sensible captain would be making for a sheltered haven.

So just where was James Skyrme and the *Great Ranger*? They had left three days ago to chase the Portuguese ship in the quest for sugar. They should have been back long since. Unless Skyrme had decided to take off like Anstis and Kennedy before him.

Not with Richard Hardy, William Main and Valentine Ashplant in the company he wouldn't. He was as sure of those three men as he was of himself, although he was not as convinced of Henry Dennis's loyalty.

'Sail ho!' The man in the maintop pointed across the spit of land that guarded the entrance to the bay. Trees hid the main part of the ship, but her sails were visible above them, three-masted, square-rigged.

Roberts felt relief replace his anxiety and then turn quickly to anger. At last! He would have something to say to James Skyrme when he saw him!

The *Royal Fortune*'s crew let out a whoop of pleasure at the prospect of welcoming their comrades back, and Roberts nodded at David Symson who joined him at the taffrail.

''Bout time too, I say,' Symson grumbled.

Roberts nodded. He was anxious to be under weigh, to get off this coast. With the *Swallow* on their trail it was getting rather too dangerous.

But the cheering suddenly faded into silence, and Roberts and Symson stared with disbelieving eyes at the newcomer. As she rounded the point it became obvious that she was another, much smaller ship.

Roberts knew a stab of disappointment, the frustrating anxiety returning with renewed force. He tried to reason it away. Perhaps

Skyrme had come across another ship and given chase. Or perhaps the Portuguese had resisted and the *Ranger* was crippled somewhere. He gripped the taffrail and struggled to squash the sense of doom that settled in his belly. 'Damn!' He couldn't wait for them here at Cape Lopez forever. Not with Ogle on the prowl.

He peered at the newcomer. She was a small ship, a slaver, flying English colours.

'Do we take her, Cap'n?' Magnes asked.

Roberts took a breath. 'Naturally. But there is no rush. We'll wait until she is riding quietly at anchor. Tonight.'

Capturing and looting the newcomer would give his men something else to think about.

Lúcia sighed and turned away from her reflection. She was no longer beautiful, she thought. Not with those great dark circles around her eyes, and she had lost weight so that her skin was stretched over her face, causing her cheekbones to stick out, her chin to be pointed, her cheeks to be hollow. It was the worry, the heartbreak, the grief. She longed to be home where she hoped her mother would take care of her.

She looked out of the small stern window at the sea. It was dark, and the sea appeared like black tar, but with small ripples in it where the light from the ship bounced off the wavelets. She longed to go ashore, but Captain Hill had expressly forbidden it. 'You can't trust the natives in these parts, *senhora,*' he said. But it was all right for the men. It was always all right for the men!

'What is that?' Maria stood beside her, also looking out of the window. Lúcia hadn't actually seen it until then, but now she could distinctly make out the shape of a white sail reflecting the stern lights.

'I don't know. A boat?'

'The Captain hasn't sent anyone ashore, has he?'

Lúcia frowned. 'I don't think so.'

'So who are these people?'

'Perhaps one of the other ships . . .' Lúcia had noticed the other ships at anchor in the bay, but even as she said it she knew it unlikely that they would send out a boat at night unless . . .

'Pirates?' she queried. Her heart began to thud in her chest and her knees weakened. *Is it him? Is it really him?*

The boat changed course and she lost sight of it.

She heard a commotion through the hull of the ship, and her stomach knotted. Someone knocked on the door, and shouted through it for her to stay in her cabin, and lock the door.

Maria went to the door, but Lúcia stopped her. 'No.'

'But *senhora*! Pirates . . .'

Lúcia threw her *mantilha* over her head, and wrapped it around her shoulders, and at that moment Rodrigues burst into the cabin.

'You must stay here, *senhora*,' he said.

Poor dear faithful Rodrigues, what did he know? *I missed him last time, I shall not do so again!*

'I am going on deck,' she said and added: 'With permission?' She was asking Rodrigues to step aside, but he stood his ground.

'*Senhora*, you do not understand. The captain has yielded to pirates.'

'You mistake the matter, Rodrigues. I understand perfectly.'

'She has taken leave of her sense,' Maria sniffed.

Lúcia ignored her. 'Out of my way, Rodrigues,' she said.

'I cannot let you go, *senhora*.'

She brushed past him, but he grabbed her upper arm, and held it in a strong grip. '*Senhora,* you do not understand.'

'Let me go.'

'*Senhora*—'

'If you do not let me go, Rodrigues, I shall scream.'

She knew he would not want her to do that, that it would bring others running. 'Besides, if you think the pirates will not cover every single corner of this ship in a minute's time you know nothing of the matter! We will not remain undiscovered. So, let me go.'

Reluctantly he released her.

On deck, the pirates had rounded up the crew. Lúcia saw them huddled in a tight group around the main mast, facing the intruders. One of them, a man she did not recognise was talking with Captain Hill. For a moment she hesitated, unsure now. Perhaps she was wrong, perhaps this was not Roberts' company after all. And if that were the case she was indeed in a great deal of danger.

She stayed back in the shadows, hidden from view and dressed in black as she was, she remained unnoticed.

The pirates sent men into all parts of the ship, down the hatch into the hold, and Lúcia slipped further back into the shadows. One of them passed right next to her but did not see her in the darkness.

Even so, it would be moments before she was discovered. She

wondered what she should do. Then a voice she recognised, the distinctive lugubrious northern accent of David Symson, and his tall willowy frame came into her line of vision.

Emboldened she stepped forward. 'Mr. Symson.'

Every eye on deck turned in her direction and she felt her colour rise. Symson stared at her, peering into the darkness, so she moved into the lantern light.

'*Senhora!*' He came towards her.

'We meet again Mr. Symson,' she said for something to say. Now she was trembling, and her stomach churned sickeningly.

Tom Sutton said quietly to Symson: 'Davy—the commander's here.'

Symson glanced at the entry port and a moment later Roberts himself came on board, his men parting respectfully to let him through.

He was a splendid figure in red damask waistcoat, a pair of pistols hanging from silk ribbons over his shoulder, a sword in the scabbard on the baldric, and the huge gold diamond-studded cross which had once been destined for the king of Portugal hanging from a gold chain around his neck. He was fearsome, handsome, magnificent, undisputed ruler of his domain.

He stood quietly surveying the scene before him the way he must have done hundreds of times before. The man Lúcia did not recognise said:

'Commander, this is Captain Hill of the *Neptune*.'

Roberts gave no indication that he had heard. Instead his eyes rested on Lúcia.

She saw the recognition there, but he turned then to Captain Hill. 'Forgive the intrusion, Captain. You will, of course, be our guest on the *Royal Fortune*.'

'I have passengers,' Hill said.

Roberts again looked at Lúcia. 'Indeed, Captain?'

Lúcia came further forward and, unsuspecting, Captain Hill introduced her. 'This is the *senhora* Lúcia Margarida Carvalho Andrade.'

They looked at each other, and she realised that she must not give herself away. So she dropped a curtsey and put out a trembling hand. 'We meet again, Captain Roberts,' she said.

He bowed over her hand and kissed her fingers, giving them a reassuring squeeze. 'Indeed we do, *senhora*. Mr. Sutton.'

'Captain?'

'Convey the *senhora* and her belongings to the *Royal Fortune* and find her a suitable cabin, if you please.'

'And my servants?'

'And her servants.'

'Thank you captain.' Oh how she longed to throw herself into his arms, to tell him how much she had missed him. But there was a certain propriety to be observed, particularly in front of his men. She understood it. So she followed Tom Sutton and allowed herself to be helped into the waiting boat where Captain Hill already was seated, and did not even allow herself to glance back at the captain.

It was some time later when Roberts came aboard the *Royal Fortune*, for there had been much to attend to. He had the usual speech to make regarding the signing on of new recruits and then there were the discussions with Magnes and Symson regarding the spoils. It was agony to be on the *Neptune* when the woman he loved was on the *Royal Fortune*. He knew he could trust Tom Sutton to see her safe, but the ritual of having to go through the motions of playing the great victor was agony.

The clock struck two bells—which meant it was ten o'clock—when Roberts finally slid down the companionway ladder to the gun deck.

Despite the rule in the ship's articles of lights out at eight o'clock, the lanterns were alight in the great cabin. It told him that Tom Sutton, with surprising tact, had put Lúcia in there to wait for him. Indeed, Sutton was sitting on the deck outside the door sleeping against the bulkhead having no doubt seen off a quantity of rum punch. He woke as Roberts approached, and with a nod, took himself off to find his hammock.

Pausing momentarily outside the door, Roberts felt the blood race in his veins. It had been more than two years since he had last seen her, and he did not know what to expect. He had longed for this moment, now he feared it. The realisation that after so much time she might feel differently now struck him for the first time. Opening the door, he went in.

Lúcia sat quite still on the long seat beneath the huge stern window, her *mantilha* pulled over her, but as the door opened she stood up.

Stopping just inside the Great Cabin, he looked at her properly.

She looked tired and drained, her beauty faded a little. He thought also that she had a new dignity. Life and hardship had aged her. She had grown up.

He said awkwardly in English: 'Lúcia! I wondered if—that is I hoped—*Hell!* I thought you were at Corso!' He took a step towards her.

She took a step away from him, keeping the distance between them. In Portuguese she said: 'I was in Whydah when you burned the slave ship.'

Although she spoke quietly, it was as though she had slapped him with the reproach, and it stopped him. Remembering that incident made him ashamed. It accounted for her coolness now. Trying to dismiss it from his own mind he said: 'You were there?'

'I was. I only learned that it was you as you sailed out!' She looked down at her hands, clasping and unclasping each other nervously at her waist. 'Everywhere I hear about Bartholomew Roberts and how the English navy is looking for him. Everywhere I hear what a villain he is. You have become notorious in my absence.'

He was silent for a moment. When they had parted at Devil's Island he had only just started out on this life. Now he was a hunted man, infamous. And clearly she did not approve. His hope for the future seemed to disappear. She no longer wanted him. And he could not blame her. He acknowledged it. 'Too much time has gone by. I am not what you think me to be.'

'That must be true,' she agreed with deceptive ease. 'The Bartolomeo I know would not fire a ship with slaves trapped on board.'

'That—that was not my order. I gave orders for the slaves to be freed, to be brought aboard the *Royal Fortune,* so that they could be set free in safety.'

'They burned to death, Bartolomeo. It was horrible.'

'You should not have seen that.'

'I did see it.' Her voice rose angrily. 'And the horror of it lives with me. How could you let it happen? You who taught me the evil of slavery! You who freed slaves and had them on your ship equal to other men. How could it happen?'

'My orders were disobeyed.'

'You are the captain. That must count for something! Ah, but I forget. You are captain of a rabble of murderers and ruffians, men who care nothing for others' misery. You and your company are as bad as the slave traders themselves. Worse, even.'

Stung, he retorted: 'I wonder, *senhora*, that you deal with such a fellow!'

'So do I!'

Standing there, glaring at each other, he could have turned and walked out on her. But then, turning away from him, she took a steadying breath. 'I do not want to fight with you, Bartolomeo. But I thought you to be different to them. There is good in you. I know there is.'

'You mistake the matter, madam,' he snapped. 'There is obviously nothing good in me!'

Turning to face him again, she crossed the cabin stopping close to him, and looking up at him earnestly. 'But there is! I've seen it.'

He swallowed, and thought that if there had ever been anything good in him, it had been buried long ago. Shame washed over him. His own father would have said much more than this woman had. He had not been brought up to steal and rob and kill. His had been a God-fearing family. What had he come to? Whatever he was now, he had given her a disgust of him.

Becoming a little calmer she turned from him: 'They are looking for you, *senhor capitão*. The English Captain Ogle is here on this coast.'

'I know it. But how do you know this?'

'He brought me to this coast, to Corso first and then to Whydah with my father. But I saw him again a short time ago at Whydah. He wanted to know if I had seen you. It was just a few hours after you sailed from there. Bartolomeo, he is close and he means to find you.'

He was rattled but he put on a show of bravado. 'Well, he shall not find me!'

Unimpressed, she told him: 'He is not a man to be crossed, Bartolomeo. He handed me over to the Phipps man at Corso to question me about you.'

'What did you tell him?'

'Nothing, of course. Did you think I would betray you? But they knew about you and me.'

'How? How could they know unless you told them?'

Her voice began to rise again. 'So you think me guilty of betrayal? Well, *senhor capitão*, I will have you know that it was my father who wrote to London complaining that you had taken me at Bahia. Captain Ogle knew about it. I told them nothing. I denied ever knowing you, but they did not believe me. In the end, they decided that I had no information that could be of interest to them, and Captain Ogle brought us to Whydah to the Portuguese governor there.'

He frowned. 'So Ogle's here.'

'If not here, then very close.' She came close to him again, and a faint fragrance that he knew well reminded him sharply of their time together on Royale at Devil's Island. 'Bartolomeo, you must leave here, go far away.'

He pursed his lips. 'We have talked of breaking up the company.'

'What does that mean?'

'Retirement. We have, each of us, enough to retire. There are places we can go, where they will never find us.'

She tried to convince him of the peril she thought him to be in. 'Bartolomeo, this Ogle will find you. He will. He will not stop searching until he captures you.'

He tried to make light of it. 'I know how to lose him.'

She took a breath and looked up at the deck head in despair. 'Bartolomeo, I do not think you understand. This Ogle is a dangerous man. He frightens me—not for myself but for you. He will not stop until he has found you.'

Seeing her distress, he put his hand out and caught hers. 'What would you have me do, *querida*?' he asked and his voice was gentle.

Shaking her head, her anger evaporated. 'Oh Bartolomeo! I would have you go away from here, leave Africa, leave piracy, go far away where he will not find you. Please, Bartolomeo, please . . .' She could say no more for tears suspended her voice.

He drew her into the circle of his arms and held her against his chest while she wept. 'You don't know how much I have feared for you,' she said when she could. 'Everywhere they talk of you. Some think you a great man, others that you are a scoundrel to be feared. And all the while I hurt inside, in here.' She clutched her hands across her stomach and wept all the more. 'The man they spoke of was not the man I knew. It was not you! Yet they said your name. They spoke of your deeds, how you were feared, how harshly you had dealt with some of them, and I did not recognise the Bartolomeo Roberto that I loved.' She searched in a pocket in the innermost reaches of her petticoats and came out with a handkerchief.

A weeping woman was enough to bring a man to his knees and Roberts was not proof against Lúcia's tears.

He drew her back to him, and this time her head rested on his shoulder.

'If I leave this life, if I go away—to Madagascar, say—will you come with me, Lúcia?'

She looked up at him, her tears suddenly arrested. 'If you leave this life, then yes, Bartolomeo, I will. But I will not be the wife of a pirate.'

'You will not have to *querida*.'

And he kissed her with all the passion of years of longing, feeling her ready response, and he knew all would be well between them.

THIRTY-EIGHT

10th February 1722, Cape Lopez

The sky had only just lightened to grey when Roberts came on deck. Heavy black clouds gathered in the west, and the wind had risen to a gale which howled through the rigging and twanged the lines and ropes as though they were musical instruments. It was said that a sailor knew how bad a storm was going to be by the sound of the wind in the rigging—and Roberts didn't like the sound of this one at all.

David Symson was the officer in charge of the morning watch, not an exciting occupation during dark hours, and even less so when the ship was at anchor, but an important task wherever they might be.

'Wind's getting up,' Roberts said approaching him on the quarterdeck.

'Aye. We're in for a rum'un, that's fer sure!'

'Any sign of the *Ranger*?' It was a stupid question. If there had been he would have been the first to know.

Symson shook his head. 'Nope. I don't like it. Looks like they've gone off with the prize.'

Roberts frowned. 'I can't believe it of Dennis or Ashplant.'

'Henry Dennis will do whatever he feels is expedient.'

'And Ash?'

'I grant you he's a good 'un, loyal to his toenails! But he's only one man.'

'There's Main, and Roger Ball, and Skyrme.'

Symson shrugged. 'I don't know. I'm pretty sure of Skyrme. But if one of 'em wants to go off with the prize, and the men are with him, there ain't much one or two men can do.' He was talking from experience.

'Could be they ran into contrary winds.'

'Aye. But Skyrme's capable.' They fell silent, and Roberts brooded. He didn't like it when a ship broke away from the company. It challenged his authority.

'Well, we can't wait forever.'

'What've you got in mind?' Symson asked.

Roberts looked at him straightly. 'The Indian Ocean.'

'Madagascar?'

'Perhaps.'

Symson nodded. He understood perfectly. 'You lucky dog!'

Roberts grinned suddenly and went below.

'You knew that scoundrel Walter Kennedy, did you not, Commander Roberts?'

Roberts paused in the act of conveying a spoonful of salmagundi to his mouth, and stared at Captain Hill. 'The Irishman? You know him?'

'He were hanged. Back in July. At Wapping dock. Said at his trial that he were one of your men. Said he ran off with a prize ship.'

It wasn't honourable to gloat, but Roberts couldn't help feeling Kennedy had come by his just deserts. 'Aye—and so he did! Hanged, eh? Well, I cannot say it wasn't what he deserved. How came he to be caught?'

'I understand he intended to make landfall at Ireland, but instead he fell in with the west coast of Scotland.'

Roberts shouted with laughter. 'I believe it! The man could not even read, let alone navigate!'

'Well, he set up a bawdy-house on the Deptford Road, and boasted that he had once sailed with the great Bartholomew Roberts. So they hanged him.'

Roberts shook his head in disbelief. 'What a fool! Always the fool! Joseph—more salmagundi for Captain Hill!'

'Who was Walter Kennedy?' George Wilson asked conversationally, delicately conveying a piece of pickled herring—a component of the salmagundi—to his mouth with a new-fangled silver two-pronged fork which had been found on one of the prize ships and which he kept for his own use

Sutton said: 'He was Irish, unlettered, dirty, a cut-throat and a brute, and a drunkard!' In short, like most of the company.

'A rogue, then.'

'Worse than a rogue,' Symson said. 'Downright evil, he was. Well, he met what he deserved. I wonder what happened to the scoundrels that went with him.'

'Well we know what happened to the ships,' Roberts said. 'We found our own *Royal Rover* burnt out at St. Kitts, and the *Sagrada Familia* he had given to Captain Cane who sold it, or so he told us when we met him again at Hispaniola.'

'At the trial, Kennedy said Cane took all his own men, and

four Negroes, and the Portuguese ship which was still more than half loaded.'

'She was a rich ship,' Roberts said. 'I should think Cane was more than pleased. It was a better deal than we got, and a much better ship than Cane's old sloop which we came off with!'

'Well, Kennedy sailed to Barbados where they fell in with a Virginiaman, a slaver, captained by some Quaker, who, having neither sword nor pistol on board, agreed to everything they said. Eight men went with him to Virginia, they being very generous to him.'

'With our gold, no doubt!' Symson said with feeling.

'Four men went ashore at Maryland. The Quaker took the rest to Carolina where Governor Spotswood had them hanged. And, would you believe it, the Quaker surrendered all the goods and presents the pirates had given to him and his men?'

'No!' It was a universal cry of outrage.

'Aye, I tell you, they did. Well, Quakers are like that ain't they? Strange people!'

He paused in his narrative at that point, for Lúcia entered the great cabin, and the entire assembly of men rose respectfully.

She wished them all good day, and took a place just to the side of Roberts who was at the head of the table, and next to George Wilson. When she sat down, they all sat down, and the surgeon helped her to some salmagundi from the dish.

Roberts thought she looked much better this morning. Her cheeks had some colour in them, and her lips had once again adopted the deep wine red that he remembered so clearly. She met his eyes and smiled, and before he could stop himself, he had done the same. Now they would be the gossip of the entire company.

'I believe I interrupted you, Captain Hill,' Lúcia said serenely.

Hill inclined his head, but he had been so engrossed in the silent message that had passed between the lady who had so recently been in his charge and this most notorious pirate that he had forgotten where he got up to. So that's the way the wind blew.

'Quakers, Captain Hill,' George Wilson reminded him. 'Strange people.'

'Ah—yes.' Captain Hill remembered. 'Kennedy fell in with a sloop from Boston, and half the company went with the sloop back to Boston including Kennedy. But his men didn't like him and were for throwing him overboard.'

'I can't think why,' Roberts said dryly.

'He was bred a pick-pocket, you know.'

'Aye, I did know.'

'And before he became a—a gentleman of fortune, a housebreaker.'

'I knew he was a rum-un,' Christopher Moody said morosely.

Lúcia asked: 'Is this the man Kennedy who was your lieutenant, *senhor capitão*?'

He raised a brow at her. 'Aye. He sailed off from Devil's Island with the *Sagrada Familia* and the goods still in the hold. Tea, *senhora*?'

'I thank you, *senhor capitão*, yes.' He poured from a delicate china teapot into a handleless china cup and gave it to her. He grinned at her as she thanked him prettily. '*Obrigada, senhor.*'

Captain Hill coughed and the others around the table exchanged meaningful glances

Captain Hill continued his yarn. 'Well, apparently his companions thought poorly of his occupations, but he pleaded with them for his life, and said he would never betray them when they got back to Britain.'

'And they believed him?' Symson asked incredulously. 'I wouldn't believe that son of a whore if he swore on the Bible! Hell—he *did* swear on the Bible! Saving your presence, *senhora*!' he added hastily and Lúcia nodded graciously, her eyes dancing.

'Well, as I said, none of them could navigate except one who pretended only and they fell in with Scotland where storms nearly took them until at last they anchored in a creek and left the sloop there. They then said they were shipwrecked sailors, but the locals were suspicious. Kennedy separated from his companions with one other man and went to Ireland. The rest travelled south to London, but they were rich and spent their money—'

'Our money!' Moody cut in.

'—like it were poison and they must rid themselves of it. Their noisy riotous ways got two of them murdered and robbed. At Edinburgh the seventeen others were arrested. But there was no evidence until two of them were encouraged to inform on them, and nine of them were hanged.'

'Hell's teeth!'

'Aye.' Captain Hill allowed himself a brief satisfied pause. 'Nine of them,' he said again. 'Kennedy came from Ireland to

London and kept a bawdy-house on the Deptford Road, now and again sailing abroad a-pirating. One of his whores—begging your pardon, ma'am—gave information against him for a robbery and they sent him to Bridewell. But she were afraid of him, as well she might be, for he was known for his bad temper, and fearing he would be free soon, she found a mate of a ship that Kennedy had taken. The man visited Kennedy in Bridewell, identified him, and had him committed to the Marshalsea prison.'

Sutton let his breath go in a whistle through his teeth, and Hill drank from his ale before going on:

'Kennedy then turned King's evidence against the others and gave a list of eight or ten. But because he didn't know where they lived, they took only one man who claimed he had been forced.'

All of them laughed at that, and Roberts said: 'No man is forced to piracy, Captain Hill.'

'Well, this man said he was, and he got off. But Kennedy was hanged, as I said, in July last at Execution Dock.'

They fell silent as they thought about what Hill had said. After all, these men had been their comrades, members of their company, and it was a salutary reminder of their own mortality.

'How did you learn all this, Captain Hill?' Roberts asked presently.

'I was at Kennedy's trial,' Hill said simply. 'He had robbed my ship.'

Lúcia said roundly: 'Well, I am glad this man is no more. I did not like him.'

Then, as the ship pitched, and everyone held tightly to cups, plates, spoons and dishes, she added: 'I think we will have a storm, *senhor capitão*, do not you?'

'I think the lady is right,' Roberts said looking across at Moody. 'Storm anchors.'

'Aye, Cap'n.'

But before he could move to give the order, the cry 'Sail ho! Sail ho!' filtered through the open balcony windows.

'At last! The *Ranger* returning,' Roberts said unable to conceal his relief. But he jerked his head at Tom Sutton who went off to see, and carried on eating.

Tom Sutton came straight back with Ben Jeffries who brought the news. 'Sail sighted across the point.'

'What is she, pray?'

'Difficult to tell. Some say Portuguese, Cap'n. Others, a French slaver. But most are for it being the *Ranger* returning.'

Whatever she was, she was coming into the bay and Roberts could afford to wait. 'Let her come in then.'

'The men want to give her a welcome. A salute, p'raps,' Jeffries said.

'I should rather want to know where they've been all this time,' Roberts said acidly. 'Keep me informed.'

With an 'Aye, aye, Cap'n,' Jeffries disappeared again, and Tom Sutton sat down.

Roberts said: 'Captain Hill, whither are you bound?'

'Prince's Island first, then the Caribbean and then Bristol,' Hill said.

'Well, you have been such an amiable guest, and you have brought the *senhora* to us, so we shall only take half your cargo!'

'The other half being the slaves, I suppose,' Hill observed dryly. 'Am I supposed to be pleased with this offer?'

Roberts grinned. 'Oh, it could be a good deal worse, Captain, believe me.'

Hill looked at Lúcia. 'Do I assume, *senhora*, that you will not be travelling on my ship after this?'

Roberts said evenly: 'The *senhora* stays with us.'

Captain Hill studied her. 'This is of your own will, madam?'

But before she could answer Thomas Armstrong burst into the cabin, his colour much heightened with alarm. 'Captain! 'Tis the *Swallow*! 'Tis the *Swallow*!'

Roberts was unperturbed. He doubted the *Swallow* could have found them here, and thought it more likely to be the *Ranger*. 'What makes you think so?' he asked.

'I served on the *Swallow* under Cap'n Ogle, and deserted at Madeira. I'd know her anywheres. I *know* she's the *Swallow*.'

Roberts felt the first glimmer of alarm. But at that distance, and with only masts visible above the spit of land, Armstrong could easily be mistaken. He uttered an oath beneath his breath and came to his feet. He would have to see for himself.

Grabbing the telescope in its leather case as he passed the cabinet he marched swiftly from the great cabin, and everyone else abandoned their breakfasts to follow him including Lúcia and the interested Captain Hill.

On open deck the wind hit them with the force of a typhoon,

and above them the clouds were thick wet rags. The ship's company leaned on the gunwales, intent on the newcomer. Roberts viewed them impatiently. 'What's the matter with you? You're all cowards, putting fear into your fellows!'

He raised the telescope. The ship had rounded the point now and was on her way into the bay. 'See Captain,' Armstrong insisted. ''Tis the *Swallow*. Can a man forget a ship he's reefed and furled and hauled?'

Roberts peered at the ship. Three-masted, a frigate-built ship. No wait! A third-rater! There was no mistaking two tiers of guns. She flew a French flag and a Portuguese flag. A trick, of course. Deep in his belly he knew that this was indeed the *Swallow*.

Roberts swore profanely. 'You are certain?' he demanded of Armstrong.

'I keep telling you! 'Tis the *Swallow*.'

Lúcia beside him said: 'I too have been on the *Swallow*, *senhor capitão*, and I am sure this man is right. That is Captain Ogle in the *Swallow*.'

Roberts felt the swoop in his belly, not of fear, but of sudden need for action. Ogle had found him. Damn the man! And if he did not act quickly they would be caught with their skirts up. He did a rapid calculation.

'Mr. Moody, call all hands to battle stations!'

Moody, acting boatswain in Main's absence, took up the cry. 'All hands! All hands!'

To the drummer James White, Roberts snapped: 'Beat to quarters!' And: 'Mr. Glasby, make all sail!'

The drum rattled adding to the general mayhem as half-drunk men ran to do their commander's bidding, already half way up the shrouds before the orders reached their ears.

Roberts turned. 'Mr. Sutton: Get the *senhora* and her servants and Captain Hill off this ship!'

He strode forward to get a better look, ignoring everyone else, but Lúcia followed him. 'I will not leave.' She had to raise her voice above the roar of the wind.

He glanced down at her, and his heart contracted. 'You must, *querida*. I cannot have you on this ship when we are under attack. For your own safety. Let Captain Hill take you to Príncipe as you intended and I will come for you there.'

Shaking her head, her lips white now and her eyes brimming

she pleaded: '*Não*, Bartolomeo! I will not leave you.'

He turned to her then, desperate. '*Querida*, listen to me.' He had so little time. 'It isn't safe. You must go with Captain Hill!'

'*Não!*'

Tom Sutton took her arm. '*Senhora,* please!'

Tears spilled down her ashen cheeks. 'Bartolomeo, please—'

'Lúcia, you have to go.'

David Symson came unexpectedly to his rescue. '*Senhora,* if you do not go, we cannot fight. And if we do not fight, we will all hang.'

She looked at him, appalled, and then at Roberts who nodded. 'It is so, *querida*.'

She nodded then, to his great relief acquiescent. She threw her arms around him, clinging to him, and he kissed her warm lips, unmindful of his men standing by. Then he put her from him. 'I will come for you in Príncipe. Wait for me there. Mr. Sutton—if you please!'

He turned away to John Stephenson who had taken the helm, effectively dismissing her. He had work to do, and she was in the way.

'Come, ma'am.' Tom Sutton pulled firmly on her upper arm. 'This is no place for a lady.'

She went with him to the entry port and as she turned to descend backwards down the ladder, she caught sight of him at the helm. He met her eyes for a moment and dread coiled around her insides like a terrible voracious serpent.

THIRTY-NINE

Roberts had no time to waste. Already his men were in the yards, making sail. As he put on the red damask waistcoat Joseph had brought to him, he discussed his plans with his officers. 'As the *Swallow* comes towards us, we will pass by her starboard to starboard.'

'She'll fire on us!' Symson said.

'No doubt on't. Chances are she'll miss. Whether she does or not we'll give our own broadside. If we're badly hit, we'll run for the point, beach the ship, and it'll be every man for himself among the natives. If we can't sail the *Fortune* at all, we'll grapple and board her, and blow up both ships together.' He buckled the belt about his waist and surveyed his officers grimly. 'If we can get clear, we will. But I do not need to remind you, gentlemen, that we are out-manned and out-gunned with the *Ranger* gone.'

Thomas Armstrong joined them. 'You wanted to see me, Cap'n?'

'Aye. Armstrong—how best does the *Swallow* sail?'

'She be best upon a wind, Cap'n. And if you want to leave her, we should run before the wind.'

Roberts allowed Joseph to put the great diamond cross around his neck and then plonked his hat on his head. He slung two pairs of pistols over his shoulders. 'Very well. Let us pray you are wrong, Armstrong, and that she is a harmless French slaver.'

The sails were ready, and Ben Jeffries bent all his young strength to hack through the arm-thick anchor ropes. The ship which had been pitching badly all morning in the gathering storm, now bucked and jerked in the current and rising waves. Harry Glasby was in charge of sailing the ship, John Stephenson at the helm, and they obeyed Roberts' orders with masterful precision. It was no easy thing, sailing a ship in a storm, judging how much canvas she could bear without driving her under, but Roberts was an experienced commander, and he knew his ship, while Glasby had a way of anticipating his orders which bordered on clairvoyance.

Up on the pitching yards, the men fought desperately to get the canvas under control as it flew from their fingers in the wind, swearing and cursing and clinging desperately to the yardarms as the masts swung dizzyingly at impossible angles until all they could see seventy feet below was grey angry sea.

But at last they made fast, and the *Royal Fortune* jerked forward as the wind took her, and Harry Glasby allowed her to pay off into the wind.

The *Royal Fortune* bucked gleefully in her new-found freedom, ploughing into the waves, green-grey sea washing over her bows in torrents and out of the scuppers. She settled quickly into a rhythm, riding up one wave, crashing down jarringly into the next. Roberts checked her sails. Her masts were bending with the strain and she could bear no more. Already he was in danger of driving her under.

Roberts addressed the man at the helm. 'Mr. Stephenson, bring us starboard to starboard.'

The *Swallow* was close enough for him to make out most of the details without the telescope, but the glass confirmed that she flew French colours. She came straight for them, head on, just inside the bay.

As they came nearer, Roberts' heart began to pound in his chest, a regular hard thud, and his mouth went dry. He knew this was no French slaver. Without doubt this was the *Swallow* sent to find him. He felt the cold chill of doom that owed nothing to the seaspray spitting in his face. They were desperately unprepared for this. The crew were still half-drunk from a night spent consuming Captain Hill's cargo of rum, wine and brandy, whereas the *Swallow*'s highly-trained recruits would be stone-cold sober. Furthermore they were trapped within the confines of the bay, having to pass the *Swallow* to escape. This would be the fight of his life.

He glanced up at the yards. Men clung in the rigging or crouched waiting for the next order to alter the sails. Others were ready at the guns, grimly awaiting their orders, the whole ship silent with tension, all of them waiting on their commander.

The *Swallow* was a hundred yards ahead.

'*Run out!*' he ordered. The *Royal Fortune*'s guns emerged from her side, the carriage wheels shrieking in the roaring wind.

Ninety yards and closing. Over the roaring wind he could hear his heart thudding in his ears. After the chaos of getting under weigh, the *Royal Fortune* was eerily quiet. They had a good speed with a following wind—ten knots by the log, and they would pass the *Swallow* at perhaps twenty. There would be no more than a few seconds to get off a broadside.

Fifty yards. He raised his sword. 'Steady,' he warned

Stephenson.

A sudden flash of lightning streaked through heavy black clouds to land in the sea somewhere beyond the *Swallow* followed immediately by a shattering crash of thunder, signalling the start of the expected storm. He didn't let it distract him, although he heard the men murmur. They were superstitious and would see it as an omen, he thought.

Twenty yards, and the rain began pounding with tropical ferocity on the decks, soaking the men in seconds.

The *Royal Fortune*'s bowsprit passed the *Swallow*'s bowsprit about a pistol-shot away, and a double row of murderous black iron guns appeared in the *Swallow*'s side.

Roberts waited for the broadside, his teeth clenched, one hand gripping the taffrail until his knuckles showed white, the only indication of the cold clutch of fear inside him.

Abruptly, flame and smoke belched out of the *Swallow*'s side, ripping down the whole length of her. The roar which tore the air followed fractionally later, and rivalled the crash of thunder which followed.

The *Royal Fortune* plunged down to the bottom of a wave, and began to rise again. 'Steady!' he ordered Stephenson. Without waiting to see whether they had been damaged, he brought his sword down swiftly.

'*Fire!*'

One. Two.

The *Royal Fortune*'s guns belched out fore to aft. The deck shook beneath his feet and shook his body to his teeth, and the *Swallow* vanished in the smoke pall.

The *Royal Fortune*'s mizzen topmast fell, and some rigging with it, but they sailed on. Already they were clear and running out of the bay for the open Atlantic.

Roberts raised the glass and looked back. The *Royal Fortune*'s guns had missed, and he swore softly. Swinging the telescope, the *Swallow*'s commander came into view, unmistakable on the poop deck. For a split second Roberts stared hard at his enemy, as Chaloner Ogle stared at him through his own telescope.

Roberts grinned to himself. He felt the full glory of relief as he watched the urgent efforts of the *Swallow*'s crew to bring her about and follow. As she turned, her deck canted sharply putting the yards under and costing precious time.

No need to beach her, he thought exultantly. They had a clear run, and he reckoned they could easily out-pace the *Swallow*.

'Get us out of here, Mr. Glasby,' he announced with a grin, walking towards the helm.

It felt good. With a following wind the *Royal Fortune* seemed to fly over the heaving sea, and the gap between the ships widened perceptibly. As the storm flashed and crashed around them, Stephenson pointed the *Royal Fortune*'s bow to the open sea, and the crew let out a cheering roar.

'You did it!' Symson shouted above the howling wind and driving rain, joining him at the helm a few minutes later, and his mouth split into a grin. But when Symson put his hands on the guard-rail, Roberts noticed that they shook as much as his own did.

'No, Davy,' he corrected him. '*We* did it. And it was a close run thing. What is the damage?'

'Just the mizzen top, and we don't need it in this wind.'

As he spoke, men began to clear away the debris of the fallen wood and rigging behind them. Then abruptly, they were clear of the bay and into the unsheltered waters of the Atlantic. Thirty-foot waves piled up on either side of the *Royal Fortune* like towers, but the ship was well-built, and rode them with ease, rising up the mounds, crashing into the depths in the usual way.

Roberts and Symson were silent for sometime, grinning at the distant *Swallow*'s efforts to catch up with them. Then Symson said abruptly: 'What do you think happened to the *Ranger*, Bart?'

Roberts sobered immediately. 'I think they have been caught by the *Swallow*,' he said. 'I think that what we thought was a Portuguese ship was actually the *Swallow*.'

'They're dead then.'

'Some maybe.' Roberts thought of the rough Valentine Ashplant, the opportunist Henry Dennis, young Richard Hardy, the irascible James Skyrme, Robert Birdson, William Main, Israel Hynde and the rest and felt a great sadness wash over him. He would miss them, brave men all.

The rain soaked through their clothes and trickled off their hats when they moved and the wind tossed the ship about mercilessly, but Roberts would not think of deserting his post to go below. The driving rain obliterated all signs of the *Swallow* but he knew she was there, like a dog on the scent.

He thought of Lúcia, and how much he loved her. They would

double back and pick her up from Príncipe later. His men owed him that much.

'Cap'n! Look!'

Sutton's cry of shock brought Roberts and David Symson to look forward. Ahead, the waves had miraculously flattened, and the sea took on a black oily texture. Already the pitching of the ship was less jarring.

Roberts knew what it was. He had seen it before. He felt his insides lurch as the rain stopped and the wind vanished quite suddenly, and the sun came out. The sails collapsed into useless limp laundry and the *Royal Fortune* stopped moving, completely becalmed.

'Sweet Jesus!'

''Tis the eye of the storm,' Harry Glasby said, and it was passing across the *Royal Fortune*, but the *Swallow* was unaffected.

Now that the rain had stopped, Roberts could see her sails bellying nicely, and she was gaining on them.

He swore profanely, impotently cursing the weather, but he could do nothing until the eye passed, and then where the wind came from would be anybody's guess.

For half an hour he paced the deck in raging impatience, and could only watch the *Swallow*'s steady progress towards them. His only hope would be that the *Swallow* would sail into the calm too, but by then they would be in range again.

'Captain! The wind!' Sutton pointed to a ripple on the sea and the wind hit them broadside with a fearsome gust for it had veered to the north.

Roberts reeled off his orders and the ready men rushed to his bidding, letting go the braces, bringing the yards round into the wind. 'Let go and haul!' Harry Glasby yelled.

Amid much cursing and swearing and shouts they brought the sails into the wind again. The *Royal Fortune* lurched and picked up speed.

From the taffrail Roberts watched the *Swallow*'s swift approach with something akin to disbelief. They were in range again.

He knew now that he could not outrun her, for the ships were evenly matched. He would have to engage in battle, for which the *Swallow*'s crew were eminently better prepared. And it would be a fight to the finish.

His heart began to thud once more, but he felt no fear. Only the exhilaration of the fight and the clear sharp mind needed to defeat the enemy.

'Mr. Symson, make ready the guns,' he ordered.

The *Swallow* fired the first of her deadly swivels, belching lethal fragments of metal and chain shot into the *Royal Fortune*'s sails.

Roberts cursed as sky appeared magically in the sails as the canvas shredded. But it wasn't enough to stop them.

'Bring her about Mr. Glasby!' he bellowed. He wouldn't run now. He would stand and fight.

Glasby and Symson bellowed out the orders.

Roberts stood alone at the taffrail, a tall imposing figure in red, with the red feather in his hat flying in the wind, his sword in his hand, the commander of the greatest pirate company in history.

As the two ships manoeuvred, the second of the *Swallow*'s swivels came to bear, its open mouth pointing straight at him. He had the fleeting impression of staring into the very mouth of Hell itself.

The gun fired. He saw the flame and smoke as it spewed out its deadly murderous grapeshot.

And a piece of metal, no bigger than a shilling, tore into his throat, sliced through his windpipe, embedded in his spine and severed his spinal cord.

He died instantly.

FORTY

John Stephenson at the helm saw the captain sit down on one of the guns. Perplexed and angry, he left his position at the helm to John Jessup and ran aft, keeping low to shield himself from the constant fire from the *Swallow*'s swivels.

Roberts seemed to be resting, his head forward as though he dozed. 'Damn you, do you rest at a time like this, you cowardly—?' Stephenson stopped abruptly. A little trickle of blood had seeped over the captain's snowy white neckcloth.

With sudden dread Stephenson crouched down beside him, and peered beneath the brim of his hat. Roberts' head had fallen forward, his chin on his neckcloth, and his eyes were open, but staring, sightless.

Gently Stephenson slipped his fingers beneath the captain's chin, feeling the hot sticky blood, and raised his head. The unseeing eyes seemed to stare through him, and Stephenson could feel the grating of severed bone with the movement. It made him feel physically sick. And then an obscene black hole opened in the captain's throat, just below the voice-box.

Stephenson gave an involuntary cry and dropped the head which fell forward grotesquely. He jumped up with sudden shock, and then burst into tears.

'The Cap'n's dead!' he wailed. 'The Cap'n's dead!' He fell to his knees again beside the body. 'Oh, Cap'n, if only the next shot could be mine that I could go with ye!'

'The commander's dead!' The news spread through the ship as men repeated it in disbelief. It couldn't be true. Bartholomew Roberts was immortal, invincible—wasn't he?

David Symson ran aft, his stomach churning. He found Roberts sitting on the gun, his head with the hat still in place, fallen forward, his chin on his chest, and beside him Stephenson, forty years old and wailing like a lost child, on his knees beside him.

'Move!' Symson ordered Stephenson, and as he did so, crouched down beside the body in his place. 'Bart?' Leaning forward, he too moved his head and felt the sick thud of shock in his belly. Already the eyes were glazed over, staring sightlessly, the pupils dilated. The captain was no longer there. The invincible Bartholomew Roberts, the man he had grown to love like a brother had gone. Only a shell remained. Nothing else.

A sob choked in Symson's throat. A sudden and terrible grief squeezed him as though in a vice. Tears flooded his eyes so that he could hardly see. Impatiently he dashed the back of his hand across them.

He looked up then, and realised that he was not alone. The company had gathered, silent, shocked. They had deserted their posts. He should reprimand them.

'Back to your positions!' he ordered roughly. 'We ain't done for yet!'

But they stood there, as the *Swallow*'s guns continued to belch out death. Another man fell. Tom Sutton wept openly, and William Magnes sobbed. James Phillips had silent tears trickling down his thin cheeks, as did others. They had all been close to him, and they had all loved him.

'Back to your positions!' Symson bellowed again, grief adding fury to the order. They began to move as George Wilson and Peter Scudamore arrived.

'He's dead,' Scudamore announced officially, and closed the lids for the last time over the sightless eyes.

The tears which flooded Symson's eyes found their way down his cheeks.

But he had work to do. The *Swallow* still dogged their stern, firing her swivels and now bringing her guns to bear. With supreme effort he struggled for self-control, wiped his face on his sleeve, and turned back to the task in hand. His was the command now. And he didn't want it.

'Back to yer posts!' he ordered them furiously. 'Move! We ain't finished yet!'

The *Swallow*'s guns belched again. A loud crack, the screeching of splintered wood, and the mainmast toppled. It came crashing to the deck in a tangle of lines and ropes and torn sail, like a falling tree in a forest.

It was the end. They all knew it.

They all looked at Symson, silent, shocked. 'Call for quarter,' he said.

He walked forward, staring hopelessly at the tangle of wreckage, and there, beneath the wood, lay Roberts' jack, with A.B.H. and A.M.H. and the Jolly Roger, with the skeleton and a man with a flaming sword, the defiance of death itself.

He picked them up, cutting them free with his dagger, and held them in his hands, looking at them, remembering the early days when the Martinicans and the Barbadians had sent ships after them, remembering how they had so often sung to the raising of them: *This flag is our Old Roger, and we shall live under it and die under it.* He screwed them up and threw them over the side where they fluttered on to the heaving sea.

Captain Ogle allowed the pirates to afford their commander the dignity of burial at sea, and the boarding party, commanded by Lieutenant Sun looked on as a sorry group assembled on the quarterdeck. They were for the most part Godless. Religion played small part in their lives, yet no man would say he had no belief. So when George Wilson suggested it might be fitting to offer a prayer, the others readily agreed.

In the renewed gale and rain, with constant lightning and the boom of thunder, with the *Swallow*'s armed men looking on, George Wilson the surgeon led them in the Lord's prayer which was all he could think of. David Symson as their most senior officer, couldn't let the commander go without a few words. He thought of when they had first found Roberts on the *Princess*, how he had rebelled at first against piracy. He thought of how angry he, Symson had been when Roberts was elected captain and not he. But his respect and love for the Welshman had grown with his many and daring successes, earning him the respect and love of the company.

He tried to sum it up. But the shock and grief prevented him finding the right words, and in any case, he was no orator. He did his best. 'He were a good captain,' he said. 'Brave, clever and fair, the best a company ever had. And we loved him dear. There ain't no-one like him, nor like to be. God rest ye, Cap'n Roberts.'

And the crew gravely mumbled: 'A-men.'

With all his pistols and sword, and the gold diamond studded cross on the chain around his neck, still wearing his red damask waistcoat, and the hat with the red feather, in stockings, breeches and shoes, they threw Bartholomew Roberts overboard to the sharks. It was what he had requested.

They stood staring gloomily as the weighted body sunk slowly beneath the Atlantic's boisterous waves, and Symson quoted the commander's own words: '*A merry life and a short one shall be my motto.*'

*****

Lúcia looked at Captain Hill. 'So, you will take me to Príncipe, captain?'

'That is what we arranged, madam.'

She nodded, and glanced again at the spit of land which separated Cape Lopez from the Atlantic Ocean. They had been gone two days. Two days since the *Swallow* chased the *Royal Fortune* in that terrible storm. Had he escaped? She prayed that he had, yet deep inside her she feared that something terrible had happened. She had a constant terrible churning in her belly, a feeling of dread which made her heart jump in her chest. She was eager now to go to Príncipe where he said he would meet her, hoping to find him there, to be reassured.

She said: 'Your men have robbed the pirates, of their gold, captain.' She had seen them poring over the *Little Ranger* in Roberts' absence, taking anything of value. They were little more than pirates themselves.

Captain Hill smiled. 'Stolen gold in the first place, *senhora*. By the time they come back, we will be gone.'

He turned from her and gave the command to make all sail.

Lúcia looked at the *Little Ranger* lying deserted quietly at anchor. *Dear God,* she prayed, *where is he? Please make him safe.*

She felt the *Neptune* jerk as the sails were loosed, and the men hauled up the anchor. In less than an hour the *Neptune* was in open sea, heading for Príncipe.

Príncipe was just as she remembered, misty and hot and craggy. But it made so little impression on her now. Nothing could replace the terrible anxiety which had taken hold of her, which boiled in her insides and stopped her eating, the awful dread that something had happened to him.

The men of the island insisted that she stayed at the governor's house, the house which had once been that of Mendoça, now long gone. There was no governor at the moment. Príncipe was governed from São Tomé by a council until a new governor was appointed, but the traders on the island thought it proper that the daughter of the King's Emissary should be allowed to stay there until a ship could be found to take her back to Lisbon.

The days passed in agonising slowness. Why did he not come? From the newly-repaired window, the same window which Roberts had blasted with cannon not three years previously, she watched the ships in the bay anxiously.

'You must eat, *senhora*,' Maria said. 'You will fade away if you do not.'

Lúcia shrugged. 'He isn't coming, Maria.'

Maria looked at her with the same expression she used for a stupid child. 'Of course he isn't coming! Don't you know he is a pirate? He doesn't care for you.'

Lúcia stood up. 'What right have you to speak like that to me?' she demanded. 'And what do you know about it anyway? You do not know him like I do.'

'I know he isn't good enough for you.'

'You think so, do you? Well, fortunately for me that is not your decision to make.'

'*Senhora*, you are making a fool of yourself over a mere sea-robber.'

'I know what he is, thank you.'

'Your dear sainted father would turn in his grave if he knew.'

'Would he? Well, you seem to know all about it, Maria.' She picked up her *mantilha* and threw it about her head and shoulders.

'Where are you going?'

'Out!'

'On your own?'

'Yes, on my own.'

She brushed past her and made for the door. Maria tried to stop her. 'I will send one of the servants with you.'

'You will do no such thing. I am going down to the harbour.'

And she was gone, out of the oppression of the house and into the bare earth courtyard.

This was where she had first seen him, crossing this courtyard, having just met Mendoça. She remembered how he had looked then, tall and dark and so fine. She had loved him even then, she thought. She had always loved him.

She took the road down the hill to the bay. There the sailors and the traders haggled over the goods the sailors brought in on their ships. And not far from there she had gone with her father and Mendoça to the English camp and haggled over a length of blue silk. *Holy Mother, where is he?*

She looked out at the bay. Two new ships had made their way into the harbour to anchor alongside a third. From this distance it was difficult to make out what they were. But there was something familiar about both the newcomers.

She climbed the hill again to get a better look, and then her stomach swooped. One of them was the *Royal Fortune*, she was sure of it. He had come for her! And the other ship? It was too big to be the *Little Ranger*. And then with sudden shock, she knew it for the *Swallow*.

Her mind raced. In a moment she realised that if the *Swallow* was together with the *Royal Fortune* it could only mean that Roberts had been captured. She could not think that Roberts, if he captured the *Swallow*, which even she had to admit was unlikely, would bring the naval ship to Príncipe. No, the worst had happened. Ogle had been victorious.

So what had happened to Bartolomeo?

She saw the *Swallow* launch one of her boats and decided to meet the occupants when they came ashore. She must find out what had happened.

She ran down again to the beach, but had a while to wait as the boat came closer. She hardly dared think, yet at the same time she hoped for the best. And what was the best? That he had got away somehow? Or did they have him in the *Swallow*'s hold, ready to make him stand trial and hang. It would be better if he had died in combat, she thought. And then unthought it. No, she couldn't bear the thought of that, but neither could she bear the thought of his being hanged.

Her stomach churned, her mouth went dry, her heart fluttered in her chest, and she had an ache in her throat. But she stood resolutely on the shore waiting for the boat.

The boat ran onto the beach and although she searched the occupants to see if he were among them, she resisted the urge to come towards it, but waited quietly. Captain Ogle, Lieutenant Sun and the surgeon John Atkins got out of the boat together with some armed men and began to walk up the beach. *Perhaps he got away.*

They did not see her, but were talking among themselves, and she had to come right up to them and stand in the way.

All of them stopped. Captain Ogle touched his hat. 'Madam.'

She stood before them, suddenly struck dumb, not able to string together a sentence in English to ask what she so desperately wanted to know.

John Atkins took pity on her. '*Senhora,* we meet again.'

She managed: 'Is that the *Royal Fortune* you have, *senhor?*'

Ogle said: 'It is, madam.'

'Then—then you have been—' she searched for the word '—victorious.'

'God has given the villain Bartholomew Roberts into our hand,' Ogle told her.

Her face drained of its colour. 'And Captain Roberts?'

Ogle said bluntly: 'Captain Roberts is dead, madam.'

Ogle moved on, walking past her with Lieutenant Sun. She was not aware of it, for she felt suddenly faint, her knees buckling, and the trees around her began to spin.

John Atkins caught her before she fell, and held her, one arm around her waist. '*Senhora*, are you all right?'

She came round then, and he sat her down on the beach and knelt beside her studying her in his concern. She trembled so much that she alarmed him.

'Is it true, *senhor* Atkins? Is he really dead?'

'I am afraid so, *senhora*. Shot and killed in action.'

She sat still for a long time, staring at the sand in front of her. She kept repeating to herself *He is dead*, but she could not really grasp it. How could someone so vibrant, so alive, be dead?

'Where is he now?' she asked.

So he told her of the funeral at sea, and how the others had surrendered. He told her that they had captured the *Great Ranger*, and left her at Príncipe with her crew chained in the hold, ready to take them all to Cape Corso for trial. She seemed, though, not to hear him. She said: 'He was a great man, *senhor* Atkins.'

'He was, *senhora*,' he agreed seriously. 'If he had been on the side of right . . .'

Two huge tears rolled down her face.

John Atkins reached out and pulled her into his arms as she began to weep.

FORTY-ONE

3rd April 1722, Cape Corso Castle

To men grown accustomed to the dark of the cells, the early sun's glare as they came into the castle's quadrangle hurt the eyes. David Symson blinked and tried to reach up to shield his eyes, but his hands jerked short, the rusty iron cutting into his wrists, his movements curtailed by the heavy manacles attached to the iron band around his waist. He cursed such an instrument of torture as those chains had become to each of them.

The guards carried bayoneted muskets, and with them waved the prisoners towards the smithy where a man waited to remove the chains. Symson waited for his turn quietly as the smith hacked though the rivets of each man in turn with a bolster.

It was a month since they had arrived at Cape Corso. Nearly two months since their defeat at Cape Lopez. In that time they had hardly seen sunlight at all, first being incarcerated in the *Swallow*'s hold, and then in the stinking prison of the castle. Not that they had not tried to cheat the gallows. The four of them, Magnes, Ashplant, Maer and Symson, realising that Ogle's crew was finely stretched because of having to man three ships, worked out a plan to kill the *Swallow*'s crew and sail off with the ship. They'd have done it too, for they had managed to slip out of their irons, only that scoundrel George Wilson had denounced them in an attempt to save his own neck. On the *Royal Fortune* surgeon Peter Scudamore had rallied the Africans, telling them he had had some knowledge of navigation—only he too had been denounced and the plan foiled.

So, to Cape Corso they had been brought, to stand trial before a court of officials presided over by Director-General James Phipps. The captain of *H.M.S. Weymouth* Mungo Heardman had been one of the judges, but Captain Ogle, as the man who had captured them, could not sit on the court.

It had been a fair trial, though, Symson thought, as trials go, better than they could have expected in England, although the outcome would have been the same. The prisoners had been given an opportunity to air their views, and some, like Harry Glasby, had been acquitted because they could prove they had been forced. Others had been sentenced to hard labour. Like Henry Dennis who had turned King's evidence against them. Henry Dennis! Who would have thought it? Even now, thinking of him, Symson felt the blood boil in his veins.

It was his turn and he held out his wrists for the smith to cut through the rivets on his manacles, and he stood quietly while he did so.

It was a relief to be rid of them; the iron belt had slipped as he lost weight, and had chafed and bruised alternately his hips and his lower ribs and spine. His wrists were rubbed raw, despite the rags and straw he had wrapped around the irons to try to prevent it. Rags. They had taken away their silk shirts and expensive waistcoats and breeches, and given them ill-fitting rags instead. Symson's made him look like a child who had outgrown his clothes, because nothing fitted him.

As he massaged his wrists the guards pushed them into line.

The sun scorched them as they stood in a row in the courtyard, a pathetic bedraggled and sick group. Hardly the dashing gentlemen of fortune of two months ago, Symson thought wryly. Not allowed a blade in the dungeon they all had straggly beards and matted lice-infested hair, and they probably smelled like the slaves usually did.

Beside Symson young Sutton shook so badly he could hardly stand. As he staggered, Symson reached out for him, and grabbed his arm, holding him up. 'Don't let 'em see,' he whispered. 'Remember—the Cap'n's already waiting for us!'

Tom Sutton nodded obediently, but his face was grey with fear, robbed in the weeks of confinement of its tan, and his eyes were sunken in his head.

'Affrighted, is he?' one of the guards mocked. 'Aw, now ain't that a shame!'

'Course he ain't,' Ashplant growled for them all. ''Tis the sickness your own dungeons breed. Ain't none of us been nothing but sick all these weeks.' In fact four men had died in prison, and everyone else had lost so much weight on the scant diet that they joked they would not weigh enough to be hanged.

The soldiers didn't believe them, and laughed and jeered at them.

Tom was only a kidwy, Symson thought paternally. 'Pay them no heed, Tom,' he whispered. 'Remember to give Roberts a thirteen gun salute!'

Sutton managed a weak smile with his lips while his eyes looked at Symson in sheer terror. It was a joke he had made himself in his bravado, cheering on another prisoner who had hoped to make his peace with God as they sat together in the *Swallow*'s hold, muttering prayers and singing psalms. 'What do you propose by so much noise, friend?' he had asked.

'Heaven, I hope,' the other had said.

'Heaven? You fool! Did you ever hear of pirates going to heaven? Give me hell, it's a merrier place; I'll give Roberts a salute of thirteen guns at entrance!'

It had done little good. The man continued to read from his prayer book until Sutton had begged to be separated from him.

It was all bravado, Symson thought. All of it. And Sutton wasn't so brave now.

Hell. Would it really be a merrier place? The stories they had heard of hell—of fire and torture and suffering—had come back to haunt and terrify all of them in their darkest moments. They had all prayed to a God they hardly knew, begging for mercy. Even Sutton himself.

Symson's own guts boiled with fear as they waited. On his other side, Ashplant's breathing came fast and heavy, rattling in his throat as though he had run up to the top yard and back. Poor Ashplant. He had lost so much weight, his skin now sagged on his face and on his belly. Harry Glasby had tried to save him from the gallows, telling the court of the time Ashplant had done as much for him. It had done no good.

The waiting was the worst part. Why didn't they get it over with. Not for the first time Symson envied Commander Roberts his quick fearless exit.

Grave John Atkins came towards them and took up a place in front of them. In the absence of a cleric, John Atkins as surgeon took on the duty of bringing them to a sense of their iniquities. 'You are pirates,' he said, 'and have acted together in piracy to the detriment of all those who make a living by transporting goods by the sea. Nothing can be more detrimental to a trading nation than piracy. You have preyed on the weak and needy, men who are trying to earn their bread in the most hazardous conditions. It is a crime against man and against God and I urge each of you to repent before you stand before your Maker.'

Sanctimonious fool! Symson knew his sort, a 'gentleman' from a noble family, perhaps a younger son, sent to Oxford or Cambridge to learn doctoring. Thought he knew all about mankind, and knew very little.

An insolent grin spread over Christopher Moody's lips. 'I need a drink,' he said carelessly.

Taken aback, John Atkins glared at him. Symson could see he did not like them. He considered them rogues, blackguards, villains and cowards. 'Do you have no appreciation of your sins, man?' he demanded roughly.

William Magnes addressed the nearest soldier. 'I want a cap.' He meant a hood to cover his face with.

'You'll get one when you're on the scaffold!' the soldier told him.

Symson smirked. *Thought they would bring us down did they? They will find out that Bart Roberts' men are no cowards. That's it men, make 'em see we're not scared.*

Atkins gave it another go. 'Do you not feel, gentlemen, that you should acknowledge the justice of the court which has passed sentence on you?'

The sheer hypocrisy brought bitter anger into David Symson's throat. He looked across the quadrant to where the fat Director-General Phipps had appeared in the doorway to his offices, the man who, as governor of the castle, earned two thousand pounds a year while lesser men starved, the man who traded in human lives, and not just slaves, the man who extorted, which was as good as stealing, money and goods from visiting ships, and the artisans who worked at the castle, the man to whom human life meant nothing. This same man—James Phipps—had been one of the officiating judges at the trial, who had condemned them to death.

'Justice?' he cried out suddenly. 'Justice? You call this justice? Be damned to you, sir! May the same justice take this court!'

'Dammit, we're poor rogues,' Ashplant growled.

Symson took it up again. 'Aye, and we hang, while others, no less guilty, but in another way, escape!'

'Enough!' Atkins cried. 'You should remember that in a few minutes you will meet your Maker. Your state of mind should reflect that!'

Symson squared his shoulders and put up his chin, looking young Atkins defiantly in the eye. What did he know?

John Atkins lowered his gaze, unable to meet the accusation in Symson's eyes. *Poor fools*, he thought. *Poor brave fools.*

He nodded to the soldiers. 'Take them away.'

At once to the beat of a drum, they ushered the prisoners through the gates, and along the shadow of the walls to the small rocky peninsular where the sea crashed against the rocks, sending spray high into the air. David Symson watched it and felt the pull of the sea as he had as a boy, and took a great gulp of the fresh salty air.

The gallows had been specially made for them. A platform with a cross beam with ropes and nooses in place. At the sight of it he shuddered involuntarily, cold hard fear clutching at his insides. He didn't want to die. He wanted to live with a fierce desperate wanting.

A small crowd had gathered, mostly members of the castle community, soldiers of course, some of the men from naval ships, some artisans from the castle, a few women and a few curious natives. They seemed to make a collective groan as the prisoners came into view. There wasn't room for more people on the small spit of land beneath the castle walls, below the high-water mark. Seaman must be hanged between the flood marks, for that was where the Admiralty had jurisdiction—in the sea.

They were led to the scaffold in single file, six of them: Valentine Ashplant, William Magnes, Thomas Sutton, Christopher Moody, Richard Hardy and David Symson. Tom Sutton, white-faced with fear, stumbled and fell, and once again David Symson took his arm. But his own knees were weak, wobbling as though he had the ague. Despite the bravado and the careless attitude, he thought the fear boiling in his insides would choke him. And the glance Ashplant shot at him told him he was not the only one. But he wouldn't let them see. He had taken the risk, knowing the penalty for piracy and accepted it. He wouldn't give them the satisfaction of a public repentance now, or show them that he was afraid.

They stood on the platform, and their hands were tied tightly behind their backs. The ties cut into Symson's wrists again, aggravating the sores and cutting off the circulation to his fingers. Well, it wouldn't matter soon.

Richard Hardy protested. 'I've seen many a man hanged, but this way of tying hands behind the back, I'm a stranger to, and never saw so before in my life!' But then John Atkins had never hanged a man before.

The drumming stopped at last.

Determined to do his duty, John Atkins now stood in front of them. He approached Ashplant first. 'Name?'

'Valentine Ashplant.'
'How old are you?'
'Thirty-two.'
'Where from?'
'Minories, London.'

Atkins noted it down. 'Valentine Ashplant, have you repented of your sins?'

Ashplant said nothing.

Atkins gave it up. 'May God have mercy on your soul,' he said.

He passed on to the next man. 'Thomas Sutton . . . Berwick . . . twenty-three.' Sutton's voice, barely audible, shook.

This was unbearable. In an effort to distract himself, Symson looked around the crowd. From the platform he could see them all clearly, with their eager ghoulish faces, waiting for the entertainment. There was nothing quite as entertaining as a good hanging. Often thought so himself.

And there, at the back, half-hidden, but distinctive in the all-enveloping black lace *mantilha* was the captain's woman. Instantly Symson was transported back two years to Devil's Island and Captain Roberts, flushed with success from taking the *Sagrada Familia*, and how they had feared he would marry her and leave them. Happy times. The best of times. He wondered what would become of her now. She was weeping, and he was puzzled. She had not come to gloat. Did she really weep for them?

And then suddenly his heart jerked, for he saw Elizabeth Trengrove standing pale and elegant in the sunlight. She looked tragic, forlorn. Hated life at the castle, did she? Well, she had got only what she deserved. It did not occur to him that she might be weeping for him. He remembered only the pain of her rejection, still so raw that it was as though a blade seared him anew.

John Atkins asked him his name, but he paid him no attention.

The little whore. She hadn't even visited him in his cell, nor even made a gift of mercy to the prisoners.

Intent on doing his duty, John Atkins asked him his name again.

Symson looked at him then. It wasn't Atkins' fault. He was only doing what he had to do. 'David Symson. From Berwick. Thirty-six.'

'You will repent of your deeds, David Symson?'

Symson looked at him scornfully. Public repentance was for weak men, an admission of guilt, a begging for forgiveness. And that he would never do. They could break a man's body, but they would never break his spirit.

He put up his head and met Elizabeth Trengrove's eyes across a hundred other heads. 'Hey!' he called out as though unconcerned. 'I've lain with that bitch three times and now she's come to see me hanged!' And he laughed unkindly, even as unmanly tears came into his eyes. He saw the expression on her face change, saw the pain flit across her features, the quick glance of alarm towards her husband, and he wished he had not said it.

John Atkins could barely conceal his disgust. Without another word he went on to the next man. 'Name?'

'William Magnes, thirty-five, Minehead in Somersetshire.'

'Christopher Moody. Twenty-eight.'

John Atkins looked up, and Symson too looked across at him. 'Where are you from, sir?' Atkins demanded again.

Moody swallowed, glanced at Symson, and then gathered himself together. 'And what's that to you?' he demanded with sudden bravado. 'We suffer the law and we give no account but to God.'

Good man! Symson thought.

'And have you repented of your sins?' Atkins demanded.

'Go to hell!'

Atkins left him and went on to the next man. 'Name?'

'Richard Hardy . . . twenty-five . . . Wales.'

'And have you repented of your sins?'

Richard Hardy did not answer.

Atkins turned away. There was no more he could do. These men had committed their crimes and they would now have to answer to God. He had done all he could.

The drumming began again, not with a rhythmic beat now, but a roll. As they came to put the hood over his face, Elizabeth Trengrove looked directly at Symson. She was weeping. He still loved her. He knew it as he had always known it. Even though she had rejected him. Hers was the last face he saw.

Inside the hood it was chokingly black and hot. He began to panic. He couldn't breathe. He felt the rope now tightened around his neck. Outside, a long way off, he heard the surgeon reciting the Lord's prayer. Beside him he heard Sutton's voice, quiet and trembling:

'Oh God! Dear God! Sweet Jesus! Have mercy on me, a sinner!'

Ashplant too muttered. They all did. The drum roll stopped.

'Dear God!' Symson whispered. 'Please make it quick! Oh God have mercy—'

And suddenly the platform vanished from beneath his feet.

EPILOGUE

Fifty-two men were executed at Corso, including John Walden, James Skyrme, William Williams, Benjamin Jeffries, Peter Scudamore, the three men who had sailed with Blackbeard: Israel Hynde, James Phillips, and Peter DeVine, as well as the men already named in the last chapter. Thomas Armstrong was hanged on *H.M.S. Weymouth* as a deserter from the *Swallow*.

Henry Dennis turned King's evidence and, together with nineteen others was sentenced to seven years as an indentured labourer for the Royal Africa Company on the coast. All of them died before they had served their time. Harry Glasby, the only genuinely forced man, also turned King's evidence, and was acquitted. Seventy-three others were also acquitted, mostly the newer recruits, those taken from the Frenchman at Whydah, and the musicians, those who could either 'prove' they had been forced or who had been so little time with the pirates that they hadn't taken part in any action. Twenty were sent to serve sentences in the Marshalsea Prison, and the seventy Africans were re-sold as slaves. The surgeon George Wilson, and another man, Thomas Oughterlaney, the pilot, were respited awaiting His Majesty's pleasure. George Wilson died shortly after, while still on the Guinea Coast, while Oughterlaney was freed.

Altogether, including the men who died in action and those who died before they could be brought to trial, the pirate company numbered two hundred and sixty-seven men.

Captain Chaloner Ogle sailed with two of his prizes, the *Royal Fortune* and the *Little Ranger*, to the West Indies, where on 28th August 1722 both ships were wrecked in a hurricane at Port Royal, Jamaica. Captain Ogle was knighted for his success against Roberts. He became Rear Admiral in 1739 and then Admiral of the Fleet. He died in 1750.

AUTHOR'S NOTE

The skill of a historian is in discovering the accuracy of facts. The work of a novelist is to interpret those facts into an entertaining story so that the reader can experience the events as they unfolded.

The story of Bartholomew Roberts is based on fact. However, where history has been ambiguous, or historians do not agree on the timing of events, I have felt free to interpret. The reader is at liberty to agree or disagree with my interpretations. The ill-fated first attempted voyage to Guinea, for example, is placed in a different time frame by the two major sources. Sometimes original sources themselves seem to contradict each other.

Research showed António Furtado de Mendoça to be the governor of São Tomé at the time of Davis's stay in Príncipe. Records in São Tomé and Príncipe and the University of Leiden say there was no governor of Príncipe at that time and that the island was governed by São Tomé as it is now.

And who is to say there was not an emissary to the King of Portugal with a beautiful daughter?

ABOUT THE AUTHOR

Evelyn Tidman was born in London, England in 1952 and, encouraged by schoolteachers and family, began writing at an early age. In 1971 she married David Tidman but the advent of four children and a move to Norfolk, England eclipsed her writing until an empty nest brought the freedom to put pen to paper once again.

History has always been a passion, especially the way extraordinary events affected the lives of ordinary people. A desire to bring the reader into those events prompted a return to writing. While many historical novels use fictitious characters and story in historical settings, Evelyn is particularly interested in the individuals who were there. GENTLEMAN OF FORTUNE, her first published novel, is carefully researched, the details as accurate as history attests, so that the reader is able to see events as they may have occurred. Only the heroine, her father and servants are fictitious.

Evelyn lives quietly on the West Norfolk coast with her husband David.

ALSO BY
EVELYN TIDMAN

ONE SMALL CANDLE, The Story of William Bradford and the Pilgrim Fathers

Based on the true story of the Separatists who sailed to America on the *Mayflower* in 1620 enduring untold hardships in order to build a colony in the wilderness.

Available now in Print and E book format from Amazon.com

FOR THE KING, a story of the English Civil War.

Based on the true story of the L'Estrange family and the siege of King's Lynn in Norfolk.

Available spring 2014 in Print and E book format from Amazon.com

Printed in Great Britain
by Amazon